Also by Omar Tyree

The Last Street Novel

What They Want

Boss Lady

Diary of a Groupie

Leslie

Just Say No!

For the Love of Money

Sweet St. Louis

Single Mom

A Do Right Man

Flyy Girl

The Urban Griot Series

Cold Blooded

*One Crazy-A** Night*

The Underground

College Boy

Anthologies

Dark Thirst

The Game

Proverbs of the People

Tough Love: The Life and Death of Tupac Shakur

Testimony

Children's Books

12 Brown Boys

Nonfiction

The Equation

Pecking Order

A Novel

Omar Tyree

Simon & Schuster
New York London Toronto Sydney

Simon & Schuster
1230 Avenue of the Americas
New York, NY 10020

First Simon & Schuster hardcover edition September 2008

For information about special discounts for bulk purchases, please contact Simon & Schuster Special Sales at 1-800-456-6798 or business@simonandschuster.com.

Designed by Davina Mock-Maniscalco

Manufactured in the United States of America

1 3 5 7 9 10 8 6 4 2

Library of Congress Cataloging-in-Publication Data

Tyree, Omar.
Pecking order / Omar Tyree.
p. cm.
1. Accountants—Fiction. 2. African Americans—Fiction. 3. New business enterprises—Fiction. 4. Parties—Planning—Fiction. 5. Branding (Marketing)—Fiction. 6. Success in business—Fiction. 7. Millionaires—Fiction. 8. California, Southern—Fiction. I. Title.

PS3570.Y59P43 2008
813'.54—dc22
2008012091

ISBN-13: 978-1-4165-4193-6
ISBN-10: 1-4165-4193-4

Are we still thirsty
for knowledge?
Or
are we already saturated?
You tell me.

Contents

Part I
The Start-up

One

Downtown San Diego

BETWEEN THE HOURS of eight and nine PM on a Thursday evening, a black Nissan Altima traveled through light traffic, heading southbound on Interstate 5 toward downtown San Diego. Overhead, a US Airways commercial airplane zoomed down toward San Diego International Airport, less than a mile west of the highway. And as the sun continued to make its descent across the far west side of the Pacific Ocean, the night lights of San Diego's downtown skyline began to flicker into an evening glow.

Inside the fairly clean two-year-old Altima was dead silence. The driver was not in the mood for music at the moment; too much else was on his mind.

He checked the clock on the dashboard for the fifth time to make sure he was still on schedule for his date at Hooters on Fourth Avenue. He wasn't particularly in the mood for flirty young women serving drinks, burgers, chicken wings, and fries in skimpy orange shorts with white tank tops. But a commitment was a commitment, so he continued on his way.

Exiting the highway on Second Avenue, the black Altima traveled southbound toward Horton Plaza, a downtown shopping center with a multilevel parking garage. When he arrived at the garage entrance, the driver stopped and rolled down his window to receive a ticket at the gate. He then accelerated past the rows of parked cars to find an open space.

Once he had found a parking spot on the third level of the garage, the driver checked the time for a final countdown. It was 8:43 PM.

"Right on time," he mumbled. He climbed out of the car and straightened out his button-up shirt of light blue pinstripes. His pants were dark blue denim, and his shoes were soft brown leather. He had dressed down on purpose for a casual date.

At 8:47, Ivan David strolled out of the parking garage exit. He was a light brown black man of medium build and medium height, with light brown hair and multicolored eyes. Some people described his eyes as rainbows, with rings of color from blue to light brown to green.

He looked around for a second to peruse his surroundings and sniff the downtown air. The nighttime temperature was at seventy degrees. *Perfect.* As soon he stepped out into the street to cross it, a yellow Ferrari Spider raced around the corner from his left and forced him to freeze.

Shit! Do I move forward or backward? Ivan asked himself. He had already made it halfway across the street. *Move back,* he decided.

As soon as he stepped out of the way, the yellow Ferrari sped past him with a California license plate that read TOO SLOW.

Ivan got the message and grinned. "Maybe I am," he grunted before continuing across.

Hooters was two blocks away. Ivan proceeded to enjoy his evening stroll past the young and old couples who walked in and out of the restaurants that populated San Diego's downtown strip.

"I'll have a glass of Chardonnay," a gray-haired businessman ordered at his outside table at Buenos Días Café. His young-as-a-daughter date sat across their small table with a controlled smile.

Ivan looked into her calculating green eyes and wondered whether she loved her older man or his older money.

The dirty-blond beauty looked up at him momentarily, as if to read his skepticism. Then she looked away, unconcerned by it.

Ivan chuckled to himself as he passed them by, outside the waist-high black iron gate that separated their table from the sidewalk. All he could think about was the numbers game: a fifty-two-year-old man, earning a mid to high six figures, and a twenty-eight-year-old date, earning a low five figures.

"I gotta stop thinking like an accountant," he reminded himself as he walked.

When he arrived at Hooters and stepped inside, he blinked and readjusted his eyes. *Damn.* The bright orange was enough to blind a man.

"Hey, Ivan, over here."

He turned to his left and spotted Catherine Boone, an old friend and fling from his undergrad days at San Diego State. She wore a lime-green dress, full of cleavage and curves, with matching lime-green heels. Her hair was shoulder length and straight, ideal for no-nonsense business. Her medium brown skin remained flawless.

As she stood up from her chair and table to greet him with an open hug, Ivan could see and feel that she had put on a good ten to twenty pounds of maturity.

"Whoa, you're filling out a little bit," he told her.

She smiled. "And?"

He hesitated. "And, what?"

"And, what does that mean?"

Women were finicky about their appearance. So Ivan remained coy.

"I don't know. You tell me," he responded.

Catherine broke away. "Ivan, is it a good thing or a bad thing? Because I like my new weight. I always thought I was too skinny in college."

"You thought you were skinny?"

"Yeah, you didn't think so?"

Catherine sat back down. Ivan sat in the chair across the table from her.

He shook his head and answered, "No, not really. Your weight was always fine to me."

Catherine grinned at him. "It's good to see that you're still the same Ivan. You're as vague and as noncommittal as ever. And no new girlfriend yet, right?"

Ivan smiled back. "I like keeping my concentration."

Catherine grinned even harder. "Are we that bad, Ivan? I mean, really?"

She got all serious and stopped smiling. She wanted a sincere answer from him. A Hooters waitress broke them out of their groove before Ivan could grant her wish.

"Welcome to Hooters, my name is Claudia." She immediately wrote her name down on a Hooters napkin in front of them. She was a breezy brunette in the bright white and orange uniform.

"Are you guys ready to order yet?"

The Hooters menu sat out in front of them on the tabletop.

Ivan frowned and squinted his eyes. "Ahh . . . I really didn't get a chance to look at the menu yet."

"I'll have a beer and some fries," Catherine ordered overtop of him.

"Okay," the brunette perked. She wrote it down on her order pad. Then she looked back at Ivan. "I'll be right back in a minute," she promised him.

Ivan nodded. "All right."

As soon as the waitress left them, Catherine changed her tone and reached her gentle hands across the table to place over Ivan's. "I'm sorry to hear about your mother," she told him. She had compassion in her dark brown eyes. She had heard about his mother's funeral in Los Angeles through mutual friends. But her apology caught Ivan off guard. He froze for a second and daydreamed in her direction, before he shook it off and looked away.

He grunted, "It was gonna happen sooner or later." He looked back into her eyes to finish his statement. "When you got any form of cancer, you're fighting it to win or fighting it to lose."

Catherine squeezed his hands tighter. "I know how much she meant to you."

"Yeah," Ivan grumbled. Then he forced himself to perk up. He said, "But the good thing she told me was to go ahead and live my life now, you know. I mean, I had been holding on for so long . . ."

"I know," Catherine responded. She remembered it through their college years. Ivan's mother had begged him several times each semester to stay away from home in South Central L.A. to finish his schooling in San Diego. She knew that her illness would be too much of a strain on him at home. And when he was offered an accounting job at the firm of Hutch & Mitchell in North Clairemont, his mother advised him to take it and stay there.

Now Ivan felt guilty about everything. Although returning home may not have changed the end result, he would have at least been able to see his mother more before she was confined to her deathbed.

Finally, he pulled his hands away from Catherine at the table.

"Look, we're not here to talk about that. So, what's up with this new job you got?" he asked her, changing the subject.

Catherine nodded and followed his lead. She wanted to make sure she got her empathy out of the way early. She had other plans for them that evening.

"Well, I may be moving back to the San Diego area if everything goes right," she told him. She was originally from Sacramento. She said, "I had my interview this morning in Oceanside, but I made sure they put me up in a downtown San Diego hotel instead of all the way out there."

Then she giggled. "I can get my way when I want it."

Ivan sat back in his chair and smiled. "Yeah, I know it already."

Catherine was a whiner, beggar, wheeler-dealer, or whatever else it took to get her way. She had worked her magic all throughout college as a business management major. And she was always in the middle of things.

Before she could get another word out, her conversation with Ivan was interrupted again.

"Hey, Ivan David. What's going on, man?"

Ivan turned to his right and looked up. He'd recognize the Spanish-American accent with the rapid-fire tongue anywhere. It was Emilio Alvarez, an excitable rookie shortstop for the San Diego Padres.

"Hey, what's going on, E.A.?" Ivan addressed him with an outstretched hand.

They had met a few months ago at the accounting firm offices. Emilio was a new Hutch & Mitchell client of Dominican descent from Texas. He was as brown as Catherine, with jet-black wavy hair. A happy-faced date stood attached to his right arm. She was as light as Ivan, with straight brown hair, and was Mexican.

"Hey, you tell me, I.D.," Emilio responded. He had to pull his date loose to shake Ivan's hand with his right.

Ivan joked, "You're out here just walking around with no bodyguards? You could get mobbed."

Emilio frowned. "Mobbed? Man, I'm just a young rookie trying to make a good name for myself. Nobody really knows me yet."

As soon as he said it, the Hooters waitresses began to smile all around him.

"We know who you are, E.A.," Claudia teased him. She spotted the rookie baseball player as soon as he walked in. She returned to the table with Catherine's mug of beer and set it down in front of her.

Once Claudia spoke to Emilio, a few of the other waitresses breezed by.

"Yeah, rookies are still impressionable," a bold blonde flirted, and laughed.

Emilio's date didn't look too pleased about that statement. But at least the blonde didn't stick around long.

Emilio laughed it all off. He said, "Hey, Ivan, you know we have a big party down here tonight. You guys should come hang out with us. Big Deke is throwing it. So we're gonna grab something to eat on Fifth Ave., then I can get you guys in VIP as my guests."

Catherine listened as she sipped from her mug of beer. She immediately shook her head before Ivan could respond to him.

Ivan caught her response to the invitation and agreed to turn it down.

"Maybe another night, man. We're just old friends over here catching up. But thanks for inviting us."

"Oh, no problem. Anytime," Emilio told him.

"Make sure you give me and my girls a few autographs before you leave," Claudia commented to the rookie.

Emilio looked confused. "Ahhh . . . okay."

His date said nothing the whole time, but her face said everything. She was just getting to know Emilio and had no idea how to respond to anything around them yet.

"Hey, rookie! What are you doing in here?" someone yelled from the doorway. The place was so bright that anyone could look straight through the glass windows and see everyone inside, just as Emilio had done to spot Ivan.

Ivan looked up again and recognized "Butch" Clayborne, a third baseman in his fifth year with the Padres. Butch had just signed a new multimillion-dollar contract earlier that year. He was a big, strong black man with two women: one white and one black. They were both proud to be his giddy companions for the night. And once the waitresses spotted Clayborne yelling through the doorway, several of them lost their cool.

"Oh, my God! Butch, are you coming in? Are you coming in?" they asked him with the double-talk of excitement.

He waved them off. "Nah, we don't have time for that. Maybe another time."

His two dates were already on their way in before he grabbed them back out.

"Hey, come on, let's go," he told them. Then he yelled back at Emilio, "Let's go, rookie!"

The two women stumbled back out to join him awkwardly.

"Damn, my heel," the black companion complained at the door.

The white companion laughed at her. In a flash, they were out of the doorway and headed up the street for Fifth Avenue.

Emilio looked back at Ivan and shook his head with a grin. "You see what I mean? I'm just a rookie this year. I got a long way to go to get to where he's at. I'm just lucky he's taking me under his wing."

When Emilio left with his date, the Hooters establishment returned to its normal chatter. The surprise visit from the Padres' baseball players had added a spark of insanity to the place. But as quickly as they had entered, they were gone.

"So, how do you know Emilio?" Claudia asked Ivan at the table. She had yet to receive an order from him. And she could see that the Padres rookie had a lot of respect for him. He had made it his personal mission to walk inside and say hi. He even invited Ivan and his date to a Padres party.

Ivan was still confused by all of it. "Ahh . . ."

Was it any of her business how he knew Emilio? How was he to respond to that?

Catherine was still shaking her head across the table with her beer. Things were getting a bit out of hand, from what she could see. Everyone was losing their focus.

She asked the waitress, "Are my french fries on the way out?"

Claudia caught her cold drift and got back to business.

"Oh, yeah, let me go get those for you."

When the waitress left them alone again, Catherine said, "Now, that was just crazy. Did you see how they started to act in here? They act as if they never saw a baseball player before."

Ivan smiled it off. "Yeah, but Butch Clayborne is more than just a regular player. He's one of their bona fide stars now."

The hype was no big deal to Ivan. He had been around plenty of wealthy and famous people. It was part of his job to go out and find new clients who had money. And they were all human. But what he didn't understand was why Catherine wanted to meet him at Hooters in the first place. They would never have any privacy there.

"You wanna go somewhere else?" he asked her.

Catherine's dress code surely didn't fit Hooters. Her lime-green dress was more than casual.

She took a deep breath and calmed her nerves. She asked him, "How do you think my body compares to theirs?"

Ivan stared across the table to make sure that he had heard her right.

"What?"

"You heard me. How does my body compare to theirs?"

She bobbed her head to the left in reference to the Hooters waitresses, who were scampering around the tables, filling orders, and cleaning up.

Ivan couldn't believe it. He shook his head and smiled. He said, "So that's why you wanted to meet me here, to do a body check against Hooters waitresses? Are you kidding me?" He was halfway laughing. He said, "If you really wanna do a body check, then let's go to this Padres party and do it for real. I mean, come on, none of these girls wanna wear the stuff they have to wear in here. It's just a job."

Catherine grinned back at him. She said, "I have my reasons."

Ivan blew it off. "Anyway . . . next question."

It was no competition in his book. He was embarrassed to even look at the waitresses. And Catherine was pleased to know it.

"Thank you," she told him. A nod of confidence meant the world to a woman.

BY THE TIME they had left the place, it was well after ten o'clock, and Catherine was good and tipsy. It became obvious that Ivan would need to help her walk to wherever they were off to next.

"So, what hotel they got you up in?" he asked her.

Catherine was secure in his arms as they walked down Fourth Avenue.

"We're almost there," she told him. "And it's a surprise."

As they walked, a white stretch Hummer passed them by in the street and turned left down Fifth Avenue.

Catherine watched it and grunted. "Hmmph, I bet you think that's more of your baseball players, don't you? But if the *Chargers* were throwing a party, that would be a *real* party. I would have been interested in going to that."

She added, "But it's only, like, four or five black players on the whole Padres team. And I don't count the Spanish guys. They're not really down with us. But on the Chargers, more than half the team is black."

Ivan only listened to her, amused by it all. He was slightly embarrassed by their night so far. What was her purpose for the evening; to get drunk while comparing her body to Hooters girls? That didn't make any sense.

The next thing he knew, Catherine had him walking her along Harbor Drive.

Ivan said, "I could have gotten my car if I would have known we were walking this far."

"It's not far," she told him. "All we have to do is cross the street and we're almost there."

Ivan looked across the street in the direction where they were headed and spotted the twin towers of the Manchester Grand Hyatt Hotel. The towers were set on prime real estate, right off the San Diego Bay. It was an immaculate hotel from the outside alone. Ivan had no idea what it looked like on the inside. He had never had any reason to stay there. But he could imagine it.

"Oh, shit, don't tell me they got you staying here," he responded.

Catherine giggled and said, "Yup. I told you I can get what I want when I want it. I couldn't wait to show you this. But . . ."

She stopped herself momentarily before she mumbled, "You really wanna know why I took you through that whole Hooters thing?"

Ivan didn't care. It was all trivial in his opinion. He decided to hear her out anyway.

"Yeah, what was up with that?" he asked as he continued to help her walk.

She said, "Okay. When I was back home in Sacramento, I found out that my ex was crazy about a girl who worked there. And he actually left *me* for *her.* And I was like . . . *why?*"

Ivan started to chuckle and couldn't help himself. *Women!* Their insecurities were amazing.

Catherine promptly stopped them from walking. "I don't see why that's so funny, Ivan. My feelings were very hurt by that. *Very* hurt," she told him.

"*I'm* college educated. *He's* college educated. *I'm* a professional. *He's* a professional. *I'm* good looking. *He's* good looking. And *still,* he picked a *Hooters girl* over me? *Why?*"

Ivan said, "Trust me, Catherine, it's not about the restaurant, it's all about the girl."

She said, "But why do guys like to see young women dressed so . . . *provocatively?* I mean, it's so *tasteless.*"

Ivan didn't feel like dealing with any of that. It was all meaningless. He thought more about seeing what the inside of the hotel looked like. So he ignored her question.

As they neared the front entrance, Catherine made sure to straighten herself up to walk in on her own. She didn't want the hotel staff and guests to consider *her* tasteless.

"Good to have you back this evening," the uniformed valet greeted Catherine from the hotel drive-through.

"Thank you," Catherine told him.

Ivan only nodded to him. They then nodded to the uniformed bellman as they entered the grand lobby.

For Ivan, a modest penny-pincher from South Central L.A., the

Manchester Grand Hyatt was immaculate. Top-of-the-line hotels allowed the imagination to run wild, with marble floors, rich carpet, giant chandeliers, crown molding, artwork, candles, exotic wood, interior plants, soft music, and tall ceilings. It was all there. The difference between a five-star hotel and an off-the-road inn was like the difference between heaven and hell.

"They actually put you in here just for an interview?" Ivan asked as they wandered through the lobby. "Which building are you in?"

"The Seaport." She grabbed him by the hand to lead him in the right direction. She said, "It has the better view. And it's the newer building."

As they strolled toward the Seaport building elevators, Ivan looked more like an amazed gawker than a guest.

Catherine read his wide, colorful eyes taking it all in. She yanked his arm for a dose of reality. "Come on, you know they're getting corporate rates. They're not paying what *we* would have to pay for this. They never do. So I told myself, 'Take advantage of it from the company now. Because I may not get another chance to.'"

Ivan nodded and agreed with her. "You're right. This is another tax write-off."

When they stepped into the elevator, another display of first-grade hotel quality, Ivan was inspired enough to go for broke.

He said, "Hell, why not just stay up in here for a night or two like it's a vacation? You only live once, right? I got a thousand dollars in the bank for a vacation, don't you?"

Catherine looked at her old college man as if she no longer recognized him.

"What, and this coming from the cheapest man I knew on San Diego State's campus?" She said, "I remember you used to sneak out of line with your food at the cafeteria to save six dollars."

Ivan laughed hard. He said, "That's when I was holding down the fort. I had to do what I had to do. I was working a full-time job, going to school, and still sending money back home to my mom. But . . . like she said . . . I can live now."

Ivan felt guilty even saying it. He could hardly get the words out of his mouth. But he did. The reality of the hotel had smacked him in the face with a cold hard hand of what he had been missing all of his life, an opportunity for luxury.

DINNNGGG!

The elevator doors opened to the hallway on the fourteenth floor.

"Here we are." Catherine spoke up with a chuckle. "Wait till you see the view I have from the room."

Ivan said, "We should have had our dinner date over here. They got restaurants downstairs, don't they?"

Catherine looked at him, amused. "And you would have paid the prices for the restaurants in this hotel? And then turned around and tipped the waiters? Because this is not fries and chicken and burgers over here."

Ivan smiled broadly, knowing better. He said, "You would have paid for it. Corporate rates. They got you in here, right? And you gotta eat."

"Yeah, and I'm sure they're looking to see exactly how expensive I can be, too," she commented. "I don't have this job yet, and I'm not a fool like that. So if we need to bring Chinese takeout back to this hotel, then that's what we'll do."

They shared a laugh as they reached the room. As soon as they walked into the king-sized suite, Ivan walked straight over to the window view of the bay and just stood there. He could see clear across to Coronado Island to his left, or view the boats, piers, smaller islands, and seafood restaurants to his right.

"They call this the corner room," Catherine told him.

Ivan looked out at a lone boat in the middle of the bay and wondered if it was the yacht of a rich man out on a private date. What a life that would be. He stood there stunned by the infinite possibilities of real wealth.

Catherine joined him at the window. "It's beautiful, isn't it? The windows even open up so you can smell the air."

She unlatched the large window and pushed it open for him to see. But Ivan remained speechless. The calculations were all running through his mind again as he idled there at the window. How could he afford to remain there at the hotel? How could he afford his own boat, property, leisure, travel, and custom designs?

Catherine moved to wrap herself within Ivan's arms, as if they were still an on-fire college couple.

"What are you thinking about?" she asked him.

Ivan heard her question in his mind and ran with it. Problem was, he was thinking about too many things at once. So he settled on the most recent idea as his mind slowed down and came to a rest to answer her.

"I'm thinking about that Padres party." He wondered what it was like and who all would be there to link up with. Maybe Emilio would introduce him to more of the major players on the team.

Catherine broke away, irritated by his answer. How could he still be thinking about a party when he had her all alone in a five-star hotel bedroom, with a dynamite view, wearing a dynamite dress, and horny to boot with alcohol in her system? What the hell was wrong with him?

"You really wanna go to that party that much, Ivan?" she snapped at him.

Ivan was surprised by her outburst. He hadn't been paying her physical attractions much attention. He'd had a lot on his mind, with the thoughts of his mother passing away, before they had even met up that night. Now he had even more on his mind concerning how he planned to live out the rest of his life.

"I mean, I don't have to go to this party, but . . ."

He stopped and thought about his dilemma. How exactly could he tell Catherine that she was old news, and that the party seemed more interesting to him at the moment? He wanted to get up close and personal with the people who could really afford to live. And he had been invited to do so.

Catherine looked into Ivan's eyes, flickering in the moonlight from the window, and she decided to do something desperate to pique his interest. She wanted him to sleep over that night and give her his full attention without any distractions. So she massaged his crotch, kicked off her heels, and sank to her knees in front of him at the window.

She looked up and asked him, "Would this be your fantasy?"

Ivan could not deny that her spontaneous exuberance excited him. His manhood would surely respond to a blow job. But then he thought about their past. Catherine was a credit card woman. Whatever you spent with her, you would be forced to pay back later, and with interest. So Ivan shook his head and backed away from the purchase.

He told her, "Nah, I'm not really . . ."

He stopped and looked into Catherine's determined face. Ivan knew who she was, and there were no surprises to her.

"I just know how you are," he concluded. "And I'm not trying to go there."

She ignored him and reached to unzip his pants zipper anyway.

Ivan stepped farther away and continued to deny her. He even put his hands in front of his pants to protect himself. "Yo—"

Catherine was incensed. "Just let me do what I want to do, Ivan. It may be *my* fantasy. And I promise not to hold you to anything."

She was saying this from her knees, and the irony did not pass Ivan by. So he continued to shake his head.

"Look at this, Cat," he commented, referring to her college nickname. "This ain't a good picture," he told her. "I mean, just look at you."

Catherine heard him out, took a deep breath, and climbed back to her feet. Then she couldn't even face him.

She sat on the edge of the king-sized bed and mumbled with her head down, "You're still the same old Ivan . . . won't break for nobody."

Ivan didn't respond. But she was right. He was a man who stuck by his principles.

She added, "I was hoping that you had changed a little bit."

He didn't have a response to that, either. The truth was, he hadn't changed. He was still as strong willed as ever.

After another minute, the silence of the room increased the awkwardness for both of them.

Catherine finally decided to let the fish off the hook and send him back into the water.

"Well . . . if you wanna go to that party so much . . ."

Ivan jumped at his chance to leave with no shame. "Are you still gonna be up?" He knew he had to at least make his exit sound good.

Catherine looked at him and asked, "What, after the party? No." She didn't care about a consolation prize. She had lost him.

"I mean, just to call you up and make sure everything is all right," he told her.

"Ivan, I'm a grown fucking woman, okay?" she snapped at him. "So you go do what you need to do and don't worry about me."

Ouch! He should have quit while he was ahead. Now he felt awkward again. Instead of saying anything else, he nodded and headed for the door.

"I'll call you," he said on the way out.

When the door closed behind him, Catherine took another deep breath and dropped her head even lower. All of her plans were out the window, falling fourteen stories down.

"Shit," she grumbled into her lap. "I would have been better off at the fucking Days Inn . . . and could have saved them a bunch of money."

IVAN WAS OUT of the hotel in a flash to hustle his way back to the action on Fifth Avenue.

"You're leaving us already?" It was the same valet who had greeted Catherine when she and Ivan had entered the hotel.

Ivan faced him and answered, "I'll be back." He added, "Not to-night, but I'll be back, though, for sure." He planned on it. Then he laughed as he made his way back up Harbor Drive.

He felt like a college student again, rushing to make his way to the clubs. And on a Thursday night, he was sure that the Padres party would have few competitors.

When he arrived back in the Gaslamp Quarter, what San Diego referred to as its main restaurant and nightclub district, the stretch limos, luxury sedans, and exotic sports cars that lined the valet parking spaces outside the Market Street Hotel told him exactly where the party was.

The long line along the outside wall of the hotel made the party look more like a Saturday. But on a Thursday night, only the able people partied: those who didn't have to clock in in the morning, those who didn't care, and those who planned to work it all out.

Ivan fit the last group. He would definitely make it to work in the morning. He would just have less sleep to count on. But he was too curious that evening to let the opportunity of the Padres party pass by.

"Come on, just let us in, it's only the two of us," a pair of long-legged twins, wearing revealing dresses, begged the doormen at the front. The time was fast approaching midnight.

"In a minute," the husky doorman responded to them. He stretched out his thick right arm in front of them, wearing the same professional black suit as the rest of the men who worked the party. Their orchestrated job looked like the set of a *Men in Black* movie. It was a doorman's extra duty to deal with the begging types. So Ivan studied the scene to see how he would plead his own case. He definitely wasn't planning on walking to the back of the long line and paying. However, he figured he at least needed to know what the cost would be.

"Hey, what's the price to get in?"

The doormen looked him up and down before anyone answered. Who was he? Was he dressed correctly? Was he coming in? Or was he staying out?

Once they all established that Ivan David was a nobody, they gave him the price of general admission.

"Cover charge is twenty-five dollars. The line is that way," one of the men piped up to him, and pointed. They continued to guard the entrance without missing a beat.

All right, here I go, Ivan told himself as he prepared to address the doormen with more information. He noticed that they marked off a guest list held just inside the doorway.

I hope Emilio has a list of names, he thought. From there, he would have to work it out himself.

"Actually, I'm here as a guest of Emilio Alvarez, the rookie shortstop. Tell him Ivan David is here."

Ivan spoke with such presence and authority that the two brown-haired twins turned to look him over for themselves. A few of the other anxious line-waiters looked in Ivan's direction as well. Who the hell was he?

"What's your name again?" the first doorman asked him. He continued to hold the twins at bay in front of him.

"Ivan David."

"Ivan *David?*" the doorman repeated in confusion. "You got two first names?"

Ivan grinned. "Yeah."

The doorman cracked his first smile. "Okay. Hey, check the list for Ivan David."

Ivan stood there knowing that his name wouldn't be on the list. He wished he had told Emilio to look out for him just in case he swung past the party later. But he planned to argue his point to the doormen anyway. All he needed was someone to go inside and find E.A. for him.

As he waited there on the sidewalk for the inevitable, the valet staff sprinted to the curb, where another stretch limo was pulling up.

The crowd got excited in anticipation. Even Ivan watched to see who it was. Was Big Deke Walker, the superstar slugger, at the party yet? He was never known to attend a party early.

But when the valet guys opened the limo doors and let out its passengers, there were only sexy women inside. They climbed out one at a time and stood on the sidewalk until the last one had joined them. There were seven of them in all, the perfect number to pack inside their stretch limo. And they were all of different races: white, black, Latina, Filipina, and exotic mixtures in between.

Were they a cheerleading squad or models? No one was sure until their leader stepped out last and was immediately recognized by the doormen.

"Lucina," one of the doormen said to her.

"Hey, Matt, how's it going?" she addressed him with a light hand to his arm.

"You know the party don't get started until *you* arrive," he teased her.

"Stop it," she told him, and laughed. "Then again, don't stop," she teased.

Ivan heard a slight accent in her voice, but it didn't sound Mexican or Filipina. It had more of a Mediterranean swagger to it. Maybe Italian or Greek.

"That's Lucina Gallo," he overheard one the twins comment from behind him.

Ivan stared at this Lucina Gallo woman up close and was impressed with her immediately. She wore a thin silky dress of a dark blue and baby-blue mix that stood out from the mostly solid colors of the other girls. Her sparkling purse, necklace, bracelet, watch, anklet, and heels all glittered in the night, like a live advertisement for a glamorous fashion magazine. And her height mixed in well with the others'. She was not the tallest or the shortest, but she definitely had the most presence. She looked no older than he was, twenty-eight. However, Ivan only gave her that because she was in a position of authority. Otherwise, she looked a spoiled twenty-two, a rich man's college-aged daughter.

Then she looked in Ivan's direction to survey the crowd. When she did, he noticed that her eyes twinkled with a multicolored hue of their own. Her eyes were in contrast with her moody, olive-toned skin and thick, dark, two-toned brown hair.

Ivan was frozen stiff just from looking at her.

Damn, she bad!

Lucina looked right through him and into the crowd behind him as if he were the clear glass window of a department store.

"Nice line," she said to herself with a nod. Then she turned back to her girls. "Let's go inside."

Ivan watched them all walk into the hotel party past the doormen, and he missed them already, especially Lucina. As he continued to stand there on the sidewalk, he felt as cold as a lone man at the North Pole.

"Shit," he mumbled to himself. He thought again about what it would take to become an insider with the movers and shakers of San Diego. The doormen then snapped him out of his daydream.

"There's no Ivan David on the list."

Ivan said, "Well, can one of you go get Emilio and let him know that I'm here?"

The lead doorman shook his head. "That's not our job. Call him up on his cell phone." He was finally ready to let the twins in. "Okay, you can go," he told them.

Ivan watched the girls pay their twenty-five dollars inside the doorway, and he realized the only way he was getting into the party free was if Emilio happened to walk outside for some reason. But why would he do that in the middle of a jam-packed party?

Ivan looked to the back of the line again. It had grown longer since the last time he looked. The doormen didn't pay him any more attention. His case was closed. They had jobs to do. So Ivan shook it off and accepted his defeat.

Let me get the hell out of here, he told himself. He figured that going through too much hassle to get in would kill his excitement at being there.

Just as he began to walk away, the lead doorman called out his name again in jest. "All right, Ivan David. You make sure you make that list next time."

A few of the other doormen laughed, but Ivan didn't find it funny. The joke registered in his mind as a challenge. So he responded to it that way.

"All right. You can count on that."

Two

Back to the Office

IVAN MADE IT to his car in the Horton Plaza parking lot and was still grumbling to himself about the doorman's slight outside the party.

"So he thinks it's all a joke, hunh? We'll see," he told himself as he climbed back behind the wheel of his Altima. Then he thought about the slight from a different perspective.

"At least they know my name now," he stated. "They're gonna know it a lot more real soon, too. Watch what I tell you."

He was that irritated by it. How dare some lowly doorman make fun of him? Who the hell was he to joke? All he did was watch the door like a human guard dog.

FOR HIS TWENTY-MINUTE DRIVE back home to the La Mesa area of northeast San Diego, Ivan decided to drive through the scenic Balboa Park before connecting east on Interstate 8.

This time, he wasn't in the mood for silence. To drown out his own doubts and insecurities about where he stood in life, he pulled out a rap CD and slid it into his audio system below the dashboard.

He needed to solidify his thoughts of rebellion against the status quo, and rap music was sure to do the trick.

"Truck Volume," a musical progression track from legendary producer Dr. Dre, was just what Ivan wanted to hear, while the famously obnoxious rapper Busta Rhymes screamed, yelled, and hollered at the top of his lungs, *"Truck shit now! Turn my music up! Truck volume! Truck volume!"*

Regardless of the rapper's overstated screaming and yelling, the Dr. Dre production pushed the mind forward through an organized sequence of keyboards, bass, and drums, as if an army of ideas was advancing forward on an enemy. As the overpowering music pumped out of the speaker system, Ivan's tense body began to bow forward behind the wheel, like an obedient soldier ready to carry out his mission.

The musical adrenaline was so strong that Ivan replayed the song five straight times, until he had pulled into the driveway of the modest three-level apartment complex where he lived.

Finally, he turned off his stereo system after parking inside the lot. "That shit is *blazing,*" he told himself of the track. It was nearly two o'clock in the morning. Nevertheless, Ivan felt as if he had just worked up an afternoon sweat. Relevant music was that energizing.

As soon as he climbed out of his car, one of his neighbors addressed him from where he stood on the second-level walkway.

"That's that Busta Rhymes album, isn't it? *Genesis.* My cousin played on that song you were just pumping. It's called 'Truck Volume,' right? That's song's pretty hot."

Julio was a Mexican-American in his early thirties with his hair cut low. He was wearing no shirt with his beige khaki pants. Colorful tattoos adorned his slender chest, and his left hand held on to a blunt of marijuana. He was still smoking it.

Ivan looked up at him and nodded while heading for the staircase.

"Yeah, that's it," he responded. "But who is your cousin?"

Julio smiled and took another hit of the blunt before he answered. "Mike Elizondo. He plays bass on a lot of Dr. Dre's songs." He held the blunt between his lips to play an imaginary bass guitar with his hands.

Ivan made it to the staircase and laughed on his way up. He lived only three doors down from Julio and his family. The two men shook hands when Ivan reached him.

"So, the bass player is your cousin?" Ivan asked him again.

"Yeah," Julio answered proudly. "And that Jewish kid from Philadelphia plays on the keyboards. Scott Storch. That kid is nasty wit' it."

He held his blunt tightly between his lips again and stretched out his free fingers to play an imaginary keyboard progression:

"Derrrnt . . . darrrnt . . . derrrnt . . . darrrnt . . . derrrnt . . . darrrnt . . . durrrnt . . . durrrrnnt." He hummed the notes as he moved his hands left and right.

Ivan started to laugh again.

Julio said, "That's that Jewish kid, man. Scott Storch. He's *nasty.* He was the one who played those wicked piano notes on *Still D.R.E.*

"Bling-bling-bling-bling-bling-bling-bling-bling-bling-bling-bling-blinnggg . . ."

Ivan said, "I didn't know you were into music like that." He figured the effects of the marijuana were helping out his neighbor's free expression that evening. It was a strong grade, too. Ivan could smell it.

Julio nodded and uttered, "Yeah, man, I love music." Another cloud of smoke left his mouth and floated up into the night air.

Ivan continued to think about that. He said, "It's just something about music that gets everybody open."

Julio continued to smoke and said, "Yup." Then he considered Ivan. "You want some of this?" He extended the blunt in his right hand.

Ivan turned it down. "Nah, man, I gotta be back at work in six hours. And Fridays and Mondays are the worst. You can't wait to get the hell out of there on Friday, and you can't believe you're back there already on Monday."

Julio said, "I gotta be at work in six hours, too. But at least you got weekends off. I only get Sundays off. And you work inside. I'm outside all day in the heat."

Julio worked for a groundskeeping company. And in the state of California, groundskeeping was an around-the-clock job.

Ivan thought about it and nodded. "I guess we all got our own medicine to swallow, hunh?"

Julio held his marijuana up in the air. "I'm swallowing my medicine right now."

Ivan laughed and shook it off. He started to walk to his apartment with his key out. Once he reached the door, he figured, *What the hell? Go ahead and get some. It'll help you make it through Friday.*

He looked back to Julio and said, "Yo . . . let me get some of that."

Julio studied him first. He asked him, "Are you sure? I mean, they don't do no urine tests where you work, do they? I wouldn't want to be the one who gets you fired."

Ivan smiled. "You wasn't thinking about that when you first asked me."

Julio looked confused for a second. "Well, I wasn't thinking until you said something. But you work at an office. Grass don't matter where I work. We all smoke a li'l bit of herb."

Ivan said, "Nah, that ain't no li'l bit of herb you smoking. That smells like you got some good shit."

Julio chuckled and said, "Yeah, this is the best. It's all green leaf, straight off the stems with no seeds." He looked at it in his hand and asked Ivan, "Are you sure you can handle the rest of this? It's even stronger at the end."

Ivan hesitated. Julio was right. The end part of a blunt was the more potent because the smoke had made it more concentrated. But Ivan decided to go for broke anyway.

"Fuck it, man, I need to change up my ways. If you keep doing what you've been doing, then you'll keep getting what you've been getting," he stated to himself.

He reached out his right hand and accepted the rest of the marijuana. About a fourth of it was left.

"All right. Good luck, then, man," Julio told him carefully.

Ivan asked him, "You don't want any more of it?"

Julio shook it off. He said, "You gotta know your limit. I've been smoking that stuff all night. But I gotta get to bed now, man. I need to get at least a good four hours."

Ivan grinned. "All right, so now you're gonna leave me with the shit, hunh?"

"You asked me for it. But I'll take it back for tomorrow night if you don't want it," Julio told him.

Ivan stepped away with it and took his first hit. "Nah, I got it. She going home with me now," he joked, sucking the smoke in deeply.

Julio looked him over and said, "All right, man, just don't get her pregnant."

They shared a laugh.

Ivan shook his head and responded, "Nah, I ain't doing that. This here is just a one-night stand, and I'm definitely wearing a condom with her."

Julio laughed even harder before they went their separate ways.

IVAN LET HIMSELF into his apartment while still smoking the potent strain of weed.

When he walked in, he left the lights off and turned on his stereo system from inside the entertainment cabinet. He had a thirty-seven-inch color TV, DVD player, videocassette player, stereo system, cable box, and five remote controls.

After turning on more music, he sat down on the comfortable

sofa facing the entertainment system and continued to smoke in the dark. Instead of listening to the brashness of rap, he clicked on the timeless jazz of Donald Byrd, *A New Perspective.*

Ivan sucked up the marijuana smoke that began to hit him like a torch, igniting his brain, while the harmonizing jazz voices, horns, chords, bass notes, and percussion beat patterns of rampant thoughts into his consciousness. No lyrics were needed.

What the hell I am I doing here? he asked himself in his high. *What is the meaning of my life? I'm twenty-eight years old now, in the year 2003, and I'm still living in a damn two-bedroom apartment in San Diego with no plans for the future.*

He thought about that as he finished smoking the rest of the blunt. He climbed to his feet and stumbled inside the kitchen to put it out in the sink before it would burn his fingers at the nub. Since he didn't usually smoke, Ivan had no ashtrays sitting around. And when the full high hit him, he walked gingerly to the sofa, where he crashed back down into his seat.

"Shit!" he told himself, feeling the disorientation of his mind and body. "I'm high as hell in here."

That's when his doubts and paranoia kicked into overdrive.

Damn! I got a job that I might get fired from tomorrow if they ask me for a urine sample . . . Please don't ask me for no urine sample. I don't even get high like this. This is not normal for me. I'll never let it happen again in my life. Honestly.

Then he began to laugh at himself.

"They won't do that shit. For what?" he mumbled aloud. *I have no history of doing any drugs. They don't check up on you for that shit, no way. What the hell am I thinking about?*

As the jazz music continued to open up his mind from the background, Ivan began to think about his present and future.

Am I gonna be somebody? he asked himself. Then he paused for what seemed like an extralong time. *Nah, who am I kidding? Ivan David is a nobody. I'm a fucking joke. I'm no better off than my brother. I just got a college degree and a job.*

Then he thought about it again.

But at least I don't have no kids and three baby mommas in my way. Maybe I can make it. If anybody else can make it, I can make it, too. Ain't nobody better than me. What makes them better than me? You just gotta stand up and do something.

He even stood up in the room to make a statement to himself. Or stumbled up.

I'm gonna make a name for myself, he declared. *And they're gonna know me in this town. They're gonna know me! San Diego's Ivan David . . . the party promoter.*

As he stood there thinking to himself about his declaration, he closed his eyes and began to sway blindly to the jazz music. The high was pulsating in his nerves, creating an insane energy of randomness.

Suddenly his skin felt cold; he rubbed his arms and shoulders for warmth.

"Shit. It's cold in here," he mumbled. *Somebody hold me,* he thought. *Mom, I'm cold. I need to turn the heat up.* But his mother didn't respond to him.

Then he visualized the girl at the party. Lucina Gallo. She was right there on the sidewalk in front of him. He asked her, *Ain't you cold?*

She answered, *No,* with her hard, colored eyes right on him.

You're not? Then how come I'm so cold? he asked her.

She continued to stare at him. Then she asked him, *What is wrong with you?*

Ivan didn't understand her question. *Hunh?*

What is wrong with you? she repeated. He was making a fool of himself out in front of her.

In his delusional state of mind, it all seemed real . . . for a second. Then he snapped out of it. He grabbed his throbbing head and asked himself, *What am I talking about? I'm bugging, man. I'm high as hell in here. I don't even know that girl.*

He fell back down on the sofa and began to rub his temples, with the jazz music still talking to him. The harmonizing voices made him feel as if a thousand eyes were watching him make a fool of himself. And he was powerless to do anything about it. The high had him stranded out in the desert.

When is this gonna wear off? The insanity had gone on long enough. The slithery, snakelike energy continued to run up and down his body. Ivan moved his hands from his head to his arms and shoulders, and then down to his legs.

"Fuck! What am I so cold for? I got clothes on."

Maybe I just can't handle this shit. You can't OD off of weed, can you . . . ? SHIT!

Ivan had only been high a few times before, in his college days. But the strain of marijuana he had tried back then was not half as potent. He didn't even cough with Julio's strain. It went down smooth and kicked in hard.

Ivan forced himself up a third time to pull out a comforter from his hallway closet. He carried it back to the sofa to stretch out with it across the couch, while wrapping it around himself like a mummy.

Man, if I make it through this, I'm never getting high again, he told himself as his body continued to twitch. *This is crazy! I just wanna go to sleep now. I just wanna go to sleep . . .*

MIRACULOUSLY, when his alarm clock went off at a quarter to seven in the morning, Ivan felt sane again. His body was worn out from the uncontrollable movement, his eyes were bloodshot from the smoke, and his hair was mangled from the craziness, but other than that, he had survived his spontaneous experimentation. So he climbed up from the sofa, where he had slept and listened to music all night, and he smiled to himself.

"What don't kill you makes you stronger," he mumbled through his grin. He was overjoyed to still be alive. "But I'm not doing that shit no more," he stated. "I got too much to do."

In opposition to the dark, sporadic energy and paranoia the marijuana had given him the night before, when the high had faded in the morning, Ivan felt light-headed and optimistic.

He walked into the bathroom to take a long leak. "I hope they don't ask me for a cup of this," he told himself with a chuckle. Then he flushed it away.

He clapped his hands in the mirror and said, "I made it back down to earth," as if the weed had taken him on a journey to outer space. "Now I just need a shower, some eyedrops, brush my teeth, get some breakfast, and I'm off for work as usual."

AT TWENTY MINUTES TO EIGHT, Ivan walked out of his apartment in a white office shirt, royal blue tie, and dark brown slacks and shoes, while carrying his black leather briefcase.

When he passed Julio's apartment three doors down, he could hear the kids up and about, playing inside. He then looked down in the parking lot and saw that Julio's pickup truck was gone.

That guy is up and out like clockwork, he thought. *And so am I. The world keeps going no matter what.*

Back out on the highway, Ivan took Interstate 8 toward the Beaches of west San Diego before connecting to Interstate 5 North for the offices of Hutch & Mitchell Accounting in North Clairemont. He needed silence again, while thinking about the ideas he had floating around in his mind before, during, and after the high.

So how do I promote parties? I haven't even thrown a party before, he mused as he drove. *I got the perfect company name for it, though. I.D. Promotions. I got E.A. to thank for that. My initials sound as good as his do. And since I'll be throwing parties with drinking involved, you'll need an I.D. to get in.*

"You can't beat that." He grinned from behind the wheel. I.D. Promotions was a solid brand name. "There's a ton of different ways I can spin that."

But first I gotta make sure the name is available online this morning.

Then he wondered about Lucina Gallo again.

"That's a bad ass girl," he stated. "And the party don't start until she gets there, hunh?"

I'm gonna have to invite her and her friends out to my parties, then. But would she even come . . . ? I'm still a nobody.

He had to deliberate on that for a minute. As he thought it over, his eyes swayed to the houses on the hills that overlooked Interstate 5. Ivan had to drive past the hilltop houses every day to and from work. The mountainside houses had a clear view of the highway traffic, the downtown skyline, the airport, SeaWorld, Mission Bay Park, the Beaches, and the Pacific Ocean. And although Ivan remained curious about them, he had never even priced them before.

You're talking about a million dollars for the basic ones, he assumed. *But maybe I need to ask somebody.*

When he pulled into the parking lot of the industrial park of North Clairemont and found a space, he thought of all the people from the various industries who worked inside the office buildings there.

Somebody owns every last one of these buildings, and all we're doing is working in them, he contemplated as he walked inside and headed toward the elevators.

Hutch & Mitchell Accounting rented half of the fourth floor in a nine-story building.

Ivan stepped off the elevator and walked into the office past the receptionist at the entrance. She was an alert college intern who liked to be at work earlier than everyone else. She wanted to prove that she was willing to put in her dues.

"Good morning, Ivan," she greeted him.

Ivan smiled and nodded to her on his way in. "Good morning."

The accounting office was set up in rows of cubicles, highlighted in royal blue. Surrounding the cubicles were the conference rooms, the manager and supervisor offices, and the attorneys' offices. They all had the window views. At the opposite corners of the building were the partners' offices, with John Hutch at one end and Barry Mitchell at the other. Their offices had the most window space and the best views.

The cubicles were grouped in four areas: the accounting staff, who input all of the numbers; the audit staff, who checked and rechecked the numbers; the tax staff, who applied the proper tax codes; and the general staff, which included the secretaries.

Ivan was one of only three African-Americans at the firm of more than thirty employees. He had served his time at Hutch & Mitchell—a public accounting firm—before passing the California Board of Accounting exam to become a certified public accountant two years ago. Now he worked in the tax department with an income of more than fifty thousand dollars a year. But while his mother continued to suffer from cancer, Ivan had been forced to spend a large portion of it to pay for her medical needs.

Time for me to start making this money work for me, he told himself.

The first thing he did at his desk that morning was go online to search for "I.D. Promotions" as a possible name for his limited liability company for party throwing. As an accountant, he understood firsthand that the primary execution of any business was to secure an attractive and taxable name. As soon as his internet search for "I.D. Promotions" came up empty, Ivan filed online immediately to secure the name with his credit card.

"Hey, Ivan, what are you up to?" someone asked from behind him.

Ivan turned to see who it was before he answered. He wasn't online for work purposes.

"Oh, what's up, Chip? I'm just locking up a business name on this thing," he stated.

Chip Garrett, another CPA, worked in the tax department as well. He was in his early thirties, still single, and his desk was only two cubicles down from Ivan's. Chip was one of the more sociable white guys at the office.

"Oh, yeah? Who for?" he asked Ivan.

The natural assumption was that, as an accountant, you did everything to benefit your clients, especially while at the office.

Ivan told him, "This is actually for me."

That caused Chip to raise his eyebrow with interest.

"Oh, yeah? What kind of business?"

As more of the staff began to arrive at the office, Ivan told him, "I'll tell you at lunchtime." Everyone didn't need to know.

Chip froze for a second before he nodded in agreement. What was Ivan up to?

"Oh, okay. I'll see if we can take our lunch breaks around the same time then."

"Yeah, I'll see you then," Ivan mumbled to him. He wanted to rush the credit card process and get back to work before anyone else could catch what he was doing online.

As soon as he had finished, Dwayne Bellamy, a middle manager, appeared behind him. Dwayne was one of the three African-Americans at the Hutch & Mitchell offices. The third was a filing secretary.

"Ivan, we have a tax staff meeting at ten this morning inside Conference Room B. Would you let everyone know for me?"

Ivan nodded to him. "All right." He studied Dwayne as he walked back toward his office in a dark gray business suit. Dwayne's office was small compared to the other offices, but at least it wasn't a cubicle. He made over six figures in his managerial position. Nevertheless, the man seemed beat down and lifeless.

Shit, I don't want to be like that when I get to his level. That brother acts like he could use a party, Ivan thought.

He got started on his work that morning on tax forms before his cell phone went off on vibration mode.

Ivan looked down to his hip at the number and recognized Catherine Boone's.

Shit! I never called her last night. He panicked. *Do I even answer it?*

Out of courtesy, he decided he would. He planned not to mention anything about not calling her. He would let her bring it up instead.

"Hey, how are you doing? You're on your way out already?"

"Yeah, I'm on my way to the airport now. How was the party last night?" she asked him.

"I couldn't even get in," Ivan admitted. "And I didn't have Emilio's number with me to call him."

"Oh . . . so, what did you do?"

It was an awkward moment. Obviously he didn't call to do anything with her.

He said, "I ended up just driving back home and brainstorming about my plans. I think I want to get involved in throwing some. But I'll tell you about that later. So call me back when you get in."

Catherine wouldn't let him off the phone that easy. "What, you're talking about throwing your own parties now? Is that what you're talking about?"

Ivan figured he had said enough at the office already. He declined further comment.

"I'll tell you about it later when you get in. I have a staff meeting this morning."

Catherine backed off. "Okay."

Ivan wouldn't mind running his party promotion ideas past her for a pros-and-cons discussion, he just didn't want to do so while he was still at work.

IT WAS AFTER TEN O'CLOCK and the tax staff meeting had not yet started. Dwayne Bellamy was having a long, closed-door conference with the supervisors. Since Ivan didn't want to start on anything new that he would need to break away from, he idled doing nothing before the meeting.

He then eyed Mike Adams, an accountant from the audit department, who was working feverishly at his station. Mike was still in his midtwenties, married, with a young child, and had not taken the state exam yet. But he was sure to pass it. He was all work and no play. He took his job very seriously.

Chip noticed Ivan watching Mike and walked over to make a comment on it.

"That guy's going to work his damn fingers to the nub, right?" he joked to Ivan loud enough to be heard.

Ivan chuckled.

Mike overheard them laughing at him. "I heard that," he commented. "But you're both gonna be happy to have someone like me on your side one day."

Chip said, "Oh, I'm already happy you're on my side, buddy. I'm ready to pass you some of my work right now."

Ivan grinned it off before heading to the men's bathroom down the hall. It was right across the hallway from Barry Mitchell's corner office. The partner had his office door wide open that morning while he chatted with another future account, a young Filipino man.

"You know how the government finds a way to tax and ride the proverbial backs of the middle class?" Mitchell asked the young Filipino rhetorically.

Ivan had heard it all from his silver-haired, well-dressed, black-Mercedes-driving boss before. Barry Mitchell was the partner who liked to talk. John Hutch, on the other hand, talked a lot less. Ivan didn't expect the young man inside the office to get many words in as he sat in the tall, comfortable leather chair across from Mitchell's king-sized desk. Hutch had even joked that maybe his partner should have been more of a financial advisor than a tax man, since he liked to talk so much.

"Well, in several ways," Mitchell began to answer for himself. "First of all, since the majority of the middle class is employed by America's larger companies, the government is able to take the money right out of their checks. So they don't have much of a choice. But the rich, who receive the majority of their income through cash receipts, business deals, dividend payouts, real estate sales, and contract payments, are given the opportunity to determine when they want to pay their taxes. By the time that happens, with what's left of it, they can then decide with us how they'd like to shelter it. And with your extreme poor, you'll find that a large percentage of them are paid under the table with cash, which they're not gonna report for taxes. Nor are the poor going to report cash gifts or any kinds of illegal monies.

"So, who ends up paying the majority of the taxes?" he concluded. "You guessed it. The middle class." He said, "The middle class also like to overuse credit, and they always pay the highest rates for it. But you're not gonna give a credit card worth any value to the extreme poor. And with the rich, well, of course, they know better, so they're always going to negotiate the better credit rates."

On that note, Ivan slipped into the restroom and remembered when Barry Mitchell had made a similar speech to him more than five years ago.

"I still haven't been able to get the government off my middle-class back," he mumbled.

When he walked back out of the stall to wash his hands at the sink, he thought, *There are no more excuses for me now. I have all the information I need to make my money work for me. And what I don't know only takes a phone call or a sit-down to find out. So it's all about my willpower now.*

When Ivan exited the bathroom, Mitchell was still going strong in his office.

He said, "The American dream has become such a strong illusion for the middle class that they're actually willing to accept their position as its mule."

One of the older secretaries, who worked close enough in her cubicle to hear every word of Mitchell's lecture, met eyes with Ivan as he walked by.

She shook her head with a frown and was tired of hearing it all. She even let Ivan know her opinion on the matter.

"It's not everyone's goal or purpose to be rich," she stated.

Ivan heard her out and chuckled as he walked by. But he didn't necessarily agree with her.

Is it our goal and purpose to remain mules? he contemplated. *What is our goal and purpose, then? I know I'm not planning to be a mule all my life, while the rich ride my back.*

He reflected on the past nine years that he had spent helping his mother fight cancer. If he had to do it all over again, he would. But that was no longer the case, and his mother had told him in her own breath that he could live his life now.

And that's what the hell I plan to do, he told himself as he arrived back at his desk.

"Hey, Ivan, we're all ready for that meeting now," Chip told him. He was already headed for the conference room.

Ivan nodded and followed him.

When they walked into the conference room, they were joined by a staff of six, with two supervisors and Dwayne Bellamy as the middle manager to oversee the meeting.

They all sat down in dark leather chairs at a cherrywood oval table that seated ten—four on each side, and one at each end.

Kevin Edison, a supervisor and the spokesman for the meeting, shut and locked the conference room door for privacy before he launched into his thoughts.

"Ah, as some of you have already heard, our contracts with Watkins Financial Group, Pellman Developers, Harvey Furniture, and Williams School Supplies are all in their last year, and the clients have not been, ah, considerably pleased with our efforts of late to save them money."

Kevin was a straight shooter in a business that needed and appreciated it. There was no beating around the bush with accounting. The numbers and tax laws spoke for themselves.

No one said a word as he continued.

"So, over the next few weeks, our efforts as the tax staff will be to turn over every new stone to find ways in which we can squeeze another pint or so of orange juice out of the city, state, and federal tax laws—as we know them to be—to try and maintain these very, ah, important clients."

Chip frowned, smiled, and shook his head with a chuckle of sarcasm.

Dwayne read his disturbance and asked him about it. "You have some questions, Chip?"

"Well, yeah, I mean, with all due respect, I understand how important these guys are as clients, but as their accountants, I feel that the auditing department should be the ones to go through all of their books and tell them how they can save more money on *their* end, instead of them coming down on us to find more loopholes in the tax laws.

"I mean, if you ask me, it just doesn't seem fair to put that kind of pressure on us," he commented. "I mean, the tax laws are the tax laws."

Kevin said, "Well, the auditing department is already working on their end. We met with them yesterday."

Dwayne said, "Obviously, you haven't spoken to anyone in the auditing department."

Chip looked confused that they were assumed to have known everything already.

"Well, isn't that what we're ultimately paid to do, to work as a team? But if we weren't told about this in the meeting yesterday, then how are we to know that?"

Ivan stared at Chip and knew better. Chip just didn't want the extra workload. He argued about everything, things that it didn't make any sense to complain about.

Amy Ashford, a tax veteran in her early forties, spoke up to stop Chip's nonsense.

She said, "Well, I did hear about it, and I assumed that we would have our meeting before the week was out, and lo and behold, here we are. So we should all be on the same page now for next week."

Dwayne nodded to her. "Thank you." He looked as if it had been a long day for him already, but it was only 10:37 AM.

Amy turned and addressed Chip before he got a chance to spit any more needless venom.

"Chip, although I see your point that auditing should be the ones to tell a company how it can benefit by tightening up within its own ranks, since we are their accounting firm, it's still considered our job to do everything in our power to find them every way possible to save money. Otherwise, why should they continue to choose us over any other accounting firm? It's all about going that extra mile for the client," she stated.

Ivan spoke up. "That's about it." He knew the deal like the back of his hand. It was what Barry Mitchell had always told them: the rich will bully their way to heaven, and unless their company could tax the middle class to stay afloat like the government did, it was in the best interest of the company to stay in the good graces of those who could afford to write the larger checks.

However, when the meeting was adjourned, Chip was not at all pleased with Ivan's acceptance of the matter.

He pulled Ivan aside for privacy and addressed him in low tones. "Hey, man, I mean, don't you get tired of all the extra ass-kissing they force us to do for some of these dickless clients we're under contract with? I mean, let's get real here, man. How much of that money do we even see for this extra work that we all do?"

Ivan remained silent. Chip had a point. They remained under salary no matter how hard they worked on taxes.

Ivan told himself, *That's exactly why I have other plans now. I'm gonna look out for me as hard as I look out for them.*

But instead of telling that to Chip, he answered, "I understand what you're saying, man. I do. But at the end of the day, our job is to save our clients money. That's all it is."

Chip studied Ivan's eyes and his calm demeanor, and he realized that he was unwavering. Ivan meant what he said, and a man had to respect that. So Chip stuck out his hand for an honorable handshake.

"You're right." He paused and stood there bewildered for a second. "Well, let's get back to work, then," he commented. "We're still on Hutch and Mitchell time."

Chip still managed to slip his wicked sarcasm into the mix. All Ivan could do was laugh about it . . . for the moment. But like he had told himself, he had other plans now.

Three

Black Network Parties

"SO, YOU'RE TELLING ME that you're going to start promoting parties now? I mean, come on, Ivan, are you serious? You've never even thrown a party before."

Catherine was crystal clear over the speakerphone. She made Ivan's idea sound preposterous. But he was adamant and all smiles while sitting on his sofa explaining it to her.

"Do you like the company name, at least?"

"I mean, the name is catchy, yes. But . . . throwing parties is a lot more than a catchy promoter name, Ivan," she warned him. "And I thought you told me you couldn't even get in the party."

"I couldn't. But that's what gave me the idea to throw my own." Ivan was excited by the challenge.

Catherine sighed over the phone. She really sounded concerned. She said, "You're not gonna quit your accounting job for this, are you?"

Ivan frowned at the assumption. "Hell, no, I'm not gonna quit my job. Why would I do that? This is the first time I've had the freedom to work my money."

"Okay, I'm just checking. Don't bite my head off," she told him. She said, "Well, if you're gonna start throwing parties like that, then maybe you should start off with, like . . . after-work network parties or something. Just start with something small. You know what I mean?"

Ivan thought it over and said, "Network parties? How am I gonna make any money off of that? People don't pay for those. That's just the bar making money."

"Well, invite somebody out that they'll pay to see, then. Get some of the Padres to talk about the lack of black players in baseball or something. I don't know."

Ivan thought about that idea as well. He said, "You think I can get Butch and Deke to come out for an after-work crowd? I mean, they got practice and games around that time."

"Look, Ivan, it was only a suggestion. But I think this whole thing is crazy, if you ask me," Catherine snapped.

"All right, well, the first thing I need to do is get my logo and website together. So I'm meeting up with a couple of college guys this weekend to run my ideas past them," Ivan told her.

Catherine said, "A couple of college guys?" It didn't sound professional enough.

"Yeah, I've seen some of their work online before, so I reached out to them with an email as soon as I got home, and they responded back to me to meet up with them tomorrow."

There was an extended pause over the phone while Catherine considered it all. "All right, well, it pretty much sounds like you got your mind made up. So, good luck on it."

"Thanks," Ivan told her. "And what about your job interview? You think they're gonna hire you?"

"We'll see. But I hope they do, though. Because I can't wait to see how you're gonna try and pull off this party promotion thing."

"*Try*? Sounds like you don't believe I can do it."

"Well, you're not exactly Mr. Party Animal, Ivan. Or should I call you Mr. I.D. now?"

Ivan chuckled. He said, "I don't have to be a party animal. All I need to do is put on the party. And I'll find other people to do all that other stuff."

"Can you even dance now, Ivan?" Catherine teased him.

"Yeah, I can still dance. I'm gon' dance to this new money. *Ching, ching, ching, ching-ching, ching, chinnggg,*" he sang in his response.

Catherine chuckled over the phone. She said, "Well, I'm glad you have confidence about it, because you're gonna need it."

Ivan thought hard after that. How much confidence did he have?

"Yeah." That's all he could say. He had done enough talking already. He needed to start putting his plans into motion.

"All right, so, call me up and let me know how this job situation works out," he told her.

"I will. And you let me know how things work out with you."

When Ivan hung up, he was surprised at how well their conversation had gone, considering he had dodged her advances the night before. In the past, Catherine wouldn't call him for a week if she was upset with him, let alone talk to him for an hour.

"I guess she's growing up now," he assumed to himself. Then he pondered his own maturity. "And so am I," he mumbled with a nod.

He figured it was time to move away from the safe road that he had traveled on for so many years and start taking new chances. And he was excited about doing so.

IVAN DROVE THROUGH the familiar territory of College Avenue on San Diego State's campus before reaching University Boulevard. He was en route to make his Saturday meeting with the undergraduate web team of TheFreeWorldWizards.com. They had built a high-adrenaline website that loaded up fast and flashed a constantly changing scenery of graphic designs, photography, and artwork. Ivan had been tipped to check out their energizing site at his office months ago. But he'd had no reason to contact the guys who set it up until now.

He pulled up to the address off of University Boulevard and immediately spotted two college-age white guys sitting on the elevated patio of the apartment. They sat in white beach chairs in front of a plastic white table, awaiting his arrival. In the driveway below them was a light green Camaro emblazoned with superheroes and cartoon characters.

"Ivan David?" one of the college guys asked him as soon as Ivan climbed out of his car. The two partners were total opposites in appearance. One was a heavyset blond with long hair past his shoulders, while the other was slim, with short dark hair and glasses. However, they both wore casual T-shirts and shorts with their loafers.

"So, who is Paul and who is Jeff?" Ivan asked them as he approached the stairs to join them on the patio.

The heavy, long-haired blond answered first. "I'm Jeff and he's Paul."

Ivan nodded. "Okay. Well, I'm Ivan."

They shared a chuckle as Ivan reached them on the patio and sat down in an extra white chair.

Paul told him immediately, "I love your company name. We can do a lot with I.D. Promotions."

"Lots of things," Jeff added. "But what are your ideas for it?"

They were hitting him upside the head fast.

Ivan responded, "Well . . . first of all . . ." He slowed things down a bit. "I want to create a logo where the 'I.D.' part is big and stands by itself. And the 'Promotions' part should almost seem like an afterthought. So in other words, when you're looking at a flyer, as soon as you pick it up, you should be able to read 'I.D.' immediately, and then 'Promotions.' You know what I mean?"

Paul had a large sketch pad and a black pen right there on the plastic white table. He grabbed them both and said, "That's easy." He drew a large, extrathick "I" with a matching period and a large, extrathick "D" with another period. Once he finished that, he wrote the word "Promotions" across the center of the "I" and the "D."

He said, "If you do something like that, all you have to do is change the background colors of the letters, and your brand will pop off of any flyer as soon as you look at it."

Paul then made a large box around the I.D. Promotions logo with enough space to draw a dancing couple to the far right side. At the top of the box, he wrote "Party Downtown," and across the bottom he created scribble-scrabble to represent the other important information.

When it was all finished, Ivan looked at the mock-up of the flyer and grinned. "Damn. Just like that, hunh?" He was impressed.

"Yeah, man, that's easy," Jeff said. "And what we can do is use that same logo for the website, and we can move it around every five seconds or so. So it'll read 'I' period, and then 'D' period, and then we freeze it for a few seconds, before 'Promotions.' Then we move it to the next spot and do it again. You know what I mean?"

Ivan nodded to him. "I can see it already. Top. Bottom. Left. Right. Corner. That's a good idea. It'll really push the name in their heads."

Jeff said, "Yeah, but this is what we were thinking about. With the whole I.D. thing, man, you're sitting on a gold mine. Now, you want to promote parties and other events and things, right?"

Ivan nodded, wondering where the college guys were going with it. "Yeah," he answered.

"Okay, so you're going to be collecting, like, an email list and population data for all of your promotions, right?"

Ivan was still studying him. "Yeah, of course."

Jeff then got excited. He said, "Okay, so that's the coolest part of your company name, because you're basically asking people, 'Who are you?' Like, 'What is your I.D.? Tell us about you.' You know what I mean? And then they'll go online and tell you. And you collect all of their data. And everyone will come to your site and sign on, because they want everyone to know who they are. Being popular is the American way."

Jeff looked at his partner Paul. Paul was all smiles. Then Paul took over with his own excitement.

"So, what we came up with, and what we can do, is, like, have random spotlights of the people and businesses, celebrities and musicians who come out to your parties and events. And, of course, the people who come to the website. And once we build up that list, in no time you can write your own meal ticket for sponsors and advertisers who would love to be a part of what you're building."

Ivan nodded and kept his cool as he ran the concept through his head. He realized that San Diego was a multicultural city, but what audience did he want to attract? Two white college guys pushing his website could very easily lead him to the wrong demographic of people. And although their energy, intentions, and theory were all sound, Ivan had to make sure his new business had a core group to start with. That way he wouldn't end up courting whomever with no particular focus. He summed up all of his own ideas before he responded to them.

"What do you think?" Jeff asked him. He and his partner both looked anxious.

Ivan looked at them both and joked, "If I wanted to sell you this company name for five hundred dollars, would you buy it?"

The college undergrads looked at each other and froze. Jeff was the first to speak up.

"Are you serious?"

Ivan started laughing and paused for effect. "Nah, I'm not serious," he told them. "I'm just tripping off of how you two came up with all those ideas in one night."

"Hey, that's what we do, man," Jeff told him. "Ideas are priceless."

Ivan said, "Okay, well . . . your ideas sound good for later on down the road, once I see where I can go with it. But for right now I wanna build my core audience with the African-American professional crowd, twenty-five and up. And I know it's not a lot of us here, but that becomes my advantage to make sure I hit 'em and I hit 'em hard to get them behind me."

Jeff and Paul listened to where Ivan wanted to go with his website, and it looked as if all of the energy had been sucked out of them.

Jeff was first to speak up. "Well, it's your site, man, we'll do what you want us to do with it, but you can always market and promote to whoever you want. I wouldn't limit who you invite to your site, though. Why would you want to do that?"

To explain himself more clearly, Ivan said, "Okay, let's take your idea for a minute. Now, let's say that we end up spotlighting a blond-haired white girl, who is twenty-two years old, and she likes rock music and skydiving."

He looked them both in the eyes to make his point. "You see where I'm going with this? How in the world am I gonna benefit from that when I know I'm not promoting rock parties and skydiving?"

Paul said, "You never know. But you mainly want to let the site create its own audience. Then you find out where your strongest support is. That's what we did with our site."

Ivan said, "Yeah, but you're not gonna be paying for locations, DJs, security, celebrities, and all the other things that I'll need to pay for to get these parties off the ground. So my website needs to cater to the audience that I'm going after. And once we're able to do that, if we find that the site is attracting other people than what I expected, then we'll find a way to cater to them. And we can sit down and do that together. But I'm not a college student anymore, and I don't have time for this website not to do what I need it to do, especially while I'm paying you for it."

Jeff nodded and understood Ivan's point. He said, "Okay. Well, let me ask you this: If you don't have a lot of time right now to build your own list, would you be willing to buy a data list of African-American professionals in San Diego? Because we can research that for you."

Ivan was still amazed. These guys were fast on their feet.

He said, "You can buy a list like that?"

"That's what telemarketing companies do," Paul answered him. "And now the internet companies are doing it."

The plot thickened.

Ivan nodded and said, "All right. Well, let's try that. In the meantime, what kind of price are we looking at to set up my logo and create and manage my website?"

The college partners discussed all of their price tags, including the management of the website, and nothing jumped out as outrageous, so Ivan planned to agree to most of it. At the same time, good business sense included negotiation, and Ivan wanted to make sure the two college students had an extra incentive to work hard for him.

He said, "Okay. I'll pay you for creating the logo, and I'll give you what you need for creating the site, but I can only pay you so much each month to manage the site until it begins to pay for itself. So the more traffic you create for me with all of your ideas, the more I can agree to pay you for management. Does that sound fair?"

Jeff looked at Paul and didn't see a problem with it. They both had ideas for traffic already.

Paul looked back to Jeff and nodded.

"All right. We could do that," Jeff agreed.

They then discussed putting everything in writing to sign for their next meeting.

Jeff stood up from his chair and said, "Okay, since we're officially gonna be in business with each other, we can show you our lab now."

Paul stood up with him, and that made Ivan stand.

"Follow us," Paul told him.

They walked into a basic college apartment of makeshift furniture, a large-screen TV, video games, and schoolbooks before they led Ivan into a darker, secluded family room. In the darker family room, they had three LCD screens, several computer towers, scanners, a color printer, a fax machine, CDs, DVDs, several office chairs, eccentric posters all over the walls, and plenty of gadgets, artwork, and books all littered around the room.

"And this is our lab, where all of our creativity comes out," Jeff told him.

Their work space was five times more cluttered than what Ivan liked for his personal taste, but he wasn't a graphic designer or webmaster. So whatever worked for them, worked for them.

Ivan smiled and said, "It's amazing how different cultures can be so . . ." He searched for a word to use. *"Different,"* he said with a chuckle.

Jeff jumped in and said, "Hey, man, it's all gonna come together one day," and he locked the fingers of his two hands together.

Paul agreed with a nod. "Like The Matrix," he commented.

Ivan grinned and held back his laugh. *As long as they do what I need them to do, it don't matter much to me,* he told himself. *They can talk about The Matrix all they want.*

IVAN STILL HAD TO BRAINSTORM what his first party would be. So he called some friends who were members of the San Diego Urban League to meet up with him for lunch.

They met at Carol's Soul Food Restaurant, a new establishment in Old Town, off of Interstate 5. The place was only a few exits south from where Ivan worked in North Clairemont.

"Now, when are you gonna stop messing around and join the Urban League, Ivan?" Thomas Jones asked him. He was an older black man in his fifties, with the enthusiastic energy of a thirty-year-old. He didn't let the gray hairs of wisdom slow him down. He was a tireless believer in the old-time religion of black solidarity. Thomas wasn't known to hold his tongue, either. He said what he wanted to say and how he wanted to say it. So Ivan realized he wouldn't be able to get around an Urban League membership.

He sat at a window-view table, enjoying barbecued ribs with

Thomas and Henry Morgan. Henry was in his midthirties. He and Thomas worked for the same real estate firm. In fact, Thomas had recruited Henry a few months before attempting to recruit Ivan.

"How much is the membership again?" Ivan asked them.

"Fifty dollars to become a Young Urban Professional," Henry answered.

"And what are my duties?"

"You don't have any duties unless you want to become an officer, Ivan," Thomas told him. "All we ask for you to do is come to the monthly meetings and participate in some of the community events that we organize."

Ivan figured he had no choice. He had not joined the Urban League before, but now that he wanted them to help him, he would have to join them in some of the things that they wanted to accomplish. Business was business.

He nodded and mumbled through his food, "All right. I can do that."

"Good. We're glad to finally have you on board," Thomas told him. "Now, what's this new promotion business you were telling me about?" he asked before stuffing his mouth with ribs.

Ivan wiped his fingers and lips with a napkin before he spoke. "I want to start organizing events where we can pull together—you know, different people from San Diego's black business community."

Henry looked at him, confused. "That's what we do in the Urban League. You're trying to start your own Urban League now?"

Ivan smiled it off and was ready to explain his ideas again. "Well, it's not just the business community, but the black people of San Diego in general. I wanna give them different places and events where they can come together and enjoy themselves for a few hours. And what I would do is use my website to promote the events and give spotlights to the movers and shakers of black San Diego. I can even set up an events calendar page to push the Urban League meetings."

That gained Thomas's full attention. He nodded and said, "That makes good sense. So basically, you wanna be a San Diego mixer man."

"Whatever you wanna call it," Ivan told him.

Thomas looked around their surroundings and said, "Well, you can start that with this place right here. They're in the middle of a bunch of Spanish restaurants. Carol could use an event here. And I know her personally."

Ivan nodded, thinking it over. He said, "I've always liked the Old Town area. It's in the perfect spot, right off the highway and only minutes away from downtown."

The restaurant had a nice size to it, with paintings of African-American historical figures on the walls. Since the furniture was lightweight and modern, Ivan figured they would have no problem rearranging the place for dancing if they needed to.

Thomas moved on the idea fast. "All right, well, let me introduce you to Carol, then." He stood up from their table and waited for Ivan to follow him back toward the kitchen area. He hadn't even finished with his food yet. He addressed one of the cooks, who was wearing a white apron and a hairnet.

"Hey, Jesse, let Carol know I got somebody out here to meet her. He wants to throw a networking party over here in a couple of weeks."

Jesse heard that and started smiling from behind the tall counter that separated the customers from the kitchen. But Ivan didn't even have a date yet.

"All right, that's good. I'll go and tell her," Jesse commented.

When he disappeared farther into the kitchen, Thomas looked back at Ivan and grinned.

"That's a good idea you came up with, Ivan. Perfect timing, too. I was just telling Carol we need to do something for her over here. All I was doing was telling people about the place. But if you promote a big party . . . now, that's something different."

Thomas was moving full steam ahead with things, but Ivan still needed to calculate it all. How could he make any money off of it?

Will she let me charge people to get in? I wonder how much she makes on a regular Thursday night. He surely didn't want to compete on a weekend. Thursday night was a safer bet.

Before he could finish thinking it over, Carol Henderson, an attractive reddish brown woman in her sixties, with dark eyes and long salt-and-pepper hair, moved out of the kitchen office to meet the young man who wanted to throw a party to promote her new establishment. Thomas told her all about him.

"Hey, Carol, this is Ivan David, a young accountant out of Los Angeles, who went to school down here at San Diego State. He works with the big accounting firm of Hutch and Mitchell. But now he, ah, wants to start promoting parties to spotlight black businesses in the San Diego area, to help bring us all together."

Carol set eyes on him and was pleased already. Ivan had a colorful look that stood out in a crowd.

Carol nodded to him and gave him some of her own history. She said, "It took a long time for my children to convince me to open up this restaurant. But I just told myself that I would do it now before I'm no longer here. And that way I can give my children something that they can continue going with."

Her easygoing talk and position as the family matriarch made Ivan rethink his business ideas. He immediately wanted to help her out and make her proud of her decision to open a restaurant. He had just made the same decision to reach for higher goals himself, only he was less than half her age. She even reminded him a little of his mother.

Yeah, I got plenty of time to make money, he told himself. *So let me just go ahead and put on a good event to start pushing my name.*

He took Carol's soft hand in his and made his pitch. "Well, at I.D. Promotions, what we want to do is identify community people and businesses who deserve attention. And I've always liked Old Town. So I'm glad we have a business like yours in this community."

Carol was speechless, just staring at the young man. His sincerity and colorful eyes were mesmerizing.

Thomas looked over at Ivan himself and held back his thoughts for the moment.

Carol told him, "Well, whatever you need from me, just let me know."

Ivan had to hold his tongue. She was giving him an open door to ask her for a cover charge for a Thursday. But how would she respond to that? Would she think of him as a charming snake and kindly chase him out of her garden? Or would she view it as simple business and take a chance with it? And what would Thomas think?

With all of his thoughts running through his mind at light speed, Ivan opened his mouth and said, "Well . . . what I want to do is promote an 'Old School Eat and Greet After-Work Jam at Carol's Soul Food Restaurant in Old Town.'"

Thomas heard that and shortened it. "An 'Old School Eat and Greet Jam at Old Town'? I like that. But what kind of 'old school' are you talking about, your 'old school' or my 'old school'?" Thomas teased him.

Ivan smiled. He said, "I'll tell the DJ to make sure he mixes it all in."

Carol continued to look him in his eyes. "Well, you just let me know, and whatever you need, we'll set it all up for you. Okay, honey?"

Ivan nodded to her. "Okay."

And that was it. It was a done deal.

Thomas walked Ivan back over to their table and chuckled to himself on the way.

"What's so funny?" Ivan asked him.

Thomas stopped and looked him in the eyes. Then he whispered, "Now, Ivan, I've been selling real estate for twenty-two years, and I know good bullshit when I see it. So I'm standing here the whole time, thinking to myself, *If Carol was just twenty years younger, she'd be all over your yellow ass.*"

Ivan started smiling and shook it off before Thomas could finish.

Thomas said, "Now, you wait until you meet her daughter. You all could pass for family, outside of them light eyes of yours."

Despite their laughter, Ivan got down to business. He said, "Well, what I'll need from you, to pull this thing off, is an email list of people to invite." He stopped himself short of naming the Urban League. He figured he would let Thomas make the connection for himself. Thomas also knew black professionals who were not members of the UL.

Thomas took the bait and said, "Oh, don't worry about that. I got all of that. But I'ma tell you what, Ivan. I think that accounting thing, with you sitting behind a damn desk all day, was the wrong career for you. You need to be out here in front of people. I can see it now. You real easy on the eyes and quick on the conversation. That's why I tried to get you to sell real estate years ago.

"But you gon' do good at this promotions thing," Thomas continued as they reached the table and sat back down. "You mark my words."

IVAN EVENTUALLY worked out a deal with Carol and her business-savvy daughter Ida to charge a five-dollar "donation" that he would share with them after the party. He didn't have the ice in his veins to ask for a full cover charge yet. And just in case his first event was a dud, he wanted to make sure he still had something to offer them for their efforts.

The total expense of the party, including promotional flyers, email blasts, and website updates, was close to eight hundred dollars. Two days before his first big Thursday event, Ivan sat alone at home inspecting the artwork of his first promotional flier. He was very pleased with it.

The flyer mimicked the initial idea that Paul had come up with in his mock-up drawing. On the back of the flier, Ivan allowed them to promote their plan to pull in a broader San Diego email list through the website. So Paul and Jeff enlarged the IDPromotions.com brand across the back, with "Who are you?" slanting across the top left corner, "What do you do?" slanting across the top right, and "Let us know!" across the bottom.

Ivan had to admit that it was a clever idea. They had street teams passing out fliers all over the city. Once they attracted high traffic to the website, they had all the right questions set up to collect the needed data.

The biggest decision was whether or not Ivan wanted to promote himself on the site. But he decided not to. He wanted to get his promotion business off the ground first. He forced himself to rationalize that it wasn't about him yet; it was all about the promotions idea.

As soon as Ivan set his flyer back in the pile of a hundred or so that sat out on the coffee table in front of him, Catherine Boone called him on his cell phone. She had gotten the job in Oceanside and was moving back to San Diego that same week. She was extra excited about it.

"Isn't this perfect timing, Ivan? I fly into San Diego on the same day that you kick off your first party," she told him.

Ivan wasn't as excited. Just as Thomas had told him, Carol's daughter Ida was a good-looking match, and he looked forward to working with her. However, if Catherine showed up, with her familiarity with him, along with her control issues, he figured she would get in the way of his plans to charm Ida.

"Does your flight get in early enough for that?" he asked Catherine. He hoped that it didn't. Or at least that she would cut it close. That would leave him no time to worry about her.

Catherine answered, "Yeah, I land at eleven in the morning. I wanted to make sure I had enough time to get in and get settled. I got my outfit and shoes ready and everything."

Ivan said, "Yeah, well, you know I won't have time to pick you up or anything—"

Catherine cut him off. "Ivan, please, I know that. I have a rental car set up. I mean, it's not as if I'm unfamiliar with San Diego. I know how to get around. Old Town is right off the damn highway."

She was biting his head off with her assertiveness already. He could just imagine the amount of his time she would want to consume at the event. So he hated the idea of her being there.

I'm just gonna have to be frank with her, then, he told himself. Any attempt to beat around the bush with Catherine would be in vain. The woman didn't respond well to hints.

Ivan said, "Well, I'ma let you know right now, when I'm doing this party, I won't have time to be locked up in a corner somewhere. I need to be able to meet and greet with people."

Catherine paused for a second. "So, what are you trying to say, Ivan, that I'm gonna be all over you or something? Because it's not even like that. I just want to see you pull this thing off as a friend. But if you don't want me to come, then just let me know."

Ivan was already shaking his head and breathing deeply to compose himself. He said, "Catherine, I'm just letting you know beforehand that my attention is all on this business right now, and I don't want you getting your feelings hurt or being offended by me not paying enough attention to you."

"Ivan, what did I tell you inside the hotel room when you left me to go to that party?"

He remembered it like it was yesterday. "You told me you were a grown fucking woman."

"And that's what I meant," she told him again.

Ivan nodded with his cell phone in hand. "All right."

WHEN THAT THURSDAY ARRIVED, Chip Garrett was more than curious to know why Ivan was dressed so nicely and why he was rushing around the office to leave an hour early.

"What you got going on tonight, Ivan? You're obviously dressed and ready to do something."

Ivan wore a navy blue pin-striped suit to work that morning, with black leather shoes, a stylish multicolored tie, and a baby blue dress shirt. He had gotten a fresh haircut that Wednesday. But he was still hesitant to let anyone at the office know too much about his promotion plans, especially while he was just getting his business started. He didn't know how the bosses would respond to any gossip about it yet. And with Chip complaining about their workload, Ivan didn't want to add any fuel to the fire about his moonlighting with a new hustle.

"I'll tell you in a few more months after I see if this goes anywhere with her first," Ivan insinuated on purpose. He never had come clean with Chip about his new business plans. They had so much work around the office that Chip forgot to ask him again. But when Ivan began to mislead him about a woman, his teammate in the tax department looked surprised.

"What, all this over a girl? Are you kidding me?"

Mike Adams overheard the conversation on his way past the cubicles and stopped to put his words in.

"Don't worry, Ivan. I got your back on getting serious. Chip only knows how to speed-date. He doesn't know what getting serious is all about."

Chip said, "Yeah, I know what it's about, it's about busting your ass prematurely for a wife and kids, that's what it's about."

Mike shook off the personal slight. He said, "Just imagine if your dad had thought that way. You possibly wouldn't have made it here."

"Actually, my dad had me when he was thirty-five, so I'm right on schedule. Maybe I'll even wait until I'm *forty*-five," Chip teased.

Ivan grinned and said nothing. He was admiring his curveball. He did think of telling Dwayne Bellamy as a member of his core audience of African-American professionals over twenty-five, but since Dwayne was a middle manager, he was not safe to trust. Furthermore, Dwayne had previously kept his race a nonissue, so Ivan had no idea where he stood on color codes or social settings away from work.

On the way out of the office at slightly past five, John Hutch caught up with Ivan at the elevator and gave him a word of advice.

"Just keep your focus, Ivan. You've been doing well." He gave Ivan a smile and a thumbs-up before the elevator arrived.

"That's all in my plans," Ivan told him with a smile of his own. As soon as he walked onto the arriving elevator and the doors closed behind him, he began to wonder what his boss really meant.

Was that a real pat on the back or a warning? he pondered. *Does he know that I'm about to start up something else? Or is he thinking that I'm lovestruck for a girl like the rest of them?*

Ivan wondered about that for the rest of the elevator ride.

If the word travels that damn fast at the office about my personal life, then I can never tell these folks what I'm really into. What would they think about me throwing parties?

When he walked out of the elevator with employees from the various floors and industries, Ivan was still thinking about his dilemma.

I need to figure out a way to work this all out, he told himself on the way to his car. *But hell, if this party shit don't even work, I could put myself in a bunch of extra confusion for nothing.*

As soon as he made it to the highway on Interstate 5, heading south for Old Town, he landed right in the middle of rush-hour traffic. He called Carol's Soul Food Restaurant to speak to Ida.

"Hey, Ida, this is Ivan."

"Oh, hey, Ivan. This phone has been ringing off the hook like crazy today, so we just might have a good crowd tonight. And the DJ is here setting up his equipment already."

Ida Stewart—her father's last name—was two years older than Ivan at thirty, but she didn't look it. She looked no older than twenty-five, with smooth light brown skin, a slim frame, long dark hair, and the dark eyes of her mother. She had never been married or borne any children.

Ivan heard her out and said, "That's good. I'm on my way, but I'm making it through slow traffic right now."

She chuckled. "Yeah, I can imagine, at this time of day. But that's the beauty of this location. All you have to do is make it halfway downtown, or halfway away from town."

Ivan said, "That's a good way of looking at it. But, umm, at six o'clock, if I'm not there yet, you won't have a problem collecting the five dollars at the door, will you?"

Ivan still had to build a full staff.

Ida told him, "Excuse me? Oh, honey, I have no problem at all asking folks for money. We think way too much about freebies as it is. Five dollars is just like you said on this flyer, a 'donation.' And it's not hardly a big one. So don't worry about the door money at all. I got you."

Ivan laughed. "Okay. It's good to hear that."

"All right, well, let me get back to answering this phone, because people are ringing me on the other line already," she told him.

"Okay, I'll see you in a minute."

Ivan hung up his cell phone and smiled from ear to ear. "Now, that's the kind of woman I need on my team, right there," he told himself.

When he got off the highway at Old Town and made his way to the restaurant, he found that a parking spot had been reserved for him right out front.

"You're Ivan David, right?" one of the restaurant workers asked him through his open window as he pulled his car into the spot.

"Yeah."

"Well, come on in, brother, we getting the place good and ready for you."

Ivan liked that feeling of importance already. He climbed out of his car and walked into the restaurant all smiles. As soon as he walked in, The Notorious B.I.G. was blasting through large speakers, *"I love it when you call me big pop-pa . . ."*

"It's a five-dollar donation tonight, sir," Ida teased him through the music. She was sitting behind a small table right inside the doorway, wearing a colorful flower-child dress, straight out the seventies.

Ivan laughed and dug into his pocket to pay her. "Boy, you took that term 'old school' to heart, didn't you?" he asked her, noticing her dress code.

"Yeah, I figured I'd dig into my closet and see what I could come up with," she responded. Then she waved his money off. "Go 'head, I was only teasing you."

Ivan refused to take his money back. "Nah, nah, I like that policy. Nobody gets in free, not even me. So when the hookup patrol shows up, we'll tell them that we paid to get in, too. So you put your five dollars in," he told her.

Ida said, "Yeah, like they're gonna believe us, right? But okay." She dug into her small purse to add a five-dollar bill to his before tossing them both into the cash box with the rest of the money. About seven people had shown up and ordered food, ten minutes before six.

Ivan looked around the place and noticed the chairs and tables pushed closer toward the walls for an open dance floor. There was darker lighting than usual, with the DJ equipment and speakers set up toward the back corners.

Ivan nodded his head and liked what he saw. *This might work out all right in here tonight,* he figured. Capacity was enough for two hundred. Ivan just hoped to see over a hundred to cover his flyer costs, after sharing half of the total with the restaurant.

By seven o'clock, more than a hundred people were already there enjoying themselves, including white Americans, Latinos, and Filipinos, who loved old school music, soul food, and a good time after work as well.

Thomas, Henry, and quite a few of the San Diego Urban League members were excited by the turnout. Catherine showed up with an attention-getting yellow dress to engage the crowd on her own, and without Ivan needing to babysit her.

Thomas and Henry even asked him who she was. Ivan laughed and told them he had gone to college with her and no more than that. All the while, Jeff and Paul were there snapping pictures to document it all for the website.

At the height of the party, around eight, when the restaurant was nearly filled to capacity with supporters, great food, conversation, business-card-passing, and dancing, Thomas pulled Ivan aside. He said, "I told you you're gonna do all right with this. Now what you need to do is stop the party, the music, and the dancing, and let everybody in the room know who you are before they start to leave."

Thomas had a point. It was a grand opportunity for folks to celebrate the man who put the idea together. Nevertheless, Ivan remained hesitant. He tried to shake it off with a grin.

"I don't mind if they don't know. As long as they all signed the email list at the door and they know that I.D. Promotions was behind it, I can continue to be a mystery," he commented.

Thomas stared at him and didn't go for it. He said, "Ivan, if your ass don't get up in front of all these people and let them know you and like you, then you's a damn fool. I thought you told me you wanted to be the San Diego mixer man. Well, you better get ready to act like it."

Ivan argued, "They'll find out eventually. This is just the first one. Let's just let them talk about how much of a good time they had."

Thomas continued to stare at him. He couldn't believe it. So he backed up and tried another route.

He said, "Well, that's real humble of you and everything, young man, but you at least need to thank the people for coming out here tonight, Ivan. And what about thanking the host, Carol's restaurant, and that fine daughter of hers? Hell, you can even thank me and the members of the Urban League for coming out here to-night, and for sending out email blasts about it."

Shit! Ivan thought. Thomas had him. He couldn't back away from thanking everyone. It was the right thing to do.

Just as he got ready to accept his fate, Ida stopped by to talk to him.

"Can I borrow Ivan for one minute?" she said to Thomas.

Thomas told her, "Yeah, after he introduces himself to the crowd and thanks everybody for coming out here tonight."

Ida said, "Perfect. So you have the DJ stop the music, and I'll go in with Ivan to bring my mother out, and we'll do it all together."

Thomas looked at Ivan and grinned, knowing that he had him now.

"That sounds like a plan to me," he told Ida.

"Good. We'll be right back out."

As Ida pulled Ivan back into her mother's office past the kitchen, he could see Catherine watching them from the dance floor in her yellow dress.

I can't worry about her right now, he mused. *I told her what time it was before she came out here tonight.*

When Ida got Ivan inside the back office with her mother, she closed and locked the door behind them and pulled out a roll of money from her small purse.

She said, "My mother and I want you to keep all of the door money, Ivan. You've earned it. We've already made nearly three times what we expected on food and drinks tonight."

Ivan looked at Carol, sitting behind her desk in the small office. She was nodding with a smile, happy but exhausted from supervising all of the extra cooking.

She said, "You really did it for us tonight. And we are just so grateful that we wanted to donate our share back to you."

Ivan was speechless. He would do more than cover expenses now. And though it wasn't a lot, it was a positive start for him.

Finally, he said, "Thank you. And we plan to post the pictures of this first event on the website and continue to promote the restaurant for you."

Ida asked him, "Well, how much would that cost us, Ivan? Because I already told you, we expect too many freebies from our people as it is."

Ivan hadn't even thought about a rate for advertising on his website yet. He didn't know where to start. But since he was thinking about breaking even, he came up with, "Two hundred dollars for a month," the exact cost of his website management.

Ida asked him, "That's all? Well, we can do that tonight."

Ivan smiled. He said, "That's actually a discount price because I don't know what to charge yet. You would be my first advertiser."

"And we were your first big party," Carol told him. "So we both start off together."

Ivan nodded. "That's cool with me."

Ida said, "Okay, Mom, I know you're tired and all, but I need to borrow you for one more second so we can all thank everyone for coming out to support us tonight."

Carol nodded and grunted, "All right."

Ivan and Ida walked out with her back to the main floor. Thomas had already asked the DJ to stop the music and get the microphone ready. Once he spotted Carol walking out with her daughter and Ivan, he got the microphone and brought it over to them.

He then addressed the anxious crowd. "If I can, I'd like to have everyone's attention . . . I want to introduce the owner of the restaurant, her daughter, and the young man who helped us all to organize and promote this wonderful event this evening."

"YEAH!" a bunch of the supporters yelled out with hand clapping.

"Great food!" someone else yelled.

"Thank you!" Ida yelled back for her mother. They had plenty of relatives who worked in the kitchen and at the cash register, but Ida had been the most vocal spokesperson for the business.

"So, without further ado, I give you Carol Henderson and her daughter Ida," Thomas told the crowd.

Some of the supporters roared again before Ida took the microphone to introduce her mother.

She said, "It's been thirty years of my life, eating my mother's delicious food, and *finally,* after I begged her to open a restaurant for nearly *ten years,* she went ahead and did it, with the help of friends from the Urban League and the local banks, earlier this year."

"YEAH!" the crowd roared again.

Ida continued, "And I must admit that it has not been easy, but it has been well worth it. But I'm gonna stop right there and let my mother say the rest, because I can get to talking, which my family already knows."

"Unh-hunh," one of the family members belted from the kitchen.

"I heard that," Ida teased. "Anyway . . ." She turned to her mother and kissed her on the cheek. "I love you, Momma. And I am so proud of you. I'm proud of *all* of us."

The crowd watched, inspired by it. Even Ivan felt choked up.

Carol held the microphone and looked at all of the people who came out in support of her restaurant, and she paused to compose her words.

She said, "I wanna thank . . . first of all . . . God, for giving me the talents to cook. Then I want to thank my family . . . for always telling me how good it was."

The crowd laughed and continued to listen. Jeff and Paul were all over it, taking pictures of everything.

Carol said, "I want to thank my friend Thomas and the Urban League for being so supportive . . ."

Thomas held up a raised power fist with his head down for the members of the Urban League to yell out their continued support.

"YEAH!"

Carol said, "And I want to thank all of you for coming out and enjoying my food this evening," for more yells. Then she looked at

Ivan. "But without this young man and his ideas to promote community businesses through his website and network parties, some of you would never know that my restaurant was even here."

When Jeff and Paul heard that, they wished they had enough light to record it all on video camera instead of just taking pictures. But they were excited just the same.

Carol continued, "So, I want *all* of us to thank Mr. Ivan David and his I.D. Promotions company for bringing us all together tonight."

"YEEEAAAAHHHH!" the crowd roared nice and long for him. Ivan got the biggest applause yet. Catherine was beaming at him right in front of the crowd in her standout yellow dress. And by the time Carol passed the microphone to him, Ivan was a nervous wreck.

He'd had no idea how it felt to be at the center of attention in front of a supportive crowd like that. Only a few of his friends and relatives were there to cheer him on at his high school and college graduations. And he had never done any public speaking. It was one thing to dream about having a name that inspired a supportive crowd, but it was something else to actually acquire it.

Ivan held the microphone in front of his first crowd of people and felt nauseous. Everything stood still and seemed deadly silent for a minute. He felt them all around him, awaiting his voice. Then he looked forward at Catherine. She was nodding her head to him to go ahead and speak. *You've done it!*

Shit! Here we go, Ivan told himself with a deep breath.

He opened his dry mouth and said, "I, ah, just had an idea . . . to do something extra. And sometimes you don't really know how it's all gonna come together, but you just try to go out and do it. So . . . that's what I'm doing. And I want to thank everybody in here for coming out and showing that we're alive."

Once he got his nervousness out of the way and the people started cheering and clapping again, Ivan made sure to revert back to his calm business mode.

He said, "So, if you all don't mind, I want to make sure that everyone signs the email list at the door, so that we can contact everyone and do this again."

Jeff and Paul were cheesing like circus clowns. That was just what they wanted to hear from him.

"But I don't want to take up too much more of your party time," Ivan told the crowd. "So please, go back to eating, greeting, drinking, dancing, and just . . . having a good time."

Part II

The Pros & Cons of Partners

Four

The Intimidator

After Ivan finished his short speech at his kickoff event, Thomas took the microphone back from him and addressed the crowd again for himself.

"There you have it, folks. Ivan David from I.D. Promotions. And you all remember that name, because we're going to be doing plenty more events with him."

Thomas looked back over to the DJ, a young Puerto Rican man in his midtwenties. He called himself the Red Face Lion. He had agreed to spin at Ivan's first event for free. The trade-off was promotion from the website, and a promise from Ivan that he would use him for future events as they both built their business brands.

"All right, put that music back on," Thomas barked at him.

The DJ was already set to play the old school classic "Joy and Pain" from Maze. When he spun the popular record, the crowd broke into a frenzy and went back to the dance floor.

Ivan took a deep breath and was glad his speech was over. He hugged Ida and her mother before they returned to their back office. He then apologized to Thomas.

"Hey, I'm sorry I forgot to thank you and the Urban League, but I was a little nervous, and I felt like we had already stopped the party long enough."

Thomas told him, "You don't have to apologize to me. I understand. Carol had already thanked us anyway." He said, "But I will tell you this, though, you better get good and used to speaking out in public. Because if you're serious about the promotion game, you can't afford to be shy. You know what I mean?"

Ivan smiled it off. He was already thinking of ways to minimize his need to be at the center of attention. He would rather the events go over well instead.

Jeff and Paul rushed over to him next. They had taken plenty of photographs of the event, and they couldn't wait to start uploading the best pictures for the website.

"Hey, you did it, man. And this is just the first one. How do you feel?" Paul asked him.

Ivan nodded. "I feel good," he told them, especially considering he would make a small profit. That was better than he expected.

"Well, we got plenty of pictures, man. So we're gonna head back and download them on a disc so you can tell us what images you definitely want for the site," Jeff told him.

As his young webmasters walked out, more of the crowd approached Ivan with their business cards, event ideas, and basic small talk. Catherine watched from a distance, aroused by everything. Ivan was the big man on campus for the night. But Thomas stepped in to intervene.

He calmly pulled Ivan aside from all of the hoopla surrounding him in the room to speak to him in private.

He said, "Now, here's the hard part, Ivan. I know everybody in here is gonna have a business idea for you. But most of them are gonna be blowing a cloud of smoke up your ass. So you can't deal with everybody. You hear me?"

He continued, "The oldest rule in business still applies, Ivan: money talks, bullshit walks. So you're gonna have to put on a tough coat of skin real fast and get used to telling a lot of people no."

Ivan grinned and reminded him, "I told you no, several times. I just wasn't into joining things then."

Thomas nodded. "That's good. A lot of people who make it big are not joiners. They always got their own ideas. But they do understand when they *need* to join."

"Yeah, like I joined up with you now," Ivan told him. It had been perfect timing for both of them. However, Ivan didn't feel like hearing a business lecture from Thomas in the middle of the party. He planned to cut their talk short until a better time.

He said, "We'll talk about it. But let me finish meeting some of these people in here before they leave."

Thomas looked and noticed a line forming in the background to speak to the young promoter. He shook his head and knew better. He said, "All right, but you're gonna need an assistant for all that real soon. A good gatekeeper."

BY THE TIME IVAN had spoken to the dozens of businesspeople who wanted to meet him, it was well after nine o'clock. He felt drained. He had barely slept the night before while preparing his mind and body for the event. But when he observed Ida admiring him from behind the counter with a smile, he felt an extra tingle of energy to extend his night if needed.

Right on cue, Catherine stepped out in front of him in her yellow dress.

"So, what are you doing afterward?"

Ivan was caught off guard. "I, ahh . . . I really don't—"

"You wanna go get a drink?"

Catherine looked as sexy as ever and was begging for his personal attention again.

Ivan used his peripheral vision to notice if Ida was watching them. She appeared to be counting their take for the evening behind the cash register.

Yeah, she saw it, he told himself. *She's only counting that money to play it off. She already knows how much they made tonight.*

He focused back on Catherine. He answered, "I'm a little tired in here already. Then I would have to drive back home afterward."

"Not if we have somewhere to go. We can take it wherever. I don't start work until Monday," she hinted with a sledgehammer.

Shit! Ivan panicked. She was making things awkward, just like he knew she would. He still didn't want to deal with her on a physical level anymore.

He said, "You're not gonna hate me for saying no, are you?" He was hoping she would continue to take the mature road.

Catherine paused and kept her cool. She told him, "You do what you wanna do, Ivan. I'll be just fine." When she turned to walk away, she tossed an obvious eye toward Ida behind the counter.

Ivan caught it and shook his head. *Women,* he thought. *You can't live with them, and I'm having a hard time living without them.*

As soon as Catherine walked out the door, Ivan thought about speaking to Ida again. She walked away and headed back toward the kitchen before he could make his move.

Just my luck, he thought. *So I end up home alone again. At least I got a pocketful of money and people know me this time.*

Once Ivan turned to gather himself to leave, Ida was there to whisper into his ear. She approached him swiftly from the back room.

"It's tough juggling so many women, isn't it?" she assumed.

He was caught off guard again. He chuckled and shook his head. "It's not even like that. You see I'm all alone now, right?"

Ida looked at him curiously. She asked him, "Are you sure?"

"Yeah."

She grinned and said nothing else before walking away from him.

Ivan stood there feeling useless.

Is she toying with me or what? he asked himself. Ida seemed interested enough to engage him, but to what extent? *Maybe I just need to back off and see if she gets in touch with me on her own,* he thought.

With the party winding down and the restaurant preparing to close at ten o'clock, he felt no reason to remain there. Thomas and most of the Urban League members had already left. So Ivan walked back toward the kitchen to let Ida and her mother know that he would be leaving.

Ida walked into him before he made it back.

"Oh, hey, I was just about to come and get you," she told him.

"Come and get me for what?" He wanted to hear her intentions.

"Well, I wanted to take my mother home and then see what, you know, you were getting into. But I have to warn you, I can't stay out too late," she told him.

Ivan smiled. "Me either. I still have to work in the morning."

"I know that's right. Bills are bills. But anyway, I was just gonna come back out and ask, you know, what you were doing."

Ivan nodded. He thought, *I wanna be doing you,* but of course, he couldn't say that to her. Instead, he told her, "I'm open. It's whatever."

"Okay, so, I'll call you as soon as I drop off my mother."

Ivan held in his smile to hide his eagerness. "All right, you do that. But actually, I wanted to tell your mother bye for myself."

Ida looked him in the face and cooed, "Aww, isn't that so sweet of you. Come on back."

He chuckled and felt like a member of the family.

WHEN HE WALKED OUT of Carol's Soul Food Restaurant, slightly before closing time, Ivan stopped outside his car, looked around, and sniffed the night air.

Yup, he told himself. *I can get used to this. This feels good.*

He drove off for the highway and slid in the upstart rapper 50 Cent's groundbreaking CD *Get Rich or Die Tryin'*. It was a perfect title for Ivan's present state of mind.

However, as soon he arrived at home and began to feel good about meeting back up with Ida, she called him with bad news.

"Ivan, I'm sorry, but I won't be able to make it back out tonight. It's already ten thirty and I'm exhausted. So I wanna make it up to you this weekend. Is that all right?"

What could a guy say to that? He had to agree to it.

"Hey, it's all good, we're all worn out. Just call me tomorrow and we'll figure something out," he told her. Quick and to the point was the best policy. That way he wouldn't sound disappointed.

But when he hung up his cell phone, he was.

"Shit! I'll just have to wait for tomorrow, then," he lamented. Not that he expected anything major on their first date, but just knowing that Ida wanted to extend the night with him was sexy. But, with the prospect of his extended evening gone, he felt anxious with unused energy.

I hate when I feel this way, he admitted. *Now I won't be able to sleep good tonight.*

"Unless I call Catherine back," he joked aloud. He shook it off and laughed. "Nah, that wouldn't be right."

When his cell phone went off a few minutes later, Catherine was calling him.

Ivan read her cell number before he answered. He couldn't imagine another positive phone call from her after he'd turned her advances down twice in a row. But he wanted to hear her out anyway. So he answered his phone.

"Hello."

Catherine wasted no time digging into him. "You know, I tried not to say anything about this, I really did. But it's really fucked up how you treated me tonight after *I* gave you the idea to start off with a small after-work network party. So I hope you're enjoying yourself. And by the way, thanks for the gratitude."

She hung up on him before he could get a word in. Ivan sat there in his usual spot on the sofa and wondered if he should call her back.

What the hell am I gonna say to her? he wondered. *It's probably best to go ahead and do her tonight. That's what she really wanted, right? That would have been her thank-you.*

Only he couldn't force himself to do it. He knew that if he did call her back and went through the process of pleasing her, he would create more guilt for himself that she would use against him later. So Ivan forced himself to leave it alone.

AFTER THE SUCCESSFUL NETWORK PARTY, the IDPromotions.com website was loaded up with an event photo gallery, a spotlight section on Carol's Soul Food Restaurant, pop-up floaters on where else to eat, where else to drink, where else to party, what else was hot in San Diego, an event calendar page, and floating announcement banners.

Ivan went online to check out his new website three times a day, morning, afternoon, and night, just to admire it.

"I don't know how they do it, but I'm loving it," he commented. Jeff and Paul had designed the website's energy and sizzle. The vivid pop-ups made sure that you never got bored. And with Ida being so open to advertising, it gave Ivan plenty of confidence that others would follow suit. Jeff and Paul were sure of it. So they plugged in an "Advertise Here" pop-up on the site.

But instead of taking advertisement money immediately, Ivan wanted to create a waiting list so they could adjust the prices. By making them all wait, he could see who had the longest money and serious intentions. As with most advertising vehicles, long-term deals and up-front money would receive the best rates.

With no time to waste, Ivan planned a second meet-and-greet event with another friend and business associate of Thomas Jones. A Filipino owner of Raymond's Hot Spot Lounge, a large new bar on San Diego's southeast side, was willing to allow Ivan to keep a cover charge, as well as receive 25 percent of the bar.

Thomas said, "That's an offer you can't refuse, Ivan. Or else I wouldn't have bothered you with it. Most of these owners want you to pay a bar guarantee after they charge you a rental fee to keep the door. But all he wants to do is let folks know that he's there," Thomas explained.

Ivan was skeptical of such a great deal so early in the promotions game. What glitters ain't always gold. So he checked the place out, believing it was a hole-in-the-wall establishment in a dead location. But when he saw the place, he loved it. It was much larger than he expected, and the place was easy to find, with plenty of parking available.

"So, you just want me to turn this place out with a drinking crowd, is that it?" Ivan asked the owner.

Raymond was a short, handsome Filipino man with slick, combed-back hair who had married a black woman and liked to mingle in different crowds.

"If you can do it, let's make it happen," he challenged Ivan.

Ivan looked around at the place again and thought about it. *Since his spot is new and he doesn't have a crowd yet, he'll use me to create one, and then he'll act like the rest of the owners. So I may as well take advantage of this while I got it,* he reasoned.

Even though he was new to the promotions game, Ivan was no fool. So he pitched his deal.

He said, "I'll do it, but only if you let me do at least three more events the same way, my door and twenty-five percent of the bar."

Raymond stopped and thought it over. Three events wouldn't kill him. And just in case the first one didn't do the trick, maybe they could use more.

"All right. I can do that," he agreed.

That sealed the deal. However, Ivan was also skeptical of the crowd that came out to Carol's in Old Town. An "Old School Eat and Greet Jam in Old Town at Carol's Soul Food Restaurant" had a ring to it. Old Town was also a centrally located area. But a bar on the southeast side would be different, especially for an after-work crowd. Raymond's Hot Spot Lounge was more like a Friday night sweatshop, not a meet-and-greet event in business attire. So Ivan had to brainstorm a minute to come up with the correct promotion for it.

After a few hours of writing ideas down and scratching them out over his coffee table, he decided to call it "Old School Jam Part II—A Throwdown at Raymond's Hot Spot Lounge." He used the same flyer layout as the first one, but with fiery reds and neon greens and blues to represent the sexy nightlife. Paul drew a new couple in party clothes, dancing with drinks in their hands. He and Jeff also added the tagline "Music by Red Face Lion" for the DJ.

The event was set for "9 o'clock Until You Drop" with a "$10 a Holler" cover charge on a "Friday Night." The back of the flyer remained the same as the first one: "Who are you? What do you do? Let us know! @ IDPromotions.com."

It was another attractive and workable flyer. Ivan thought so, and Raymond absolutely loved it. But when Thomas saw it over at the Urban League offices, he felt embarrassed to hand it out. He looked at it, flipped it over a few times, and winced.

"I don't know about this new flyer, Ivan. It looks like you're getting a little too, ah . . . hip-hoppy for the real old school."

Ivan laughed and remembered how old Thomas was.

"Nah, man, this is a different crowd from an eat-and-greet event at Carol's. This is a bar on the southeast end, Thomas. I gotta bring it how they're gonna want it," Ivan reasoned. He said, "They don't want to sip no drinks on a Friday night wearing business clothes to a bar in the 'hood. They want to throw the drinks down, party hard, get sweaty, and take somebody home to make a baby."

Thomas chuckled, but he remained reserved. "Now, you know you're stereotyping a little bit there, Ivan. Some of us black folks still like a nice time out without all that funk and sweat."

Ivan stopped and thought. He said, "You know what, you're right. We do like nice affairs. So when I do a ballroom event for fifty dollars a plate and invite Jesse Jackson to speak, then I'll promote it that way. But for a bar on the southeast end, this is how you promote it."

Thomas looked at Ivan and asked him, "So, when did you become an expert on parties, after one damn event, Ivan?"

Ivan had to laugh at the audacity of it himself. After scoring just one lucky touchdown, the rookie receiver was already speaking as if he had been to five football Pro Bowls in Hawaii.

He said, "All right, you got me on that. I'm not the expert yet. I'm just following my gut on this. I've been around black people and enough parties to know a li'l something. I mean, I'm from LA, and my older brother partied hard all the time. So I guess I just picked up on a few things that I never had a chance to use before," he explained.

Henry Morgan walked into the offices in the middle of their conversation and picked up one of the flyers to look at for himself.

"Hey, fellas," he addressed them both with a nod. "So, this is your new event, Ivan?"

"Yeah. What do you think about that flyer?" Thomas asked him.

Henry studied it in detail before he answered. "It looks like it fits the audience."

"And what audience is that?" Thomas questioned.

"You know, that Friday night, boogie-woogie-woogie crowd," Henry answered. He even did a dance move with it.

Ivan broke out laughing. He said, "I'm trying to tell him, Henry. That's the crowd that do their thing at bars."

Thomas stopped the clowning. "Well, here's my thing, Ivan: what crowd do *you* want to be known for? That's the more important question."

It was a good question, too. Ivan approached it from a different angle. He said, "The way I look at it, I want to have enough of a following for I.D. Promotions where I can promote different events to different crowds. My goal is to have three parties for three different crowds on the same night."

The bigger ideas of Jeff and Paul were beginning to rub off on him.

Henry looked at Thomas and said, "Whoa, the man got big

ideas. But I think it can be done. Especially how you have your website set up. You got it set up to appeal to a lot of different people."

"That's the point," Ivan commented. "I want to be like a shopping mall for parties. That's why I'm not really pushing *me* so much. It's all about the brand."

"Yeah, but you don't want your brand confusing folks, either," Thomas argued. "Because you can't be all things to all people."

Ivan said, "Well, right now I'm focusing more on black people. But who's to say where you can go with it? San Diego is that kind of town. I even want to do some military parties.

"But *you* brought me to the table on this, Thomas," he reminded him. "What kind of party did you expect me to throw at a local bar?"

Thomas answered, "Not one where you need a roomful of security and metal detectors, that's for sure."

Ivan said, "Now, whose stereotype is that?"

"Well, that's what you're gonna get if you push it that way," Thomas argued. "You keep trying to invite everybody and see what happens."

Ivan looked back at Henry. "What do you think, Henry?"

Henry shrugged. "Well, I wouldn't go to that party, that's not my crowd. But if you're gonna throw a party in that area, then you need to make sure that it appeals to the people who live there."

Ivan looked back at Thomas and concluded, "That's all I'm saying."

Thomas didn't have any more to say about it. "All right. We'll see," he grumbled.

WITH A CAPACITY of nearly three hundred at Raymond's Hot Spot Lounge, Ivan hoped to make two thousand at the door and another five hundred from the bar, more than double what he had made at Carol's. Then he would ask Raymond for three to five hundred dollars for an advertisement banner on his website.

In preparation for his second event, Ivan spent additional money for liability insurance to protect his company from any nonsense that might occur at the locations. Then he promised to pay Red Face Lion out of the door and bar take, and also Ida, who agreed to show up and help collect the cover charge. Security was supplied by the lounge.

On the marketing end, Ivan had street teams pass out his flyers, specifically in the south and southeast San Diego regions, as opposed to all over the city like the first flyer. He expected Raymond's to be a more localized event. He put his website on full blast to promote it. The word continued to spread about the website. And after the first month, Jeff and Paul were ecstatic about the new traffic.

"Dude, we're getting nearly *six thousand* unique hits per day," Jeff stated over the speakerphone. "It took us nearly *two years* to get *half* of that."

Ivan could hear Paul agreeing excitedly in the background. "Yeah!"

"Six thousand hits per day, hunh? How did we manage to do that?" Ivan asked them. He realized that his party promotion and street teams would hardly drive that much internet traffic. Something else was empowering the site.

Paul said, "It's all about working the right search engines, my friend. So anything people search for in San Diego, we need to have a page up to identify it."

"Yeah, because we're I.D. Promotions, baby!" Jeff shouted in the background. "And we're *new.* Internet viewers always want to check out what's new."

"Hey, Ivan, you still want to sell this site name to us?" Paul asked him.

Ivan laughed hard at that. He answered, "Like I told you before, I was only joking."

"Are you sure?" Jeff pressed him. "We haven't even made any official offers yet."

"No offer would apply," Ivan told them. "My name is priceless."

"Well, we don't want your name, we just want the I.D. Promotions," Jeff responded.

Ivan continued to smile. At his apartment, he thought, *They're gonna want me to pay an arm and a leg to manage this website now. But they obviously know what the hell they're doing. And a deal is a deal. So if what they're doing makes me money, then it makes them money.*

Finally, he told them, "I'll tell you what, after about five years, we'll see where we are with this thing, and I'll let you make me an offer then."

Paul said, "Five years? The world could be over by then. You see all of the problems going on in the Middle East right now?"

"Yeah, the Third World War is supposed to start over there. It's been prophesied in the Bible," Jeff added. "Maybe we're already in it and we don't know it yet."

Ivan said, "Yeah, well, in the meantime, let's keep on living. All right, fellas? We still got a lot of work to do. You guys haven't even graduated from school yet. You got a lot left to live for."

IN HIS QUIET TIME, only days before his second big event, with leftover tax work from the office out in front of him, Ivan daydreamed about how long it would take for him to become intimate with Ida. He had been so busy over the past few months with his mother's funeral in L.A., his extra tax crunch at the office, and now with his new promotion company that he had gone without the naked touch of a woman for a while.

Ida seemed to be moving real slowly and carefully with him on purpose. She always seemed to have something to prepare for whenever they got too comfortable on their dates.

Does she want to deal with me or not? he asked himself. *She probably still thinks that I'm a player because of Catherine that night. But she's been around me enough to know that I'm too busy for that. What is she waiting for?*

Ivan was itching to call her and go for broke that night. Then again, he didn't want to seem anxious and ruin the rapport that they had established.

Is she looking at me only as a friend? he questioned.

He forced himself to call Ida anyway, only for her to answer her cell phone with the same brevity that he had gotten used to from her.

"Oh, hey, Ivan, are you ready for another big night this Friday? I'm just doing some last-minute running tonight. Is everything okay?"

No, it's not okay, he wanted to tell her. *I need to touch a woman right now.*

Instead, he answered, "Yeah, I'm good. I was just wondering what you were up to tonight."

"Well, that's nice of you. I'm around. But I guess I'll see you on Friday."

Ivan paused. He said, "Well . . . I was hoping I could see you before Friday."

"Yeah, I know, but between my day job and helping out my mother at the restaurant and a few other things I'm trying to do, I just run out of time."

Ivan thought, *Okay, so I just need to leave her alone, then, and keep it business.*

"All right, I'll see you Friday, then," he responded.

When they hung up, Ivan shrugged it off and went back to work on the tax papers.

THAT FRIDAY NIGHT at Raymond's Hot Spot Lounge in southeast San Diego, no more than sixty-five people had shown up to party by midnight. Nearly half of the people who did show were die-hard supporters of Thomas Jones and the San Diego Urban League.

Needless to say, Ivan was disappointed.

"Well . . . what do you think now, Ivan?" Thomas asked him near the bar. His purpose was not to rub it in, but to see how Ivan would respond.

Ivan stared into the crowd, wearing a silk red shirt under his charcoal-gray sports jacket, a combination he had come up with for that evening. He had been doing his mental calculations when Thomas approached him at the bar.

Ivan wouldn't break even on this event. He still had Ida and his DJ to pay. He was already thinking about the next promotion and how to plan his way back into a profit.

"Looks like you were right," he finally admitted to Thomas. "Maybe you can't get all the crowds." He was swallowing his first piece of humble pie.

Thomas slapped a comforting hand on his right shoulder. He said, "No, you can get this crowd, you would just have to do more than a couple of parties to get them. You already realized that when you made the additional party deal with Raymond. A bar crowd parties mostly from word-of-mouth, and in places that they're already familiar with. So it'll take a while."

He continued, "But my point is still what I asked you in the beginning: do you even want this crowd? Come to think of it, even though Raymond is happy with the turnout, I'm wondering if maybe we shouldn't have even thrown this party."

Ivan looked Thomas in his eyes. Was he admitting fault?

Thomas nodded to him and read it. "Yeah, I'm admitting it, Ivan. It was my mistake to drag you into this. My eyes got too big on the money you could make. We *both* got big eyes. But you were right, a lot of professional folks won't wanna party here. And they only showed up tonight out of respect for us."

Even Henry had shown up to support them with his wife. They were having a great time dancing, and they preferred having the extra room to move around in.

Ivan nodded to Thomas and squashed it all. "I'm thinking about throwing a network party downtown next. You were right, too," he told him. "I'm an accountant, and I need to stick to meeting professional people. That's where all the real money is. This right here would be nothing but pocket change anyway. But at least my guys took some more good pictures for the website."

Thomas grinned and said, "It's all a learning curve, young man. If you never fail, you never learn how to succeed."

Then he looked over behind the bar. "Hey, let me get a rum and Coke, Raymond."

AT THE END OF THE NIGHT, Ivan didn't feel up to chasing Ida anymore. It would have been nice of her to give him a small consolation prize of a woman's attention, but he was no longer pressed about it. Where Catherine had been all up in his face with her advances, Ida seemed to be the running-away type. So he paid her, he paid his DJ, he told everyone good night, and he took the remaining three hundred dollars he had left in his pocket home with him to brainstorm the next goal: an event in San Diego's Gaslamp Quarter downtown.

When the going gets tough, that's when you find out who the real players are, Ivan told himself on the drive back home. *I got no excuses to watch from the sidelines anymore. So I'm staying in this damn game until I win it.*

BY THE END OF SUMMER, Ivan landed his first event downtown. He found owners of a wine lounge on Sixth Avenue who were willing to allow him to bring his old school R&B music and a professional African-American crowd to their establishment on a Wednesday night. He even got in touch with Emilio Alvarez to invite him and a few of the Padres to stop through.

He called it "Old School Jam Part III—The Business Network Toast." Instead of one featuring more dancing, Paul created a sophisticated flyer with a group of business folks drinking wine and mingling, with the skyline of San Diego above them. The cover charge was "$10 with Free Wine Tasting." At the very bottom of the flyer was printed, "Meet Us in the Gaslamp."

In his steady growth, Ivan picked up a few more young and eager teammates from San Diego State University to work with, and he jumped back on his promotional horse with class and poise.

Thomas was pleasantly impressed by it all.

"Looks like you got the stomach to ride the waves of business," he mentioned to Ivan.

Ivan grinned and said, "I got plenty of time to learn it. I plan to suck it up like it's college all over again."

Among other lessons, he reminded himself to use his profession as an accountant to work more relationships in his favor. So he began to contact the professionals he met and casually offer them tax and accounting advice, while asking a few of them to consider the firm of Hutch & Mitchell for their accounting work.

He also offered his services to the Young Urban Professionals at the Urban League in a free lecture at one of their membership meetings. Thomas was surprised by that move as well. Ivan had gone from a man who barely spoke out in public to engaging a crowd regularly in a matter of months.

"The business made me do it," he joked to all who noticed the change.

All the while, his website at IDPromotions.com continued to draw increasing traffic. So even though his first downtown promotion at the Wine Cavern would not earn him much of a profit, Ivan felt relaxed and progressive, while making his supporters feel welcomed and appreciated.

He stood before the crowd of nearly a hundred, with a glass of red wine in his right hand. He wore black on black, blending in perfectly with the elegance of the dark cherrywood background.

He said, "I wanna thank you all for coming out tonight and looking professional, grown, and sexy."

He stopped there and allowed everyone a chance to laugh and gloat while feeling good about themselves before he continued.

He smiled and said, "I mean that," to produce more laughter. He told them, "But I also wanna thank you all for supporting my goal to create a promotional vehicle that continues to bring like minds together for business here in the city of San Diego."

Thomas joked from the crowd and asked him, "What, are you running for mayor now?"

Ivan ran with it and joked back, "You give me five more years of your support, and I'll let you know by then."

The man was becoming a natural crowd-pleaser.

I knew he had it in him, the gift of gab, Thomas thought as he watched Ivan woo the crowd.

As the network function wound down and a professional photographer documented the event through his camera, Ivan talked business with one of the lounge owners off to an empty corner of the room.

"So, you don't have to advertise at all?" he asked the co-owner.

"Well, our clientele already knows us, and they get the word out quite effectively for us through word-of-mouth."

He was a slim, clean-shaven man with graying hair, wearing a white shirt with no tie under his dark blazer.

"What about being a wine sponsor if we agreed to buy a few cases for a much larger event?" Ivan asked him.

The partner hesitated. That was a good thing.

"Ahh, I would have to talk to Dale on that, but what . . . what would a sponsorship entail?" he stuttered.

Before Ivan could answer him, he felt the presence of a tall woman waiting patiently behind him. He turned, looked, and failed to recognize her. But she was definitely striking, a caramel-skinned black woman, wearing a daring red dress and professional makeup with seductive long lashes.

"May I help you?" Ivan asked her. Was she coming on to him? He wouldn't mind it if she was. However, she didn't even smile when she spoke to him.

"I have someone here who wants to meet you."

Ivan froze. Whoever it was had excellent taste in women, because the messenger was a hell of an attention getter.

The wine partner looked Ivan in his dazed and confused face. He told him, "Go ahead, Ivan, we'll catch up. This is your party."

Ivan hesitated before he nodded. He followed the woman to a lone table at the back end of the room. On the way over, she didn't even bother to make small talk with him. Then she stepped aside to her left at the table, where Ivan came face-to-face with Lucina Gallo. She was having a bottle of Chardonnay. An extra empty glass sat out on the table across from her.

Ivan panicked. *Oh, shit! Is that who I think it is?*

She stood up from her seat and extended her delicate hand to him. She was wearing an expensive multicolored dress. It looked like Versace.

"I-van Da-vid, I'm Lucina Gal-lo," she said with an accent. They looked into each other's eyes with a double sparkle.

Ivan took her hand and nodded. "Yeah, I know who you are."

"Good. We talk, then." She pulled her hand back and sat down across the table. Her messenger walked away.

"Have you had enough wine? Or do you want more?" Lucina asked him.

Ivan sat down across from her. He still couldn't believe that she was actually there in front of him. He nearly forgot to answer her question.

"Oh, ah . . . nah, I'm good right now with the wine," he finally answered.

Like her messenger, Lucina refused to smile.

She asked him, "Where are you from?" and took a sip from her glass.

"L.A. Where are you from?"

"I'm from Bra-zil," she told him. "But much of my family is Italian."

Ivan nodded and smiled at her. He said, "I was thinking something like that. Your accent don't sound Spanish or Filipino. But you look like you could be anything," he told her.

Lucina ignored his comment. She said, "I like your website. I think it has a lot of pa-tential."

She made Ivan's small talk seem meaningless. She was there for strict business.

"So, you've been checking us out? How'd you find out about it?" he asked her. He was flattered by her research on him, to say the least.

"I see you plan to be very busy," she responded. "So you want to throw parties now?"

It was a rhetorical question.

Ivan looked into her colored eyes and answered it anyway. "Yeah."

He wondered what she thought of his eyes. The two of them were definitely close enough to get a good look at each other. However, Lucina stuck to her script, as if Ivan were faceless.

"I hear you work as an accountant. Are you any good?"

Ivan still couldn't believe it. She had done her research well. With each new question she asked him, he kept thinking that he would wake up soon. But he couldn't let her know that. So he grabbed hold of his emotions and rode out his excitement.

"I don't think they would have hired me if I wasn't," he bragged.

However, he didn't feel so secure after noticing Lucina's sustained grille of icy demeanor. She took another sip of her wine and said nothing.

Damn, she's just like she was in my dream, he told himself. *She's making me feel stupid over here. And I'm not even high now.*

Before either of them could get another word out, a few of the people in the crowd called for Ivan's attention.

"Hey, Ivan, we're out of here, man. It's a workday tomorrow."

He felt hesitant to move. He looked into Lucina's eyes first, as if asking to be excused. She had that kind of hold on him.

"Go ahead," she told him. "I will wait for you."

Ivan was still hesitant, glued to his chair. Then he shook it off. "Yeah, let me see them all out," he told her.

When he got up to walk away, Lucina's eyes followed him across the room. She studied his mannerisms and how people responded to him. But every time he glanced back in her direction, she made sure that he never caught her staring.

After another minute in his absence, she called her messenger back to her table.

"What do you think about him?" she asked her. "And don't look," she warned.

"Umm . . . I mean, I don't know. He has nice eyes, I guess."

Lucina frowned at her. "But do you trust him?"

"Do I trust him?" her girlfriend repeated. *How am I supposed to know if I trust him? I don't even know him,* she thought. But she wouldn't dare say it.

"Yes," Lucina pressed her. The girl was so irritating. She had so much to learn.

"Umm . . . I guess. I mean, he looks right at you when he speaks. That's usually a good sign, right?"

"Yes, thank you. Bye," Lucina responded, and brushed her away. She saw that Ivan was headed back to the table. It was time for her to get to the point of the evening and test his will with her pitch. So as soon as Ivan sat back across from her, Lucina looked around the room at the majority-African-American crowd, who were sipping wine, conversing, and listening to the music. Then she looked back into Ivan's eyes.

"So, I-van, are you throwing parties for business, or just because you like parties?"

Ivan frowned at her and got back to business himself.

"Nah, I'm not throwing parties just for the hell of it. I got major plans," he told her. "But it's just gonna take time. So I'm learning to be patient."

When he said that, Lucina stared at him. "Patient?" she repeated.

Ivan caught on to her objection. "What, is that a bad thing? I thought patience was a virtue," he commented.

"Virtues don't make money," Lucina told him.

That comment caught Ivan off guard. He laughed it off. And it was true. People seemed to want the forbidden fruits ten times more.

But while Ivan laughed and grinned across the table, Lucina remained about business. She said, "Let me ask you *this* question. Are you just trying to make *black* money, or do you want to make *money money?"*

Ivan looked into her colored eyes and was speechless. He couldn't even think for a few seconds. When he finally did think of something, all he came up with was, *DAMN!* In real life, Lucina was icier than she had been in his dream.

Before any words could tumble out of his mouth in response to her, she pulled out a business card from her expensive purse and placed it on the table in front of him. Then she stood up to leave him there.

"You call me and we'll talk. Okay, Ivan? Because I need a new partner."

The more she said his name, the more normal it sounded.

Ivan heard her out and nodded, while holding her business card in hand.

"Okay," he mumbled. And he still had no response to her question.

Five

Family Ties

After Lucina's swift exit, Ivan continued to think to himself in silence.

Black money or money money? he pondered. *But money is all green,* he argued to himself. He continued to sit there at the table with her business card in hand.

"What was that all about?" someone asked him from behind. Ivan had begun to flip Lucina Gallo's business card over and over in his right hand. But when he recognized Ida standing there beside him in her tasteful black dress, he slid the card into his jacket pocket.

"Oh, she was just asking what my plans were in party promotions."

"She wants to partner up with you?" Ida assumed.

Ivan nodded. "I guess so."

Ida studied his thoughtful posture. "So . . . what are you planning to do?"

Ivan was thinking more about Lucina's questions than an immediate partnership with her.

He shrugged. "Well . . . I guess I'll investigate it first."

Ida nodded to him and grinned. "She's been a part of some big parties in San Diego. I've seen her around before. You're gonna have to step your game up to deal with her," she challenged him.

Ivan laughed it off nervously. "Yeah, I think I know that already."

Ida said, "Well, make sure we talk before you leave tonight, okay?"

He nodded to her and stood back up from the table to rejoin the crowd, only for Thomas Jones to pull him aside again.

"Now, this right here is more your style, Ivan. Get used to this kind of party and do it more often," he commented.

Ivan grinned, but his mind was already traveling elsewhere. The fact was, he still couldn't turn much of a profit while throwing polite business functions. Like Lucina had told him, virtuous affairs often didn't make money. But Ivan wasn't ready to express his thoughts on any of it yet. He continued to think it all over.

AT THE END OF THE EVENING, Ivan stopped to chat with Ida, like he had promised her he would.

"All right, I'm ready to head on home now," he told her.

"Wait a minute," Ida responded to him with a raised index finger. She waited for more privacy before she continued. People were still saying their good-byes near the doorway. When the opportunity presented itself, she asked Ivan, "You feel like having any company tonight, or are you on empty?"

Ivan was shocked. He stopped and stared at her before he commented. "Are you sure you don't have to make any runs before or after?" he asked. He had become leery of Ida's disappearing acts. He had little faith in any of her intentions. It was already approaching eleven o'clock.

Ida smiled and told him, "I'm taking off of work tomorrow."

Yeah, but I'm not, Ivan thought. Since he was curious and surprised by her spontaneous proposition, he asked her, "Are you sure *you're* not on empty tonight? I don't wanna start something we can't finish," he hinted.

He figured he would be as bold as he needed to ward off any disappointments.

Ida grinned at him. "I guess we'll find out," she said, and left it at that.

IDA FOLLOWED HIM back to his apartment complex in La Mesa. During the drive, Ivan continued to wonder what had sparked her sudden assertiveness. He kept wondering if she would call him up on the cell phone with a change of heart again. But she never did.

"My place is not even ready for this," he mumbled to himself behind the wheel. He still had flyers, tax paperwork, food, and clothes that littered his apartment from the week's work.

Then he began to think of his image. Although his apartment complex wasn't all bad, he figured a successful accountant and party promoter should have a snazzier place to rest his head at night.

To make things worse, when they arrived in the parking lot of his complex, Ivan spotted his neighbor Julio, smoking another blunt on their second-level walkway.

"Shit!" Ivan grumbled to himself. *Now I gotta walk past Julio with her, with weed smoke all in the air. But it's too late to do anything about it now. She's here.*

Ivan had turned down his neighbor's offers to smoke another one after the first time, but he hadn't had company since then, either. So as he climbed out of his car, before Ida could climb out of hers, he attempted to make eye contact to tell Julio to clear out of the way for him.

Julio caught Ivan's eye and understood his gesture of concern immediately. He could tell by their dress that it was an elegant affair. So with a nod and a knowing grin, Julio calmly put out his blunt and walked back inside his apartment. He agreed to allow Ivan to walk by with his dressed-to-impress date in peace.

As soon as Ida reached the second level of the apartment

complex beside Ivan, she was still able to smell the lingering smoke of the weed.

To Ivan's surprise, she inhaled deeply and commented, "Somebody has some strong reefer around here."

Ivan chuckled guardedly. He joked, "It sounds like you want some."

Ida looked at him and grinned, with no verbal response.

What does that mean? Ivan asked himself. *Does she smoke . . . ?*

He ignored his question and made it inside his apartment with her.

Once inside, he clicked on a dim lamp in the living room to maintain an evening mood.

Ida noticed the laptop, pizza box, tax papers, and old work clothes that were strewn around his living room floor, sofa, and coffee table, and chuckled at it.

"Looks like somebody's been working overtime in here."

Ivan grinned. "Yeah."

Ida walked over to inspect the family photos that Ivan had set out on the open spaces of his entertainment center.

"Your mother and brother?" she asked him.

"Yeah," he answered, while cleaning up his work area.

"Looks like those eyes of yours run in the family," she mentioned. "How much older is your brother?"

She could tell that his brother was the oldest by the swagger in his stance and the seriousness of his grille.

Ivan answered her while cleaning up. "He got me by five years."

"That makes him thirty-three?"

Ivan joked, "Yeah, so you want him now instead of me?"

Ida picked up the sarcasm and read the story inside of the joke. "So, your brother's the real player," she assumed. "And let me guess; he's been stealing all of your girlfriends since your late high school years?"

Ivan laughed while walking off toward his bedroom. He carried old clothes in hand.

"Not exactly," he told her. When he returned empty handed, he added, "But he has had his share of women."

Ida continued to stare at his family photos. She said, "But your mother still gave you the bulk of her attention." She concluded that from the smiles that Ivan and his mother held in the picture, while his taller and older brother looked too bothered to smile.

Ivan hesitated. "Well . . . I guess you could say that," he conceded. "But not really. She just gave us attention in different ways. But *he* would probably say that," he admitted to her.

"So, in his eyes, you were the spoiled little brother who got a chance to go away to college," she assumed again.

Ivan grimaced and turned his scowl into a grin. "How are you coming up with this?" he asked her.

Ida walked toward him and away from the photos when she answered him. "Well, I notice that he has the tattoos and such on his arms, with a long, counterculture hairstyle, while you're pretty much a clean-cut corporate college boy all the way."

Ivan laughed. But he didn't like all of her insinuations. He felt he needed to add a bit of spice to his image for her.

"I'm not that clean-cut," he told her as she approached him.

Ida walked right into his face. "I wouldn't want you to be." She took ahold of his waist to get closer to him. She said, "But I've been watching you, Ivan. And I do like what I see."

He stood his ground and looked into her dark eyes with his light ones as they closed in on each other.

"Sometimes I couldn't tell," he told her. "Seems like you wanted to run away from me."

Ida finally kissed him on the lips and moaned, "Mmm, I had to make sure first."

Ivan kissed her back. "Make sure of what?"

"That you were who I thought you were," she answered. "So I had to wait you out. But I liked you. And I see that you're very determined and focused."

She kissed him again.

Ivan asked her, "You couldn't tell that from the beginning?"

She stopped and stared at him. "Men can seem like a lot of things in the beginning, things that don't pan out in the end. But now I've been around you enough to know. You're stable. And I like that. But let's not talk anymore. Your cologne is killing me."

She went after his neck with a passionate tongue, while reaching with her hungry hands to unbutton his black shirt.

Ivan responded by reaching his hands around to her firm ass to caress both of her cheeks.

She probably likes it a little rough, he assumed from her assertiveness. So he reached down to the bottom of her dress and pulled it up enough to grab ahold of her thong panties.

"I've been waiting for this," he told her.

"I know," she moaned. "Me, too."

Ida stepped out of her thong while still kissing him. Once she had unbuttoned and pulled off Ivan's dress shirt, she went after his pants.

In minutes, they were both naked and dripping with lust, right there in his living room.

Ida pulled out her own protection from her handbag to roll down on his throbbing erection. And instead of them hiking back to the bedroom, Ivan took the initiative to bend her over his living room sofa and take her from behind.

"Ivan, what are you doing?" she moaned. "We can't do it like that. I'm a lady."

However, she failed to put up a fight to stop him. So Ivan ignored her and continued his rough play.

"Yeah, and I'm a *man,*" he told her with his first stroke inside.

Ida moaned and took his pounding from behind, moaning louder with every stroke. *"Unh! Unh! Unh! Unh . . ."*

As it began to feel good to him, Ivan poured on the heat with more speed and pressure, grabbing her firmly by the hips with both of his hands.

"Oh, I-van! Oh, I-van . . ." she moaned to him as he continued to

pound into her. But as Ida began to call out his name in both of its syllables, Ivan flashed back to his brief conversation that night with Lucina Gallo.

I-van Da-vid, I'm Lucina Gal-lo, he heard her voice addressing him again. In a flash of mental distortion, Ivan began to imagine that he was taking Lucina Gallo from behind instead of Ida. And he began to talk to her.

"You want me, don't you? You want me."

"Yes, Ivan. *Yesss!*" Ida squealed.

"I know you do. But you were fronting on me, weren't you?"

"I didn't mean to," she told him. "I had to make sure first. *Ooooooh,*" she moaned to him, and shook in her stance.

Ivan held on to her and closed his eyes, still thinking of Lucina.

God, this feels good! he told himself. He could feel the pressure of his climax beginning to mount. With his eyes closed, the image of Lucina's stern, seductive glare was crystal clear to him.

I want you so bad, girl, he imagined telling Lucina, while he continued to push himself inside of Ida from behind. *I want you as bad as you want me.*

When the climax hit him, Ivan lost control of his stroke and began to bounce on his toes in a hot, naked, and sweaty convulsion.

"Oooohh, shit, baby," he moaned back, gritting his teeth and squeezing Ida's body into his. The climax was so strong it felt as if he would fill up her entire body from the tips of her fingers down to the curls of her toenails.

Ida squeezed her own eyes so tightly that tears of joy leaked down her face.

When it was over, Ivan slumped limply over her body, exhaling loudly from the back of the sofa.

"Okay, Ivan, let me get up," she told him.

She pushed him away and straightened up. She headed toward his hallway bathroom. "Do you have a washcloth and a towel I can clean up with?"

Ivan stretched back up himself to answer, "Yeah."

He headed toward his closet to get her what she needed.

When Ida closed the bathroom door to take a shower, Ivan stood naked inside his living room. He began to shake his head at how insane his thoughts had been.

"This is crazy," he mumbled to himself. *That damn girl got me wide open. And I don't even know her like that.*

He was referring to Lucina. He then thought about the obvious disrespect to Ida, who had waited patiently for him in vain.

Ivan shook his head, knowing himself. *If I'm already thinking about someone else on my first time with her, then Ida don't have a chance in hell at keeping my attention.*

"Damn," he grumbled. "That's just fucked-up timing."

After Ida took her shower and joined him naked in bed, Ivan remained conflicted with guilt. Nevertheless, with a naked woman in his bed all night, he took full liberties with her body whenever he found himself aroused again.

IN HIS CUBICLE at the offices of Hutch & Mitchell the next morning, Ivan continued to feel guilty and confused about Ida. His thoughts had even distracted him from his work. He had been going over the same pile of paperwork at his desk for an hour.

There's nothing I can do about how I feel, he argued to himself. *If you slow, you blow.*

He now thought, nonstop, about a possible business and pleasure relationship with Lucina Gallo. How exactly would that work?

A woman like her probably has a man already. Then again, maybe she's strictly a businesswoman, he told himself.

So I could end up doing a partnership with Lucina and still have Ida right in the middle of things, collecting money at the door. How would Ida take that? Would she care? I know she has to feel some way about it. Lucina would end up being her boss.

As he continued to be distracted that morning, Dwayne Bellamy approached him at his cubicle and broke through his ruminations.

"Hey, Ivan, can I see you in my office a minute?" he asked.

Ivan looked up and snapped out of it. "Oh, yeah, just give me, ah, a few minutes."

Dwayne nodded and walked off toward his office.

Ivan gathered himself for the meeting. *I wonder what he wants.*

As soon as he entered Dwayne's office, he was told to close the door behind him.

Right outside of the door, Chip Garrett walked by and noticed the privacy. He wondered what was going on as well.

Ivan sat down in the chair across from Dwayne's desk and continued to imagine what he was there for.

Dwayne, wearing a typical dark blue business suit, looked over at Ivan across his desk and nodded stoically. "So, what have you been up to lately, Ivan?"

Ivan shook his head, still wondering where Dwayne was going with this.

"Nothing much, man. Business as usual," he answered.

"That's not what I hear," Dwayne commented. "I hear that you're the new party man around town. IDPromotions.com, right?"

Dwayne was all smiles with it. But Ivan had no idea what his smile meant. His heart leaped into his chest as he felt blindsided. The last thing on his mind was the guys at the job figuring out his extra hustle that morning. Every other morning he had been prepared for it.

It figures. As soon as I let my damn guard down, I get the hammer, he thought. *This is great fucking timing!*

He played it cool and said, "Oh, yeah, well, you know, it's a pretty good way to meet other professionals in San Diego."

Dwayne continued to smile and nod. "I see," he commented.

Ivan wondered if the fellow black man felt slighted. Ivan hadn't invited him out to any of his functions. So he continued to wonder where Dwayne was going with this.

He said, "Yeah, I didn't want to make a big deal out of it at the office. I didn't want it being a distraction to anyone at the job concerning my work. Because I always get my work done," he quickly defended himself.

Dwayne sat there and continued to grin, while watching Ivan squirm. Finally, the middle manager chuckled. He said, "I know you carry your weight well around here, Ivan. You don't have to defend your work record to me. That's why I always lean in your direction to set examples for the other staff members. You're not one of the complainers. You just get it done."

Ivan nodded to him. "Thank you."

Then Dwayne let him have it. "I'm just wondering why you never invited me out."

Ivan felt another sack of guilt tossed on his back to carry around that morning.

He said, "Well, can I be frank here?"

"That's why I asked you to close the door," Dwayne told him.

Ivan nodded. "Okay, well, you know, you and I haven't really had that kind of relationship here, and I felt that if I invited you out to something and not Chip and Mike . . . You know what I mean? So I just decided not to go there."

Dwayne heard him out and continued to nod. He said, "I understand. Trust me. I often go through that dilemma myself. Am I a black man today or just a professional accountant? Am I a professional accountant today or just a black man? It still gets confusing sometimes. I just figured I would ask you about it, that's all. I was curious."

"Yeah, well, it was nothing personal against you, or any of the other guys at the office. But at the same time, like I said, I didn't want anyone complaining about me doing a little something extra after work," Ivan explained.

Dwayne said, "Well, that's why I called you into my office. It seems you brought in a few new clients from your network parties, and we're still discussing it with a few others."

Ivan perked up and smiled. "Oh, yeah, I figured since I'm around professionals who are making good money, why not ask them about their accounting. So, I'm kind of, like, working my business links at the network parties instead of out at the golf course."

"Whatever works," Dwayne told him. "But we're giving you the company standard of ten percent on each new client, so just continue doing what you're doing. And I totally understand if you need to exclude me because I'm at the office. Jealousy and envy are still very much a part of the corporate structure. So keep your extra business to yourself, and I don't know anything about it."

Ivan felt uplifted. He had no idea Dwayne was that cool. He looked across the man's desk and beat his heart twice with his balled fist. "That's love, man. I appreciate that."

Right as he said it, his cell phone vibrated against his hip, but Ivan ignored it.

Dwayne warned him, "Just don't slack off on your tax work. Or if you *do* slack off, just make sure you bring in enough new clients where John and Barry won't mind as much." Then he smiled again. "That's when they'll move you up to manager and ask you to explain how you did it. So begin to prepare yourself for that conversation. I had to do that myself years ago. Along with pulling on a tougher coat of skin that I have to wear now."

Ivan heard Dwayne out and understood him a lot more now. He nodded thoughtfully and said, "I'm glad we finally had this conversation, man. Because, to be honest with you, I had no idea who you were or what you represented."

Dwayne heard that and held up an index finger of caution. He said, "Ivan, just like I'll maintain your business as your business, I'll expect you to do the same with mine. So I don't want you treating me any differently now. That means no 'What ups,' no 'Hey, brothers,' no funny handshakes; none of that stuff. You understand me? Because I don't need any of that extra attention around here."

Ivan understood his point and laughed. Then he deadpanned with a final nod, "Okay . . . *sir,*" he joked.

Dwayne stared at him to settle him back down from the humor.

Ivan understood his glare and repeated, "I got you. This meeting was about nothing more than our usual tax work."

Dwayne nodded and remained stone-faced. He said, "You get yourself prepared to explain your methods, Ivan. And I have nothing to do with it."

He then closed the paperwork on the new clients whose folders sat out on his desk and stood up to show Ivan back out of the office.

"We'll have you sign off on the new clients by the end of the week."

Like clockwork, as soon as Ivan stepped out of the private meeting with Dwayne, Chip appeared behind him at his cubicle.

"Hey, Ivan, what was that all about?"

Ivan looked up at him and let out a long, tired sigh. "Just your typical tax issues, man. Nothing you want to know about."

Before Chip could ask anything else, Dwayne called him out.

"Chip Garrett, you're next. My office, please."

Chip looked in his direction. "Okay." As soon as the middle manager walked back inside of his office, Chip complained to Ivan again.

"Shit. I don't need this, this morning," he grumbled.

When he walked off, Ivan was all smiles. *If Chip only knew,* he told himself. *He's probably the main guy that I have to watch out for. Me and Dwayne.*

Ivan then looked at his cell phone to see about the call he had missed a minute ago. He read the 310 area code of the phone number and froze. It was his brother calling from L.A.

"Now, what does he want?" he asked out loud.

He's not calling me in the middle of the day just to say hi. He can do that after work.

Ivan called his brother back for a heads-up. They hadn't spoken at length since their mother's funeral months ago. And their relationship had been stormy before then.

Ivan took a deep breath and waited for his brother to answer his call. He had his whole conversation down already. It would be quick and to the point, until he could get back to his brother later.

OUT ON THE SAN DIEGO FREEWAY of Interstate 405, at the southern tip of Long Beach, California, Derrick David drove a gray Impala with the windows down while smoking a cigarette in his left hand. He drove the old car with his right, heading south. He had slightly browner skin than Ivan's, with the same colorful eyes, and a longer growth of light brown hair. His dress code was more rugged, with the beige khaki pants, white tank top, and basic white tennis shoes that were popular within the urban street culture of South Central Los Angeles.

When his cell phone went off, he switched hands to drive with his left, answered the phone in his right, and held the cigarette tightly between his lips.

"Yeah," he answered gruffly.

"What's up, D.? I'm at work. What's going on?"

Derrick frowned at his cell phone. He recognized his brother's brush-off move immediately.

"I'm coming down there to see you, man. It's been a while," he responded.

"What? For what?" Ivan sounded disturbed.

Derrick began to shake his head. Momentarily, he took both hands from the wheel so he could flick the ashes from his cigarette.

"What'chu mean, 'for what'? To see my little fucking brother. I can't see your ass no more? I should have brought one of your nephews with me," he commented.

Ivan asked him, "You're doing that right now?"

"Doing what?"

"Driving down here?"

"Yeah, I'm passing through Long Beach right now. So I should be there in, what, another hour and forty-five minutes?"

Ivan hesitated. "I mean . . . let me call you back in a few. But this might not be a good time—"

Derrick cut him off and said, "All right, I'll just see you when I get down there. I'm just calling you to let you know. So I'll probably go to one of the malls or stop through Horton Plaza downtown to pick up some pussy or something." He laughed through his smoke and said, "You know, get me some of that wet Filipino pussy."

Ivan heard that and cut the conversation off. "All right, I'll call you back."

Derrick closed his cell phone and went back to his smoking and driving. He clicked on his stereo system to blast his latest Snoop Dogg CD. He sang along with the chorus while enjoying his late morning drive down the San Diego Freeway:

"Beautifuuulll / you're my favorite girrrlll . . ."

BACK AT THE OFFICE, Ivan went into panic mode. *This mother . . . He needs more money already. That's all it is,* he suspected. *Why else would he want to see me out of the blue?*

Ivan was ready to take an emergency break outside of his office to call his brother back and tell his ass not to come. He wanted to let Derrick have it. But his efforts would have been meaningless. If D. was on his way, he was on his way, and that was that. Nothing would make him turn back.

I should just ignore him once he gets here, then, Ivan told himself. But he knew better than that. Derrick knew where he lived, and he was an impossible man to ignore. That would only make things worse. The best solution was to hear his brother out and get his checkbook ready.

Needless to say, with so much on in his mind, Ivan couldn't possibly get much work done.

AT A QUARTER AFTER SEVEN, when Ivan arrived home from work, Derrick was already waiting for him on the second-level walkway. He was socializing there with Julio.

"What took you so long, Ivan? You still letting that job control all your time, hunh?"

Ivan took a breath and kept his poise as he approached them.

"It is what it is," he answered. "What's up, Julio?"

"What's up, man? I didn't bust your groove last night with the smoke, did I?"

Ivan shook his hand and said, "Nah, she was cool with it."

Derrick shook his brother's hand next and frowned at him. "You had a girl over here last night? What was she, your first one? Let me see the sheets," he joked.

He understood Ivan's hesitancy with women. He didn't want to get any of them pregnant.

Julio chuckled with Derrick, but Ivan wasn't in the mood. He led his brother toward his apartment with no comment.

"I'll catch up, Julio," Derrick told Ivan's neighbor. "I wanna try some of that weed you was telling me about."

Ivan looked back at Julio and stopped himself from saying anything. He thought, *Yeah, I need to get D. out of here as quickly as possible.*

As soon as they walked into his apartment and closed the door, Ivan looked his brother in the face and asked him, "How much do you need from me, man? And I'll see if I can do it."

Ivan had a nice nest egg of investments and savings, but not like he wanted to have. However, his brother's economics were an entirely different story. With makeshift employment and the needed financial support of three sons from three mothers, Derrick was in a deep hole. Nevertheless, he felt offended by the question.

"So, that's all I am to you now?" he asked Ivan. "No 'How are you doing? I love you. Let's hang out and kick it. Go get some girls.' None of that brotherly love shit, hunh?"

Ivan said, "You tell me, man. You don't call me for none of that."

"Yeah, and you don't call me," Derrick threw back at him.

They were at a stalemate.

Derrick looked at his brother's dress code, all nice and neat in his business attire. He said, "I see you still taking good care of your business."

Ivan nodded. He said, "And I see you still . . . doing you." That was all he could say about his brother. He hadn't done much of anything but make babies and hang out in the streets of Los Angeles. It was a wonder that he hadn't been killed or sent off to jail yet. He had had a few close calls, however.

Derrick told his brother, "I'm always gon' *try* and do me." Then he added, "But I never really had that chance to get away from it all and do *me* like you do *you*."

Ivan began to shake his head, predicting where their conversation was headed. He said, "Don't even start that shit again, man."

"Start what?" Derrick asked him.

Ivan used his right hand to make his point as he spoke. "Mom's cancer didn't have shit to do with you fucking up your life, man. And I'm tired of hearing that shit. It ain't like she gave me some extra push to go to college. I had the grades for it. But you didn't even finish high school," he commented. "Now how you gon' blame that on Mom's cancer? She didn't even have cancer when you fucked up."

Derrick snapped, "Yeah, but she had all kinds of other shit going on that you don't know shit about, Ivan, because you were too *young* to know. So your ass got a chance to go to school and all of that other shit without being bothered by it. And who stayed home to be close to Mom while you did you?"

"Aw, here we go," Ivan told him, walking away inside the room. He faced his brother again and said, "That's a real convenient excuse for you, ain't it; blame everything on Mom? Well, that's *bullshit* to me, man, 'cause I've *seen* what you do. And if anything, you made Mom's situation *worse* with the shit you kept taking *her* through. So don't stand here and try to blame Mom for *shit!* You'll make her roll over in her grave."

Derrick heard that and went crazy. He rushed across the room toward his brother, hollering, "You little motherfucker! I'll kick your fucking ass in here!"

Ivan skittered away and around the living room sofa to keep his distance. He then raised his hands to defend himself, but only after he had escaped his brother's reach.

He said, "That shit won't work no more, D. We can kill each other in here if you want, and it won't change nothing. Mom was giving you money out of everything that I was sending her the whole time, and I know it. So now you gotta come to me for your living. And beating my ass ain't gon' change that.

"*If* you can even do it now," Ivan added. "Because I really don't wanna go up against you that way. But this shit is childish, D. We ain't kids no more, man. So don't fuck up the hands that's gonna feed you unless you gon' find another way for you and your kids to eat."

Derrick listened to him and realized that he was right. But how could a grown man admit his economic dependency on his little brother? So he calmed down and nodded his head. Then he tried reverse psychology.

He said, "Okay, you live a nice fucking life now, Ivan. You a grown-ass man now, and I'm a grown-ass man. So I won't bother you ever again. You hear me? You did this all by yourself."

When Derrick rolled out the door to leave, he slammed it back so hard that every resident inside the complex could hear it.

BOOM!

"Shit!" Ivan cursed as his brother left. Derrick was famous for making scenes. He was the main reason why Ivan hated bringing unnecessary attention to himself. Nevertheless, he was his only brother, and Derrick was now in desperate need with their mother no longer there to help him.

I can at least find out how much he needs. It may only be a few thousand. But what if it's more than that? Ivan questioned.

He went back and forth trying to decide whether to let his brother leave or to chase him down and figure things out.

Finally, Ivan told himself, "Shit, I'm an accountant. I gotta make this shit work somehow." *Mom would have begged me to,* he realized. *Otherwise, what is the point of my education?*

"Fuck!" he cursed himself. He hated the reality of his decision already. He dashed outside and ran his brother's car down before Derrick could leave the parking area.

"D., hold up, man, come on. Let me ride with you."

At first Derrick looked tempted to run his brother over. But he backed down and stopped the car just long enough for Ivan to climb inside the passenger seat. Then he zoomed off.

"What the hell you want, man? You got your life now and I got mine, right?"

Ivan ignored his pouting. He said, "So, you had *your* six thousand, and *my* six thousand from mom's life insurance policy, right? How did you spend it all?"

Derrick looked at him and said, "Come on, man. How long you think twelve thousand dollars is gonna last me in Los Angeles? Think about it. I got three sons from three greedy-ass mothers to feed."

Ivan figured twelve thousand dollars could last his brother a lot longer if it was budgeted properly. So he thought it all over. He said, "You got the mortgage payments for Mom's house, your regular bills, your life, health, and car insurance, and a minimum amount that you owe each month for the mothers of your three kids. We can figure out a way to work that all out into a budget. In the meantime, you're gonna have to find steady employment, man, to help *me* out."

Derrick asked him, "Doing what? Janitorial shit? Like you said, Ivan, I don't have no education, right?"

Ivan said, "Look, if that's what you gotta do, then do what you can, man. At least to keep your own pocket money."

Derrick said, "I got my own fucking pocket money, Ivan. I can do that. But it's mainly the house and these kids that I gotta take care of now."

Ivan nodded and pulled his thoughts together. He said, "Okay, we can work on that. We gon' figure it all out."

Then he looked over at his older brother, who continued to drive aimlessly.

"Are you hungry, man? Let's stop and get something to eat," Ivan suggested.

It took a minute for Derrick to respond to him.

"Yeah," he finally grumbled. "Let's do that."

Six

Football Party

When the two brothers made it back to Ivan's apartment that evening, both with full stomachs from dinner, Derrick noticed the collection of flyers Ivan had held on to from his first three promotion events.

He picked one up from the coffee table and asked, "What is this? You're throwing parties now?"

He looked at Ivan for an explanation of the obvious.

Ivan grinned. "I'm just trying to do a little something extra, man. So I came up with the idea and ran with it."

Derrick broke out laughing. "Ivan, you don't know shit about throwing no parties. What made you decide to do this? But I like this name, though," he commented. "I.D. Promotions is a good look. I like how you used your initials on that."

Ivan told him, "Look, I'm just learning on the job right now. But I just started this hustle, and already I'm meeting the right people to help me blow it up."

His brother asked him, "You made any money off it yet?"

Ivan couldn't lie about that. "Not really," he answered. "But I haven't really lost any money, either. Everything is breaking even. In the meantime, I'm building a strong website."

Derrick flipped the flyers over to view the website brand on the back and nodded. "I see." He said, "But if you wanna make the real money in the party game, invest in a liquor license." He took a seat on the sofa. "You need any help with this hustle?" he asked.

Ivan thought about how unreliable his brother had been over the years, but it didn't matter anymore. He needed to help out to manage his mess of a family, as well as to maintain their mother's house in L.A. So he came up with a workable plan.

"I could make you a special events advisor and put you on salary. That way I can pay your insurance, taxes, and child support, and they won't have to bother you about money anymore. And from there you can just be a father to your kids."

Derrick frowned and said, "How much are you talking about paying me for that?" He didn't want all of the money going somewhere else.

Ivan sat down on the sofa beside him. He said, "We still have to run through all the numbers and figure that out. But I'm looking at somewhere around . . . three to four thousand a month."

That was nearly as much as Ivan's salary at Hutch & Mitchell. But he offered it anyway.

"Are you sure about that?" Derrick asked him. He didn't believe his brother had it like that. He would have been satisfied with one or two thousand. That's all he was there to ask for. The rest he figured he would scrape up for himself.

Ivan said, "If I'm able to make that happen, would you be all right with that?"

Derrick said, "Three, four thousand a *month*? Hell, yeah! That would be good looking out."

Ivan nodded and said, "That's what I need to work on, then. And that would take care of Mom's house, too."

Derrick nodded and changed the subject. "So, who you had over here last night?" he asked his brother. "Some girl you picked up from one of these parties?"

Ivan grinned. "That's a wild story that I don't feel like talking about right now. So ask me about it again later, like in a couple of weeks."

Derrick laughed it off and left him alone. "All right, then, suit yourself."

IVAN WAS ANXIOUS for the rest of that night. He was trying to decide when would be the best time to call Lucina about her ideas for their partnership. By the time he had settled in with his brother and went over the hard calculations of his monthly business goals, it was eleven o'clock. Was eleven o'clock at night too late to call on business?

What the hell, she throws nightclub parties, Ivan argued to himself. *This is not a nine-to-five job she's pushing. And it's a Thursday night. She's probably out somewhere right now herself.*

So he decided to call her that late from his bedroom while Derrick crashed on his sofa. He took a couple of deep breaths to compose himself and get his thoughts ready while the line rang, only to receive a recorded message. The message didn't use her voice or even identify whose number he was calling.

"Shit, how do I even know this is for her?" he mumbled. He went ahead and left a message anyway. "This is Ivan David from ID Promotions.com. I'm calling for . . . Lu-cina Gallo," he said with hesitation. He nearly screwed up her name. "Ah, anyway, call me back . . . and we'll talk."

Ivan hung up his cell phone and said, "Shit. That was a terrible message." Then he felt anxious again, wondering how long it would take for her to call him back.

As soon as he began to strip out of his clothes, his cell phone rang. He grinned and moved to answer it from his bedroom dresser, assuming it was Lucina.

"That was fast." However, when he read the number, he recognized that it was Ida calling him.

He stopped and stared at the phone with a new dilemma. *Do I even answer it? I'm ready to talk business right now. What if Lucina calls me back while I'm shooting the breeze with Ida?*

He decided not to answer, still hoping to get his call back from Lucina. When he remained up, doing business projections for his website, and eleven o'clock turned to eleven thirty, Ivan called it a night and climbed into bed to rest.

"I guess she'll call me tomorrow, then," he figured. He pulled the sheets over his boxers and white T-shirt. *I need to call Ida back tomorrow, too,* he mused. *I'll just tell her I went to bed early after an extralong day.*

As soon as he got good and comfortable with his eyes closed, his cell phone rang again and startled him.

"Shit!" He stumbled back up to answer it.

He looked to read the number and found that it was restricted.

"Okay, this must be her now," he assumed. "Hello."

"I-van Da-vid, what are you doing right now?"

It was Lucina Gallo, as he had guessed. Her question sounded urgent. Ivan could hear faint music blaring in the background.

Okay, how do I answer that? he asked himself. He mumbled, "Ah . . . actually—"

Lucina cut him off. "How fast can you get downtown?"

Ivan hesitated again. "Ah—"

Lucina cut him off again. "I-van, I'm going to have a mee-ting with a couple of football players from the Chargers at the Trea-sure Grill. And I want to throw a big birthday par-ty. If you can make it here in no more than thir-ty minutes, I can let you pitch them with me."

What was an eager businessman to do . . . ?

"I'll be there," he told her.

She said, "O-kay. I'll make them wait for you."

As soon as Ivan hung up the phone, he cursed himself again. "Shit!" It was twenty minutes to midnight. Then he wondered, "What should I wear?"

He froze for a minute, standing in the middle of his bedroom while he thought it over. *Football players, hunh? . . . Wear something flashy,* he told himself.

He walked into his closet and pulled out a colorful party shirt he had bought for himself after graduating from college. But after putting it on, he decided that it was too bright and loud.

"Yeah, that's too much . . . but maybe I could put a blazer over it." He grabbed a navy blue sports jacket to wear over the top. He liked how the combination looked with his dark denim jeans and brown leather shoes.

"Not bad," he decided, looking it over in the bathroom mirror. With no time to waste, he brushed his teeth, tossed on a dab of Escape cologne, and headed for the door.

When he walked out into his living room, Derrick was sound asleep on the sofa. The cable TV was on an HBO adult series.

Ivan chuckled and went on about his business.

AT SEVEN MINUTES AFTER MIDNIGHT, Ivan found a parking space off of Fifth Avenue and rushed into the Treasure Grill to meet up with Lucina and the Chargers.

"May I help you?" the hostess asked him at the front entrance.

Ivan looked like a man who was late for a hot date that had cooled off. The place was nearly empty.

"Yeah, I'm looking for a, ah, pretty Brazilian girl with some football players."

The hostess smiled at him. She was a college-age blonde in all black.

She said, "You must be Ivan David."

"Yeah," Ivan answered her with a nod.

She nodded back to him. "They're in the back. Follow me."

She led the way to a secluded section of the restaurant where they had pulled two tables together to accommodate a group of eight. But at the moment there were only seven; three football players, Lucina, and three other drop-dead-gorgeous women.

Lucina caught Ivan's eye as soon as he approached them at the table. She stood up to greet him by taking his left hand with her right. Then she introduced him to everyone.

"O-kay, everyone, this is I-van Da-vid, from IDPromotions.com, one of the best upcoming websites for San Diego par-ties."

The biggest football player looked impressed and nodded. "Is that right?" He had to be at least six foot seven and three hundred pounds. He sat at the far end of the table to give himself plenty of uninterrupted space. They had left an open seat at the closest end for Ivan.

Ivan pulled out a stack of flyers from his party at Raymond's Hot Spot Lounge and passed them around the table. He still liked the flyer, the party just didn't turn out right.

They all checked out the flyer, while Ivan took a seat in the empty chair. Plates of steak, shrimp, chicken, mashed potatoes, and vegetables littered the table along with drinks.

"So, how did this party turn out?" a much smaller and younger football player asked him. He inspected the flyer front and back.

Ivan answered him quickly. "It was basically a party for a new friend who wanted more late-night traffic for his bar. So we gave it to him. That's what we do."

His answer was satisfactory enough for a nod from the three Chargers. The third Charger continued to observe him in silence. He was smaller in size than the first, but larger than the second. His age seemed to fall in between theirs as well. He looked to be in his late twenties, like Ivan. They were all casually dressed. But with the extra sizzle of their jewelry, confidence, wealth, and the hot women who surrounded them, they produced an overload of energy in the nearly empty room.

Lucina said, "Zachary is the birthday boy. He's turning twenty-four in two weeks. And we want to throw a *big* par-ty for him."

"Go, Zee-Dog! Yaaay!" the hot women cheered. As Lucina's signature, her girls were a mixture of races and nationalities.

The smallest and youngest player grinned sheepishly at their excitement for him.

The big guy in the back belted, "Yeah, Zee-Dog's from Chi-town. He's trying to go after ten interceptions this year. He set a new rookie record last year with seven."

The silent player still had nothing to say. He looked on and smiled, taking everything in. In many business transactions, the silent ones were the deal killers. So Ivan paid him the most attention.

"Well, how big of a party do you want to throw for him—two thousand people at a hotel ballroom? Or do you want to stay classy with five hundred, special guests only?" Ivan asked Lucina. He tried his best to appear professional.

The big guy spoke up first again. "*Five hundred?* That ain't enough people. We'll fill up that party just with the team and everybody's girlfriends," he joked.

They all laughed.

The big guy added, "We need more like *three thousand.*"

"Yeah, that's *much* more like it. He needs a *big* par-ty, I-van," Lucina commented. Ivan could read the hint in her language: bigger was better. Then he looked at the silent one to see what he thought.

"What do you think?" Ivan asked him.

Finally, he got the guy to speak. "Well, either way, I feel it should be a controlled setting so things don't get out of hand. And it's easier to control the smaller parties."

He was exactly what Ivan thought he would be, a cautious over-thinker. Just because they were all on the same football team didn't mean they were cut from the same economic class. Ivan suspected that the silent dissenter was more money and image conscious than the other two players, so he had just the right approach for him. He had just learned the class lesson himself.

Ivan nodded and said, "I know what you mean. There's different events for different crowds." Then he pulled out a flyer from his most recent event at the downtown winery.

The silent one looked at it and cracked a grin. He said, "I've been to this place with my fiancée before."

Bingo! He was also getting married soon. The hot women Lucina had surrounded them with after midnight meant this was not his ideal business meeting.

The big guy cut him off. He said, "Look, Jeffrey, just 'cause *you're* gettin' married now don't mean you should stop *Zee-Dog's* fun. He's just gettin' his feet wet in the league. You go somewhere and have your own small party and leave his alone."

Ivan grinned and pulled out his business card from Hutch & Mitchell while the rest of the table laughed and made fun of the party pooper.

"Boooo, a married man is no fun," one of the hot girls commented.

"Who told you that?" one of the other girls responded.

Ivan ignored it all and handed Jeffrey his card across the table. He said, "I'm an accountant with the Hutch and Mitchell firm. I also work with the San Diego Urban League. We should talk. I could save you a whole lot of tax money."

Jeffrey took his card and was now impressed with him. Ivan was more than just a slick party promoter.

Jeffrey nodded and said, "Okay, I'll call you."

Zachary overheard it and asked him, "You a tax man?"

Lucina bragged, "He's one of the *best*."

Zachary said, "Well, let me get one of your cards, too. I could have you double-check what my agent does," he joked.

Ivan smiled as he pulled out another card. He said, "We already represent some of the Padres players, so we know just what you're up against as young athletes with money."

The big guy looked on and hesitated from the far end of the table.

Jeffrey told him, "If anything, you *really* need to get his card, Perry. You spend money out here like it's water."

Ivan jumped on that, too. He said, "If you create a business, and you put it all on a debit or credit card, we'll help you work it out for taxes."

The big guy couldn't turn down good money advice out in the open. He at *least* had to make it *look* like he was listening.

He said, "Okay, give me one of your cards."

Ivan took out another one and passed it over.

"What about us? We wanna save money on taxes. I want a card," one of the hot girls whined.

Ivan pulled out his small stack of business cards and handed one to everyone but Lucina.

"He's already helping me with my taxes," Lucina lied.

Jeffrey opened up and asked him, "So, how did you get into the party promotion game?" The veteran football player was used to meeting loud, drunken ramblers and shady hustlers who threw parties, but not young, professional tax accountants.

Ivan told him the truth. "I just got tired of sitting on the sidelines, basically. I wanted to meet more people and make a name for myself. So I figured, why should I sit back and watch all these guys, who know nothing about stretching money, blow it all right in front of me? So I'm out here making new friends, connecting all the dots, and becoming who I want to be: a hardworking man who makes money while taking care of people's money."

Everyone was sold but Jeffrey. Ivan's honesty brought to mind a bigger question for him.

Jeffrey asked him, "But isn't that a conflict of interest for you to make money with your clients?" He figured he had a gang-busting question on his hands. A tax man would know every extra dollar that a client had to spend.

Ivan didn't flinch. He said, "Is it a conflict of interest for Nike, Reebok, and Adidas to make money with you? They know how much you're making, too. But the more money you make through the things you do off the field, the more popular you become, and the more money *they* make through your sponsorships."

Ivan went on, "Well, think about it the same way with your tax man. The more money you make in diversified ways, the more we can figure out how to save for you. That's how we stay valuable to our clients. And that's how we attract *new* clients."

Jeffrey heard that and went silent again. It sounded good to him so far. But . . .

"Isn't getting involved in too many business ideas a risk to the client?" Jeffrey asked him. "I've heard about plenty of guys who nearly lost it all by being advised to do too much."

Ivan looked the man in his eyes in silence at the table. It was an easy question to answer. But his patience made Lucina nervous. Everyone else was awaiting his answer.

Ivan said, "Jeffrey, every time you step onto the football field, there's a risk that somebody's gonna try and knock your head off. But you get your heart up and you tell yourself, 'I can play this game. And *win.*' Otherwise, you may as well stay on the sidelines with the equipment managers."

There was a pregnant pause at the table before Perry and Zee-Dog looked at each other and broke out in laughter.

Perry said, "Shit, brother, that's the truth right there. Everything's a damn risk. Every time Jeffrey catches a pass across the middle, my ass is on the sidelines praying for him."

Zee-Dog said, "Every time I'm one-on-one down the field, it's a risk that I might get burned for a touchdown. But I go after them interceptions anyway."

Perry said, "Football is the riskiest sport there is. Either you got the heart for it or you don't." He looked at his cautious teammate and said, "You gotta admit that, Jeffrey. That's going all the way back to Pop Warner days. He's right."

Ivan jumped back in to simplify things. He added, "Basically, we're just talking about one party here, Jeffrey. We're not talking about a car dealership or a pyramid scheme. Just *one* birthday party."

Finally, Jeffrey looked across the table at Lucina and gave in. Then he nodded and grinned to Ivan. *This guy represents himself well,* he admitted. *So let's do this one party with him and see how it goes.*

* * *

AT CLOSE TO TWO O'CLOCK in the morning, Ivan sat across from Lucina in a downtown bar that was still open.

Lucina cradled her drink in her right hand and told him, "You did good. But at first . . . I was very nervous. I did not know where you were going," she told him. She said, "I was thin-king, 'Oh, my God! What have I done, to invite him here and mess up my business?' But then . . . you did all right."

Ivan took a sip of his drink and chuckled. "That guy Jeffrey was gonna break the deal. That's why I concentrated on him. I know that quiet type. You know how I know?"

Lucina looked at him and asked, "How?"

"Because I used to be him. I was skeptical of everything." Ivan leveled with her. "I kept my money in my pocket unless it was for family. But at the end of the day, you can't do business like that. You gotta go for it and learn your lessons on the way. That's what I'm doing right now," he admitted.

It's nearly two o'clock in the fucking morning and I still have to go to work, he kept saying to himself.

Lucina tilted her glass to her lips and made her comment over the rim. "You are right. That is what I did with you." She took a sip of her drink and said, "I took a chance."

With that, Ivan got back to business. His fantasizing about working deals and romancing Lucina Gallo were over, for the minute. He was now sitting next to her with a major event to put on.

He said, "Okay, so, how is this gonna work? Do you have a venue already?"

Lucina said, "I have several to choose from."

"And how much do they cost?"

"From two and a half to five thou-sand dollars."

Ivan nodded. "What are the other expenses?" He knew what he needed for his parties, but a three-thousand-capacity crowd was way out of his league.

"We need radio, your website, promotional flyers, catering,

security, my girls." She stopped and said, "I always pay my girls."

"What about the DJ?" Ivan asked her.

She said, "No more old school, I-van. This is a regular par-ty."

Ivan laughed and said, "That was just for the older crowd that I was catering to. But you still gotta mix the new songs in with the classics."

Lucina said, "I know plen-ty of DJs. I even know DJs out of L.A."

"Yeah, but what would they cost us?" Ivan asked her. "My DJ would only cost five hundred dollars. You bring a guy from L.A, that's a thousand just to bring his equipment down."

"That's part of the budget," she told him sternly.

Ivan slowed down and said, "Okay, so what is the budget?"

"Twen-ty thou-sand dollars," she told him.

Ivan was shocked. He repeated, *"Twenty thousand dollars?"* He figured they would need *half* of that. He said, "These guys are gonna give us twenty thousand dollars for a *birthday* party?" That was more than a quarter of a year's earnings for him at Hutch & Mitchell.

Lucina frowned at him and said, "That's *nothing*. I was gonna ask them for *for-ty* thousand. But since this is your first big par-ty, I want to make sure they are sa-tisfied with you."

Ivan sat there and thought, *Shit, I should have teamed up with her a long-ass time ago!*

Then he asked her the obvious question. "So . . . why are you willing to partner on this with me? I mean, it's obvious you already know what you're doing."

She took another sip of her drink and told him frankly, "It's too much work. Most promo-ters have partners."

Ivan couldn't argue with that. He had run around like crazy just trying to pull off his small events for *three hundred,* let alone three *thousand.*

He said, "Okay. But why me? I mean, I'm just getting started in this thing. I really don't even know what I'm doing yet," he acknowledged. "I'm still on my learning curve."

Lucina looked at him through her colored eyes and said, *"That's* why. Because you are *new*. So I have a chance to *trust* you. But the other promo-ters I know . . ." She shook her head and said, "They *all* change, and I no lon-ger trust them."

But you're gonna trust a guy you don't even know? Ivan asked himself. That part of it didn't make any sense.

Lucina read his mind without him asking her the question.

She said, "Do you trust *your-self* with other people's money, I-van?"

He was an accountant. It was his *job* to trust himself with money. He had just sold the Chargers on his trustworthiness to secure the party less than two hours ago.

He answered, "That's all day, every day. That's what I do. I've been watching a dollar since I was a kid. That's why I became an accountant in the first place."

She said, "Well, then trust *me* now to know what I am *do-ing*. I just had a *fee-ling* with you. And I met you and went with my gut. Now, if I *can't* trust you, I-van, then you tell me right now."

Damn, she was intimidating! A snappy little rich girl from Brazil, with a full Italian ego, and exotic eyes like his own to boot.

Ivan kept his composure. He looked back at her and said, "I didn't climb out of my bed and get dressed near midnight to rush down here and meet up with you if I wasn't serious. So just like you trust *me*, I gotta trust *you*. And we're in this thing together now."

Lucina smiled, the first innocent smile that Ivan had seen from her. And it melted him.

She said, "You were in bed? Oh, my God, you're an ear-ly bird."

Ivan was so turned on by her smile that he thought of ignoring her question to lean over and kiss her lips. Or maybe the effects of the alcohol had made him feel that way.

He caught himself instead. He answered, "Yeah, I was halfway out of here. But I'm glad I came out, though. Damn, I'm glad."

Lucina continued to smile. She said, "Me, too," in her accent.

That's when Ivan began to reflect on how badly he would love to lay her down and spread her open for heavy moaning and groaning.

Right on cue, Lucina broke him away from his daydreams. "Anyway, back to biz-ness. So, we charge twen-ty-five dollars per head, times two to three thou-sand, and we make fif-ty to seven-ty-five thou-sand, mi-nus the for-ty thou-sand we pay the football players back. And once we add in the VIP, we can split fif-teen to twen-ty thou-sand apiece. Is that good enough money for you?"

Ivan couldn't believe his ears. If they partied like that just twice a month, he could buy a house on La Jolla in a year and look down from above Interstate 5 for the rest of his life.

To keep himself from sounding too excited, he held up his drink and asked her, "What about the liquor? Do you have a liquor license? My brother said that's how we can make even more money."

Lucina frowned at him. "And have a big-ger head-ache," she commented. She said, "I have another partner who does that. But to have your own liquor li-cense, you need in-surance, trained bartenders, storage for the al-cohol, a truck, and your own security team unless you sell drink tickets."

She shook her head and said, "That's way too much has-sle for a girl. I just want to throw the par-ty."

Ivan had to agree with her. Or at least for the moment. He had to study it more.

She said, "And by the way, we don't spend all twen-ty thou-sand dollars up front. This par-ty should cost no more than twelve. So we take four thou-sand apiece off the top. That's how you do it. Otherwise, you throw par-ties with no money left. And I never do that. You should *al-ways* have money left after budget."

Ivan took it all in with a nod. By that time, he was glassy eyed from drinking.

Lucina asked him, "Do you need to stay a night here? You don't look like you can drive."

Ivan grinned at her. "Are you staying here?"

"No. I have to get up to-morrow and get ready. You have to book the radio spots in ad-vance to get the best times and rates."

Ivan told her, "I have to get up tomorrow, too. I gotta go back to work at the accounting office in the morning."

"Well, may-be one day you will have your own firm. Then you won't have to show up un-til late."

Ivan chuckled at the thought. "Yeah, those days are coming. But not yet," he told her.

AFTER LANDING a major party and a partnership with Lucina, Ivan's next important meeting was with his two young webmasters. Jeff and Paul had produced phenomenal traffic for his start-up website. And that allowed Ivan to pitch solid advertiser rates.

They all sat down to discuss it over a dinner meeting at a seafood restaurant near campus. The college partners were eager to negotiate a fair share of revenue for their successful management of the website, based its outstanding traffic, like Ivan had promised them. They were up to an average of eight thousand hits per day.

Paul spoke first, without touching his food. Ivan had already handed them the proposed ad rates for comment. "So, you want to charge three hundred dollars per week, a thousand dollars per month, twenty-five hundred for the quarter, and four thousand for a half a year?"

Ivan nodded while cracking open his giant snow crab legs. "That's reasonable, right?" he mumbled through his food. He wiped his lips with his napkin and said, "I'm basically charging a dollar for each one hundred eighty hits. In other words, for the eight thousand daily hits that we get, I'm charging about forty-five dollars per day until we saturate our ad space or increase our hits. Then we'll have to raise the price and charge them more. And we always give the better rates to the longer-running advertisers."

Jeff did his own calculations. He said, "So, that's a dollar per two hundred forty hits for the month, a dollar per two hundred ninety hits for the quarter, and a dollar for every three hundred and *sixty* hits for a half a year?"

"If we can get a company to commit for that long," Ivan answered.

"What if we continue to increase traffic past ten thousand hits per day?" Paul quizzed him.

Ivan said, "Then we'll raise the rates every three months as the traffic continues to grow. That's like in any other business. And we still give the most faithful companies the better rates."

Paul and Jeff understood it with a nod. It was all basic numbers. Jeff then began to pick through his food, while Paul continued to read from Ivan's printout.

Paul said, "You're only raising our maintenance fee to *five* hundred dollars a month?" He sounded slighted. Jeff hadn't read that far yet.

Ivan answered, "Plus twenty-five percent commission on all created ads. Because you'll need to keep upgrading the site every time we put up a new one. And I understand that that's a lot of work," he admitted to them. "So keep reading."

Jeff raised his head from his plate. He said, "So we get twenty-five percent of every ad that we create for the site?" It sounded like a sweet deal to him.

Ivan joked and said, "Unless you don't want it. And not only that, if you actually *sell* an ad, you'll pick up the other twenty-five percent commission that I'll be offering to salespeople." He continued, "Because I don't have the time to do it all. So I'm planning on taking out ads for professional salespeople to help us."

Paul and Jeff looked at each other with nothing to complain about. They could make thousands of dollars per month. So they continued to read through Ivan's deal memo in silence.

Jeff added, "You know we can create our own help-wanted ads for the site."

"That's what I need," Ivan told him. "How many different advertising sections or pages can we put up?"

Jeff started counting on his fingers. "We have the home page, the party page, restaurants, things to do, calendar, hotels, concerts, the picture gallery. Ah . . ."

Paul cut in and added, "Travel, sports—"

"Sports?" Ivan hadn't seen that on the site yet.

"Yeah, we started building it a couple nights ago to add it to the search engines. The more subjects the site offers about San Diego, the more traffic we can direct to it."

Ivan said, "So, we have about ten pages total on the site now? And we can get up to, what, three to five banners or pop-ups to rotate on each page?"

"Yeah, about that," Paul mumbled. He finally began to eat his lobster tail. Ivan was paying for it all.

He said, "That's pulling in anywhere from thirty to fifty thousand per month, at full website capacity?"

"At full capacity, yeah," Paul answered him.

Ivan said, "Ironically, on the sports angle, I just did a meeting last night with a couple players from the San Diego Chargers about throwing a birthday party for their second-year cornerback. They want us to do it during their bye week next month. I'm teaming up with this party promoter Lucina Gallo on that."

Jeff said, "Lucina Gallo? Dude, she's like Brazilian or something?"

Ivan smiled and said, "Yeah, that's her."

Jeff got excited. He said, "I just read about her in *944* magazine. Man, she's *hot*. You're doing a *Chargers* party with *her?* She knows all the hottest girls, too."

Paul grinned. "We'll be there bright and early with the cameras out."

IVAN AND LUCINA RECEIVED the twenty thousand dollars cash from the group of Chargers that next week and went right to work preparing for the "Rights of Passage Birthday Bash at the Waterview." It was to take place at a hotel venue off the San Diego Bay that held exactly three thousand in its grand ballroom. Lucina worked out a three-event deal with the management to help drive traffic back to their renovated hotel. She and Ivan then paid for an aggressive radio campaign. They printed ten thousand flyers to work the entire San Diego region, including the military bases. They set up the catering. They contracted a popular radio DJ for additional promotion, while still adding Red Face Lion to the flyer and website as a co-DJ—a deal Ivan had pushed in order to bring his young entrepreneur more marketing exposure. They sent out several email blasts, hired extra security for the star athletes, and paid for Lucina's list of "girls," for an exact budget of twelve thousand dollars.

"I told you," Lucina gloated to Ivan.

Ivan grinned and was pleased to pocket his half of the eight thousand in cash that was left.

Lucina also had him post some of the more glamorous party photos of her and her girls on his website to solidify her crowd. Jeff and Paul were more than happy to do that. And they had finally talked Ivan into using a few imagery-branding photos of himself on the site.

"Trust us, Ivan. We want to make you the King Kong of the San Diego promotions game," Jeff stated to him. "So just sit back, relax, and ride the wave."

Ivan and Lucina rode the wave of their first major Saturday-night party to the tune of twenty-three hundred general paying customers, and another two hundred who paid double for VIP status. Including the athletes and their entourages, the place was packed to near capacity with a multicultural crowd. Hundreds more were turned away at the door.

Jeff and Paul documented it all with their digital cameras, especially the diversity of the crowd. They explained to Ivan that it was time to stretch to the largest possible audience for the website, particularly when dealing with San Diego–based advertisers. So Ivan finally agreed to it. He had no choice. Money was money.

"Now, *this* is a fucking party, man!" Jeff exclaimed. He even took pictures of the disgruntled crowd who never made it in.

The wide-open ballroom had an elevated DJ platform at center stage, giant speakers in the corners of the dance floor, catered food against the left and right walls, and tables and chairs surrounding the edges of the room. The VIP areas were roped off with security to the left and right sides of the DJ booth, with more expensive catering, more tables and chairs, and large, comfortable sofas for the athletes and their special guests to relax in. Two bars were stationed at opposite ends of the VIP, and a third bar was stationed near the general entrance.

All night long, Lucina dragged Ivan around the room and introduced him to the important notables within the crowd. She wanted to make sure that everyone knew who he was for their next big event. She had no interest in him playing the behind-the-scenes partner. She needed the money people to feel comfortable with him for their next pitch.

"Hey, this is new my partner in crime, I-van Da-vid from L.A. And we're gon' to be do-ing *lots* of big part-ies to-gether. So make sure you add your email ad-dresses to his website at ID-Promo-tions-.com. It's a won-der-ful website for you to promote *all* of your biz-nes-ses."

Over and over again, she repeated her introductions like a seductive robot, while adding touches of improvisation to her script whenever needed. Ivan did his best to keep smiling and talking his way into the memory banks of each new potential client. And at the grand moment of the party, Perry Browning, the hulking defensive end, stormed center stage in front of the DJ booth and grabbed the microphone to address the crowd in a near-drunken stupor.

"Yo, we wanna thank everybody for coming out here tonight and sharing this rights-of-passage party for my man Zee-Dog."

"Yeeaah!" the crowd cheered him.

"Whoop, whoop, whoop!" the football players yelled.

"Go, Zee-Dog!" Lucina's girls filled in.

Lucina made her way next to Zachary in his dark blue jeans, sports jacket, and eye-catching jewelry before he was called onto the stage.

Perry said, "But you know what, we're a year late with this one, 'cause my man ain't a rookie no more. That was last year. But anyway . . . hey, Zee-Dog, come up here and say something to the people, man. Represent Chicago. And tell them how you plan to break your interceptions record this year. He got three in our first five games already."

Lucina held on to Zachary's hand at that exact moment. She told him, "Make sure you thank *Lu-cina* and *I-van* for the par-ty." She said it with authority and made sure that Zachary made eye contact with her before she released his hand.

Zee-Dog looked at her and then to Ivan, who was standing nearby. He grinned and nodded to both of them. "Oh, I got you. I know what time it is."

He walked up onstage as the crowd and his teammates cheered him on.

Ivan stood there and wondered if Zachary would do what Lucina had told him.

Knowing these football players, he'll probably thank everybody and his momma first, and then plug us in last, if he even remembers, Ivan assumed as he looked on in curiosity.

However, Zee-Dog flipped the script at the microphone and thanked them *first.*

"Hey, um, before I even talk about all that, I want to thank my girl Lucina Gallo over here, for putting on this hot-ass party for me, right."

"YEEAAAHHH!" the crowd yelled even louder.

Perry grabbed the microphone back from him and belted, "Oh, yeah! Everybody knows Lucina. Hey, come on up here, girl. And bring your boy Ivan with you."

He then gave the microphone back to Zee-Dog to help Lucina up. Lucina grabbed Ivan's hand and pulled him along with her.

Oh, shit! Ivan panicked. *Here we go again.* He felt for sure that he could play the background, with so many celebrity football players in the house. But it was not to happen.

Zee-Dog said, "I wanna thank my teammates from the Chargers: the 'Shockwave' defense."

"THE SHOCK-W-A-A-A-AVE!" one of the football players yelled at the top of his lungs.

"That's 'The Big Bad Hitta,' Herman Seaford, over there," Zee-dog responded to him with a laugh. "He's going for twenty sacks this year."

"Whoop, whoop, whoop!" the rest of the Chargers teammates hollered again.

By that time, Lucina and Ivan had reached him at center stage. Zee-Dog acknowledged them. He said, "Yeah, let my girl Lucina say something before we get back to this party."

But instead of Lucina saying anything to the crowd, she told Ivan, "Just thank every-one and talk about your website."

Ivan stood there confused as hell as she passed the microphone directly over to him.

FUCK! he screamed to himself. Nearly three thousand people were waiting, watching, and listening. Ivan immediately thought of hip-hop mogul Russell Simmons and his famous underscored sign-off from HBO's *Def Comedy Jam*. The thought just jumped into Ivan's head. *Be short and get it the hell over with!*

He opened his mouth to the crowd, with his heartbeat thundering inside his chest again. He said, "I want to thank everybody for coming out tonight. I'm Ivan David from IDPromotions.com. And make sure you sign our email list for the next big party promotion."

Then he raised two fingers of his right hand with the microphone in his left and added, "Peace out," before pointing with his index finger and concluding, "Party on."

On cue, the DJ began to spin his next record, 50 Cent's "In Da Club." He had been holding the popular record on his turntable while they used the microphone to address the crowd. Once he let it spin, the crowd went crazy and got back to dancing.

In confusion, Zee-Dog and Perry looked at each other and

shrugged. It was not Ivan's intention to end their stage presentation with such authority, it just happened that way. All the while, Lucina stood at his side in silence, with a grand, money-getting smile.

When Ivan realized he had cut the football players short, he tried to apologize to them offstage. "Hey, man, I didn't mean to cut y'all off like that, I was just—"

Zee-Dog stopped him and said, "Shit, man, I didn't want to be up there no way. I'm glad you did that."

Perry added, "Yeah, they already know I'm halfway damn drunk in here. And this is the perfect shit to get back to the party with. Girls love this damn song."

Zee-Dog stepped right into a circle of three excited girls and started dancing in the middle. Perry joined him and did the same. The party was back into full swing.

Ivan looked at Lucina, who barely moved to the beat. She seemed above dancing. She was only teasing the music.

He asked her, "How did that look when I did that?" He was still self-conscious about his short address to the crowd. He didn't want to seem like a showboat or a control freak. But how did the crowd view it?

Lucina smiled at him, beaming away. She pulled his left shoulder down toward her to speak directly into his ear through the music.

She said, "I-van, you don't even realize your full po-tential yet. But for-tunate-ly, I *do*. For *both* of us."

Part III

Learning to Deal

Seven

Like a Pimp

As soon as Ivan stepped away from Lucina at the Chargers party, he walked into Jeffrey Morefield, the overly cautious wide receiver, who had been able to play the background more successfully that evening. Jeffrey wasn't even dressed for a weekend party. In his tailored suit and button-up shirt, he was only a tie away from a corporate business meeting.

He nodded to Ivan and told him, "That was good. It was straight to the point and no-nonsense." He extended his hand for a shake.

Ivan took his hand and said, "Actually, I would have rather been in the crowd like you were on this one. I had no idea they were gonna pull me up there for that."

Jeffrey smiled at him. He shook his head and said, "Naw, brother. You can't hide in business. In business, you're *supposed* to be on the field. That's just who you are, Ivan. You were right where you needed to be to police things back in the right direction." He jokingly added, "Those *defensive* guys can easily get out of hand on you."

Ivan smiled back at him. "Thanks. I appreciate that. And I thank you again for working with us."

"No problem. You'll be hearing from me," Jeffrey told him. He quickly disappeared into the crowd.

Ivan watched the reserved football player in a daze for a minute, while ignoring several admirers who hovered nearby for his attention. His eager webmasters were able to break through his haze.

"Hey, Ivan, that was awesome, man!" Jeff shouted at him over the music. "We need to make that your end-of-line slogan: 'Peace out, party on.' Did you feel the moment of that? That was out of this world."

Paul added to his energy with a wide smile of his own. "We have it all on camera."

Ivan nodded, noticing more people in the crowd who begged for his attention.

He told Paul, "That's good. We'll talk about it for the website this week," and he moved on to meet and greet a few folks. He couldn't continue to ignore them.

Catherine Boone was there in the crowd as well, dancing with his brother, Derrick, who had driven down from L.A. just to see his brother pull it off. Derrick knew Catherine from Ivan's college years.

As soon as Ivan approached Catherine and his brother, Derrick told him, "Shit, you the man now, ain't you?" his open hand extended.

Ivan took his brother's hand and grinned. "Believe it or not, I didn't mean for that to happen that way."

"Yeah, but it did," Derrick told him. "You shut the shit down and started the party back up again."

"Actually, Perry Browning shut the party down," Ivan stated.

"Yeah, and how many of us really wanted to listen to that football shit?" Derrick commented. "This ain't no football field. These people paid their money for a party, and that's what the hell you gave them. You saved us all from hearing that bullshit."

Ivan smiled it off and addressed Catherine. She was looking special as usual, wearing bright colors to pop off of her smooth brown skin.

"How have you been?" he asked her.

She shrugged. "I'm hanging in there."

Derrick felt the crowded space through their unspoken words. They needed more privacy.

"Yeah, well, let me let you guys catch up while I catch on to something else in here," he hinted.

When Derrick walked away, Catherine said, "So, you end up with a San Diego Chargers party, and then you go from high yellow to foreign now. I guess blond and blue is next up, hunh?"

Ivan chuckled. He said, "I see you still have your candor. So, who's been occupying your time lately? And by the way, Lucina and I are strictly business. Even Ida knows that."

Ivan figured there was no sense in hiding anything from her. They were all adults in the room. And adults made adult decisions.

Catherine said, "Does she really? Because I've heard a few things about *Lu-cina,*" she insinuated.

Ivan laughed off the venom again. He asked, "Is that the direction we're headed in now? Because I still consider you a good friend. We have a lot of great memories together."

Catherine looked into his face and snapped, "You know what, Ivan, spare me the bullshit. Okay? Because I'm not from San Diego, and I can clearly see the direction you're headed in now. I thought you, of all people, wouldn't go for that. But I guess I was wrong."

Ivan frowned at her. "Go for what? Look, all I'm trying to do is grow my business in here."

Then he stopped and realized that he was in the middle of a crowded event, where people were still watching him. How would it look for him to have an argument? So he smiled it off and said, "I'm obviously the bad guy now. Is that it? Is that what you're trying to make me out to be?"

On cue, a Filipina assistant asked him politely, "Do you need anything, Ivan?" She was easily one of the most eye-catching girls in the room. At five foot five with three-inch heels on, she stood eye to eye with Catherine.

Catherine responded by looking through the crowd for Lucina.

She figured, who else would send a pretty foreign girl to interrupt them? Lucina had nearly twenty associate girlfriends around the room. They were swarming the place. She even knew most of the Chargers cheerleaders who were there.

Ivan said, "Naw, I'm good right now. But thanks."

"Are you sure?" the assistant pressed him.

Catherine looked the girl in her face but failed to get any eye contact from her.

"Yeah, I'm sure," Ivan told her.

"Okay, well, you let me know if you need anything." Then she looked at Catherine. "Hi." She never waited for a response. She was there to assist Ivan and nothing more. Catherine wouldn't have responded to her with anything positive anyway.

Ivan's college girlfriend looked back at him and was convinced by the whole scene. He had crossed over into a different world. She told him, "You be whatever the hell you want to be now, Ivan," and walked away.

Instinctively, Ivan wanted to reach out and secure her arm. He wanted to know more about what she felt. But he restrained himself. It would have given Catherine too much of his attention again. However, he still felt an impulse of loyalty to their friendship.

"Shit," he cursed himself. He had only a second of private time before Henry Morgan from the Urban League appeared in front of him with his wife.

"Hey, Ivan, you're moving on up fast now. This is *huge.*"

"Yeah, it really is," his wife agreed.

Henry added, "Too bad Thomas couldn't make it. He's out of town this weekend. But I'll be sure to tell him what he missed."

Ivan smiled and said, "I know you will."

Then he noticed the Filipina assistant was back.

"Ida and Lucina are waiting for you at the front," she told him.

Henry overheard her. He said, "Well, go 'head and do your thing, Ivan. I know you're busy. But we're *proud* of you man. *Real* proud."

Ivan continued to smile and nod. "Thanks."

As he followed Lucina's assistant to the front entrance of the ballroom, he grinned at the many well-wishers who continued to eye him and randomly call out his name.

"All right, Ivan! Great party!"

"Thanks!"

At the front entrance were Ida, Lucina, an assistant from Ivan's camp, two girls from Lucina's camp, and three beefy security men in black. They were awaiting his arrival with two metal money boxes and two dark leather money bags.

"We need to count everything up," Lucina told him.

Ivan nodded and followed them all to a smaller, private room of the hotel.

"Only me, I-van, I-da, and May-ya in the room," Lucina told them all. Maya was her most trusted friend, a Colombian woman with the dark hair and eyes and the olive-toned skin of people from her native country.

The three security men stood guard outside the closed door, while the other assistants returned to the party.

Ida opened her metal money box on an empty table and kept her poise. Maya did the same with her box. They then opened the leather bags and poured the money out onto the table.

Ivan looked down at the overflow of cash money in front of him and couldn't believe his eyes. He had never seen that much hard cash in his life. Before the party, he had never seen twenty thousand dollars in hard cash, which the three Chargers had shelled over to promote it.

Damn! he thought. He forced himself to keep his cool like the rest of them.

Lucina, Ida, and Maya had all been around hard cash before, but not quite as much as they now had out in front of them.

Ivan took the lead. "Okay, so let's count the hundreds, fifties, twenties, tens, fives, and ones all in separate piles, from left to right."

"You got it," Ida told him.

"I'll take the hun-dreds and fif-ties," Lucina commented. "You two girls take the twen-ties. And I-van, since you are the a-ccoun-tant in the room, you count the fives and sin-gles, and add it all up with the cal-cula-tor," she joked with a smile.

"Yeah, leave it up to the accountant to do all of the grunt work with the bills, hunh? That's typical," Ivan joked back.

Lucina had brought a calculator and a thick bag of rubber bands to group the money with. They started their count by first organizing the bills into their separate piles.

They all began the exciting count of hard American cash in the San Diego hotel room. As expected, the twenties outnumbered all of the other bills. So Ida and Maya had their hands full.

When they all had finished, after two recounts, they had added up and grouped more than sixty-eight thousand dollars.

"Se-parate the first for-ty for the investors," Lucina told Ivan.

Ida beat him to it, grouping twenty rubber-banded stacks of twenty-dollar bills. Each stack was two thousand dollars.

Ivan said, "Naw, don't give them that. Give them the stacks of hundreds and fifties to make it easier for them to count."

Lucina argued, "No, you *want* them to think about coun-ting. That way they know how much money they made with us."

Ivan frowned and said, "These guys have all counted money like this before. They're professional football players. Giving them twenty stacks of twenties will only make us look small-time."

Ida and Maya looked at each other as if their argument was frivolous.

What the hell difference does it make? Ida mused. *Money is money.*

But Lucina insisted. She grabbed the stack of twenties and said, "Trust me on this, I-van. It's much bet-ter to give them more to count. They are much more generous when coun-ting more than they are when coun-ting less."

Ivan thought about that and froze for a minute. Maybe Perry and Zee-Dog would spend more with twenties, but Jeffrey would prefer his in a check if possible. Then again, Ivan could explain his

own preferences to Jeffrey later. So as a team player, he agreed with Lucina.

Ivan nodded, understanding her game. "Okay, you're right. Let's just give them the twenties, then."

"Thank you," Lucina responded. Then she looked at her thin Movado watch. "It's getting close to two o'clock. Let's go say our good-byes now."

AT THE END OF THE NIGHT, everyone was paid well, San Diego had enjoyed a hell of a football party, Lucina's girls were out entertaining more of the players, and Ivan was headed back home in his car carrying a purse of more than twelve thousand dollars, while Ida followed him in her car.

Ivan's brother Derrick was nowhere to be found and would not answer his cell phone. But that was all right with Ivan. Knowing D., he would tell him all about his adventurous night in the morning. Or more likely during that next afternoon.

Ivan was all smiles, driving in silence as he made his way back home. He had heard enough loud music to last him for the rest of the weekend.

"This has been a good damn night," he told himself. "Now we have to make enough to throw parties without so much overhead." He grumbled, "She should have negotiated *thirty* thousand back instead of *forty,*" in reference to the football players' payout.

But we'll work on that for next time, he thought.

As he continued to think it over on his drive back home, Lucina called him on his cell phone.

"So, what do you think about the big-ger crowd?" she asked him.

"It's much bigger money," Ivan answered immediately.

"That's what I al-ready know. And we made a lot of *big* noise tonight, I-van," she told him. "So now it will be ea-sier to throw more par-ties. Al-ready I have cli-ents li-ning up."

Ivan jumped on that and said, "Hey, before you lock up more of these deals, you need to talk to me about the payouts first. Because these football players didn't need to make back *forty* thousand dollars. They already got money."

He thought the return was a stretch when she first told him about it. But now that he saw forty thousand dollars walk back out the door, it made the point even more evident. They needed the lion's share of the money for doing the lion's share of the work.

Lucina responded, "I-van, if you want more of the money, then you put up your *own* money. That's the way it goes. But I am *not* in this biz-ness to risk my own money if I don't have to."

Ivan began to calculate immediately. If he put the twelve thousand he had just made into another major event, and made at least sixty-two, he could walk away with *fifty* thousand dollars instead of sixteen. Or if he split the deal down the middle with Lucina at six thousand apiece, they could each make twenty-five thousand off of their six.

In the middle of Ivan's thoughts, Lucina told him, "I-van, *please* don't get ahead of your-self. You have to re-mem-ber that this was a Char-gers par-ty, and al-though people did come to dance and to have a good time, they still came to par-ty with the stars of the field. Otherwise they would not have paid twen-ty-five dollars and left their usual down-town clubs. O-kay? So, un-less you have a ce-leb-rity showcase like we had to-night, please don't think you can draw the same crowd and make the same money."

She continued, "That is why I worked so hard to have this par-ty du-ring foot-ball season when the Chargers are the spot-light of the ci-ty."

After Ivan listened to her explain things for a while, Lucina's accent became normal to him. And she made good business sense. So Ivan nodded and reminded himself, *Trust your partner.*

He said, "So it's all about having a celebrity draw?"

"Yes. Definitely," she told him. "And celebrities cost money. That is why you use other people's money and take less of a risk. And yes, you may earn less for yourself, but in the meantime, you lose less or nothing."

Ivan chuckled and said, "Yeah, you lose all that setup time and effort, that's what you lose."

Lucina paused for a spell. She said, "Ivan, I hear so many people say that time is money in America. But in Brazil, we learn that time is only wasted when you do nothing at all. So as long as you are busy having a good time with your life, then you are not wasting time."

Ivan had no comment. He thought, *This girl has an answer for everything.* And since he was almost back at home with Ida, he wanted to end their phone call.

"Well, anyway, I'll talk to you tomorrow. Are you in for the night?" he asked her.

"Are you?"

Ivan paused. She had to know that he was attracted to her. But he had spent enough time just trying to figure out Ida. Lucina was another long-term project. Nevertheless, he asked her, "Should I be?"

She chuckled. "You have a good night, Ivan. I'll talk to you tomorrow."

When they hung up, Ivan wished that he had never asked her. Now she was on his mind again, and in more ways than just business.

When he reached the parking lot of his apartment complex and climbed out of his car to walk up with Ida, he saw Julio step back inside his house. It was nearing three o'clock in the morning.

I wonder if he was out here smoking weed again. But I can't smell it, Ivan thought.

Ida wondered the same thing. She smiled and asked, "Does your neighbor always smoke weed out here at night?"

Ivan laughed as they climbed the stairs together. "I was just wondering that myself. But I don't really know. I don't see him every night."

Then he thought about Julio's connection to super music producers Dr. Dre and Scott Storch through his cousin Mike Elizondo.

Shit, I wonder if Julio could get me in touch with any of those guys for a party. I could have one of them show up to be a special guest DJ or something.

His wheels were still turning late at night. He made a note to ask his neighbor more questions about his connected cousin whenever he bumped into him again.

As soon as Ivan walked into his apartment with Ida, she asked him, "So, Ivan, what do you think about all of these girls Lucina has around her?"

Ivan hadn't given it much thought. They were all pretty girls, but he was more focused on making money with the queen bee.

"I mean, they like her. She takes care of them," he answered blandly.

He walked into the kitchen, pulled out two glasses from his cabinet, and got out a large container of cold springwater from the refrigerator. He then began to pour them each a glass.

Ida walked over to him and stated, "That's what I mean. She takes care of them *how?*"

Ivan said, "The same way I take care of *you* for helping *me:* a couple hundred dollars here and there when they need it."

Actually, Ivan had given Ida more than a few hundred dollars. But loyalty was priceless, and he had no complaints about her efficiency on the job, or her added perks.

She said, "But for what? I mean, you can *see* what *I'm* doing. And a few of her girls were busy tonight, but a lot of them were just . . . *there* doing whatever."

Ivan frowned and said, "So, what's the big deal? Obviously she uses these girls to get the crowd that she gets. And nobody's complaining about it. We're all used to seeing pretty girls around Lucina. They gravitate toward her. But I mean, what are you trying to say?"

He took a long swallow of his water and waited. He didn't believe Lucina was a lesbian or anything. She was simply working her social network game.

Ida swallowed from her own glass of water. She asked, "So, why do you think she was so adamant about giving those football players a bunch of twenties to be 'generous' with? Generous *how?*"

Ivan laughed nervously at what Ida was insinuating.

"Come on, Ivan. Do I need to come right out and say it? It's obvious."

Ivan opened his mouth and said, "You think she's passing these girls off to make more money? Is that what you're saying?"

Ida just stared at him. "I mean, we're grown people here, Ivan. And I don't like how she kept referring to *me* as a *girl,* either. How old is she anyway, twenty-five, twenty-six? Well, she has a lot of damn *nerve.* And I don't *care* where she's from. She acts like a spoiled-rich girl. Everybody's supposed to move to her drum."

Ivan was getting more nervous by the minute. Ida talking about Lucina so passionately was turning him on, and he didn't want her to notice it. But Ida had to admit it herself, the Brazilian girl was interesting.

Ivan shook off his excitement and kept his cool. "Naw," he responded. "Something that obvious would be crazy."

Ida stared at him again. "Okay. You just remember I told you so."

Ivan drank his water and remained silent. He told himself, *I guess I'll have to find out now.*

OVER THE NEXT FEW DAYS, Ivan spent time interviewing several website salespeople who had responded to his solicitations for help. He had already sold a third of his ad space just from the waiting list that he had kept. But now was the time to go all-out. With the buzz they had created from the Chargers party, the entire city was becoming familiar with his website brand. IDPromotions.com was set to blow.

Instead of offering salaried positions, Ivan wanted commissioned hustlers who earned from what they brought in. Only problem was, he had no idea who could really sell. So he made note of the most organized applicants with long résumés of experience. In the meantime, he continued to master the website jargon: banner ads, skyscraper ads, pop-up ads, pop-under ads, text ads, content pages, public domain information, subscriber information, unique site articles, click-through sites, visitor impressions . . . There was plenty of it to learn.

Ivan kept his poise through the process. As Lucina had told him, time does exactly what you choose to do with it. So he remained active and kept his interviews productive.

Near the end of his first week, he had spoken with twenty-four prospects over the phone, internet, and in group lunch and dinner meetings. By that Thursday night, Ivan was exhausted.

He sat down to dinner with his new partner, Lucina Gallo, downtown to discuss it all.

"So, are you going to use all of them?" she asked him over steak, potatoes, and wine. Ivan was having the same, Lucina's treat.

"I have to see what they can do first," he answered. "I mean, a qualified résumé is one thing, but a check in hand is the real deal."

She said, "Well, I'm sure that the most qualified people will bring you those checks."

"We'll soon see," Ivan told her.

"So, how much are you giving them to sell each ad again?" she asked him.

"Twenty-five percent for new ads, fifteen for recurring ads."

"And how much would you give me?"

That caught Ivan off guard. She had slipped it in effortlessly. But he should have known to include her. Ida was already included as a salesperson. Ivan had given her the benefit of the doubt.

Ivan answered, "I'd give you the same thing," and grinned at her.

Lucina didn't flinch. "You'll give me the same as everyone else? I didn't give you twenty-five percent of the party."

Ivan caught on to her point. He said, "I can't give you fifty percent of ads. I still have to pay the web designers to put them things up."

"And how much are you paying them?"

"Twenty-five percent for newly created ads and fifteen percent for maintenance," he answered.

"Well, you give me half of what *you* get."

Ivan looked across the table and said, "Shit."

Lucina told him, "What's fair is fair, Ivan. I give *you* half." She only budged to eat a piece of her steak.

Ivan started smiling and thinking about the suspicions that were surrounding her. It was best to talk about them with her face-to-face. He had waited all that week to confront her.

He said, "So, who are you gonna get to sell these ads, your girls?" He ate a piece of his steak while waiting for her to respond to his sarcasm.

"You'd be surprised at what beauty can do for business," she told him.

"Oh, yeah? Tell me about it. I got all night," he responded.

Lucina stared at him. "What do you want to know?"

Ivan paused and wiped his lips for the grand moment. He said, "Well . . . I've just heard some things about you and your girls, that's all."

"Things like *what*? Be up-front with me."

Ivan was suddenly nervous. He felt ridiculous bringing up suspicions and opinions, but he had to. Partners needed to know what they were getting into.

He said, "I've just heard that things may be a little loose around you."

"A little *loose*?" she asked him, and frowned.

"Yeah."

Lucina took a breath and said, "Let me tell you what I've learned. As a woman who looks good, I know that guys are always interested in talking to me if they think they can take me to bed. So, while I have their attention, I talk business. But as soon as they feel that they will never get me in bed, some of them no longer want to talk business. So I've learned how to let rumors fly where they fly, while I find a way to make my living here."

Ivan said, "So . . . what does that mean, 'find a way to make your living here'?"

"I work whatever angle I have to work," she told him.

He said, "Well, be frank and up-front with me. I mean, what are you really talking about? Are you and your girls sleeping around for deals or what?"

Lucina told him, "The most important business of a woman is never to tell. Just like an accountant can never tell on his clients. But if I say I don't play the game at all, will the client still be interested in business with me? You tell me *that,* Ivan."

It was a good question. Ivan said, "A *good* businessperson *would.*" And he considered himself to be one.

Lucina asked him, "Then how come I've lost so many partners?"

"You've been meeting the wrong ones," Ivan answered. "But not anymore," he hinted.

She smiled and grunted, "Hmmph, we'll soon see. Already you want to treat me like everyone else, with twenty-five percent instead of what I give you."

Ivan smiled back. "I told you already I'd do half."

"No, you *cursed* at me," she reminded him.

He felt embarrassed. "That was just a knee-jerk response. But I agree to it. What's fair is fair, right?"

"Not with men and women," she told him. "Men can always go further."

"You don't really believe that, do you?"

"Yes, I do. I've seen it happen too many times." She said, "I did plenty of meetings with those football players, then I call you for *one* meeting with us, and finally they agree to do it."

Ivan felt duped. "Is that right?" He'd believed that her deal was practically done already. He'd thought he was only the icing on the cake.

She told him, "Yes. In desperation, I called you to test out my idea that night, and it *worked*. The Chargers' week off was coming, and we were running out of preparation time. That's also why at the party I knew that it was better for me to stand next to you as just the pretty girl and let you take the glory, rather than to step out in front of you and be recognized as the bossy bitch."

She continued, "And although I can be the bossy bitch behind closed doors, I do not want the crowd to think of me that way. But as long as they believe that me and my girls are *loose,* I can still keep them interested in my parties. And it may sound sad to you, Ivan, but it is the truth. So please tell me something differently. I want to believe in something else."

Ivan was stunned. Lucina held more layers than he could cut through. He felt like leaning across the table and giving her a hug. But she had long become too hardened for hugs. How hard had her business life been as a pretty girl? She made him think again of Catherine. How hard had her life been trying to find and keep love? So Ivan felt guilty about everything. Maybe Lucina was right: the world of men was despicable for a woman.

He shook off the chill he felt inside and said, "It's a cold world out there." Then he drank some of his wine to warm his own cold heart.

OVER THE COURSE of their evening dinner, Lucina disregarded several of her phone calls, only responding to situations of urgency. Ivan gave her an open door to excuse herself from the table when she needed to. And she explained to him that she looked out for pretty girls because they all reminded her of herself in her younger years of dreaming to become an international model.

"I was only fourteen back then and very hungry to succeed," she told him. "I traveled around the world and spoke parts of six languages: Portuguese, Italian, English, some Spanish, some French, and some Russian. But for whatever reason, international fame does not happen for everyone. So once I reached a certain point in my modeling career, I just got tired of trying so hard."

It seemed that every pretty girl at least fantasized about being a model at some point. So Ivan listened to her with open ears, trying to get a fuller understanding of who she was.

"I moved to the United States in California by myself at eighteen," Lucina continued. "And I worked many odd jobs: as a waitress, hostess, shoe salesperson, in clothing department stores, anything where I could make money with my charm. Then I started doing parties in L.A."

When she mentioned L.A., Ivan raised a brow. She had never spoken of it before. But she always made sure to speak about *him* being from L.A.

"And what happened with that?" he asked her.

Lucina shook her head. She stopped and said, "At first I loved the attention. There were so many stars and so many things to do if you followed the party crowd there. But then I noticed that girls there were willing to starve for the dream of becoming Hollywood stars. They were coming from all over America and every country. Well, I had already been through that. And I was not coming to the United States to do it all over again. I wanted *real* money that I could *count*, not promises to be a star in movies and videos," she told him.

Ivan smiled. He had never tried the Hollywood thing; just living in L.A. allowed him to know that all the glitter was not gold.

Lucina continued her story with rising animation. "So then I came down to San Diego, and I demanded *real money* from promoters to fill up their clubs with hot girls. And at first they would not pay me. So I would take all of my girls to an empty club and make *that* club hot. And soon the promoters got my point. You *pay me* for what *I do.*"

She said, "So then I became a promoter myself. But my expertise was not really the money side. I just dealt with my girls and how to sell the crowd on a good party. So I always had male partners who would set up the parties and do the deals. But as my popularity in this city grew, I noticed that I was still not getting the money that I deserved from these partnerships."

She told him, "The promoters, they all had excuses to pay me less. I felt like they had all met in a big room and decided that they would refuse to pay me equal money. And then the rumors started. 'I hear Lucina does this and that.' And at first, I tried to fight them. But then I decided to continue to focus on making money and meeting new friends."

Ivan heard all of that and was hooked. As far as he was concerned, Lucina had finally met the right man. It was perfect timing for both of them. And if she could take care of her part, he would take care of his.

He nodded and said, "That all makes perfect sense for me now. I get you. But, ah . . . were these promoters all white guys, or have you dealt with brothers before?"

Ivan had some hunches of his own.

Lucina answered, "I've dealt with *all* promoters and every crowd: hip-hop, rock and roll, pop. And they *all* act the same: *greedy*. But me, I try to be fair with all people and not get stuck on race, class, or social politics. Especially since I'm from Brazil." She said, "I am very used to all races and all classes of people. But money has no race. You get it from who's willing to give it to you."

Ivan nodded. *One question down, one question to go,* he thought.

He said, "And what are your real thoughts on me?" He wanted to hear that he was more than just a random promoter that she would move on from if things didn't go her way. He wanted to know what her long-term intentions were.

She smiled at him again, that naked, guard-dropping smile that seduced him. But then she took a breath and her smile quickly disappeared. She returned to her business mode.

"The truth is, when I first looked at you, I thought to myself, '*He is just like me. He can go anywhere he wants to go. All he has to do is cut his hair down low like Vin Diesel.*' "

Ivan frowned and said, "Vin Diesel?" He didn't follow her on that.

She said, "Ivan, one thing that I've noticed in this country is that everyone must use their own advantages to get ahead. That is what I tell all of my girls. If you have a certain look, then *use* it. And the ones who realize that quickly go the furthest. So I look across the table at your eyes—similar to mine—and your light skin, your hair, and I say to myself, '*If Ivan wants it, he can have it all.* You can go in many directions.'

She told him, "Certain looks can be from anywhere. And you have that certain look. White, black, mixed, whatever. You will always stand out. But you want to make sure that you *use* it. That is why I love my accent. It makes people know immediately that I am different, not only in how I look, but with how I speak.

"But you, your hair is the only thing that can get in your way."

Ivan began to chuckle at her superficiality. He said, "I thought you just told me you don't get into race, class, and social politics."

Lucina told him, "I *don't*, but white American owners *do*. They are not like Brazil. Americans still judge color. But if you can confuse them just long enough to get into the room, you can get deals done."

Ivan heard that and broke out laughing. He said, "Are you crazy? That's that old-time Negro religion of crossing over. That shit don't work no more. We just did a party with *jet-black* football players, and everybody was in the room. You even said that yourself. Those guys are celebrities, and they're true-blue *black* brothers," he told her.

Lucina kept her poise. She said, "And they are also *football* players. But are *you*? And are you *a rapper*? Are you a *basketball* player? Are you a *baseball* player? Are you *any* of those?"

Ivan began to shake his head, not liking where their conversation was headed.

Lucina told him, "Ivan, I have been around white men in this country who were basically nobodies. And all they did was kiss the ass of the rich and famous, drop names, lie about their friendships, and hang around the club just long enough for a big bag of money to fall right into their pockets. And I've seen it happen with my *own* eyes. But if you don't play the game the way *you* have to play it, then you can be *stuck* looking in from the outside, with no one to blame but yourself."

Ivan continued to shake his head defiantly. Even as a high-yellow, rainbow-eyed, light-brown-haired brother, he still had his black pride about him. And he would allow no foreign Brazilian girl to try to strip that pride away from him, no matter how good she looked or how much money they could make together.

But Lucina remained adamant. She flashed him that rare smile of hers and said, "I would even give you a *big* diamond earring for your left ear to add some sparkle to your eyes."

Ivan couldn't help but laugh at her. He repeated, "You're crazy." He told her, "You know what, if my look is so special, then how come you don't remember seeing me before? You looked right at me."

Ivan figured he had her. It was time to cut the cord on her bullshit. But he had to admit that she was good at it. He could imagine that other young women would have no chance with her. Women loved that kind of flattery. No wonder Lucina Gallo ruled them. But Ivan was a man—a rising businessman.

Lucina said, "You mean at the Padres party outside of the Market Street Hotel in the early summer? You were standing on the sidewalk trying to get in. And you were wearing a striped light blue shirt, dark blue jeans, and brown leather shoes."

Ivan was ready to jump up from the table. He lost all of his business savvy and blurted, "Get the fuck out of here! No fuckin' way! There's no way possible you can remember me from just a look on the sidewalk with all these new people you meet."

He started shaking his head again with an even bigger grin. He mumbled, "Naw, naw, naw, that's just . . . that's just . . ." She had to have some kind of trick up her sleeve. Had one of her girls taken a picture of him that night without him noticing? Her story was outright *freakish,* and Ivan had run out of words to express it.

Lucina told him, "I have a way of looking at people without them knowing that I am looking. And I take a mental picture. I have been doing it for years. And I can remember them down to their fingernails. It is a gift from God, so I learned to use it. But when I first saw you, I had no reason to know you yet. You were not even in the party crowd. But I could see in your eyes that you were searching for something more in your life. So I told myself right then and there, *That man has a* look *and determination about him that can take him many places* if *he decides to go there.* I said, *But right now he is still undecided.*"

She continued, "So, once I sat down with you at the wine house and I realized who you were and what you were doing, I told myself that I would save this conversation for when I need it. And I knew that you would be impressed. So hopefully, Ivan, now that you know all of this about me, you will take my advice and go as far as you can go."

All Ivan could do was stare across the table at her in a child's wonder.

He cracked another smile and thought, *Yo . . . they have no idea. This girl is just . . . fuckin' dangerous! Or maybe she's just fucking with me. Either way, I guess I'll find everything out soon. Because she can't keep saying all the right things forever.*

Eight

Deeper & Deeper

When Ivan drove home from his long fact-finding dinner with Lucina, he was still on a natural high from their conversation.

"That girl's something else," he told himself.

The whole time, she had managed to dodge answering any specific questions about the operations of her "girls." And although Lucina may have been well experienced in handling the advances of popular and wealthy men, Ivan could easily see that a number of her girls would not be as well prepared.

Nevertheless, her inspired speech on the subject of a woman's disadvantage to men made him think of apologizing to Catherine. So he called her cell phone on his way home, only to get her voice mail.

At first he hesitated. He could call her back at a much earlier hour the next day. But he decided to leave her a message instead.

"Hey, Cat, this is Ivan. I hate to call and leave you a message so late on a weeknight, but I just wanted to apologize to you for how we've fallen apart as friends. I mean, I know it's a cold world out here for a girl, but . . . it ain't that easy for a guy, either. It's a lot of tough decisions that gotta be made, day after day. Anyway . . . call me. Let's chit-chat."

By the time Ivan pulled into his apartment complex, Catherine was calling him back.

He read her number and answered, "Hey."

"Hi, Ivan, I just wanted to call you back to tell you that I'm all right," she responded. "I understand what you're up against out there. And I wish you all the best of luck. But your brother pretty much explained everything to me. I was being a typical spiteful woman. But at the end of it all, you just gotta do what you gotta do. And I need to respect that."

That all sounded good to Ivan, everything but the brother part.

He said, "My brother explained everything to you?" That didn't sound right, unless the explanation led past words. That was more his big brother's style: use whatever you have to use to hit the skins.

Catherine answered, "Yeah, that night at the party. I mean, I really got messed up, so he basically had to drive me home that night. And on the way, he told me everything that you were trying to do, you know, with taking care of his family and whatnot. I mean, he really explained a lot of stuff. And he's proud of you and what you're doing. So I really had to back up and understand the position you're in."

Ivan was at a loss for words. He thought, *Damn! My brother's proud of me? And he told her everything about his three sons and three mothers. That's crazy! I must be really doing something, then.*

He said, "So . . . *D.* told you all of that?"

Catherine chuckled. "Yeah. Why, you don't think he *should* be proud of what you're doing?"

"I mean, I guess. But you thought I was tripping when I first started talking about throwing parties."

"It was just so different for you, that's all. You never were even a party person. But it's late, so . . . I'll just talk to you tomorrow or whatever."

"Okay. Have a good sleep."

"You, too."

Ivan hung up his phone, climbed out of his car, and felt great. Everything was falling into place for him. So when he spotted Julio up on the second level of the complex, smoking a cigarette instead of a blunt, he remembered to ask him about his cousin in the Dr. Dre camp.

"Hey, Julio, what it is, what it is, man?" he asked, extending his hand for a shake.

Julio shook his hand and smiled. "You've been pretty busy around here, man. I've been busy, too," he commented. It was a little too chilly out to wear no shirt that night, so Julio wore a black sweatshirt with black jeans.

Ivan looked over his neighbor's low haircut and thought again about Lucina's comments on cutting his hair down.

"Hey, man, how long have you had your hair cut low like that? How long can it grow?" Ivan asked him out of the blue.

Julio grinned and said, "My hair would grow all the way down my back if I let it. But I don't feel like dealing with my hair that much every day. It kept getting way too dirty in the landscaping business. Too much flying dirt, and plants, trees, cut grass. It's a lot easier to wash all that shit out if I keep it low. Plus it makes me look like a badass. More macho, you know."

Ivan said, "How do you think it would make me look?"

Julio stopped and stared at him. "Ahh . . . I don't know, man, those funny-colored eyes of yours would probably pop out more or something."

Ivan nodded. "So you think they would stand out more?"

Julio took another drag from his cigarette and nodded back to him. "Yeah. You would have nothing else to look at," he answered with a chuckle.

"And what if I put a diamond stud in my left ear?" Ivan asked him next.

Julio looked at his ear and imagined it. He smiled and said, "That would be pretty cool on you. Especially if you bought one of those diamonds with the colors and shit in them. Like . . . like those blue and yellow diamonds and shit. That would go real well with your eyes. But me and my dark eyes, I might as well get a hard *white* diamond."

He asked Ivan, "Why, are you trying to change your look now or something? What would the people at your job say?"

"Man, fuck the people at my job," Ivan snapped. "I'm just thinking about *me* right now." It just came out that way. He figured Julio thought too much about authority.

Ivan's raw response made his neighbor laugh.

Julio said, "Hey, man, that's the way you gotta be sometimes. No more Mr. Nice Guy."

Just as Julio said that, his wife poked her head out from their apartment door.

"Papi, are you coming in to bed soon?"

Julio looked irritated. "Yeah, I'll be in in a minute."

His wife paused inside the doorway. "Okay, but you said that before, thirty minutes ago."

Julio said, "Yeah, but it's still *minutes,* it's not *hours.* I'll be there. Damn, I'm catching a smoke out here."

His wife looked ready to say a few more things, but then she looked at Ivan and decided not to.

"Hi," she said to him. She was a pretty woman, but extrasmall. She barely stood at five feet. Julio stood at least eight inches taller.

"How are you doing?" Ivan responded to her.

"I'm good," she said. And she closed the door.

Ivan joked, "You better get on in there, man."

Julio took a drag from his cigarette, shook his head, and slid the closed fist of his right hand up and down near his torso to simulate masturbation.

Ivan laughed and said, "Yo, man, I actually wanted to talk to you about getting in touch with your cousin Mike Elizondo. I want to see if I could hook up with some of the musicians they produce to bring them down for a San Diego party or something."

Julio got excited. "Yeah, man, how are your parties going now? I heard your ads for the Chargers party on the radio. I really wanted to make that one. I.D. Promotions is blowing up now, hunh?"

"Not if we can't keep the momentum going," Ivan said, leveling with him. "We need to start bringing in celebrities now."

"Well, just say the word, man, and I'll call Mike," Julio told him. He said, "You know, I don't really bug him a lot because he's busy all the time, but if you wanna talk business, that's different. We can call him right now."

Ivan said, "Well, just get some party price tags for now. Like, how much would some artists charge just to be at the party as a guest DJ or something? And I could just have the artists tell the DJ to play their favorite new songs while they chill and drink."

Ivan already had it worked out in his mind. A celebrity would sit in the VIP section with plenty of hot girls and his or her entourage, and he or she could get on the microphone whenever he or she felt like it. But if the artist was asked to play a favorite song or two, most likely he or she would suggest some of their own music and possibly go into an impromptu performance. Jeff and Paul or another cameraman would then be sure to catch it all for the website.

Julio said, "You got it, man."

Ivan smiled at him. "You do that for me, and you got VIP all night long with a free bottle of wine in your hands."

"And two honeys," Julio added without whispering.

Ivan chuckled. "Now, you know we got that. But let me get on in bed and get some rest for tomorrow."

"All right, I'll get back up with you once I talk to my cousin."

They shook hands on it and ended their night.

INSTEAD OF INVESTING in another big party, Ivan used the thousands of dollars he had made from the Chargers event to contact the best law firms in San Diego to represent his interests. It was easy to secure top-notch representation when you could afford the up-front retainers. The best representation would make it easier for Ivan to sleep at night when engaging in so many fast-moving deals. He even had the lawyers set up the payment terms for the mothers of Derrick's three sons.

After his new calculations, with website costs, the lawyers, and his brother on the payroll, Ivan estimated an overhead budget of seven thousand dollars a month. He added another three thousand to pay himself each month, tapping out at ten thousand. Between the website advertisements on IDPromotions.com and party promotions with Lucina, Ivan figured he could triple that in profit and shell away his Hutch & Mitchell salary without needing to touch it.

Then I can move into a nicer place to live by the end of the year, he thought. *Or better yet, buy a house near the university to use as an office. That way Jeff and Paul—or whoever runs the site—can have all of the sales and editorial staff right there with them.*

As a long-term goal, Ivan continued to think about the homes above Interstate 5.

"Damn, this feels good!" he told himself inside the bathroom at the Hutch & Mitchell offices. He washed his hands at the sink and finally felt in control of his life. He then stared into the mirror at his hair, wondering how he would look with a low cut. While he stood there, Mike Adams walked in.

He caught Ivan staring at himself and said, "Yeah, you look good."

Ivan chuckled as Mike hit the urinal to the left of the sink.

"I'm trying to decide if I should go with a new look or not," Ivan commented.

Mike did his business and responded casually, "Everything's worth a shot to see."

"What about if I put a diamond stud in my left ear?"

Mike grimaced, zipped up, and walked over to the sinks to wash his hands. "Well, an earring on a guy is a little eccentric, isn't it? But I guess you wouldn't have to wear it all the time. And definitely not while at the office."

"Well, where else would I wear it, then?"

Mike shrugged. "I guess on the club scene or wherever. Fancy dinners. I don't know. What do you single people do nowadays?" he joked. "But you're supposed to be getting serious now. What does the lady think about that? Did *she* suggest it?"

Ivan had to chuckle. Mike was wrong as well as right. Ivan told him, "Yeah, she did suggest it," and kept his office illusion going. They continued to believe he was passionate about a woman instead of business. The irony was that Lucina Gallo was both.

Mike chuckled at him and joked, "In that case, it's a great idea. The woman is *always right*." He added, "But I don't have much use for an earring in my ear. That would only give my toddlers something else dangerous to grab at."

When his coworker walked out of the bathroom, Ivan continued to stand there in the mirror. He mumbled to himself, "Yeah, well, I don't have any kids."

Next walked in Dwayne Bellamy, the middle manager. He saw Ivan there in the bathroom alone and said, "Your new clients are still rolling in, Ivan. But you make sure you get your story ready for the brass. I hear your on-the-side thing is getting bigger now."

Ivan nodded to him. "Yeah, it is." Then he decided to ask Dwayne what *he* thought about an earring. "Hey, man, what do you think about a diamond stud?"

"A diamond stud? What do you mean?" Dwayne asked him.

"An earring."

"Oh, an earring." He shrugged. "Well, that's just not my thing."

Ivan said, "Michael Jordan got *two* of 'em."

"Yeah, well, Michael can get away with it," Dwayne commented.

Get away with it? Ivan repeated to himself. He nodded and said, "All right."

He was ready to leave.

Dwayne said, "You're not thinking about that, are you?"

"Well, I wouldn't have to wear it at the job, right?" Ivan responded.

They eyed each other for a couple of seconds, as if it was a stare-down.

Dwayne finally told him, "Don't get too far ahead of yourself, Ivan. Sometimes we can jump out of the plane before we have a parachute or a landing pad ready. You catch my drift?"

Ivan nodded again. "I got you. I was only speculating."

Dwayne nodded back to him. "Okay," he said, and left it alone to do his business.

Ivan walked out of the bathroom right past Barry Mitchell's office. He wondered how his boss would take him having an earring. Would it be too much of an obvious signal of change? And how much of Dwayne's response was built around his knowledge of Ivan joining the party promotions game?

I'm not ready to do that anyway, Ivan told himself of the earring idea while on the way back to his desk. But the low-cut hair was a doable experiment. *I might go ahead and get it cut down after work tonight. Fuck it, it'll grow back!* he told himself.

AS SOON AS IVAN finished getting his hair cut down at the barbershop that evening, he received a call from Lucina.

He laughed and said, "What, are you reading my mind now? I'm just walking out from the barbershop. I'm trying that new look you suggested to me. Let's see how it works."

"Ivan, stop fighting it and go along with the flow," she told him. "Anyways, I have two new friends from out of town who want to go shopping at the Fashion Valley Mall. But I have meetings to make tonight. So I was wondering if you could be a great guy and hang out with them there for a couple of hours before the mall closes."

Ivan looked down at his Seiko watch. It was already after seven. He said, "The mall will be closing by the time we even make it over there. Where are they now?"

"They are already on their way," Lucina informed him. "They

should be there in no more than twenty minutes. And since you already live in that area, I told them they could wait for you inside the car."

Ivan didn't see any problems with it. He figured he could finally scope out a few of Lucina's girls to see what they were all about. Were they down-to-earth girls who simply needed an experienced big sister type for guidance? Or were they fast and flirty, with their own ideas about life and business? He was also curious to see how they would respond to his low haircut. So, for his own research purposes, he agreed to it.

"All right, I'll babysit your girls tonight," he joked.

Lucina corrected him. "No, they're not my girls. They're just some new *friends*. And I want to see how they are."

Ivan paused. "You want to see how they are?"

"Yes. I want to see how they treat you. I told them both that you were a very sweet and important man. And I want to see if they take advantage of that."

Ivan was confused. He made it back to his car and said, "You didn't tell them that I was your partner?"

"No, I just told them you were a good friend," Lucina answered. "But if they treat you with respect, and you still like them, I will tell them that you are my partner later. So will you do that for me?"

Ivan didn't know what to say. He wanted to slow things down and ask her more questions. But he figured it was best to gather his own information by going through with it.

"All right, all right," he barked to her. "I'm heading over there now. And I'll tell you how they are once I send them home. But if they're your *friends*, then you should already *know* how they are."

"Yes, but they are *new* friends. And women can always *change* to show their true colors around wealthy men."

"Oh, so you told them that I'm *wealthy*, too, now?"

"Why of course. Why wouldn't I?"

I better not let them see my car, then, Ivan told himself with a grin. His modest Nissan Altima was not a wealthy man's car.

"Okay, so meet them at the limo outside of the Cheesecake Factory," Lucina told him.

"You got them a limo?"

"It was a favor from a friend."

Ivan chuckled and said, "Okay." It was a good thing he still had his work clothes on.

When he hung up the phone, already headed in the direction of the fashion mall, he mumbled, "Yeah, she's full of it. But I'll find out what I need to know now. She still hasn't told me enough yet."

HE ARRIVED at the Fashion Valley Mall off of Interstate 8 and parked his car three rows away from the Cheesecake Factory so he could meet the girls without his car being seen.

A midsized black limo pulled up as soon as he made it over.

"Ivan David?" an older white man behind the wheel asked him at the curb. He had rolled his driver's-side window down.

"Yeah, that's me," Ivan answered.

"Thank you."

The driver double-parked and climbed out to open the back door for his two passengers. Ivan watched with anticipation along with a small crowd of waiting customers outside of the Cheesecake Factory.

The first young woman climbed out of the limo in orange strap-up heels, an off-white dress, and a large orange belt to match her shoes. She had long beaded jewelry around her neck, with matching earrings and bracelets. Her hair was bleached blond, and she had large dark eyes and tanned skin and carried a dark brown leather Coach bag over her right shoulder. She had an East Coast ruggedness about her.

"Hi," she said perkily to Ivan. She extended her left hand to him as she reached the curb.

"How are you?" he asked her. "You *look* lovely enough." Since he was supposedly wealthy, Ivan kissed the back of her hand like a gentleman.

"Oh, I'm fine, and thank you for the compliment," she responded. So far, she had good manners, but her look was over-the-top. She was trying way too hard to dazzle.

Ivan flattered her anyway. "No, you deserve it."

"Well, you don't look bad yourself," she responded.

"Thank you," he told her.

The second young woman climbed out of the limo in dark blue heels and a solid blue dress. She wore silver jewelry with a small silver purse. She was darker than tan, with black wavy hair, a sign of a mixed breed of black. Her tiny dark eyes hinted at Asian blood.

"How are you?" she asked Ivan. When she smiled, her eyes looked even smaller, with dimples on both cheeks. But she never extended her hand to him. She kept her hands wrapped around her small purse.

Ivan said, "I'm good," and he preferred her look already. She could dress up or down and still kill it with her naturalness.

Ivan's night of research at the mall had just begun, and all eyes were on them before they even budged.

He said, "Well, you both know who I am. Now I need to know who you are."

"I'm Audrey," the bleached blonde responded.

"And I'm Christina. But you can just call me Chris."

"Chris? Is that what everybody calls you?"

"Yes," she answered softly.

Ivan extended his hand forward. "Well, are you ready to shop?"

"Of course," they both answered.

The driver said, "I'll be parked right around in this area when you're ready."

Ivan nodded to him. "Okay. That's good."

The girls began to walk toward the mall. It was an outside, multilevel shopping mall of high-end fashion stores—Gucci, Fendi, Prada, Coach, Bebe, St. John, Caché—with lower-end stores such as Banana Republic, the Gap, and Old Navy. It was anchored by larger department stores—Macy's, Lord & Taylor, Belk—and mixed in were specialty stores, jewelry shops, a food court, and a movie theater on the top level. And it seemed that they had entered at the most expensive end of the mall.

"Oh, my God, this reminds me of an outside Bellagio in Las Vegas," Audrey stated. She walked right into the Fendi store and started looking at the most expensive carrybags. Ivan looked at a few of the price tags and winced. *Damn, all that for a purse?*

Chris stood close by him and smiled at his reactions.

Ivan asked her, "Where are you from?"

"Seattle."

"Do you drink coffee?"

Chris paused before she chuckled at his question. "I know, right? There's, like, a coffee shop on every corner in Seattle. Why, have you been there before?"

"No, I just have friends who told me about it. But I've been to other places."

"What's the farthest place you ever been to?" she asked him. She acted as if she were uninterested in shopping.

Ivan lied and told her, "Japan."

Chris grinned and said, "My father is Japanese."

"Oh, yeah? I thought you had an Asian look to you."

She smiled, giving her heritage away again. "My eyes, right?"

"Yeah, but you're Japanese and what?"

"Black."

"I figured that, too."

"Because I'm dark?"

Ivan said, "You're not that dark, but you're dark for an Asian girl."

"That's because I'm not Asian. I'm only half Asian. But I'm darker than you."

He said, "That's not hard to do. I'm not dark at all."

She asked him, "Are you mixed?"

"Do I look mixed?"

She looked him in his face and nodded. "Yeah."

"What makes you say that?" he asked her. He figured he was still clearly a black man, even with his hair cut low.

She said, "You have black features, but your skin is light and you have those light eyes."

Ivan asked her, "And do I look like an attractive man to you?"

She looked him right in his face and said, "Yes. I think you're *very* attractive."

He nodded and said, "Thank you. And you already know how *you* look. I'm sure that plenty of guys have already told you."

She grinned and said, "Yeah." That's all she had to say.

Boy, she knows she bad, Ivan thought. He began to feel comfortable with her, but he'd been ignoring Audrey. So he walked forward and asked the forgotten friend, "What are you about to do, buy the whole store in here?"

"Oh, they just have so many great bags," Audrey told him. "They have some I haven't seen before."

"In Vegas?" he asked her.

She turned to face him. "Yeah."

"Is that where you're from originally?"

"Well, I'm actually from Hawaii, but I've been in Las Vegas for two years now," she answered. "Do you like this one?" she asked him, holding up another large Fendi bag.

It looked like a typical Fendi bag to Ivan. It had the up and down *F*'s all over it in brown, burgundy, and beige, like the majority of them. He didn't see what the big deal was with Fendi. Most of the bags were not even leather.

He flattered her anyway. "That's all you."

Then he turned back to Chris. She had walked over to check out a lone Fendi bag on display in the middle of the store. It was the only one that looked different, a multicolored bag that didn't even look Fendi. There were no *F*'s all over it.

One of the female salesclerks commented on it. She could see that Chris was admiring it.

"That's one of our newest bags," she said. "It's our latest promotion."

Chris nodded to her. "I like it. It's different."

"Would you like to have it today?" the salesclerk asked her. She angled toward Ivan when she asked her. She was a crafty, older white woman with dark brown hair and hard green eyes.

"Sure, if I could afford it," Chris told her with a sly grin.

The salesclerk looked right at Ivan. "Wouldn't this bag look beautiful on her? She's *gorgeous.*"

That even got Audrey's attention. "Oh, my God, I didn't even see that one." She walked over to it immediately.

The multicolored bag was practically the first purse you saw when you walked into the store. Ivan didn't see how Audrey could have missed it. But Chris hadn't missed it. And all eyes were on Ivan now.

He thought, *Okay, am I supposed to buy them this now? I'm not spending thousands of dollars on these girls. Is this how Lucina hooks them up, with that "generous" shit? Because I'm not into it.*

So he came up with his own response system. He said, "I'm basically seeing what their tastes are like today. But this store isn't going anywhere, and they both plan to settle down here in San Diego. So we'll have plenty of time to come back."

"Oh, I see," the salesclerk commented with a nod. "So you two are both from out of town?" she said addressing the girls.

"Yeah," Audrey answered. "But we both would like a change of pace, you know? San Diego is nice."

Ivan didn't believe her. She seemed to have lost a chunk of her luster as soon as she realized that he wasn't buying them anything. Ivan made note of that along with everything else he observed.

When they walked out of the Fendi store empty handed, they bumped into Emilio Alvarez from the San Diego Padres.

"Hey, E.A., what's going on, man? Where have you been? I tried to invite you out to two of our last events."

At first Emilio had to look twice at Ivan's new haircut.

"Oh, shit, Ivan, you cut your hair down," he responded. "That looks good on you. You look like an agent now."

Ivan laughed it off and noticed that Emilio was with a new, white girlfriend. She had shopping bags full of expensive items with her. She had authentic blond hair and gray eyes, but she didn't look *half* as stunning as either one of the two girls with Ivan. She looked frail, with weak skin, and lacked a body. Ivan saw that and felt sorry for the baseball player immediately. He was being taken to the bank by a seven instead of a nine. Maybe he allowed it because she was white.

Audrey looked at his new girlfriend, carrying the shopping bags, and she stood right there in front of them for an introduction. Ivan went ahead and gave her one just to see what she would do with it.

"Oh, this is, ah, Audrey from Las Vegas, and Christina from Seattle."

Emilio nodded to both of them. "Nice to meet you."

Audrey stared at him and said nothing. Chris cracked her dimpled smile again.

Emilio looked at Ivan and said, "Yeah, I heard about your parties, man, but I was just busy trying to stay focused on my first baseball season in the majors."

Ivan nodded. "I understand. You gotta do what you gotta do. But I'll have some more things coming up for you."

Audrey heard that and continued to stand there, soaking it all up. Just like at Hooters, Emilio didn't bother to introduce his companion.

Finally, she said, "I need the keys. I'm going to the car."

Emilio dug into his pocket for his Mercedes key ring. He told her, "I'll be right out in a minute."

As soon as she walked away, Emilio pulled out his cell phone and said, "Hey, give me your number again, man." He peeked at Audrey and said, "I'll definitely make it out to your next one."

"What position do you play?" Audrey asked him.

Emilio looked at her and was surprised that she was talking now.

"Shortstop."

"And are you happy with it?" she asked him.

Happy with what? Ivan thought. He looked over at Chris for Audrey's meaning. Chris did her usual smiling thing. But did she know, or did she not know?

Emilio answered, "Yeah, I've played shortstop all of my life," as if Audrey were talking strictly about baseball. But Ivan wasn't so sure about that.

"And you never wanted to play any other position?" she asked him.

Chris smiled so hard that she had to turn away. Ivan caught that as well.

Emilio answered, "Well, you know, I thought about it."

Audrey looked him in his face and said, "Okay, I just wanted to ask."

Emilio looked at her and seemed stuck there for a minute.

Audrey shrugged him off and looked back at Ivan. "Okay, well, I'm ready to do some more *window*-shopping now," she hinted with sarcasm.

Ivan grinned it off and said, "Let's go. I'm following you." He reached out to shake Emilio's hand. "She'll probably be at our next event, man, if you can make it out," he told him in reference to Audrey.

Audrey and Chris caught on to that. Ivan was making his own moves now.

Emilio still seemed dazed by the girl. "Oh, okay, well, I'll call you up, man. And you got my numbers, too, right?"

Ivan nodded. "Yeah, I got everybody's numbers. That's what I do. But sometimes I can lose them if nothing's going on with them. If you slow you blow, you know."

Chris and Audrey looked at each other again. It was a game-recognition thing. Ivan had it good. His cadence was natural and realistic. He was fully believable. And he was extracalm at it, too.

Emilio smiled. He said, "I hear you, man. So, like, you know, I'll call you up, now." The rookie baseball player struggled to pull all of his words together.

Ivan told him, "You do that," and walked away behind the girls.

When they were alone again inside the Gucci store, Audrey was too curious. She stopped looking at clothing and smiled back at Ivan.

"So, you think he likes me?"

Ivan grinned and answered, "Definitely. You look better than that girl. He knows that. He plays baseball and they all have good eyes. Now he just has to learn how to catch better."

Chris and Audrey started laughing. Ivan was starting to loosen up for them and talk shit while he was at it.

Audrey stopped in front of him and said, "So, Ivan, how close are you and Lucina? Because she told us you're her *good* friend."

He had her full attention now. She had seen and heard enough for her instincts to kick in.

Ivan flipped the script and told her, "Yeah, and she told me you were both our *new* friends. So I'm here to check y'all out for myself."

Chris stopped to listen to him as well.

Audrey said, "Oh, so that's what you're doing?"

"I'm not supposed to?" Ivan asked her.

"I mean, I thought that Lucina had already did that."

Ivan figured the girl was ready to tell him something important.

"Lucina already did what?" he asked. It was his moment of truth to find out what his elusive partner's game was.

Chris kept her silence and listened to them. She had already observed enough about Ivan. Now she was studying Audrey.

Audrey took a deep breath and said, "I'm just confused right now."

"Confused about what?" Ivan pressed her.

Finally, Chris spoke up and told her, "You're thinking too hard. Just have a good time with him. If Lucina says he's a good friend, then that's what he is. Show him some respect."

Audrey looked at her and paused. Then she nodded. "Okay, you're right." She turned back to Ivan and said, "I'm sorry."

A few of the Gucci salesclerks looked on curiously, wondering when they should ask them if they needed any help with anything.

Ivan told both girls, "Let's walk out and talk for a minute."

He knew he wasn't buying anything from the Gucci store. And if neither girl had her own money, there was no sense in teasing them.

They followed him out and realized that Ivan's priority was making money and not spending it on strangers. He was incredibly poised about it. He didn't seem pressured by them at all.

Once they were back out in the center of the mall, he asked them, "So, which way do we walk and talk?" as if it made a difference.

Christina answered, "It's all on you. We're on your time. And if we're not really buying anything here, then how long do you want us to look at stuff?"

She had a point. Ivan smiled and said, "Maybe so, but I'm just trying to make sure, you know, that you see everything you came to see."

Audrey said, "We did. We checked you out, and you checked us out, right? Now we're all good. And we like you."

Ivan said, "You like me?"

Audrey nodded and said, "As a businessman."

"Basically," Christina agreed with her. "From what I can see, you're about getting money like Lucina. I mean, you stood your ground and told us what time it was, and I like that. I can see what you're trying to do. And we're trying to get money like that, too. That's why Lucina wanted us to meet you. She's clever," the Seattle girl concluded.

Ivan agreed with her. "Obviously, she is . . . And so am I," he added with a chuckle.

Audrey grinned and said, "Yeah, we saw that. We noticed how

you lured your boy Emilio. And if you're getting money, we both want to be down with you."

"And what about Lucina?" he asked them.

Chris said, "We're all friends here, right? She told us to hang out with you. And you were the first person she wanted us to meet. I think that *means* something, right? Obviously, you're the most important person to her. And now we know why."

Ivan stood still for a minute. Lucina continued to amaze him. And he continued to rise to the occasion. Not only was he there to test them, they were there to test *him*. So Ivan broke into a grin and laughed. He was tickled by the whole thing, as long as he got it right. He would settle up with Lucina later.

He said, "So you both want to help us build up this party game in San Diego? Is that it?"

"Yes," Chris told him. "It's whatever."

The girl had a baby face, but her willpower was iron. She thought fast. And he liked her.

Then he looked at Audrey, whom he liked less.

She nodded and said, "It really is. We want to help you get whatever you need."

Ivan didn't believe it as much from her, but he figured the truth would come out sooner or later. So he nodded. It was a done deal.

He said, "Well, let's go throw these parties, then."

Nine

Money Lessons

IVAN WALKED Audrey and Christina over to eat at the Cheesecake Factory, where they had a lighter conversation. He asked them all of the basic questions to get to know them better. And at the end of their dinner, including cheesecake to go, he told them he looked forward to working with them. He then sent them back on their way inside the limo.

"Another interesting night," he told himself as he climbed into his Altima. "Now what will she try to tell me about this?" he asked in reference to Lucina.

Sure enough, Lucina called him as soon he pulled out of the mall parking lot and onto Friars Road, headed for home.

Ivan answered, "Nice test this evening."

Lucina chuckled. She said, "I told them to call me when they were done hanging out with you at the mall. I already know that you're an early bird on weeknights, so I let them know that you probably wouldn't keep them out too late."

"That's not what they told me," Ivan insinuated.

Lucina paused and ignored his comment. "Well, they both said they had a great time with you. They said you were very interesting. What did you think about them?"

Ivan paused. Honesty was the best policy. "You're not gonna tell them what I say, are you?" He wanted to make sure before he said anything.

"Ivan . . . come on. What is my number-one rule? I never tell."

"But you force them to tell you everything, right?" he assumed.

She said, "Most times, I don't even ask. Why do you think I'm calling you so quickly? Once they told me that they left you, I asked them what they thought of you, and they both told me what I already know. Then I hung up with them to call you and get the rest."

"Oh, and now I'm supposed to tell?"

"You said that you would when I asked you earlier," she reminded him.

Ivan grinned. She was right, he did agree to it. A deal was a deal.

"Okay, well, let me just get it over with, then," he commented. "The first girl, Audrey, told me she was a military brat. And she's over-the-top and a little impatient. She's an all-in-your-face girl, but she's still likable for guys who like that type. In fact, I already promised Emilio Alvarez from the Padres that she would be at the next big event, to get him out there. We bumped into him at the mall, and he already had his nose open for her."

Lucina said, "I see. And you said this right in front of her?"

Ivan laughed and said, "Yeah, she's the show-and-prove type. And she wouldn't move away from us. She stood right there. She knew he liked her."

"And what about Christina? How was she?"

"Oh, now, Christina, in my humble opinion, is more seasoned. She knows how to play a better game," he assessed. "She didn't press as hard. And she won't overdo it."

He continued, "Maybe it's her Japanese influence, but she's very understated. And she reads things well. So I like her a lot more. But that's just my personal preference. Some guys like the flashy type, like Audrey, more."

"Hmm," Lucina responded. "It sounds like you read things pretty well yourself."

"Well, of course. I'm learning it from the best," he flattered her.

She told him, "Yes, well, here are more things for you to learn. Audrey is the kind of girl who you get to work the front of the party. The surface guys will be attracted to her immediately. She is very show-offish, just like they are. You are right. So you get her to work the up-front money crowds and men who like to spend lavishly. But Chris, as you have already noticed, will be better off where there is less noise. She pays more attention, and she will speak only when she has to. She is also more respectful to men with money. So you get her to work the VIP sections and men who will not spend a fast dollar."

Ivan smiled from behind his wheel. He commented, "So, you *do* know them."

"I know them enough," Lucina answered. "But like I told you before, understanding people is my expertise. I now need for *you* to know how to read them. Because you will have to learn how to make them want to work for you. That is why tonight was so important."

"Hmmph," Ivan grunted back to her. "I see your point. And you wanted *them* to learn to respect my hustle."

Lucina said, "That's right. They *all* need to. Just like they respect mine. And they need to know that you will not overextend yourself. Or else they will try and play us against one another. So we must *both* let them know that they will have to *work* for all they get. That is just how life is."

Ivan chuckled and said, "Yeah, they walked right into the Fendi and Gucci shops as soon as we made it to the mall."

Lucina chuckled. She said, "And if I know you, you probably told them they could have some of those things at a later time, *if* they work with you first."

Ivan started laughing again. He was nearly home already.

"Did they tell you that?" he asked her.

"They did not have to. I already know," she told him. "That is typical of a good businessperson. You know that everyone has their price."

She said, "But I don't want to take up too much more of your time tonight. I just wanted you to know that the best business in life is *impulsive.* That means that we want people to spend their money with us *right now.* That is why I employ so many pretty girls for business," she explained. "Pretty girls are impulsive, and they can create impulsive behavior from everyone around them. At the same time, I've noticed that when you try to get the bigger money, it's harder to find the impulse. So I now have a love/hate relationship with rich people," she told him. "Why? Because I love the lifestyle of the rich, but I hate how hard it is to get them to spend their money in my direction."

Ivan parked outside of his apartment and laughed even harder.

He said, "You're not alone with that love/hate relationship with the rich, trust me. I gotta go through that shit every day at my accounting offices. These rich clients will have you breaking your ass to do everything *they* want, just like you said, *right now,* while you gotta wait your ass off for them to pay you for it. But you wait it out for them anyway, because you *know* it's bigger money. And that's exactly where their power is, just *having it.*"

Lucina said, "I know. But in the meantime, we continue to make noise and make money so that the rich know that we are here. Okay, Ivan? So I will call you tomorrow with my new party ideas, and you call me tomorrow with yours."

Ivan hung up with her and climbed out of his car. It was late October 2003, a solid five months since he had started his new promotions brand in June. And he had made great progress. But patience was indeed a virtue. He still lived at the same apartment, with the same car, the same clothes, and the same day job. However, his income potential had significantly increased.

"Just keep doing what you're doing over time, big guy. It's all about growth and stability. That's all it is," he mumbled to himself as he climbed to the second level of his complex.

Julio ran out to catch him before he reached his door.

"Hey, Ivan, I talked to my cousin for you, man."

Ivan stopped and was all ears. "Oh, yeah. What he say?"

Before Julio answered, he noticed his neighbor's new haircut.

"Oh, shit, you did it. You cut it all down."

"Yeah, man, it was impulsive," Ivan responded with a grin, using Lucina's words.

Julio nodded and said, "It looks good on you." He sized Ivan up in his light brown sports jacket and usual business clothes. Ivan was standing there waiting for his information, looking leaner and more important. Julio told him, "You look like a kick-ass businessman now. Like, my time is my money, you know, so don't waste it."

Ivan laughed. "So, the hair makes that much of a difference to you?"

Julio answered, "Yeah, it really does. Especially when you're still in your business clothes. But anyway, I talked to my cousin Mike last night, and he basically said that it all depends, man. Sometimes they'll just show up at a party for nothing. But if you invite them there and put them on a flyer, first you have to make sure they get there. So, like, you have to pay them for travel, and for the hotel rooms. And they don't usually travel alone, man. So you can expect to pay for three or four tickets and rooms for their boys. And the hotels they stay in are usually nice, you know. Then they get the limos, groupies, good weed . . ."

Julio stopped and said, "Now, I can get you the good weed." Then he looked around at their apartment complex. He said, "But you're not living like that for all the rest of the things they want. So, unless you give them cash money up front to show them you're serious . . . I mean, it's nothing personal, man, but they get asked to show up for parties and stuff like that all across the country. So, unless they just happen to be in this area . . . I mean, you gotta understand that my cousin's down with Eminem, D12, Xzibit, Snoop Dogg, Kurupt, Nate Dogg, 50 Cent, the G-Unit. And those are not, like, regular people there, man. They're, like, *superstars.*"

Ivan took all of the information in with poise. He nodded and said, "I understand. So what was the price?"

Julio looked embarrassed to even tell him. "My cousin said they can get up to *fifty* thousand dollars. And that's just to *show up*."

Ivan didn't blink. The football players made *forty* thousand. However, they used their own money for the setup.

"Well, what's the starting price if they're already in the area? I mean, if those guys are already recording right in L.A. . . ."

Julio shrugged. "I guess *thirty* thousand or so would do. I mean, its, like, easy money for one night, right? Just to guest-DJ? That's what I told him." Then he asked Ivan, "How much did that Chargers party cost you?"

"About the same, or ten thousand less," Ivan answered casually.

"Yeah, but the Chargers are *local*. These guys are not."

Ivan asked him, "What about Scott Storch? I mean, I know he's not local, but he could use a little attention to his name. What would he cost?"

Ivan was already thinking about a pitch to spotlight the Jewish hip-hop producer on his website. He fit more of the crossover demographics of San Diego.

Julio said, "I can't see him costing more than any of the others right now. I mean, people are starting to get to know him right now, but—"

"Ten, fifteen thousand, right? And we blow up his name as a producer," Ivan suggested.

Julio looked at Ivan and grinned. "Ivan, this guy was all over Dr. Dre's last album. You're not gonna get any more blown up than that."

Ivan said, "Your cousin's not blown up, and he's on Dr. Dre's albums more than any of them. He's like the other half of the Neptunes. What's Pharrell's partner's name?"

"Umm . . . Hugo."

"That's what I'm talking about. It took you a minute. But the Neptunes would do well out here, too." Ivan said, "I don't see San Diego as a hard-core rap town like L.A. is. I see it more as a crossover town."

Julio agreed with him. "Yeah, you're right."

"So I have to focus more on the people that I can get here who are less pricey and who fit the demographics of a crossover. Because if you're talking about *fifty* thousand dollars and whatnot, then we don't need a party, we need a *concert.*"

Julio nodded. "That's big." He had never really talked to Ivan about business before. He knew that his neighbor did accounting work, but talking about the hard cash of party promotion was different. He was growing new respect for Ivan now.

He joked and said, "See, that new haircut fits you already, man. You sound like a man who's ready to go after the world."

Ivan responded with a smile, "Yeah . . . I am." And he wasn't joking.

WHEN HE SETTLED in for bed that night, Ivan couldn't get Lucina's ideas out of his head. What was the common impulse that forced the rich to spend? And how did the rich become wealthy in the first place?

"Sound investments that make them long money is the only thing they're interested in," he answered in the darkness of his bedroom. He was in bed with the sheets up and the lights off.

He told himself, "The rich find or create profitable assets that make them money, and then they keep more money than they spend. It's that damn simple. These are things I already know."

So, how do I make that knowledge work for us? he mused.

Ivan thought about it for another few minutes before he hopped out of bed to write his thoughts down on paper.

He walked back out into his living room, clicked on the lights, and leaned over his coffee table with several sheets of blank white copy paper and a black pen. He wrote the words "Balance Sheet" at the top, drew a large rectangle up and down the page, and split it down the middle with a straight line. At the top of the left side he wrote the word "Assets." At the top right he wrote "Liabilities."

Then he began to list the liabilities that cost him money on the right, and he listed the assets that made him money on the left.

Ivan stayed up half the night working out all of the intangibles of his business until he fell asleep on his sofa.

IN THE MORNING, Ivan wrote a checklist of the things he needed to do over the next few days to work his business plans. He booked lunch hours all that week for face-to-face meetings at the Subway sandwich store that was five minutes away from the Hutch & Mitchell office building.

First he hired Edward Kennison, a forty-two-year-old white man who was a fifteen-year advertising veteran from the *San Diego Union Tribune,* as his advertising sales manager. "Eddie K." was a real money getter who was excited by a change of pace. He was a recent divorcee, and his only son had received a full academic scholarship to attend college at the University of Southern California that fall. Eddie used this opportunity to quit the newspaper business and jump headfirst into the website game with a 25 percent new ad commission, plus a 10 percent management purse of all ads instead of a salary.

Ivan had to trust someone to collect and deposit all of the ad revenue, while he continued to spend the majority of his workdays as an accountant. He realized that Ida would be too gun-shy to quit her day job for the heavy responsibility of the position. And Eddie was already experienced at putting together ad pitch tools for the sales staff. So Ivan introduced his new ad sales manager to Jeff and Paul and told them all to get familiar with each other.

"AT THIS POINT, the four of us make up the four corners of this website: the ad management, the general management, the ongoing creation, and the overall promotion," Ivan told them over another dinner meeting in the university area. He said, "Next, I'll need to hire a content editor to make our pages more client driven. That means the majority of our content and the spotlights that we post will surround the businesses that advertise with us."

He said, "We can't afford to keep posting random information like we do now. Everything we decide to post has to help us to make this website more profitable."

Paul grimaced. He said, "Ivan, you don't want your viewers to start feeling like the site is all business. That tends to turn people off. I mean, website viewers *like* random information. That's what the Information Age is all about. But if we make the site too structured around businesses, we'll start to lose a lot of the curious new traffic that we get."

Jeff said, "Not only that, but you'll set up a situation where the advertising businesses will become far more aggressive about when they receive their spotlights. And if we run their spotlights before we get their ads, they may not advertise with us at all. We'll be creating our own mess."

Eddie chuckled at the argument. He said, "That right there is a major difference between websites and newspapers that will allow me to bring plenty of new business to this site, my friends. There's always been a bitter struggle between the editorial staff and the sales staff to try and negotiate some kind of peace between the people who advertised with us and the people who didn't. But with the internet, I believe that we can re-create our own rules."

He said, "There are plenty of solutions in which we can satisfy everyone. Well, not *everyone,* but enough of the viewers for the site to continue to grow. So what I'll do is work hand in hand with whoever's the content editor to create an organized schedule of who comes first and who comes next on these spotlights. But you definitely want to mix it up. And Ivan's right in regards to random spotlights. We need to let a business know beforehand because you never know when their spotlight could coincide with a special promotion. That tends to work better for them."

Ivan said, "And as far as creating a balance for our viewers, it'll also be up to the content manager to respond to our emails and know exactly what the viewers like or dislike about the site. Then we respond to them accordingly. Whatever they tell us, that's what we'll respond to. That's interactive strategy, right? Because ultimately, it's *their site* for San Diego information."

Paul began to see the idea and nodded. Jeff accepted the plan as well. It wasn't as if they had a choice. Ivan was still the boss, and they all had to find out if his plans would work.

Eddie smiled and said, "I feel really good about this. We can all work this out. And I have a big list of advertisers lined up to pitch to."

That's what Ivan wanted to hear. Business was business.

Paul asked them, "What about the random spotlights for the *people* of San Diego?"

Ivan answered, "I still want to do that. And we'll have it represent *all* of San Diego: black, white, Filipino, Mexican, Italian, military, whatever. Who are you? What do you do? Let us know at IDPromotions.com, right? So just let's do it and work out all of the details."

Jeff smiled and said, "Okay, you're the boss. Paul and I still want this site to be as successful as you do."

Paul told him, "By the way, I like that new haircut. It makes you look like a slicker businessman."

"Thanks," Ivan told him. "Now I'm thinking about whether I should get a diamond earring or not."

Jeff looked at him and said, "Oh, that would be cool on you, man. *Real* cool."

Even Eddie grinned. He was still a straight by-the-book newspaperman with a no-nonsense haircut and a clean-shaven face with his crystal-blue eyes.

He said, "That's another great perk of being an entrepreneur. You can be as eccentric as your clients allow you to be. And ultimately, that makes you more interesting."

Ivan responded, "As long as you're making money with it. Because if it stops you from making money, then it stops you from being interesting."

Eddie told him, "Well, you don't have to worry about not making money, my friend. Because if that's the only way that I get paid, then it's definitely gonna happen."

"And the more money *you* make, the more money *we* make," Jeff added with a chuckle.

"Let's all drink to that," Paul commented.

They all toasted with their glasses of nonalcoholic drinks.

RAYMOND'S HOT SPOT LOUNGE on the southeast side still owed Ivan a few more events for the door and 25 percent of the bar. Ivan called them up with a new idea to host *Monday Night Football* parties with the Chargers, the Padres, and Lucina's girls.

Ivan said, "We kick it off with strong radio promotions, and we'll have ten weeks left of *Monday Night Football*. Then we can host the playoffs and the Super Bowl for four more weeks."

He continued, "And all I want is the door and ten percent of the bar. And you know how those athletes can drink when they get excited, man."

Raymond said, "I didn't promise you that many events with bar money, especially not now, because I'm no longer getting the discounts that I got two months ago."

Oh, so that's why he gave me that deal, Ivan thought to himself. *He was getting his own damn deal.*

Ivan argued, "But Raymond, I'm only asking you for ten percent now."

"Yeah, but ten percent for *fourteen* weeks. That's one hundred and *forty* percent," Raymond calculated.

"But look at it this way," Ivan told him. "We're also going to be marketing your bar for the next *fifteen weeks* over the radio and on our website. That's not worth *ten percent* a night, Raymond? With what I'm bringing you, you can get *new* deals. We might even pick up a liquor *sponsor* after a couple of weeks. In fact . . ."

Ivan stopped himself. He felt that he was overpitching his idea. He wanted to keep the sponsor possibilities to himself. So he backed up and took another angle.

He said, "Look, Raymond, I'm even willing to pay for a large projection TV screen. So ten percent is a very small fee of everything I'll be bringing to the table here. I mean, think about it. I'm bringing the *Chargers* and the *Padres* to your lounge *every* Monday night."

Raymond went silent for a spell. The reality of the deal was sinking in.

"Let me talk to my wife and think about it."

AFTER IVAN'S CALCULATIONS, he projected pulling in three to four thousand dollars each week from "*Monday Night Football* at Raymond's." And the sports crowd could party afterward.

"That ain't bad money for a built-in party," he told himself. "And if I can get a few extra grand from a liquor sponsor, that could make it five to six thousand every Monday night."

He called up Lucina and explained his new plans to her.

He said, "The idea is to create as many small cow parties as possible a week to promote from the website. And as long as we promote at least one of them on the radio, we can push all of the traffic back to the website, and then we use our traffic numbers to get in on all the other parties around San Diego."

Lucina caught on to his grand idea. She said, "So you want to use the website to get everyone to advertise their parties with us?"

"That's it, girl. In the meantime, we do at least three to five events of our own to pull in twenty thousand dollars each week, regardless of whether we have celebrities in town. It's all about consistency. Then when we *do* have celebrities, we make sure that we funnel all of the party traffic back to our main event. That way we lock in our money every time."

Lucina listened to all of his excitement and asked him, "Ivan, do you really think the other promoters are going to allow you to do that? They're not going to advertise their crowd with you. That would be stupid. And they would see what you're trying to do immediately."

"Well, we'll just see how long they hold out, then," he responded. "But once we start making money through consistent events, you mark my words, more of them are gonna decide to deal with us than not. They'll have no choice."

Ivan was all pumped up optimistic adrenaline. Thinking about new ways of making money was energizing.

Lucina said, "Well . . . I see you've been very busy."

"Yeah, I've been busy. You told us to stay busy to let the rich know that we're here, right? Well, that's what I'm doing. I can't even sleep at night. No more early bird for me. So anyway, the guy we used at the Chargers birthday party for the liquor, he has a direct relationship with the liquor companies, doesn't he?"

Lucina paused. Ivan was rushing way ahead of himself. "Yes, he does," she told him.

"Well, we need to talk to him about sponsorship opportunities and buying large volumes. And eventually, I might still have to break down and get our own liquor license and team. So we need to start asking more of these girls of yours to become trained in bartending."

Lucina said, "Ivan, *please,* slow down. You're asking for a whole lot of maintenance with all of these ideas of yours. And that does not mean that they are not *good* ideas, but each one will take time."

Ivan caught the irony of the moment and chuckled. He said, "You remember I told *you* that? And you told me that virtues, like patience, don't make money?"

Lucina was forced to chuckle herself. She admitted, "I do remember."

Ivan said, "Well, now that I'm fully awake on the job, I see how this thing is supposed to work. You have to be *impatient* and *patient* at the same time. If that makes any sense to you."

Lucina said, "It makes perfect sense. We make impulsive money for today, so that we can take our time to make long money for tomorrow."

Ivan got real excited again. He screamed, "That's my *girl!* We gon' get this money, baby! You got me turned on now!"

AT LUCINA'S COZY, small home across the San Diego Bay in Coronado, she ended her call with Ivan David and smiled. Then her smile quickly faded away. To add to his opposites of patience and impatience, she felt happy and sad. She was happy that she had chosen the right man to partner with, but sad because she still could not bring herself to trust where they were going.

She paced her well-designed living room, which featured a California stone fireplace, exotic Italian furniture, a colorful Persian rug, and international artwork and accents, while thinking deeply about her predicament.

She shook her head and mumbled, "He is running way too fast." Then she stopped and stood still. "But is that all my fault?"

Now he scares me more than anything, she thought. *Because if he decides now, like a typical businessman, that he can run much faster without me . . . how long will it take before I will need another new partner?*

"Shit!" she cursed herself. "I should have taught him *nothing.* Or at least not so fast." Then she had to admit to herself with a pause, ". . . But I like him."

Part IV

Life & Money Management

Ten

Narcissism

RAYMOND AND HIS WIFE agreed to Ivan's *Monday Night Football* deal. The husband-and-wife team came to the conclusion that if his football night was not as successful as he had hoped it would be, Ivan would lose a lot more than they would. A mere 10 percent of the bar would hardly break their business. So with Ivan bringing the crowd and the large projection TV screen, and paying for all of the promotion, added security, and pretty party girls to boot, unless no one showed up, which was highly unlikely, they had everything to gain from the popularity of professional ball players and their entourages becoming regulars at their lounge once a week.

Once the deal was sealed, Ivan met up with Lucina downtown and told her that he needed two party girls who were familiar with the ethnic crowd of southeast San Diego, preferably Filipinas and Mexicans.

"Why?" Lucina asked him curiously. "Is that who you want to attract?"

Ivan explained, "Look, I can't really count on these athletes to come out here every week. They might start off well in the beginning, but they're gonna have their own parties and other things to do. So I mainly want to introduce this idea to the guys on the street level. They'll come in there and try to spend the same kind of money as the athletes do. It's impulsive spending, right? But you can count more on the local baller types to make it their regular hangout."

He continued, "You already know we're gonna get the brothers. But on that southeast side, you got Mexicans and Filipinos over there. And I want them all to come together, watch the game, drink, and talk shit just like they would at Jack Murphy Stadium watching the home team. The Chargers have a *Monday Night Football* game left themselves."

Lucina asked him, "But what if they all don't get along? Then you have them all in there drinking with pretty girls around." She frowned and said, "I don't like it. It sounds like trouble waiting to happen."

That only made Ivan smile. He liked the idea even more now.

He said, "And you know what, that's exactly what urban men gravitate to, that sense of danger. The ones who don't like danger don't spend money like that. I learned that from being around my brother's crew in L.A. So I wouldn't even want a safe crowd over there. And it'll be my job to make sure that we all *do* get along. That's *my risk.*"

Lucina looked at him as if he were crazy. She said, "Well, I don't want any of my girls mixed up in the middle of that. And the two hundred fifty dollars apiece you offer is no money for them. Some of my girls can make up to two hundred dollars *per hour.*"

Ivan repeated, "*Per hour?* Is that what you pay them? Modeling rate? That's crazy. That would be eight hundred dollars for *one girl.* We would never make any money like that."

"What about if I had my liquor friend sponsor two thousand dollars toward the party?" Lucina suggested.

Ivan thought about it. He said, "And then pay the girls out of that? But would your guy offer us two thousand every week? He could advertise for two months on my website for that price, and you would keep nearly eight hundred of it. Then you can pay your girls extra from that if you want."

Ivan was turning into an experienced wheeler and dealer overnight.

Lucina told him, "I don't know. I'm just trying to work this all out in my head."

He said, "Well, you gotta understand that I'm trying to create enough party connections for your girls to work more regularly. And we may pay them less, but they'll have a lot more opportunities to make money. That just makes more sense for *all* of us, to me. The more they're seen, the more promoters will want to hire them."

Lucina argued, "It's not about the *quantity,* Ivan, it's all about the *quality.*"

"Yeah, but we can do *both.* We can even host a second *Monday Night Football* spot downtown if you can work a deal that makes sense there. But if you're only gonna make two or three thousand dollars a night, and then turn around and pay your girls two hundred an *hour* . . ."

"I usually pay them that for the much bigger parties," Lucina explained.

Ivan said, "But, these are not the home-run hits. These are singles, doubles, and triples that all add up on the scoreboard."

Ivan was becoming frustrated with her hesitation. His plans were based on understandable math: create the lowest-priced parties to run up your profits.

However, on Lucina's end, she was already predicting Ivan's greed. It had happened to her several times before. But what could she do about it? They still had to move forward with a profitable partnership, and his plans were sure to make money. She had to admit that much herself.

Finally, she took a deep breath and agreed to it. "Okay, but I'm letting you know *right now* that I will give my girls the *choice* to work your venues at your price or *not.*"

Ivan nodded. "That's fair. And like I said, if you want to pay them more out of your share, then you're free to do that."

Typical! Lucina thought in a huff. *He's already becoming bigheaded. And now I can see his head more. Which was my idea.*

TO LUCINA'S SURPRISE, two of her girls who were familiar with the Filipino and Mexican crowd of the southeast agreed to work with Ivan. And once Audrey and Christina had settled into the San Diego area as roommates, they were in on the deal as well. A thousand dollars a month to host wealthy, bodacious men during *Monday Night Football* once a week was an easy decision for all of them. Their rents would all be paid with just sixteen hours of work.

Ivan even had the girls do photo shoots wearing the featured teams' opposing jerseys for the flyer, with Pittsburgh and Dallas as their first game. He then had Eddie K. work a deal to feature a sporting goods store on the sports spotlight page of the website, with a promise from the store's manager to advertise their next sales specials on the site.

Ivan then solidified commitments from some of the Chargers he had met at the birthday party, as well as Emilio Alvarez and a few of his friends from the Padres, to attend his "*Monday Night Football* Bash at Raymond's Hot Spot Lounge."

Ivan even invited Julio out, while his neighbor promised to spread the word to more of his Mexican friends.

Thomas Jones called him from the Urban League offices after he had heard the ads on the radio.

"So, I see you worked out another deal with Raymond," he commented.

Ivan told him, "Hey, man, I had to learn to get back up and ride that horse. It's too much money to be made over there to leave it alone, you know."

Thomas said, "Brother, you ain't said nothing but a word. Get back over there and make it happen."

* * *

On the night of the first big event, Ivan left work at the accounting offices early to make sure the large projection television was set up right and connected to the stereo speaker system at the lounge. Before the game started, some of the crowd began to show up after work to catch the *ESPN Countdown* show.

"Make sure we block off that left corner area as a restricted section for the Chargers and Padres," Ivan told Christina and Audrey. He wanted them both to work the VIP section, while the two other girls worked the general floor, closer to the Filipinos and Mexicans he hoped would show up to join the crowd. And each of the four girls would spend time at the door passing out I.D. Promotions flyers.

By game time, Ivan had his wish. Emilio Alvarez showed up with Butch Clayborne, Big Deke Walker, and two other Padres players. Perry Browning, Zee-Dog, and three other Chargers showed up, including Herman "The Big Bad Hitta" Seaford. They all took chairs on the left side of the room, with a few girls and other guys who accompanied them. The Filipino locals, Mexican locals, and local blacks showed up with their money, jewelry, and girls to claim their areas of the room to watch the game. And before the Pittsburgh Steelers had even kicked the ball off, premium bottles of expensive liquor were already being ordered and popped from the tables.

The lounge was filled to capacity by the end of the first quarter, with a line still waiting out front. A hired cameraman took shots of it all for the website, while Jeff and Paul had other work to do.

"What do we do when we run out of room?" Ida pulled Ivan aside to ask him near the door. She was pleased with the turnout, but also worried about the overflow.

Ivan shrugged and said, "They're just too late. There's no more room in here."

He wore a gold knit tennis shirt under a dark gray sports jacket to keep his professional look, even among the jersey-wearing sports crowd.

Ida told him, "Well, you need to go out there and tell them something. It's a whole lot of people still waiting to get in."

"About how many?" Ivan asked her.

"I can't count them. They're all over the sidewalk."

Ivan walked out to view the crowd for himself. Sure enough, there were plenty of latecomers outside, admiring the luxury and sports cars of the athletes and other high rollers who had arrived early enough to park and make it in. They were also pleased by the girls who walked out to pass them flyers.

"Hey, Ivan, what's going on, man? Am I still good?"

It was Julio and three of his friends, including his little brother, all standing out in the crowd, late. Julio was wearing Dallas Cowboys gear, all pumped and ready to watch the game.

Shit! Ivan cursed himself. *How am I gonna work this line out?*

Everyone outside wanted to get in, but the place was fast running out of room. *And what if a few of the Padres or Chargers come late?* Ivan worried.

He thought fast and told Julio, "One minute, man." Then he grabbed the first security guard he could reach to walk inside with him.

Once they were inside the door, Ivan told him, "Hey, man, do me a favor and grab the guy with the Cowboys jersey and his friends in here. And if any other professional athletes walk up, you let them in as our special guests. But we need to tell everyone else to come earlier next week and enjoy the game somewhere else, because we're filled to capacity already."

Ivan didn't want to max the place out to elbow-room. That would only make it more ripe for a disaster.

The security guard smiled and said, "I got you, man," and walked back out to do his job.

Ida overheard him and smiled herself. She said, "You sure got your wish tonight, hunh? So I guess we can close the cash box now."

Ivan chuckled and said, "I guess so." He went back to working

the crowd on his own that night. Lucina wanted no part of it. She didn't even bother to witness her partner's smashing triple. The only thing that stopped it from being a home-run hit was the small capacity of the lounge.

"Hey, what up, man? I'm Ivan David," he introduced himself to the crowd, shaking hands. He wanted to make sure they all remained sociable.

"Yeah, we know who you are," some of the crowd responded to him. "From IDPromotions.com, right?"

"Yeah," Ivan answered, grinning. "Y'all need any more bottles of that good stuff?"

"Is the next bottle free?" someone joked loudly.

Ivan answered, "Naw, this ain't the place for that, nephew. This is high rollers only in here. So put your money where your mouth is, and we'll send one of the pretty girls over to collect it."

They laughed out loud over the football announcers on TV. And they respected Ivan as the chief of the party.

Perry Browning yelled out from the players' section on the left, "Hey, Ivan, how come you didn't bring *ten* of Lucina's girls? I don't see enough of 'em in here to go around for me."

Ivan hollered back to him. "Oh, that'll happen for you next week. We wanted to see what we were working with first." Then Ivan addressed the crowd. "But now we know. So make sure y'all show up bright and early again next week. The only reservations we're taking up in here is cash money."

"I heard that!" Herman the Big Bad Hitta yelled out.

"THERE GO THE BUS! THERE GO THE BUS!" Perry yelled toward the screen in reference to the Pittsburgh Steelers' massive running back Jerome Bettis. Bettis rumbled over several Dallas defenders in the secondary for a touchdown, to give the Steelers a 16–3 lead in the second quarter.

As the crowd responded to the replays on the large screen, Perry boasted, "You wait till we play his ass in week twelve! I'm gon' knock his damn wheels off!"

The Big Bad Hitta hollered right behind him, "THE SHOCK-W-A-A-AVE!" and high-fived his teammates.

OUTSIDE AT THE INTERSECTION of the street, Lucina pulled up in her black E-Class Mercedes and eyed the dense crowd of sports fans and exotic cars that surrounded Raymond's Hot Spot Lounge in the parking lot, as well as on both sides of the street.

"Oh shit, it looks like they did it tonight," her passenger commented. It was her girl Maya, the dark-haired Colombian.

Lucina remained speechless at the wheel. She pulled up to double park outside the lounge entrance, next to a dark blue Bentley. She pressed her hazard lights on.

"I'll be right back out," she told her girl.

"You're going in to see Ivan?" Maya asked her.

"Of course," Lucina answered snidely. *Why else would I go in?*

Maya didn't think anything of it. "Tell him I said hi."

Lucina closed the car door behind her without responding.

Out in front of the lounge, the security guards were still trying to clear the disgruntled crowd.

"Look, you all just need to clear away from here. There's no more room to stand inside."

"Man, you don't own this sidewalk," someone jabbed from the crowd.

Lucina walked right past them all.

"Hey, Lucina Gallo," one of the security guards noted.

A dark brown baller, draped with jewelry around his neck, in both ears, and across his front teeth, turned to recognize the Brazilian beauty for himself. He had only seen the much-talked-about San Diego woman before from a distance. *Twice.*

He responded, "Oh, shit, she's up in the flesh out here."

Lucina wore another expensive, eye-popping dress, with heels to match. As she walked by, she ignored the men out front as if they were all shadows in the dark.

"Is Ivan still inside?" she asked the security. She wanted them all to know who she was there for. It was more marketing for the future.

"Oh, yeah, he's still in there," the security told her.

"Take me inside to see him," she ordered.

The security guards didn't say another word. One turned to lead her inside.

One of the other ballers said, "Yo, I thought you said it wasn't no more room in there," to the remaining guards.

"There's always room for her," one of the guards deadpanned.

A few of the crowd started to chuckle. Someone said, "Well, goddamn, I wish I was Ivan."

INSIDE THE LOUNGE, Lucina strolled into the middle of the room and immediately called the attention of her four girls. All eyes were on her, just as she liked it, especially since the game had reached halftime. Her four pretty workers scrambled in her direction from their separate sides of the room, all wearing curve-hugging jerseys and heels with tight blue jeans. Then the whispers started:

"Hey, that's Lucina."

"You know who that is, don't you?"

"That's Lucina Gallo right there."

"Is that Lucina?"

"Yo, she da *baddest* bitch."

"That girl looks skinny to me."

"That's a nice-ass dress she's wearing."

"Who the fuck is she?"

"Damn, my dick is hard just looking at her, homes."

"Yeah, she's *very* pretty."

"I guess she's the boss bitch, hunh?"

"Why is everybody staring at her?"

There were nearly three hundred opinions of her inside the room.

Perry Browning hollered out above the crowd, "LU-CI-NAAA! You bring six more girls with you? I told Ivan he went cheap on us in here tonight!"

Lucina only smiled in the football player's direction. She had little tolerance for him that night.

She asked her girls in their huddled circle, "Is everything okay?"

"Yeah, we're good," they all answered.

"And are they treating you right in here?"

"Yeah, they're treating us good."

Lucina nodded to them. By that time Ivan had spotted her. She made eye contact with him and proceeded to send her girls away. "Okay, everyone go to their *own* homes tonight. Now let me talk to Ivan," she told them.

As soon as they all left her, Lucina stared at Ivan through the crowd and gave him a come-here finger motion.

Ivan saw it from across the room and froze.

God knows, I wanna fuck the hell out of that girl, he mused of Lucina's sexy grandstanding. *I thought she said she wasn't coming tonight. Let me go over here and see what she wants.*

When Ivan reached her in the middle of the room, Lucina turned to walk toward the exit, expecting him to follow her. And as soon as he followed her as she expected him to, he met eyes with Ida and felt a lightning bolt of guilt and shame strike his heart.

Shit! he cursed himself in a panic. *I wonder what Ida's thinking right now. I look like a fucking dog following his master out of the rain.*

To make it all seem harmless, Ivan pointed to Ida and stated, "I'll be right back in. All right?"

Ida made him feel better by nodding to him. "Yeah, okay," she told him. *Whatever,* she thought. *I know you like that damn girl. Cut your hair down for that bitch and everything. Didn't even ask me about it. But that's okay. You won't be fucking with me tonight. So you best hope she wants to give you some of that South American pussy, because you won't be touching me. Ever again!*

And as Ivan walked out of the lounge behind his seductive partner, the whispers started up in the room again:

"What the hell was that about?"

"You think he's fucking her?"

"So they're supposed to be just partners, hunh? Yeah, right."

"Man, she looked like she was mad as hell at him."

"I thought he was with the light-skinned sister."

"That's a lucky motherfucker right there, homes. Let me tell you."

Ivan walked outside of the lounge behind Lucina and was disturbed by her. She'd made him look weak in front of Ida at his own event. Then she had the audacity to walk away from him as he continued to follow her like a sidekick.

When she finally stopped and turned to face him a little ways up the street, Ivan asked her in irritation, "What's going on?" She was acting as if they were a couple who had had a fight.

She stared at him and said, "I just came to check up on you."

Ivan stared back at her. He frowned and asked her, "And that's how you do it? You looked like you were having a tantrum in there. What I do to you?" he asked her. "You wanted me to fail? I thought we're supposed to make money together."

Lucina continued to stare at him without words.

Finally, she told him, "I don't want you to fail, Ivan. I'm just concerned about my girls tonight."

"Bullshit, man. You're actually jealous that I pulled this shit off without you."

"That's not true."

"Yes, it is," he argued. "You were mad when your girls even agreed to do it with me. What do you think, you're Mommie Dearest and they gotta listen to everything you say? They're trying to get money, have a good time, and live out here, Lucina. That's all."

He calmed himself down, realizing he had said enough. He wasn't even sure if Lucina could take that from him. Was she ready to move on and mark him off as another lost business partner?

She nodded to him and said, "Okay. You did a good job. Just make sure they all get home safe tonight."

She started walking back toward her Mercedes parked in the street.

Ivan said, "You're not staying? You can make sure they get home for yourself if you stay."

Lucina looked back at Ivan from the street and shook her head. "Maya and I are expected at another event tonight."

Ivan was ready to ask her more about it, but what difference did it make? She had promised to attend someone else's event on a night when he had set up a party for them to make easy money. He thought about that and was irritated again. It seemed disrespectful to him. She knew he had planned the "*Monday Night Football* Bash." She could have at least supported him on the first one.

Nevertheless, he nodded and blew it off. "All right, then. Y'all have a good time tonight."

"Thank you," she told him.

Ivan headed back inside the lounge without another word. The third quarter would be starting after halftime.

Lucina watched her determined partner walk away and felt betrayed by her pettiness. She wanted to hurt him just to see if he would bleed. She wanted to know if he still had a heart outside of business. And if he bled, then it proved that he cared. But was it fair for her to test him in that way just to satisfy her own insecurities about their partnership?

When she climbed back into her black Mercedes she felt guilty about it. She sat there in silence for a minute behind the wheel.

"Of course, he wanted us to stay," she commented to Maya.

Maya read Lucina's volatile emotions and already knew.

She likes him, she thought with a silent nod. *So she's going through a power struggle with him now.* But there was no sense in her speaking up about it. Maya knew that Lucina liked to keep her intimate emotions to herself until she expressed them on her own. Even when they were obvious.

Finally, Lucina took a deep breath and said, "Let's go," before she restarted the car to drive off.

IVAN WALKED BACK inside the lounge and made his way over to Ida to calm the rough waters he could sense between them. Ida had already begun to complain about Lucina's blatant disrespect of her. She also hinted that Ivan gave the woman far too much leeway in their partnership. But the power-play antic Lucina had just pulled inside the lounge may have been the straw to break the camel's back.

"What did I miss?" Ivan asked Ida in reference to the football game. The game had moved into the third quarter now.

Ida shook off his question. She answered, "I wasn't really watching it." She said, "But since you have everyone in here now, I'm getting ready to go. I have some other things I have to prepare for." She handed him the cash box and the money bag.

Ivan didn't like how that looked or felt. He asked her, "What's wrong?" as if he didn't know.

Ida refused to talk about it. "Nothing's wrong, I just have some other things to do tonight."

Ivan stared at her. "Are you sure?"

He was itching to get told off, but instead of taking the bait, Ida took a breath to compose herself. She wanted to remain civil.

She nodded and said, "Yeah, I'm sure. Let me just go ahead and go now."

Ivan took a deep breath and looked away in frustration for a second and caught Christina eying them from across the room.

He turned back to Ida and nodded. "All right. I'll call you when I get in tonight."

When Ida left the lounge, no more than five minutes after Lucina had left him, Ivan felt alone in the crowd, and with a load of money in his hands.

Fuck it, let me go count up this loot, he told himself, moving toward Raymond at the bar.

As he made it through the crowd, he watched all of the girls to see how they were making out. They all looked to be enjoying themselves and working the crowd effectively. He could also see that Audrey was continuing to work her charm on Emilio. She made sure she passed him with every move she made inside the players' VIP area. Then he watched Christina to see what she was up to. As he studied her from a distance, he noticed that she seemed distracted.

She knows I'm watching her, he told himself. *And she knows that Ida is pissed at me. She's smart like that.*

"Hey, Raymond, can I use your back office for a minute?" he asked behind the bar area.

Raymond was working his ass off behind the bar, with boxes, bottles, and glasses everywhere. But he was pleased as hell to be doing so.

He looked up at Ivan while filling another drink order and noticed the metal cash box and money bag in his hands.

"Oh, sure, Ivan, one minute," he said, finishing up the drink. He grinned and led Ivan back to his office. "You really did it tonight, man. I mean, *really.* This is gonna be a great deal for us."

His wife was hard at work, filling drink orders with two other bartenders. Three waitresses and Lucina's girls all worked the floor.

Ivan smiled at Raymond and said, "I'm just glad you decided to do it."

"Oh, me, too, man. Me, too."

Ivan closed and locked the door behind him before spreading the money out across the floor. He sat in Raymond's office chair, leaned over, and separated the hundreds, fifties, twenties, tens, fives, and ones as usual. But this time he did it by himself. And when he did his recount, the take from the door came to exactly $5,238.

Ivan grinned and mumbled, "Either Ida let somebody in for eighteen dollars, or she took or lost two singles out of the cash box."

He wasn't going to make a big deal over that. But Ida had left without even being paid that night.

"Yeah, I know something's up with her now," he assumed.

He set the metal cash box and the money bag in a corner of the room and returned to the bar to have Raymond lock the office back up until they were ready to close for the night.

"What are you guys looking like tonight?" he asked Raymond in reference to their take at the bar.

Raymond looked at him and said, "So far, thirteen thousand."

Ivan smiled, feeling like a contestant on the game show *The Price Is Right*. His estimates were right on target. It felt like he was taking candy from a baby.

He nodded and said, "Okay." *Another G for me,* he thought. *But just imagine if I owned the lounge.*

He stepped away from Raymond and pulled Christina from her VIP duties to speak to her in private for a minute.

"Are you all right over there? You doing okay?"

She looked at him with all of her girlish innocence. "Yeah, I'm okay. Why do you ask me that?"

Ivan felt her steadiness all over him. That was what he was used to from her. But he couldn't see it from her when he was staring at her.

He said, "Maybe it's just me, but you seemed to be . . . *distracted* tonight."

She shook it off again. "No, I'm good. But how are you doing? Is everything all right with you?"

Ivan looked into her small dark eyes, surrounded by her beautiful brown skin and dark wavy hair, and he began to think with the wrong head. He felt like reaching out and pulling her sexy frame into him and telling her the blunt truth at that moment.

After making this easy money in here tonight, I feel like I deserve some good pussy. Seriously!

Since Ida and Lucina had left him there alone, Ivan had no other bumpers to keep him away from a payout from Chris. So instead of him playing it all business, like his normal MO, Ivan changed up his script.

He told Christina, "Don't leave here tonight before I talk to you."

She paused and then nodded to him. He was in authority.

She said, "Okay." And that was it.

When she walked away to return to the VIP area with the ball players, Ivan told himself, *Yeah, she knows what time it is. And I'm not playing Mr. Nice Guy tonight to let her off the hook, either.*

THE PITTSBURGH STEELERS held on to win the game 37–31, after a furious late comeback by the Dallas Cowboys. When the game was over, the customers continued to party, drinking and talking shit. But there were no fights, no escalating arguments, and no embarrassing incidents.

So Ivan thanked everyone for coming out, reminded them to show up early for the game next week, and made a gang of new friends. Then he went through the final bar numbers with Raymond.

The bar total came to more than fifteen thousand dollars, increasing Ivan's take to close to seven thousand. After subtracting his expenses, he and Lucina would net close to four grand to split.

At ten o'clock at night, Ivan stood out on the sidewalk with Audrey and Christina. He had already paid them all, and Lucina's other two girls had left a few minutes earlier.

"So, you're driving, Audrey?" Ivan questioned. He had to set up his getaway plans for Chris.

"Yeah, I got a little Pontiac convertible," she responded with a chuckle. "What are you driving, Ivan?" she asked him.

Audrey had watched Emilio pull off in a red Maserati with plenty of fanfare. The Latino crowd had been excited to see him there and to take pictures with him. Audrey couldn't wait to catch back up to him. She had his personal numbers now.

Ivan smiled at her and answered, "I just drove my company-man car, a black Nissan Altima. All that other stuff can wait."

Audrey heard him out and agreed. "I know that's right."

Ivan then looked at Chris. She was doing her normal silent-smile thing.

He said, "So, we're all grown people out here, right?"

He waited for them both to respond.

"Yeah."

"And grown people's business is grown people's business?"

Audrey and Chris looked at each other, wondering where Ivan was going with it all.

"I mean, what are you trying to say, Ivan?" Audrey asked him. She had a feeling of where he was going. She also had a response to it if he went there.

I hope he's not thinking what I think he's thinking with us, she thought.

Christina had a feeling as well. But she waited hers out to see what Ivan had to say first.

Ivan said, "Well, if it's all right with Chris, I'll take her home."

Both girls froze and looked at each other. Ivan didn't have to do that out in the open. He could have pulled Chris off to the side and let her tell Audrey something on her own. Even Chris was shocked by it.

Why did he make it so obvious? she asked herself. At the same time, it turned her on a little. He was getting rather bold. And he was making it known that he wanted her.

On Ivan's side of the coin, he also wanted to test Lucina's rules.

We'll see if she doesn't ask them now, he told himself. *But if I'm gonna be around all these girls all the time, they're not all gonna tell me no.*

Audrey opened her mouth and said, "Well—"

"Let me talk to him," Christina commented, cutting her off.

Audrey looked at her and said, "Okay." She figured Chris would handle it on her own. Ivan was off base.

Chris walked forward with Ivan for their privacy.

She asked him immediately, "Why did you do that?" He had put her smack inside of a dilemma. What would Audrey think? Lucina had told them all to make sure they returned to their *own* homes that night. She didn't say that for no reason. But there was Ivan, deliberately complicating things for all of them.

Ivan said, "If you don't wanna go, you don't wanna go. Just tell me you don't like me that way."

He doubted she would tell him that. He already *knew* she liked him. And he was not letting her off the hook.

Christina told him, "It's not that, it's just . . . I mean, we're all in business together, Ivan."

Isn't that why Ida walked out on you earlier? she assumed. *Mixing business with pleasure is just bad. It doesn't work.*

Yet she was highly attracted to Ivan's individual hustle.

He asked her, "You think my business is gonna stop because I take you home tonight?"

She knew better than that. "No, of course not."

"Are you gonna stop doing business with *me*?"

Chris had to stop and think about that one. What if she started to hate his guts for some reason? Or what if Lucina began to dislike her? She could tell that Lucina had an attraction to Ivan as well. Maybe she had even ruined his relationship with Ida on purpose.

Christina had read the whole thing. Now Ivan was attempting to take his emotions out on her. She expected that as well, just not as boldly.

She shook her head and told him, "I just don't want to be in the middle of anything."

"And how is that gonna happen?" he asked her.

Somebody would have to tell. Who would it be? Audrey?

Christina said, "I have to respect everybody in this, Ivan. I just can't up and do that."

"Up and do what?" He wanted her to spell it out to him. He said, "If you don't like me like that, then it's not an issue, right?"

She told him, "But you know I like you. I told you that already."

He said, "You told me you liked me in *business*. But my *life* is *more* than just business."

"I know that."

"So why would you let me go home alone tonight if you like me?"

He was killing her. But she already knew that Ivan had it in him. He knew how to press people's buttons to get them to move. She had watched him in action all night. Now he was turning his focus in her direction.

She read the situation and said, "I just don't want to be anybody's substitute, that's all."

He smiled and said, "Oh, so now you're not good enough? What, I'ma put you back on the bench after the game? You can't handle being a starter?"

Chris smiled back, knowing that he was wrong. Now he was attacking her ego.

He said, "Shit, if I got my chance to start after watching from the sidelines, I'd take that chance and go to the championship with it. But maybe that's just me."

Chris was still standing there in silence on the sidewalk. Either she wanted him or she didn't. But Ivan was going to make her choose *right now. Impulsively.*

He said, "But if you don't want me like that, then go on back home with Audrey. She's still here."

It was a big risk to go that hard on the girl. Nevertheless, Ivan was training himself. Business was a hard man's sport. There was little room for softness. Softness either lost the business or ended up on the liabilities column instead of the assets. And Ivan was only thinking about making money now, the assets.

On Christina's side, she couldn't take the rejection from him. What if he meant it? And what if she never got another chance to get that close to him? She was certain that he was on his way up. There was no question about it. So she would hate herself for turning her only opportunity down. But it still felt wrong.

She squirmed and said, "Ivan, I really do like you, but—"

Ivan cut her off with a raised hand and said, "Let me let you go, then."

Christina stopped and stared at him. "What does that mean?"

Her heart was pounding in her chest. *Did I fuck it up? I just don't . . . feel sure about it yet,* she told herself. *I mean, I want to, but . . .*

Ivan told her, "Go on back to Audrey. I'm done."

His rejection was even stronger now. She could hardly breathe.

She pleaded, "Don't be that way with me, Ivan. I'm not like that. If I say I'm down with you, I'm down with you to the end."

Ivan remained as stony as a downtown building with her.

"Well, show me, then."

The clock stopped ticking. It was all on Christina. She sized up her chances and gave in.

She took a deep breath and said, "I'll go tell her I'm going with you."

AUDREY WAITED down the street for what seemed like forever. When Christina finally returned to her, she asked her, "So, what did you say?" She assumed that she had turned Ivan down.

Chris took another breath and answered, "I'll just, um . . . see you later on or whatever. Okay?"

Audrey looked at her, confused. She said, "What, you're *going* with him? You know Lucina told us—"

"I know what Lucina said," Chris argued.

Audrey whispered, "And you're gonna fuck with her partner in business anyway? I mean, how is that smart?"

"Are you gonna tell her that, Audrey?" Chris asked her.

Audrey frowned and said, "Hell, no. But what if she calls tonight and asks to speak to you?"

"You just tell her to call me on my cell phone."

"And what are you gonna say when she calls?"

"You let me deal with that. It's not your concern."

Audrey backed off and said, "Okay." *I just thought you were smarter than that,* she thought. *But that's a dumb decision. You could have any of those guys in there before Ivan. Ivan is, like, off limits.*

Even Audrey could tell that Lucina liked her partner in more ways than just business. Lucina was very protective of Ivan's image. But like Christina had told her, it was not her concern.

IVAN TOOK CHRISTINA HOME with him to solidify his confidence in everything. He wanted to feel like he deserved it. And he wanted to teach everyone around him to give in, starting with the black and Japanese beauty.

But there were no more dreams about Lucina while he did her. Ivan had his full focus on the beautiful mind, body, and soul of Christina, who accepted his passionate weight.

"You like me for real, hunh?" he asked her with a strong thrust of his naked pelvis into hers. They were dead center in Ivan's king-sized bed.

Christina winced, whimpered, and moaned, *"Mmm-hmm."*

"Can I have this whenever I want?" he asked as he continued to push.

She took it and whined with her eyes closed, "If you want to."

"But do you *want me* to *want it?*"

"Oooh," she moaned, feeling it.

"Hunh?" Ivan asked her, pouring on his weight. *"Do you?"*

"Yesss," she hissed back to him, *"I want you to want me."*

Ivan was not interested in making their romp into a talkathon. Business was about action. The talk was over. So he pounded into her body without pause. And he planned to continue having things his way.

Eleven

Moving Forward

THROUGH THE FALL and into winter, Lucina fell in line with Ivan's small cow party idea, making two to five thousand dollars off each event they partnered in to promote. Using his model of consistency, the small parties added up to an average of twelve thousand dollars a week. As Ivan had planned, a few of the other small promoters of San Diego agreed to use IDPromotions.com to increase the awareness and traffic at their events.

The consistent party activity also increased the popularity of the website. But despite the immense traffic, Ivan's ad manager, Eddie K., still found that many businesses were hesitant to advertise on the site. So Eddie applied the idea of using printout coupons for website viewers to receive 10 percent discounts on selected items bought from the advertising businesses. His plan was to prove the site's traffic value to the advertisers. However, the price tag was steep, a 25 percent discount off of the website ad price.

At first, Ivan balked. "Damn, twenty-five percent? Why not just match their ten percent?"

Eddie K. explained, "With some of the higher-end retailers, our website costs are not high enough yet to do that. Our ten percent discount wouldn't be worth the value of a ten percent discount at their stores. At least not right now. But at *twenty-five* percent it works."

He said, "What I've done is basically swapped the discounts you were trying to give to frequent advertisers, and instead, we use the coupon so we can encourage viewers to utilize the site for retail action. Because if a business can see that an extra two hundred people are walking into their stores each month to buy something because of the coupons on our website, then obviously it makes sense for them to continue to advertise with us."

Ivan agreed with the philosophy and loved the idea. He said, "That's why it's good business to hire the right people."

Eddie chuckled and said, "You betcha."

By the end of the year, the discount coupon idea had caught on to help the sales team to pull in thirty advertisers from general retail, restaurants, party promotion, community events, San Diego sights and travel, specialized services, and general branding, producing nearly thirty-five thousand dollars a month in revenue, of which Ivan netted thirteen thousand.

Since the initial ad rates were based on eight thousand unique hits per day and forty thousand daily impressions of visited pages, the end-of-year numbers of ten thousand unique hits and eighty thousand daily impressions of visited pages would allow them to increase their rates another 25 percent in the next quarter.

With a 25 percent ad increase and the same thirty ads, Ivan projected his website could generate more than forty-three thousand dollars a month in revenue, of which he would net nearly twenty thousand. An increase to forty ads a month at the same rate could generate close to sixty thousand, of which Ivan would close in on thirty thousand a month.

If Ivan could also reach his small cow party goal of twenty thousand dollars a week with Lucina, they could make over eighty thousand dollars a month, of which he would net more than forty thousand. Combining his website projections and party promotions for the year 2004, Ivan estimated that he could pull in seventy thousand dollars a month by the beginning of summer.

"That's good money. And that's not even including my increased salary now at Hutch and Mitchell," he told himself from the balcony of a new downtown apartment.

From his party introductions to new friends, associates, and businesses, Ivan had brought in twenty-three new clients for Hutch & Mitchell Accounting. The commission on those new clients earned him another seven thousand dollars before taxes and increased his general income by two to four thousand dollars a month.

Pocketing a total of sixty-five thousand entrepreneurial dollars after taxes for the year 2003, plus twenty thousand added to his retirement fund, Ivan had never done so well in one year in his life. So to make himself feel worthy of his new progress, he moved into a two-bedroom apartment near the downtown Gaslamp area. He then paid an interior decorator friend of Lucina's to furnish his new pad, creating a luxurious appeal for a sane price. And as he overlooked the San Diego skyline from his new high-rise balcony downtown, Ivan felt invincible.

"Yeah, this is the life, right here," he told himself, grinning, with both hands clasped behind his head. His move downtown was only the beginning of his ambitions. Ivan still had a short-term goal to buy property in the university area to house his website offices. And he still thought of owning a home in La Jolla, with a half million dollars needed for a down payment.

"Why not?" he asked himself out loud. *At seventy thousand a month by this summer, I'll be able to do that by next year,* he plotted. He could even see the hills of La Jolla from his downtown balcony, facing north.

He then looked out to his left to the nearly completed downtown baseball stadium for the Padres. Several other downtown apartment complexes, condominiums, and hotels were all under construction.

"Real estate and development, hunh?" he questioned. "Maybe it's time to have another talk with Thomas."

Ivan's phone rang in the living room, breaking him from his ruminations.

He walked back inside and answered it. "Hello."

"Yes, Mr. David, this is the front desk calling. We have a Mr. Emilio Alvarez here to see you. Shall we send him up?"

"Oh, yeah, send him right up."

Ivan hung up the phone and smiled. The gatekeeper system was another perk of wealth. He had never had such a luxury before.

Emilio arrived at his door a few minutes later. Ivan planned to receive a lot more company after moving into his new two-bedroom apartment. The downtown location was more convenient for business, and the new pad allowed him to feel more confident about having folks over to entertain. So he took the leap from less than a thousand dollars a month for rent to double that and change.

Emilio walked in and commented, "Hey, man, this is a nice place."

"I'm sure it's nothing like your place," Ivan assumed. Emilio was a two-and-a-half-million-dollar-a-year baseball player. His signing bonus had been three million.

"Well, your place is much neater," he responded with a chuckle. "I still have to hire a maid."

He continued to walk around Ivan's new pad to check out the decor: the plush furniture, artwork, accents, rugs, vases, exotic lamps, everything.

"So, how much it cost you to decorate this place, thirty, forty grand?" Emilio asked him.

Ivan answered him with a frown, "Thirty, forty *grand*? Hell, no! Try *half* of that."

Emilio looked surprised. "You're kidding me. You did all this for less than *thirty*?"

Ivan said, "Look, man, I took a lot of the things from my old apartment in La Mesa, and I just told the guy to build around that. And that's what he did. So a lot of this stuff in here is just an *illusion* of wealth. But as long as it looks good and feels good, I'm cool with it."

Emilio took a seat on the plush beige sofa facing the entertainment center and said, "Yeah, I see what you mean."

Ivan sat on a twin sofa next to him. "So, what's been going on, man? I didn't see you at the New Year's Eve party we had."

Ivan had made another five thousand after Lucina's share. There were too many parties going on that night to make much more than that. However, his ad team pulled in another two grand for the website from New Year's Eve party promotions. Ivan even had liquor sponsors courting his business now.

Emilio grinned. He said, "To tell you the truth, man, I hung out with Audrey that night, and she, ah . . . didn't want to go to your party."

Ivan nodded. "Yeah, I understand." Audrey no longer worked with them. She got her hooks into Emilio and left with her own plans. Lucina had warned him that would happen with many of the girls. There was no way they could control it. So he felt guilty now for introducing the girl to his baseball friend. Ivan had used them both.

"So, ah . . . how are you doing with her now?" He wanted to ease into a conversation about it. It had been on his mind lately after seeing Audrey's upgrades in car, wardrobe, and appearance.

Emilio smirked and said, "Man, she's expensive as hell, but I like her."

Ivan didn't like any part of that statement. Emilio was still a client of his accounting firm.

He said, "I understand that you like her, man. A lot of guys would like her. But don't let her spend up your money, E. You gotta have a budget for everything you do with that girl. A *tight* one. And I would know."

Emilio looked at him and wondered. He figured that Ivan had had all the girls. Some guys just had that thing about them that made the women flock. So Emilio planned to ask him a few questions that night. That was why he had shown up.

He said, "Did you ever, ah, you know, bone her?"

Ivan grimaced. "Who, Audrey?"

"Yeah," Emilio confirmed.

Ivan shook his head. "Naw. I didn't deal with her like that."

"Have you known anyone who has?"

Ivan couldn't think of anyone. Emilio was the first and only guy that she had gone after.

"Naw, she, ah, pretty much just went after you, man. And I hadn't really been around her that long, to tell you the truth."

Once he said that, he felt guilty again. Ivan wouldn't have dealt much with Audrey at all had Emilio not bumped into them at the mall and fallen for her. Nevertheless, Emilio's presence at his events helped Ivan to bring in a lot of the Latino crowd. So it became a good trade-off.

Emilio said, "Yeah, man, she told me she was still a virgin."

Ivan heard that and said, "What?"

Emilio grinned. "Yeah, that's what she told me."

Ivan said, "You don't believe that shit, right? So that means you haven't done her yet? Well, what happened to the white girl I saw you with?"

Emilio shook it off. "That just didn't work out, man."

"Well, how do you think *this* is gonna work out? You planning on marrying this girl or something? I mean, she's telling you that she's a virgin, while she's spending up your money. What the hell are you doing with this girl, man?" Ivan was becoming irritated by it all.

Emilio asked him, "What are you doing with Lucina?"

"I'm making money with her," Ivan told him. "I don't have to touch her. I got over that a while ago. Lucina's a *big* asset to me. But this girl Audrey is nothing but a liability to you. She's not bringing you any money."

He added, "I thought you would just kick it with this girl, man, and move on."

Emilio repeated, "Nah, man, like I said, I like her. Everything isn't about money."

Ivan just stopped and stared at him. He repeated, "Everything isn't about money? Are you *crazy*? Money is the reason why we're both here in San Diego. You got a baseball contract, and I have an accounting job and a promotions business."

"Yeah, but we could both do that anywhere," Emilio argued.

Ivan took a deep breath, cursing himself for getting his baseball friend into trouble with a gold digger. He said, "Let me ask you an economic question, E.A. How much money have you spent on this girl so far?"

Emilio shook it off again. He said, "It doesn't really matter, man. It's nothing compared to what I make."

Ivan said, "But you could still make your money work for you instead of against you."

Emilio said, "I'm not a moneymaking guy like you, Ivan. I'm just a baseball player."

"Yeah, a *rookie,*" Ivan reminded him. "And you're acting like one, man. You think all of these girls are around me and Lucina because they just like being around us? Hell, no. They're *working,* man."

He continued, "So, just look at it this way: you play, what, one hundred-sixty games a season?"

"Yeah, if you're that healthy," Emilio answered with a chuckle. He said, "But definitely not that for pitchers."

Ivan said, "Anyway, so that's about, sixteen into twenty four . . ." He did his calculations for two million, four hundred thousand dollars divided by one hundred-sixty games, and came up with, "Fifteen thousand dollars a game. And sometimes you play up to four or five games a week, which gives you sixty to seventy-five thousand dollars with no expenses. Because the team pays for everything, right—travel, hotel, food?"

Emilio nodded. "Yeah."

Ivan said, "Well, that's a lot of damn money to make with no expenses, man." He said, "Now, if a big event promoter could flip some of that money and double it for you twice a month, while you're still flying around playing ball, that would become an asset."

Ivan caught himself and laughed it off. "Naw, let me stop that, man. I plan to make close to that myself soon anyway," he stated.

Emilio smiled and asked him, "What if you bought one of those Hooters franchises? They're popping up everywhere now."

Ivan said, "See, now you're thinking. Those things make money every day of the week. Then you can hire all of the pretty girls you want, right there. And you could pay them minimum wage, plus a couple of hamburgers, and do good."

They shared a laugh before Emilio added, "We could get Lucina to hire the whole staff."

Ivan hesitated. He said, "Naw, you wouldn't want to hire Lucina's kind of girls. They would want more money than that. They would put you out of business."

Emilio said, "Well, how do *you* deal with them?"

Ivan had to stop and think again. He said, "I just try to stick to the numbers, to tell you the truth. And if it don't add up, I tell them I can't do it. But I always let them know that I'm still here to make more opportunities for them."

He started thinking about Christina when he said that. Maybe it hadn't been the best idea for her to give in to him. Outside of being able to spend private time with Ivan, she hadn't benefited much from his personal touch. But at least she hadn't been tossed out in the street in a jealous rage from Lucina. Ivan had kept their relationship under wraps, and he and Chris continued to do business as usual.

He told Emilio, "The truth is, you just can't get caught up with it, man. Everybody wants something . . . even us. So you get what you can get, give what you give, and you move on. Just try to make sure that most of the things you choose to do will benefit you in some way."

Emilio heard him out and nodded. "Thanks, man. I really needed this talk."

Ivan looked at him and felt good about it himself. He nodded and thought, *Yeah, maybe you'll get rid of that damn girl now. That was all my fault.*

LUCINA MAY HAVE gone along with Ivan's small cow party idea while it made them money at the end of the year, but she definitely didn't plan on continuing his idea in 2004, if *she* could help it. She had much bigger plans for them, namely full-fledged concert promotions. So she set up a meeting with one of the veteran San Diego promoters that she had worked with in the past, to see what kind of interest she could drum up for the future.

However, she felt apprehension after being forced to endure a longer-than-usual wait to set up the meeting. It took her five follow-up phone calls. Even when she showed up on time for their agreed-upon appointment at the three-story office building that housed Randy & Ralph Entertainment, Lucina found herself still waiting inside the reception area with the secretary.

She looked down at her watch. It was fast approaching two-thirty.

"Would you like anything to drink?" the secretary asked her while she waited. She could tell that their guest was a little perturbed by the wait.

Lucina shook it off. "No, I'm okay. I'm just being very patient right now. *Very* patient," she emphasized.

The secretary nodded. "I understand. And I apologize. But Randy should be out any minute now."

Lucina didn't respond to her. Instead she thought, *It's amusing how even old business partners can make you play the humility game when they believe they have the upper hand.*

Finally, Randy Sterling rang his secretary.

"Yes, I'll send her right in."

Lucina looked up from her chair, where she'd been flipping through the latest issue of San Diego's *944* magazine, and caught the secretary's eye.

"He's ready for you now," the secretary told her.

Lucina closed the magazine and slid it back onto the small table in front of her. She stood and said, "Thank you."

The secretary led her into the back office, past a hallway of framed enlarged photos of Randy and Ralph with various celebrities at their past events. Lucina was surprised to see that they had not bothered to frame even one photo of her. She had been present at at least *five* of the twenty events on their hallway walls.

Typical, she told herself. *And there is no reason to even ask.* Nevertheless, she hoped he would be open to a few new business deals.

As soon as Lucina walked into his office, Randy picked up the phone again and started blabbering away.

"Justin Timberlake? I mean, is this kid for real, or will he be another solo act that goes nowhere?" He spotted Lucina on her walk in and motioned for her to have a seat in the empty chair across from his desk.

"Hey, thanks, Linda," he quickly told his secretary.

"No problem," she said, and turned to walk out.

Lucina took another seat and waited again while Randy continued to run his mouth on his office phone.

"Yeah, of course I've heard the album. But I mean, you know, the hits, they come and go. But I guess we can do something while he's still hot, you know. And he's still a little young, but the chicks seem to like him."

Randy was a brown-haired, green-eyed white man in his late thirties who was still in athletic shape with solid height and good skin. He considered himself every bit an entertainer. He gave the connected people of San Diego a premium good time at a premium price.

"All right, well, let me call you back on that. I have an old friend in my office," he commented over the phone, with a wink in Lucina's direction.

Lucina smiled at him out of courtesy.

When Randy hung up the phone, he went right at her. "So, Lucina Gallo, what brings you around? I see you're still looking hot these days. What can I do for you?"

She didn't like the tone of the conversation already. It sounded way too distant, as if they would be starting from nowhere. Lucina carried on with the bullshit game anyway.

She grinned and told him, "I see you're still at it yourself. You're still single?"

"Unless some goddess snuck a ring on my finger that I didn't notice while I got toasted one night," he joked. Then he laughed. "Yeah, I'm still the same asshole that I used to be when it comes to taking that dreaded walk to the altar. What about you? Are you still teasing them all?"

Lucina grinned and answered, "Of course. How else can you keep a man's interest?"

"By making him some money," Randy answered on cue.

"Well, I've been doing that, too," she commented.

Randy turned serious and said, "Yeah, I heard something about that. Football parties, fashion parties, food tastings. But isn't that all a little backwards for you? I thought you and your girls would have been working your way up to *our* league by now. How's, ah, Maya doing?" he asked.

"She's still gorgeous," Lucina told him proudly.

Randy grunted and said, "I bet she is," while starting to reminisce.

He and Lucina's girl had had a short affair that didn't end so well.

"So, anyways," Lucina commented, moving the conversation along, "the past is the past. But I'm here to talk about the future.

What does Randy and Ralph Entertainment have in its plans for the new year that is in the six-figure range?"

Randy looked at her quizzically and spoke on behalf of himself and his partner.

"Ah, everything, actually. If it's less than that, then what's the point?"

"Any three- or four-way splits?" she asked him.

"Not with another promoter, if that's what you mean. No."

Lucina read that and asked, "Any room for *silent* partners?"

Randy eyed her from his rotating leather chair and answered, "Not the kind of partners who refuse to be silent." He realized Lucina loved to make sure everyone knew that she was involved. So he shook it off and told her, "But we don't really do the local partnership thing anymore anyway. I mean, I'd invite you and a few of your girls out. I'd love to see Maya again. But outside of that . . . you know, we already have our hands full."

He added, "I hear you have a new partner now yourself."

Lucina nodded. "Oh, yes, Ivan. He has some great ideas. And he's just getting started. So with the right direction . . ."

Randy looked at her and nodded back. "Is he, ah, Brazilian or Italian, too?"

"No, he's all American from L.A.," she answered.

"Oh, L.A." Randy then paused a beat. "Is he black?"

Lucina told him, "You know, I never asked him that. But he is an accountant."

"Yeah, well, that's a good thing to have," Randy commented. "Is he a good one?"

"Why, of course. Why wouldn't he be?"

Randy nodded again. "That's good." But from there, it seemed the conversation had nowhere left to go.

Randy opened his mouth and uttered, "Well—"

Lucina cut him off. "If you come up with anything where you may need an extra six figures, then you let me know."

He said, "I doubt if I'll need it, but all right." He abruptly stood up and looked at his black, gold, and silver Rolex watch. "Well, I have another meeting to take at three, Lucina. So, good luck with everything, all right? And make sure you tell Maya I said hi."

Lucina had no choice but to stand up with him as he walked over toward his door to show her out.

"Thanks for dropping by," he told her.

"And I'll make sure I tell Maya," she promised him. *When all of hell freezes over,* she promised herself. But she pressed him anyway. "Just remember to call me on any new business."

Randy blew her off and said, "Yeah, I'll let you know."

WHEN LUCINA RETURNED to her black Mercedes in the parking lot, she felt foolish.

I should have never tried this, she thought behind the wheel. *What made me think that he would ever change? If business was only business, I'm sure we could all work something out and make money. But business has so many levels of nonbusiness that it all drives me crazy sometimes.*

She took a deep breath before she restarted her car and drove off with other plans boiling.

BACK AT THE OFFICES of Hutch & Mitchell, it was unrealistic to assume that Ivan could keep his good fortune away from his fellow accountants. Outside of the Nissan Altima that he continued to drive to work, everything about him had changed. His choice of clothes was snazzier, he finished his tax work a lot faster than usual, he rarely stayed late at the office or went to lunch with the guys anymore, he continued to have his hair cut low, and his confident swagger was off the charts now. The bosses had even let the cat out of the bag about his recent performance, stating that they were very pleased with all of the new clients he had brought them over the third and fourth quarters of the year. In fact, Dwayne had told him that John and Barry wanted to meet with him to address his new salary.

"You should be ready for it by now," he assumed of Ivan. He had been drilling him for it since October.

Chip was all over Ivan at his cubicle for real answers.

"So, what's going on, Ivan? What's your secret? And you're not gonna tell me that love is doing all of this for ya," Chip pressed him. "Because if that's really the case, then I'd like to meet this girl's younger sister," he joked.

Ivan was pleased he had held the guys at the office at bay for as long as he had, but even he understood that he couldn't continue to hide his promotions business from them forever. His plans for the new year were too big to get away with that.

So he nodded and took a breath to compose himself. He looked up from his desk chair and told his fellow accountant, "Chip, instead of me sitting around complaining about how hard we work in here to make sure that the rich *remain* rich, I decided to create my own vehicle where I could move in that direction myself."

At first Chip only stared at him. He said, "So, it's never really been about a girl?" He wanted to erase the thought from his head. He had really believed the hype that a good woman had done wonders for Ivan, and he was seriously thinking about going in that direction for himself. *Maybe the focus of just one woman really is good for you,* he had pondered over the past couple of months. He had even started dating one woman more steadily than he had done in the past.

Ivan explained, "Actually, I do have a female *partner* who was very influential in the process. And there's no way in the world things could have worked out as well for me at this point had I not teamed up with her."

He continued, "But we haven't been dating or anything. I mean, we both realized that making money together is more important than that. So we kind of, like, stayed away from that issue altogether."

Chip was stunned. Now he was even more interested. "So, what kind of partnership is it?"

Ivan took another breath. He said, "I'm not going into discussing it all while we're still on Hutch and Mitchell time, but you can go to IDPromotions.com and look through it yourself."

"IDPromotions.com?" Chip repeated. "I.D. like in 'Ivan David'?"

Ivan nodded to him. "Yeah."

Chip said, "All right, I'll check it out."

Ivan warned him, "And Chip, I'm not gonna talk about it here. So if you want to discuss it further, we'll have to do that after work."

Chip nodded and said, "All right, that's fair." He couldn't wait to log online immediately at his desk.

No more than a minute or two after Chip had left him, Dwayne called Ivan into his office. He closed his door behind them and wasted no words. "Well, the time is now, Ivan. John and Barry want to make you a new salary offer by the end of the day. So get yourself ready to hear them out for a four o'clocker."

Ivan was poised and ready for it. *More money, more money,* he told himself.

He nodded to Dwayne and said, "Okay. I'm ready."

Dwayne nodded back. "That's good. So, ah . . . how's the new business doing?"

"It's growing, man, just like it's supposed to. I can't complain. All I got is time."

Dwayne didn't have much else to say. He said, "All right, that's all." He added, "And let me warn you, once they make this offer to you, and you accept it, be prepared to grow a tougher coat of skin around here," he warned. "You're gonna need it."

Ivan smiled and said, "Yeah, I already know."

By the time he had returned to his desk, Chip had told Mike Adams to log on and check out IDPromotions.com as well, and they were both very impressed with the site.

Mike asked Chip, "So how long has Ivan been doing this, you know?"

"Since he first brought up this whole story about a girl, I guess," Chip assumed.

Mike shook it off. "No, this looks far too detailed for it to have only been a few months. And I love the San Diego spotlight idea. That can easily make the little guys feel a big part of the deal, you know. Then they'll have all of their friends and family members check the site out. That's a pretty clever tactic to drive more traffic."

"Pretty *clever*?" Chip responded. "Shit, man, are you kidding me? The whole idea is *genius*. No wonder Ivan's been so smug around here lately. He's ready to become another one of those filthy-rich dot-com guys. And he's been doing it right in fucking front of us."

Mike continued to check out the photo gallery, where Ivan posed in photos with professional athletes, pretty girls, San Diego small business owners, and other movers and shakers.

Mike nodded and said, "Now I see why Ivan was asking me about wearing an earring. In this crowd here, it would all fit. It would give him something extra to stand out with, you know?"

Once Chip spotted Ivan returning to his cubicle, he told Mike, "I didn't tell you any of this, all right? You just happened to swing by my desk when I was logged on. Because Ivan doesn't want to talk about it on the job."

Mike chuckled and said, "I bet he wouldn't. So, are you gonna join his email list? 'Who are you? What do you do? Let us know,'" he joked as Chip slipped away to return to his area.

"Smart-ass," Chip responded.

Ivan planned to ignore it all. There was nothing more calming for him than having new money in the bank and more money on the way. He even had a dinner meeting set that night with Thomas Jones. He wanted to discuss real estate investments at Carol's in Old Town.

When he was finally called into John Hutch's office after four o'clock for his new salary discussions, Ivan was as cool and calm as a nighttime swimming pool.

Since John Hutch was the heavy on the business side of the company, he did the majority of the talking about the salary increase, just as Ivan had expected he would.

"I guess you already know why we're meeting with you this afternoon, Ivan," he stated. "You've been performing steadily with us over the past five years, but during these past few quarters, we've noticed that you've really turned the corner and decided to become a real go-getter for the company. And since our company is always interested in expanding our client base, we'd like to reward you for that."

He went straight to the point, sitting behind his extralarge desk, while Barry sat in the second leather office chair to Ivan's left.

John continued, "As we explained when we first hired you years ago, we typically like to pay our accountants more in commissions than we do in base salary. So with that in mind, we've decided to give you a substantial pay raise to a hundred and four thousand a year, plus a *twenty* percent commission on all new clients instead of ten."

Ivan did the math and came up with roughly six thousand dollars a month after taxes. It was a dead-on estimate of what he figured Hutch & Mitchell would offer him. So he smiled and said, "That's a generous pay raise, but I'm sure you both would like to know how I've been able to spark a new client base in the first place."

Ivan was well aware of their commissions ideas. He used their model in his own business.

Barry spoke up. "Definitely. We were gonna get to that. Although we don't always expect smart young guys like you to let us in on your methods," he commented. He and his partner reasoned that if Ivan was indeed a gamer, he would have some counteroffers.

Ivan figured his website and promotional events brand was strong enough now to invite bigger fish to the party. So he told them, "Actually, I have no problem telling you my methods. I've basically started a promotional website and network party vehicle where a small staff and I have been able to generate an average of ten thousand unique hits a day and more than eighty thousand daily impressions. And through a lot of meeting and greeting at the various promoted parties and events around San Diego, I've been able to win enough faith and confidence from some of the movers and shakers here that they trust me in their financial affairs, which, of course, includes their accounting services at Hutch and Mitchell."

John and Barry stopped and looked at each other.

Barry said, "More than *eighty* thousand impressions? That sounds like an *impressive* number."

"And we're still working on increasing that number," Ivan told them. "But what I'd like to offer to Hutch and Mitchell is an opportunity for us to build a financial corner page, where you sponsor it for the first year, for fifteen hundred a month, to help increase an even stronger new client base here at the company."

He looked at Barry and added, "You could even post a blurb each month with your own financial advice page." Then he looked back to John. "My counteroffer would be a hundred and eighty thousand. We do that, and you sponsor the financial corner page for the first year, and it's a deal."

John slowed down Ivan's optimistic idealism and told him, "Well, we would need time to look at this, ah, website of yours to determine how much of a benefit it would be. And it's still a bit of a jump for us to get involved in your, ah, party promotions website at this point. We would just like to compensate you for what you've been able to do for the company lately."

Ivan nodded and said, "I understand that. Business is business. But my party promotions is how I've been able to do it. So take your time. Do your research on it. And call me back in when you're ready. But in the meantime, I still work for Hutch and Mitchell Accounting, and I plan to continue doing my job while I'm here." He then handed both of them his IDPromotions.com business card.

John looked at the card and raised his brow. "Looks like you're really putting your personal seal on this thing."

Ivan smiled and said, "Without a doubt. And if anyone else decides that they can do the same, I offer them an opportunity to try it. But at the end of the day, the real numbers do the talking. And we've been putting up the real numbers."

WHEN IVAN walked out of John Hutch's office, the two partners closed the door behind him to discuss their thoughts.

"Well, what do you think, John? Pretty bright and ambitious kid, right?" Barry quizzed his partner. He had always been impressed with Ivan. Ivan was rarely the one to toot his own horn. So the fact that he was so confident in his new business carried a lot of weight.

John was still staring at the business card behind his desk. He was definitely curious. He had noticed the confident changes in Ivan's personality around the office himself. He had been impressed with the young man out of South Central Los Angeles as well.

He said, "Well, first we'll need to investigate this website and party promotions business of his to understand it for ourselves. But for us to triple his salary, this website idea needs to be far better than average."

ON IVAN'S SIDE OF THE COIN, ad sales manager Eddie K. explained that the more well-respected businesses they could get involved in supporting their website, the easier it would become to entice other respected companies to fall in line. So it was paramount for IDPromotions.com to establish relationships with as many recognized company brands as possible, and in every professional field.

As far as Ivan's personal salary was concerned, his goal was to pull in ten thousand dollars a month after taxes, which $180,000 a year would allow him to do. However, as a compromise, he would settle for $140,000 a year, or slightly more than eight thousand a month. Eight to ten thousand a month, after taxes, would be more than enough to cover all of his personal expenses, as well as fatten up his retirement plan.

IVAN MET UP with Thomas Jones at Carol's Soul Food Restaurant that night, and they were both all smiles at their table.

Thomas shook his head and said, "I still can't believe you got folks to pay twenty dollars a head to watch *Monday Night Football* on a big-screen TV over at Raymond's Lounge. And now you got 'em doing the same shit with the playoffs."

Ivan said, "It's *thirty* dollars a head for the playoffs, including an all-you-can-eat buffet. But just look at it this way. How long have Americans been paying for bottled water now? These guys are all paying for the experience of being around a certain group and in a certain atmosphere, just like if you were going to the game. And if they don't want that experience, then they stay home and watch it."

Thomas chuckled. He said, "I'm only imagining now how much money you're gonna make once you own the place."

Ivan told him, "That's what we're here to talk about, right? Real estate."

Thomas asked him, "Yeah, so what's this big interest of yours in the university area?"

"That's where most of my help comes from," Ivan answered. "Both of my webmasters, three salespeople, blog writers, four party assistants, two photographers—they're all San Diego State undergrads or grad students. And if I set up an office over there, I don't have to worry about my interns needing transportation. They can all walk or ride their bikes to work."

Thomas said, "But what about the mature people who end up working for you? They might want a more businesslike atmosphere."

Ivan said, "The people I want to hire have to be versatile enough to fit into different crowds. I mean, we're talking about a website and party promotions here."

"So, how much are you paying these guys, if you don't mind me asking?" Thomas questioned.

Ivan looked at him and answered, "A very generous percentage of the ad money, plus five hundred dollars a month for my webmasters; a nice percentage deal for my sales manager; and different small fees to my editorial manager, photographers, and everybody else." He said, "But when you're building something without a lot of up-front capital, you gotta be real creative in how you decide to pay the good people around you."

He added, "Like my time, donations, and the calendar of events page I set up for you guys at the Urban League."

Thomas laughed. "You don't have to explain that to me, Ivan. I know how it all works. I'm just happy that you picked it all up so fast. So, how much are you trying to spend on an off-campus house?"

"Well, I could use a three-bedroom for starters. That way I can separate my webmasters, my ad sales manager, and my editorial chief in their own office rooms. Then I can set up a cubicle atmosphere in the living room and dining room areas, just like at a regular office."

Thomas said, "It sounds like you got it all worked out in your head already."

"Hey, man, most nights I'm up all night brainstorming. But what kind of damaged property or foreclosure deals do you think you can find for me in the hundred-thousand-dollar range?" Ivan asked him. "Because I figure we'll have to do a lot of remodeling and painting to get the place how I'm gonna want it anyway."

Thomas asked him, "How much do you have to put down?"

Ivan shrugged. "Forty thousand. And that doesn't mean that I want to spend it all, but that's what I have."

Thomas eyed him and said, "Ivan, let me now explain how the

game of real estate works. With forty thousand dollars, I would advise that we look for *three* off-campus deals. And if we can find three of them for one-fifty each or *less*, you put down ten percent on each, you remodel and paint all three of them, and you either resell the extra two or rent them out to pay for the one that you keep as your office."

He continued, "And once you start to get a little comfortable with this real estate machine, I got plenty of information on housing development companies who are open to private investors."

They got so heavy into talking business that they neglected to order any food. When they finally took a look at the menu, Thomas spotted Ida in the background of the restaurant. But she didn't seem too eager to make it over in their direction to speak.

Thomas asked Ivan, "So, what happened between you and Ida?"

Ivan shrugged. "We're still cool and all, but the business and personal sometimes . . ."

Thomas nodded to him and grunted. "Mmm-hmm." Then he cracked another smile. He said, "I knew that was coming. Ida's a nice girl for you, but I think you like money too much right now to get caught up in emotions with her. So you just packed it up and moved on to the next one, hunh?"

Ivan took a breath and said, "You gotta move forward, Thomas. I mean, I still like her and all. I respect her. I thank her for her support. But at the end of the day, I still got a lot of other things I wanna do. And like you said, man, all the extra emotions . . . it just ends up slowing you down."

Thomas grinned and said, "But you didn't drop that Lucina Gallo girl, did you?"

Ivan laughed it off. "Naw," he answered, "she's still making me too much money."

Thomas said, "I bet she is."

Twelve

Everybody Wants Something

JOHN AND BARRY investigated Ivan's website and promotions brand from top to bottom at their accounting offices and loved the idea. Ivan continued to impress them as a young business leader in their midst. So they offered him a $150,000 package deal that included $132,000 in salary, plus the extra $18,000 for their one-year sponsorship of his financial corner website page.

"And I'm going to hold you to that offer to post my blogs, Ivan," Barry Mitchell told him.

Ivan agreed to follow through on the blogs, but he did not agree on the $150,000 package.

He countered, "You add another eight thousand to the salary to round it up to one-forty, and it's a deal."

John Hutch quickly agreed to the revised numbers with a silent nod. There was no sense in holding up the deal over seven hundred extra dollars a month. So Ivan accepted their final offer and felt good about it.

At lunch break, he rushed out of the office to meet up with Eddie K. at Subway to discuss their sales goals, only for Chip Garrett to catch up to him outside the building before Ivan could reach his car.

"Hey, Ivan, let me talk to you for a minute, man."

Ivan looked at Chip and was prepared to brush him off. But he figured it was better to get it over with instead. Chip seemed urgent.

"All right, hop in the car with me," Ivan told him. He didn't want his coworker slowing him down.

Chip walked over to the black Altima with him to climb into the passenger seat. He looked around inside the car and commented, "Come on, guy, when are you gonna get a new car? You got things going on now, right?"

"Yeah, I'll get one soon. That's just not a priority right now. But what can I do for you?" Ivan asked him.

Chip looked at him and said, "Dude, there's this one party girl on your website that I would just *kill* to meet."

Ivan couldn't believe it. *All of that for a girl? I hope he's not talking about Lucina, though.*

"What does she look like?"

"She's a blond, with green eyes, wearing a hot pink top and a black skirt, about halfway down the latest party photo gallery page."

Ivan smiled. "Oh, that's, ah . . . Janine." He knew the exact picture.

"And there's this other girl right across the page from her in this white hat that just stands out in the middle of the crowd."

"Gretchen," Ivan told him. Then he laughed. "People really do look at those pictures, hunh?"

"Come on, man, you got the hottest girls on there," Chip responded. "And you know them all by name. So make sure you invite me to the next big party."

Ivan said, "Yeah, I'll introduce you. But I got a meeting to make right now."

"Hey, do what you do, man."

When Chip climbed out of the car, he got Ivan thinking again. *With these white girls mixed in all over the website now, I wonder how many white men are watching me. And I wonder who they would all like to meet.*

It was a thought that remained with him when he met up with Eddie for lunch.

He walked in a few minutes late and said, "Eddie, let me ask you a question. What do you think about the girls we post on the website?"

Eddie K. was already munching on a turkey club at his table. He nodded to Ivan with wide eyes and mumbled, "They're the best. We're, like, an interactive *Maxim* magazine."

"You think everybody sees that?" Ivan asked him.

"Of course. Are you kidding me? The photo galleries still get the most visits. We didn't have anything like that at the newspapers," he added.

Ivan nodded and kept his thoughts to himself. *Even legitimate businessmen are more concerned about the girls, hunh? Okay. So be it.*

Then he returned to business. "So, anyway, Hutch and Mitchell agreed today to sponsor our financial corner page; then I'll have my guy Thomas Jones to help us set up the sponsorship of the real estate page."

Eddie nodded, loving everything he heard. He said, "This thing is really shaping up to be an online magazine. We'll be posting close to fifteen pages now. And that means more space for advertisement. Me and the guys were even thinking about a few things."

Whenever Eddie mentioned "me and the guys," he was referring to Jeff and Paul, the undergraduate webmasters. They had all become quite friendly.

Ivan said, "Yeah, what about?"

Eddie looked at him and paused. He answered, "Well, we know you're being quite generous with us on the commissions and all, but we were just wondering out loud if we could buy into the company at some point. Or at least make us an offer before you make offers to anyone else."

Ivan shook it off with a frown. "What makes you think I'm ready to start offering up pieces of the company already? As far as I'm concerned, we're just getting started. We haven't even set up our office yet."

Ivan was a little defensive. His team sounded as if they were getting paranoid too early about being swindled on a buyout. He assumed that it was mostly coming from Eddie. He was a business veteran who had broken off to do something different. And maybe he was becoming greedy too fast.

Eddie grinned and took a sip of his soda from the straw. He said, "We would just like a first-option clause, that's all. With us helping you to build this thing, we thought that would be fair for all of us."

Ivan paused and calmed his nerves. There was no sense in him getting too excited over speculation. He had to manage it.

He stood his ground and said, "The first thing we need to do is focus on making sure the website continues to grow. So I'm using all of my resources, just like you are, to make sure that happens. Now, as far as me giving you guys a first-option clause, the biggest problem with that is not knowing what the value is yet."

Eddie said, "Well, we could all sit down and work that out later, Ivan. We just want to make sure that we would have a *right* to have those conversations with you."

Ivan thought it over and mellowed out. Eddie was only being a good businessman. Ivan had to admit that their input, creativity, and professional efforts had all worked in tandem to create something special.

Finally, he nodded and said, "All right, that's fair. I'll have my lawyers draw up something."

Eddie nodded back to him and grinned. "Great. Now I have a lot of good news for you. And none of this is definite *yet,* but it's *definitely* gonna happen for us in the very near future."

He pulled out several files of paperwork from his briefcase and set them all out on the left side of the table.

"After thinking about the editorial content, I went ahead and printed out some articles we could share with the writing staff that would really help us to get after these sponsorships a lot more aggressively."

Ivan looked at all the paperwork Eddie had printed out to present him, and he read the situation correctly.

Okay, the man is trying to show off all of his value to me now, he told himself. He smiled over the table and remained speechless. *And I notice he didn't show me anything until he got what he wanted on this first-option clause. I guess that's just what good businesspeople do,* he mused. *I probably would have done the same thing.*

WHEN IVAN MET back up with Thomas Jones, his real estate and business mentor had lined up six foreclosure properties to take a look at, right outside San Diego State's campus.

"Now, I would advise you to get in on these things *fast,* Ivan," he warned. "Foreclosures are not for slow movers."

Ivan told him, "I understand." He planned to waste no time deciding which three properties he would buy in his price range.

Thomas said, "And my part for doing this for you, and educating you on the deals, is a free real estate banner on that website of yours. You said you're about to start up a real estate page soon, right?"

Ivan was already thinking about a real estate sponsor for the page.

He said, "Actually, if you can get your real estate brokerage to sponsor the page, that would work out great for *both* of us."

Thomas argued, "That won't work out great for *me*. If they sponsored the page, then I would have to compete with the other agents for all of the new business."

Ivan said, "Naw, we could still put up your banner, the company would just sponsor the page. So everyone would still see your personal spotlight for business. But I can't even put up the page without securing a sponsor, because I gotta pay my webmasters to do it."

Thomas looked at Ivan and started laughing. He said, "I had no idea you would be this damn good this fast, Ivan. But come on, now, you put up this whole damn website without needing sponsors, so don't tell me you gotta wait for one now to put up a real estate page."

He added, "However, once you get this page up and running and I let them know how much business you've brought in for me, I'll be able to talk them into doing something with you."

Ivan smiled back and laughed himself. They were both running a me-first game on each other. He said, "You know I'm gonna do it, man. You've helped me out too much for me to act crazy on you. But at the same time, I can't afford to wait around for you to ask your guys to sponsor the page. So, if you don't ask them now, then that option may no longer be open."

Thomas looked at him and said, "Ivan, now, you know I understand business. Money talks, bullshit walks. So I'll ask them about it, but I wouldn't count on anything from them too soon." He said, "To be frank, when it comes to spending dollars outside the normal channels, these guys can be *reeeaal* slow. You gotta *prove* everything to 'em first. They even wanna know what color *drawers* you wear before they spend money with you."

Ivan joked, "Well, you tell them I wear money-green boxers . . . Fruit of the Loom."

And they shared a laugh.

THINGS WERE MOVING and shaking at lightning speed in the new year. Ivan had already made another fifty thousand dollars by the end of January: a split of seven thousand each week from NFL playoff parties at Raymond's, another seven thousand split each week from a combination of small cow parties downtown and around San Diego, and a more than twenty-thousand-dollar net from website advertisement.

The website ad team had reached nearly forty ads a month, with five page sponsors on board, including Hutch & Mitchell Accounting and Pacific Property Realtors for the "Financial Corner" and the "San Diego Real Estate" pages, respectively. With the additional web pages, their ad capacity and viewer impressions continued to grow.

"Now we can make close to a hundred thousand a month off the ads before we even increase our rates again," Ivan told himself while going over the numbers at his apartment. He used his second bedroom as a home office, with a large desk, a leather office chair, two meeting chairs, a large LCD screen for his computer, a color laser printer, a multipurpose fax and copy machine, and a separate phone line. He had begun the process of remodeling and painting the three foreclosure properties he had bought close to San Diego State's campus. They were on schedule to open up the home office for business by the second week of February.

Ivan leaned back in his downtown apartment office chair and propped his feet up on the desk like a big boss. He told himself out loud, "I'm turning twenty-nine this year. I'm not even thirty yet. And I'm making out like a bandit now."

Then he checked his watch to make sure he was still on time for the party he promised to stop by and make an appearance at downtown.

It was only nine thirty, right on schedule.

"I need to buy an upgraded watch, too," he reminded himself.

As soon as he stood up to get himself ready for the party, his cell phone rang from his hip. He looked down and read the number. It was Julio, his old neighbor.

Ivan answered his call. "Hey, Julio. What's going on, man?"

Julio said, "I got great news for you, Ivan. You know I've been telling my cousin about you, right? So I told him to check out your website. And when he finally got around to looking at it, he says he *loves* it now, man. So he told some of the guys to check it out, and now Busta Rhymes, Eve, and Xzibit all want to come down to San Diego and do a couple parties or whatever with you. He told me even DJ Quik checked out your website."

Ivan said, "Oh, yeah? So again, man, what's their price tags for a basic party appearance? Because I'm not paying thirty to fifty thousand dollars just for them to show up," he repeated.

"Yeah, but that's okay," Julio told him. "They're willing to work with us now. So, if you, like, can give us fifteen thousand in cash, we can work it all out."

Ivan listened closely to the language and understood that Julio and his cousin had placed themselves in the middle of the deal. And since Ivan doubted Mike Elizondo would be hurting for money with production credits on multiple Dr. Dre records, he figured that Julio was using the opportunity to jump-start a bankroll for himself.

But that's all right. I can't stop a man's hustle. As long as he can guarantee that they'll be here, Ivan reasoned.

He said, "Well, I can't send them fifteen thousand dollars in cash through the mail. They would have to be here to get it."

Julio said, "That's no problem. Just give me, like, five thousand as a down payment, and I'll make sure on my cousin's word that they'll be here."

Ivan asked him, "Will I get a chance to even talk to them first, just to say hi over the phone or something?"

"Oh, if you wanna do that, man, then yeah. We can make that happen. I just gotta let my cousin know."

Ivan didn't have the time to talk to Julio all night about it. He had a party to prepare for. So he cut their conversation short.

"All right, well, just call me back and let me know who's ready to come down first and on what date. All right, Julio? But I gotta run now, man. I got another party to attend tonight."

"Oh, yeah, where at?"

"In the Gaslamp."

IVAN STROLLED OUT of his downtown apartment building after ten o'clock that Thursday night wearing a dark blue sports jacket over a cream-colored mock turtleneck.

"Have a good night, Ivan," the on-duty security guard told him out front. He was aware of Ivan's popularity as a party promoter, and he had seen him around a few times with the pretty women who surrounded him.

"Oh, yeah—you, too," Ivan responded.

He now lived a five-block walking distance from the Fifth Avenue Gaslamp Quarter.

This is real convenient for me now, he thought as he paced forward with a wide grin.

Lucina called him on his cell as soon as he had made it halfway there.

"Are you on your way here?" she asked him. "Jeffrey Morefield from the Chargers is here with his fiancée. They have a wedding date now," she told him.

Ivan could hear the music in the background through her phone.

"Yeah, I'll be there in five minutes. So tell Jeffrey and his lady to hold tight for me."

AS SOON AS LUCINA clicked off her cell phone to return to the party, one of her girls approached her in a panic.

"Lucina, that guy I was telling you about is here. I really think he's stalking me."

She was a brown-haired white girl with very pert breasts, wearing a small top that exposed her flat stomach.

"The military guy?" Lucina asked her.

"Yeah."

Lucina had heard enough already. She wanted to get to the bottom of things. Her girlfriend had obviously gotten herself into more trouble than she could handle.

"Where is he now? Point him out to me."

Her friend looked even more terrified. "What are you gonna do?"

"I'm gonna ask him what his problem is," Lucina told her.

"Lucina, he's *crazy,* that's his problem."

"Well, you let me be the judge of that. Now where is he?"

She began to search through the partially crowded dance floor. It was a mostly red-lit club called the Red Cave.

"He's right at the bar," her girlfriend informed her.

Lucina spotted a clean-cut, clean-shaven white man sitting at the bar solo.

"The guy in the striped shirt?" she asked.

Her girl looked cautiously. She didn't want the man to turn and spot them looking at him. "Yeah, that's him."

Lucina took a breath and began to walk in the man's direction through the club. The party was too upscale for any nonsense. It was more of a business affair.

"Lucina, no . . ." her girl cried out to stop her. But it was too late. Lucina was halfway to the bar already, and she was not planning on turning back.

When she arrived in front of the young Marine at the bar, she said, "You seem to know one of my friends very well. Her name is Faloni."

The soldier, in his midtwenties, looked into Lucina's eyes and nodded. He said, "Yeah, I do know her. But she's trying to pretend now that she doesn't know *me.* And I just wanted to ask her *why.*"

"Is that why you've been following her?" Lucina asked him. "Because she does not like it. And you should give yourself something else to do before I tell security."

"Tell security what?" he asked, confused. He hadn't done anything wrong.

"That you are making a guest feel uncomfortable."

He said, "Well, excuse me, but I have the right to be here like everyone else. I paid my money to get in just like they did."

Lucina dug into her purse and pulled out a twenty-dollar bill. She held it in front of him and said, "You may leave now. And my friend does not choose to know you any longer."

The Marine shook it off and refused to take the money. He said, "Well, I still choose to know *her.*"

Lucina took a breath and decided to go another route. She said, "Look, you are an American soldier, correct?"

He nodded and answered, "Yeah."

"So, how come you don't have any respect for the citizens of your country?"

She hoped that her obvious accent would allow him to understand the ridiculousness of his irrational behavior. And it worked. He finally took the twenty-dollar bill she had offered him and stood up to head for the door.

He said, "You tell Faloni that she needs to learn how to be a real lady."

"Thank you. I will," Lucina told him as he began to head for the door.

Ivan walked in just as the Marine began to walk away. He caught the tail end of the exchange.

"What was that about?" he asked Lucina.

She exhaled and shook it off. "It was nothing important." She looked Ivan over, nodded, and smiled briefly. "You look good tonight," she told him. "Let's go find Jeffrey and his fiancée now."

Ivan followed her into another section of the darkened room.

"Hey, Ivan, how are you tonight?" Faloni asked him, grinning.

Lucina eyed her sharply and said, "I will speak with you later. Okay?"

Faloni caught on to her sharp reaction and backed off.

"Oh, okay. Well, thanks."

Ivan noticed the stiff-arm Lucina had given her and chuckled. "What did she do?"

Lucina answered, "She made her life more complicated than she needed to." She changed her tone and smiled when they reached the football player and his fiancée.

"Jeffrey, Ivan is here now," she commented.

Jeffrey Morefield turned to face them, looking professional as usual.

"Hey, Ivan. Let me introduce you to my fiancée, Lachelle."

Jeffrey had not been to many of their events lately. And when he did show, he had not brought his fiancée.

Ivan extended his hand to her and was impressed. She was a tall, slim, medium brown woman with very smooth skin and a mane of curly, reddish-brown hair. She also had small eyes like Christina's, but her cheekbones were higher.

"Hi, I-van. I've heard a lot about you and Lu-ci-na. It's nice to finally get to meet you both."

She had an accent of her own. Ivan nodded to her and grinned.

He said, "Well, I hope somebody gave me a good reputation."

Jeffrey's fiancée laughed and said, "Oh, they did."

Ivan asked her, "Where is your accent from?"

"I am from Gambia in Africa."

Ivan was surprised. He'd been thinking the Caribbean. "Oh, okay." *So Jeffrey went all the way back to the motherland. And she looks damn good,* he told himself.

Lucina said, "We were just discussing us doing something nice for their wedding reception. They're getting married in early May."

Ivan nodded. Jeffrey hadn't said much. He was being Mr. Silent again. Ivan read that and wondered what was on his mind.

He told Lucina, "All right, we'll see what we can do. We got plenty of time to plan something for that. And congratulations to you guys."

"Oh, thank you," Lachelle told him.

Finally, Jeffrey spoke up. He said, "Hey, Ivan, let me speak to you for a minute."

Jeffrey excused himself from his lady and Lucina as he and Ivan stepped away to speak in private.

Jeffrey said, "I like what you're doing with the website, man. That thing is really taking form. What are your plans for it?"

"I plan for it to keep growing," Ivan answered.

Jeffrey nodded. "You need any financial help with that? Any investor needs?"

Ivan looked at him and read his interest. With the internet boom all over America, his website must have looked plenty enticing.

He nodded and said, "I thank you for your interest." However, he was still not quick to give up any ownership of his baby. Jeffrey would definitely not ask to invest in it without wanting a piece. So Ivan figured he would test out his interest in something else.

He said, "To be honest with you, man, this internet and website game can take a while. But if you're looking for some heavy hitters to invest in soon, I may be heading in the real estate game. I got some inside tracks on development properties on the southeast side near Chula Vista. And I just bought a couple of foreclosure houses near San Diego State that we're remodeling to sell or rent right now. I'll let you check them out when we're finished in a couple of weeks."

Jeffrey's face lit up immediately. He said, "Oh, yeah? I've always been interested in real estate."

Ivan jumped on that quick and told him, "Hey, man, real estate is the oldest money game in the book. Forty acres and a mule, right? Black folks should still be looking for that. So at my accounting firm at Hutch and Mitchell, we always advise our clients to invest in the many values of property," Ivan hinted.

Barry Mitchell was working on a blog on that very subject that Ivan couldn't wait to post on the "Financial Corner" page.

Jeffrey said, "Yeah, I've still been meaning to call you up on that."

Ivan blew it off to appear less eager. "Well, like you said, during the season you're thinking about football. I understand. But football season is over with for a minute now. Now it's time to focus on the other parts of your life. And you can remind your teammates about that, too. They probably need it more than you do."

Jeffrey laughed and said, "Man, you already know that. You've been around them."

Ivan joked, "And I couldn't talk to them about a thing while they had the girls all around them. But maybe I can get through to them now."

"Good luck on that," Jeffrey told him. Then he stuck his hand out to Ivan's to shake. He said, "I'll definitely be calling you, Ivan. But let me get back to my lady before she starts to complain."

Ivan laughed back and said, "Yeah, you don't want that to happen. So just call me up, man, we'll talk. You need another business card?"

At first Jeffrey hesitated. Then he said, "Yeah, give me a couple of them."

Ivan pulled out his business cards and handed a few over.

When it was just him and Lucina again, she immediately asked her partner, "So, what did he want to talk to you about?"

"Business," Ivan told her.

"Did he mention any parties?"

Ivan looked at her, confused. Obviously she had had a different kind of discussion with Jeffrey. Ivan hadn't talked about a party with him at all. And since he didn't want to say the wrong thing at the wrong time, he figured that maybe the middle of a party was not the right place or time to talk about it.

He asked her, "Can we talk about it later?"

Lucina stared at him and didn't have a choice. They had other people to meet and talk to there. So she nodded and agreed. "Okay. We'll talk about it later."

Ivan continued going through the motions of meeting and greeting for the rest of the evening. When the clock had fallen on the other side of midnight, he was more than ready to pack it up and ship it in. Nevertheless, Lucina still wanted to talk to him about his business conversation with Jeffrey Morefield.

"You told me later, and now it's later," she reminded Ivan at the end of the party. They had collected another three thousand dollars just from showing up and bringing a crowd. But after Lucina had sent her girls home, she was not willing to let Ivan off the hook so easily.

Ivan told her, "When I said later, I meant like *tomorrow* or the next day. Because I'm tired right now, Lucina."

He realized she was used to having her way, but so was he.

"Well, do you need a ride home?" she asked him.

Ivan paused. He could use a ride. It was only up the street and around a few corners, but it beat having to walk.

"Yeah, that would be nice of you," he told her.

Ivan walked with Lucina to her parked car, and she drove him to his apartment building in near silence. But once they arrived, she parked in a no-parking area instead of dropping him off out front.

Ivan asked her, "What are you doing?"

She looked him in his eyes and said, "I'm coming up with you."

Ivan hesitated. *Okay, what does that mean?* he asked himself. He was tempted to ask her why. But he didn't. He was curious.

"Okay," he agreed with a nod.

"Welcome back, Ivan," the security guard greeted him on their way in. He nodded to Lucina and said, "And good evening."

Lucina only nodded at him with a weak smile.

Ivan asked him, "Your shift don't end at midnight?"

"Yeah, but the guy on the next shift is running a little late," he answered.

Ivan said, "Well, I'm sorry to hear that."

"Yeah, it happens."

Lucina walked inside with him, stepped into the elevator, rode it up to Ivan's floor, and still hadn't said much.

Ivan continued to think along the way. *Am I gonna find out what she's about now on the personal level? Is she just doing this out of the blue? Is this, like, her regular MO? I mean, what is on her mind right now?*

Once they stepped off the elevator, he finally asked her. "What's on your mind, Lucina? You've never been this quiet before."

She said, "I'll tell you inside," and kept him waiting.

Ivan opened his apartment door with his key, and Lucina walked right in to inspect the interior decorating job. Ivan watched her with patience, allowing her to see whatever she wanted around the room.

When she finished her walk-through, Lucina nodded and said, "He did a pretty good job."

"Well, you knew that already. Why else would you suggest the guy to me? Lucina Gallo selects nothing but the best, right?" Ivan asked her sarcastically.

His comments led Lucina right into her present thoughts on their partnership. She responded, "So, why am I allowing you to continue pulling me into doing these small, meaningless parties instead of us going after the much bigger money out there?"

Her unexpected bite caught Ivan off guard. His lighthearted smile turned into a fast frown.

So that's what she came over here to do, he realized. *She's ready to have another business tantrum with me, and at one o'clock in the morning to boot.*

Instead of adding fuel to Lucina's fire, Ivan calmed his nerves with a cool-water approach. He said, "We are just six thousand dollars away from a twenty-thousand-dollar-a-week goal. That means we can both clear forty thousand dollars *a month* without sweating the risk or all the extrahard work of these big parties. I mean, I got this idea from talking to you," he told her.

Lucina argued, "No, you did *not* get this small party idea from me. You came up with this *tedious* tactic *all* on your own, and now me and my girls have been attached to these small, *nothing* parties at least *five times* a week for *months,* without promoting *one* big party. Not even on New Year's Eve!"

She was *pissed*. But Ivan failed to see the problem. The parties were all easy, everyone was working regularly, and everyone was being paid. Ivan was even tempted to laugh out loud at her tantrum. It just didn't make any sense to him.

He said, "Lucina, if you need more than thirty, forty thousand easy dollars a month right now to satisfy you and your girls, then I have no idea what you're all spending it on. The Fashion Valley Mall? Because that's good money in *my* book. Maybe you need to hire me as your accountant, too," he quipped.

Lucina told him, "That may be good money for *you,* but my goal is to make *much more* than that. And now that football season is over, *half* of the money will be replaced by, what, *two more* small cow parties?"

She continued, "My girls and I have had *enough* of this. That is why I wanted you to meet with old friends and new investors tonight to move us closer to doing much bigger *concerts*. Now, what did Jeffrey talk to you about?" she asked him again.

As Ivan listened to her rant, the picture became clearer for him. Lucina and her girls had obviously been around a lot more hard cash than he had. Nevertheless, they had not learned how to *build* on it, so they had unrealistic ideas of how real wealth was accumulated.

Just to make sure his theory was right, Ivan asked his partner, "So, you asked Jeffrey and some of the other people in there to invest in another party with us?"

Lucina said, "Not just *a* party, Ivan, but *huge* parties. We need to get them excited about making *big* money," she told him.

Ivan looked away toward the window and shook his head. Lucina hadn't learned enough about how the rich liked to operate. As an accountant at a well-respected California firm, Ivan figured he knew a lot more on the subject.

He told her, "Lucina, those people are not thinking about investing in *parties*. And you can't get their money by *asking* them for it. I don't care what you explain to them. Rich people invest only in what they understand. So you have to talk to them in *their* language. And they really don't care about you telling them about it, they want to *see it*."

He said, "So the best way to attract investors is by continuing to make your own money first. You flip forty thousand a month into *eighty* thousand. You flip eighty thousand a month into one-*sixty*. You flip one-sixty into three-*twenty*. And you keep it going. Then, before you know it, they'll start calling *you* up. That's how it works. But you can't sit around *talking* to them about it," he explained to her. "You gotta show them the hard numbers.

"But we're just getting started here, Lucina. Give it some time."

She looked at him and snapped, "*You're* just getting started. I've been doing this for *years*. And I must be honest with you, Ivan. I am running out of *patience* with all of these *small* events, and I am losing my *passion* to continue doing this."

Ivan said, "Well, let your money work in some other avenues, then. I'm getting involved in real estate now. You could ride that horse with me. And what about my website? You told me you wanted to help bring in ad revenue for that. But you and your girls have sold, what, four or five party ads in three months? And I was giving you thirty-something percent on that."

Lucina responded, "I've noticed you spend *far* too much time concerned about your website now."

"I thought you said you *liked* my website," he argued. "Were you *lying* to me about it?"

"No, I *do* like it. But if you were to spend *half* the time preparing parties that you spend preparing your website, then we could make a lot more money together."

Ivan had to stop and think about that. His IDPromotions.com website was a long-run game, where the parties had made him much more money in the short run. Nevertheless, smart money people were long-run people. And they were asking more about his website than his party promotions. Even Jeffrey Morefield was more interested in the website. But Ivan decided not to rub that in his partner's face. He realized that Lucina was still a valuable asset to him. So he needed to manage some of her legitimate concerns.

He said, "All right, I got a guy now who can link us up with music performers and producers from Dr. Dre's camp in L.A. Now,

I haven't done any business with him yet, but if we can invite, like, Busta Rhymes, Eve, Xzibit, and people like that as our special guests for twenty-thousand-dollar budgets, and charge twenty-five dollars a head, plus VIP at the door, with a capacity of two thousand and up, we could make, what, thirty, forty thousand a night?"

He continued, "But we don't need any outside investors for that. And if you really wanna work your way up to the concert level like *you* say you do, then we're gonna have to learn how to create, manage, and finance the bigger parties for ourselves. So, again, I don't know what you spend your money on, but if you want me to move back into the bigger party game, then you have to be willing to put up your own ten or twelve thousand for half the risk."

Lucina calmed down and nodded, agreeing to it. She told him, "I also know A and R reps who could get us access to plenty of entertainers."

"That's good," Ivan told her. "But for right now, we just want to get their general appearance and promotional prices, and not that performance or concert shit. Because that's a whole 'nother ball game. You feel me?"

Lucina nodded. She was satisfied with where their conversation had ended.

"I feel you," she answered him.

Ivan joked on romantic instincts. "So, I guess you can spend the night and make up with me now, right?"

It all came out so smoothly Lucina was unable to feel offended. Instead, she smiled at him and asked, "Would you say that to me if I were a man?"

Ivan smiled back. "But you're *not a* man."

"Nevertheless, this is *business*," she told him, "and I like to *keep* it that way." She walked toward the door and said, "Good night, Ivan. I will call you tomorrow to begin making plans for the next level of parties."

When she walked out of the door and closed it behind her, Ivan took a breath and wondered about her. He nodded to himself and mumbled, "Yeah, she likes me. She just likes the money a little bit more right now."

And I can't complain about that, he mused. *I like this money right now, too.*

THE NEXT NIGHT, Ivan invited Christina over to his apartment before running out to another weekend event. Chris was not nearly as engaging as she usually was. She had a lot on her mind that Friday evening, and she would not allow Ivan to work in a quickie of sexual satisfaction.

"What's wrong?" he asked her.

Christina had settled in on the living room sofa and would not budge.

"I just don't feel like it tonight, Ivan," she told him.

Ivan waited to hear more. Christina was a woman of layers.

She said, "I'm thinking about going back to school."

Ivan looked at her and nodded. Higher education was on her mind.

He asked her, "How many years did you do?"

"Two."

"And you would go back to school to study what?"

"Business administration," she answered. She had thought about it in detail.

Ivan then wondered about Catherine Boone and how she was making out in her new job.

He asked Christina, "Were you studying business before, or you just decided you want to study it now?"

She faced him and said, "I just decided on it. I mean, I don't plan to be a hostess at parties for the rest of my life. What kind of life would that be?"

Ivan nodded again in silence. She had a point.

She said, "But I may need for you to sponsor me."

Ivan heard that comment and frowned. "Sponsor you? What do you mean?"

"I mean, help me to go, Ivan. Colleges cost money."

Ivan said, "You got money to go. You get paid every time you host. You're making a thousand dollars a week now, aren't you? Plus you work at the Thai restaurant during the daytime now."

She said, "Yeah, but that's just enough to pay for my living expenses. You know I don't share rent with Audrey anymore. She has her own place now."

Ivan did the math and said, "You're making more than four thousand dollars a month, and you're talking about me sponsoring you to go to college. What are you talking about? I had to pay my way through college with *half* of that."

She said, "Yeah, but I wouldn't be able to work that much once I start. I would have classes, homework, and other things to do full-time."

Ivan told her, "Yeah, that's what all full-time college students do."

He thought, *I'm not treating this girl like she's my child just because we've been intimate. What the hell is she thinking?*

Christina stood up from her spot on his sofa and told him, "You know what, I can make it happen on my own. I've been doing that all my life now anyway. I just wanted to *see* if you would support me to do something more, that's all. But now I know that you won't."

Ivan looked up at her and argued, "I support you as a *friend,* and I would help you out if you really needed it, but all this sponsorship talk . . . I mean, for what? You don't need me to sponsor you. You can *pay* for school."

"Okay. Bye, Ivan," she told him as she headed for the door.

"Oh, now I'm wrong?" he asked her. "I give you steady work and income, and now I'm the enemy because I won't pay for you to go back to school, too?"

"Whatever, Ivan. You can afford to do what you want. I'm just not a priority to you," she responded. "So, thanks for letting me know that."

When Christina walked out the door, Ivan stood up from the sofa himself and shook his head.

"Two nights of this in a row, hunh?" he stated. *I guess this is what I need to get used to now. I'm supposed to make everybody's dreams come true. Well, I haven't even achieved my own dreams yet.*

To add insult to injury, before he could walk out the door that night, his brother Derrick called him.

"I may need you to bail me out of a jam, li'l brother. What you got that you can spare for me?"

Ivan started chuckling to himself. *You gotta be kidding me,* he thought. He asked his brother, "Are you serious, man? I already got you on the payroll."

"Yeah, and it's all good for you to look out for me like that, but you already know most of that money is going into bills and my child support payments. It's not like I see much of that money. So I need to be able to *hold* something."

"Then find yourself a *job* to hold," Ivan told him.

Derrick cut to the chase and said, "Look, man, are you gonna help me out or what?"

Ivan told him, "I'm already helping you out."

"So that means no?"

There was a long pause over the line while Ivan thought it over. *If I help him, I may as well sponsor Christina for college, too. Then again, he's my brother. And that* is *a priority.*

But instead of him agreeing to anything too soon, he told his older brother, "I'll have to think about it."

taxes yet. I could probably save you another thirty thousand dollars or more."

Goddamn, this motherfucker's a shark! Thomas sat there and thought. He started laughing again. He said, "Ivan, you're *still* in here hustling. So, what you get, a new client commission over at Hutch and Mitchell, and now you're trying to bring everybody over there for taxes? I saw that 'Financial Corner' page on your website."

Ivan grinned. He answered, "Client commission is their whole model. I just wasn't using it. But now I use it with my own company. And you get all motivated people that way."

Thomas shook his head, grinning again. He had to stand up from his chair. He stuck his dark brown hand out across the desk and said, "Ivan, I'm on your team now. So, if you need me to sign up with Hutch and Mitchell, like I got you to sign up for the Urban League, then let's just do the paperwork tomorrow."

Ivan stood up and shook his hand on it. He said, "That's a good money deal."

When they both sat back down, Thomas said, "Now let me ask you a question, Ivan. What made you decide to just turn it on all of a sudden? I mean, I've been knowing you ever since I did that real estate lecture on campus, but you never seemed to be interested in anything. Now all of a sudden you just . . . *taking off*," he commented with a forward clap of his hands.

Ivan sat there and thought about it. He looked up and said, "I don't really talk about it much, but . . . when my mom passed away before last summer . . . she told me, man, 'Live your life now' . . . and you know, I had always felt guilty about not being back home with her while she struggled with cancer. But once she passed . . . it was like, '*What are you waiting for?*' You know?"

Thomas sat there and heard him out. He had nothing to say for a change.

Ivan shook it off and said, "So I just started seeing things that I wanted to do and that I wanted to be a part of. And I kept telling myself, 'You don't have no excuses now.' Not to say that my moth-

Ivan grinned and said, "Oh, yeah, I just . . ." He felt embarrassed and shook his head. "My bad, I was just working the sales figures."

"And the sales figures *always* include the commission," Thomas told him. "Unless you're gonna be out there selling these houses yourself. And you don't have the time for that. But I *do* thank you for giving me that ten percent. That's nice and generous of you."

Ivan told him, "It's all good, man. This is a good money deal. I thank you for putting me on to it."

Thomas responded, "This is just what the rich do, Ivan, buy low, sell high, all day long. Wait until you start getting involved in these development deals I told you about."

Ivan stopped and asked him, "So, if you know how easy these deals are, then how come you're not getting in on this for yourself?"

It was the million-dollar question.

Thomas looked at the young business hustler and chuckled again. He said, "You really wanna know the truth about that, Ivan?"

Ivan stared at him. "Yeah."

Thomas explained, "I couldn't afford the *risk* anymore. And most of the time, when I made any good money, it was already spent."

He continued, "I'm an older man now, Ivan. I got a family, kids in college, two mortgages, car notes, credit card debt, health bills, back taxes, all kinds of shit. And I'm not complaining about it. I still manage to live a good life. But if I could do it all again, knowing what I know now . . ." He shook his head and concluded, "Man, shit, I would *kill* to be in your position.

"You're young, single, vibrant, gainfully employed, with no kids, and you got *two* hustles bringing you in plenty of money. Shit, I'm ready to ride in this boat with *you*. Maybe I can get back on *my* grind now."

Ivan sat back and smiled, listening to an older man using a young man's language.

Ivan told him, "You still haven't let me help you out on your

Ivan told him, "Thank you," but he didn't get too excited about it. All he could think about was how much he had to pay for everything. Good business was not cheap.

IVAN HAD A LATE real estate meeting that same week at Thomas Jones's office.

Thomas said, "You did a damn good job putting together these first few houses, Ivan. I'm telling you, man, you should have gotten involved with me on this real estate game a long time ago."

"Not with no money," Ivan told him.

Thomas paused. He said, "Well . . . that's true," and laughed.

Ivan said, "Yeah, I'm a hundred and fifteen thousand dollars in the hole right now, and renting ain't gon' get my money back."

Ivan had spent sixty-five thousand to buy the three foreclosure properties, and another fifty thousand to paint and remodel them.

Thomas looked across his desk at how urgently his young business recruit had declared his position, and he began to chuckle.

He said, "Ivan, now you're about to learn how the rich *really* get rich. You just bought these houses at *half price,* then spent good money to make them better than what they were, and now we'll put them back on the market at three hundred and *eighty* thousand *apiece,* or a little more than the property value of the area. And realistically, you can accept anything from three hundred thousand *up* and still make a killing."

Ivan nodded. "Yeah, I know how it works. I've done the figures. So let's just go ahead and do it."

Thomas nodded back and said, "Well, welcome to the land of the rich. You're about to make yourself two hundred thirty thousand dollars and change."

Ivan frowned. He said, "I came up with two hundred *sixty-five thousand* and change."

"Minus my ten percent," Thomas reminded him. "We *did* agree on ten percent, right?" he asked to make certain.

Ivan smiled and said, "Exactly. We don't want any of that to happen. So, if anybody here has a bad memory, you need to check the website biography page once a day to remember what I look like. And Jeff and Paul have done a great job of making me look good there."

"I have a minor in airbrushing," Paul joked with his hand up.

"Well, you need to hook up my picture, too, then," Ava told him. "Make me look like Mary J. Blige's lost cousin."

Ivan grinned. He said, "Last but not least is the issue of security. If you notice, the front door is a heavy, self-closing and -locking door. And with all the valuable property on the premises, we don't want any of it deciding to get up and leave without us knowing. You catch my drift?"

"We got you," Ava responded. "So, unless all this stuff can just walk out on its own . . ."

Ivan nodded. "That also goes for damages. If anything no longer works or is broken, we need to know about it as soon as possible. And it doesn't matter who did it, as long as we know what needs to be fixed."

"Now, *that* should let a lot of us off the hook right there," Jeff joked again. "Fido did it!"

They all laughed.

Ivan said, "Well, as we can all see, we are definitely fun, hard-working, and smart people in here, so let's all keep our attitudes positive and optimistic about making IDPromotions.com one of the most talked-about and utilized websites in the San Diego area."

"Yeah!" the staff shouted, and clapped. "I.D. Promotions!"

Ivan hadn't expected all of that from them, but he was glad to hear it. Enthusiasm was a pleasant surprise.

Eddie K. pulled him aside when the evening staff address was over.

"That was very well done, Ivan," he commented. "*Very* well done."

computer industry. And although I can't assume that we all will remain with the company, with some of you guys still students here, I would love for all of us to be able to look back and consider this a start-up unit that we can all be proud of."

He said, "Now, only *five* of us are gonna have keys, and I want us all to raise our hands: Paul, Jeff, Eddie, Ivan, and Daphne." He explained, "Now, Jeff and Paul are always going to be around campus somewhere, doing homework, projects, reports, or whatever. But just like they did at their on-campus home, they will spend a lot of their time here now."

"Yeah," Jeff agreed eagerly.

"You bet. This is officially our new favorite place to be," Paul commented, adjusting his glasses.

Ivan said, "So, in the afternoons and evenings, you can always find one or both of them here to let you in. But Eddie, our ad sales manager, does a lot of outside meetings, so sometimes he's here, sometimes he's not. The sales staff will definitely need to lock in his number."

He said, "Now, Daphne, this lovely young woman to my left, who also works the doors at the parties we throw, will always be here to open up no later than nine in the morning. She seems to stay up late and still get up early, like I do," he commented. "She lives on campus and can be called for emergency or lockout situations. And me . . . don't ever call me for a lockout," he told them, "because it's not gonna happen."

They all laughed, but Ivan was serious. He told them, "I will only be here on a need-to-be basis. However, I will stop by on occasion to check in on everything and to bring potential clients over to see what we do. So if anyone doesn't know who I am when I walk into the room, somebody needs to inform them fast, because I don't want any embarrassing situations for us."

Jeff joked, "Ah, who are you again? How the hell did you get a key? You can't just walk up in here. This is a business."

IDPromotions.com the way he projected they should, he looked forward to pulling in nearly two hundred thousand in his second year.

Ava Tate, the editorial manager, was set up in the small middle room, right next to the second-floor bathroom. She was a black single mom, originally from Fort Worth, Texas, who had settled into San Diego as a freelance magazine writer. She was in her mid-thirties, divorced from a Navy officer, and looking for a more consistent position that allowed her to continue her passion as a freelance writer. Since she mainly used her laptop, she could write her blogs, edit copy, give assignments and suggestions, and email Jeff and Paul from any location to post her completed work on the site.

Although her position at IDPromotions.com only paid her five hundred dollars a week, Ava was able to create her own entertainment news page for the site, solicit freelance work, reprint her magazine and newspaper articles, and sell ads on commission. Along with the money she received from child-support payments for her two sons and daughter, Ava was perfectly fine with the economics of her new position.

She saw the placement of her editorial office and joked, "Perfect, I'm right next to the bathroom. Was that by design?"

Ivan chuckled. He said, "Not really, but if it works it works."

The downstairs area was just as Ivan had planned as well. He had an open cubicle area in the dining room, with several smaller desks, computer stations for laptops, a printer and copy machine, and several office phones. In the living room, he created a meet-and-greet lounge area, with a receptionist desk and a floor-model television set, surrounded by comfortable sofas, a coffee table, and plenty of magazines. Inside the kitchen area, he ordered a bench table, an easy-to-use microwave, a large refrigerator, and a few vending machines.

Ivan explained in his first full staff meeting of twelve, "IDPro motions.com is a great vehicle for us all to get our feet wet in the

Thirteen

Setting Up Shop

THE IDPROMOTIONS.COM HOME OFFICE, near San Diego State University's campus, was up and running by February 2004. Outside of the remodeling and painting budget, Ivan had spent an additional fifty thousand dollars in office furniture, website equipment, and supplies.

Jeff and Paul walked into their master bedroom office on the second floor of the house and were hyperventilating.

"Oh, shit, man, to see it happen is just . . . I mean . . ." Jeff ran out of words.

Paul finished them for him. "It's the shit."

"Yeah," Jeff agreed. "We're gonna graduate this year in *style.* Hey, Mom, look at my new office," he joked, aiming his small digital camera at himself behind his new desk.

Ivan watched him and laughed. He had set their twin desks on opposite sides of the room, facing each other. In between their desks were six small conference chairs arranged in an oval, two on each side and one at each end. Against the wall between two bay windows that looked out into the main street was a dual computer station with all of their needed equipment. And in all of the corners of the room were file cabinets.

Ivan told them, "Now, I know you guys like it all dark and cave-like, but you can both do that in here on your own."

Paul shook his head and said, "Hey, man, we're versatile. We don't need to be in the dark."

"Yeah, Paul never liked it so dark anyway. That was more my taste," Jeff commented.

Ivan smiled. He was happy his guys both liked the place. Jeff and Paul had already made close to twenty-five thousand dollars in their business with Ivan, and that was just the beginning of things. With Eddie K. on board as the advertising manager, and Ava Tate as their new editorial manager, Ivan projected a first-year income for Jeff and Paul in the eighty-to-hundred-thousand-dollar range.

"How's that for two crazy guys coming right out of college?" he joked to them.

They were now considered IDPromotions.com's creative executives, a fancier business title Eddie K. had given them to substitute for webmasters.

But when Eddie saw his ad office set up in the back bedroom, he was less thrilled about it.

"Oh, so I get the oldest kid's room in the back. The eccentric problem child on drugs?"

Ivan grinned and argued, "They need more room than you, Eddie. It's two of them and they have to deal with all of that computer shit."

Eddie laughed it off. "I'm just messing with you, Ivan. I understand. Those guys are the kings of the castle around here. And this place definitely creates a great atmosphere for what we're doing. It makes me feel like the leader of a college think tank."

"A think tank that makes money," Ivan told him.

Eddie had made fifteen thousand dollars in his start-up ad efforts online, but he looked to make more than a hundred and twenty thousand by the end of the year with the company, which was right in line with his salary in the newspaper industry before he left. However, if the website ad rates were able to increase at

Part V

Bigger Fish

er's cancer was an excuse, but . . . in a way, it was. It stopped me from really putting myself out there. It was like I was always holding something back. But now . . . it's like I can hear my mother in my ear. 'Do it, Ivan. Live how you wanna live.' So I just do it now, man. You know? Like you said, I feel like I got nothing to hold me back anymore."

Thomas heard all of that and was still speechless. He just nodded his head. He said, "Well . . . that's, ah . . . pretty powerful. A mother's love for her son is about the strongest love in the world. In fact, you make me want to call up *my* mother tonight and tell her that I love her for the hell of it."

He said, "But you keep on being brave, Ivan. That's what holds a whole lot of us back from making ourselves good money: a lack of courage. And a lot of folks just don't know any damn better. They're scared straight, thinking the earth is still flat and shit. Like their money's gon' fall off the edge of the world if they invest it in something."

WHEN IVAN ARRIVED back at his downtown apartment that night, Thomas's comments were still ringing in his ears. Being scared held you back from making good money.

Thomas had traveled west to California from his own roots in Greenville, South Carolina, to make himself some brave money thirty years ago.

But you gotta be smart, too, Ivan argued to himself. He figured his partner Lucina Gallo was smart. *But she still has to learn she's gonna have to be a little more patient.*

He mumbled, "It's all gonna happen in time."

Then he looked at the clock on his kitchen microwave and came up with an idea that would surely please her, another brave money deal.

It was only ten thirty, and one of the few nights when he didn't have anywhere to run out to. So he called Lucina up to chat.

"Hello, Ivan," she answered.

He said, "I got an idea," and walked toward his apartment balcony to look out at the San Diego skyline. It had become one of his favorite things to do.

"And what is that?" Lucina asked him.

He said, "First of all, we're gonna start doing those celebrity invitation parties. We can do two to three of those a month with different crowds and make up to fifty, sixty thousand."

Lucina said, "Ivan, we talked about that already. And I've already started making my contacts. So that's not a new idea."

Ivan said, "Well, I have a birthday coming up on March fifth. And I want to call up the Manchester Grand Hyatt to see what their ballroom capacity and rates would be for my own birthday party."

Lucina told him, "First of all, you can't call them only a month in advance and expect for them to have availability there. Second, the price will be high, including in-house catering."

Ivan said, "We're gonna make it all back. We can charge fifty dollars a head and make a hundred thousand."

Lucina asked him, "Are you crazy? Who are you going to invite for fifty dollars? That's a concert ticket."

Ivan told her, "All of the businesspeople who want to meet me and celebrate my birthday with me."

Lucina went silent for a minute. She was waiting for the punch line from him. But when he didn't give her one, she asked, "Are you serious?"

"I'm *dead* serious," Ivan told her. He said, "I just got a good feeling on this. You raise the price to make the real money people curious. And you said that *944* magazine wants to interview me now, right?"

She said, "Yeah, but—"

Ivan cut her off. "I'll pay for this whole party with my own money and still give you half of it. But I'll need you to really go after the money people hard and pitch this as a once-in-a-lifetime event: the introduction of Ivan David."

Lucina chuckled at him. She said, "Who is Ivan David?" sarcastically. Her partner was really beginning to smell himself that evening.

Ivan said, "Exactly. It worked for Jill Scott, right? We need to invite her out to an event one weekend, too."

"Ivan, what have you been *doing* tonight? Have you been smoking something?" Lucina finally questioned.

Ivan chuckled while overlooking the San Diego skyline from his balcony. He said, "I'm gonna forgive you for that when we make all this money. But I'm gonna create the *impulse* for the people to come out for it."

Lucina paused over the phone again. She didn't know what to say anymore. She needed time out to think it all over.

"Ivan, let me call you back in a few minutes," she responded.

"Take your time."

WHEN LUCINA HUNG UP her cell phone, she paced her living room in thought.

"What is he talking about?" she asked herself. *But he sounded like he was serious.*

She shook it off and said, "He *can't* be serious. *Fifty* dollars? Who does he think he *is* now?"

Then she called up her best girl, Maya.

"Hey, Maya, do you have a minute to talk?"

"Come on, girl. *Always*. Spit it out," Maya told her.

Lucina stopped and said, "That's nasty. I don't spit."

"You don't *shit,* either, do you? Come on, tell me what's on your mind."

Lucina shook her head against the cell phone and thought, *She's so raw. But she covers it so well in public. I never have to worry about her embarrassing me. But she does it in private all the time.*

"Anyways," she commented, breaking herself from her musings, "what are your honest thoughts about Ivan?"

"Ivan is a definite hottie. I would give him a *nine,*" Maya stated without hesitating.

Lucina said, "A *nine?* He's not a model."

"And I'm glad that he's not," Maya responded. "Male models are so . . . *iffy.* But Ivan is all man. He says what he wants to say, and he does what he wants to do."

Lucina told her, "He has a birthday coming up on the fifth of March. And he wants us to charge *fifty* dollars a head for it."

Maya paused and said, "Wow. That would make him a ten."

"Would you stop with the numbers already? Who would pay *fifty* dollars to see him?" she snapped.

Maya said, "Well, that's more like a *ticket* price. Is he going to be selling tickets from his website?"

Lucina answered, "I don't know. I just told him I would call him back. I didn't think he was serious."

"Well, is he?"

"I'm still not sure. That's why I called you. But he wants to do it at the Manchester Grand Hyatt."

Maya said, "Oh, now, that would be nice. No wonder he wants to charge fifty dollars. Is this a dressed-to-impress affair?"

"It would *have* to be," Lucina assumed. "He says he wants top-money businesspeople."

"Yeah, and that's who he would get for fifty dollars. But how many people does he expect to attend, five hundred?"

"Five *hundred?*" Lucina repeated. "He said he wants to make a *hundred* thousand dollars. That means at least *two thousand* people. And he wants to rent out the main ballroom there."

"Wow," Maya responded again. "That would really take him off the charts."

"Yes, yes, but can he actually *do it,* that's what *I* want to know."

"I know I'll be there to *see it,* that's for sure," Maya told her.

"So, a fifty-dollar party makes you want to see it?"

Maya explained, "You can't look at it just as a fifty-dollar party.

You have to promote it as if Ivan David is *royalty* or something. And when people start to ask for tickets, then you tell them it's fifty dollars. That's when you separate the money people from the people who don't have money."

"But *two thousand* people paying that price?" Lucina repeated to her friend.

"It depends on how well you promote it," Maya countered. "We've been around parties like that before. The price starts at twenty-five. Then it goes up to forty. Then they drink for fifty, sixty, and *seventy* dollars."

Maya asked her, "Is Ivan having liquor sponsors there? At that price, and for that crowd, they may be really interested."

Lucina stopped talking. She didn't know all of those details yet. But it seemed as if her girl believed the idea could work.

Lucina told her, "Let me call him back and ask him all of those questions."

"Okay. And let me know what he says."

Lucina hung up without responding. Then she paced her room again.

"Hmmph," she grunted. "I don't believe this."

WHEN IVAN'S CELL PHONE rang at his apartment, he had already made his way into his bedroom office to start jotting down all of his ideas: "Who is Ivan David? What is an I.D. Promotion? Where is the big party?" Then he wrote down a list of people to invite: advertisers, liquor sponsors, corporations, Chargers, Padres, military personnel, promoter affiliates, all of Lucina's girls, the Urban League members. He followed this with a list of things to arrange for: radio promotion, ticket access, gift bags, magazine articles, newspaper articles, website promotion, flyers . . .

Ivan looked up when his phone rang and smiled. *She's calling me back already,* he thought. It had only been ten minutes.

He answered the phone and asked Lucina, "So, what do you think about my party idea now?" He was still grinning. He figured she had thought about it more.

"How do you plan to make it all work?" she asked him. "If I know *you,* you have your own ideas already. So I will tell you which plans will work and which plans will not."

Ivan said, "First we have to use tickets, and we can give some away with a big radio promotion. And I definitely want to get the liquor sponsors involved with this one. Of course, I'll hit up our friends at the Chargers and Padres to come out. I'll get all of the Urban League members to come. I'm going to do that *944* magazine article. Eddie K. will link me up with his editorial contacts at the *San Diego Union Tribune* for an arts and lifestyle article. We'll also hit up the smaller papers in town. Then we'll give away gift bags to the first five hundred people at the party. And I'll tap into all of my website advertisers to convince them to contribute as sponsors or add something of value to the gift bags. Then we hit up all of our promoter friends to join us in the fun. They all owe us now, right?"

Lucina heard him out and responded, "You make it all sound too simple. And you can do all of those things, Ivan, but what are you really giving to the customer for their fifty dollars?"

Ivan explained, "Lucina, the one thing Americans love more than anything is a success story. That's why we have so many of these reality shows popping up nowadays. Americans love to see new faces in the limelight. So we're gonna give them one. 'The Ivan David story.' "

"You haven't done anything yet," Lucina told him. *The audacity of this man!*

"Nor have these reality show people," Ivan argued.

"Ivan, they're on national television. We get to watch them make *fools* of themselves for *free*. They're not asking us for *fifty* dollars to come to a party."

Ivan said, "When they come off them shows they do. They get

all the money they can get. And we may *think* we're watching them for free, but the advertisers and networks have already paid for it."

He continued, "Those shows had to be *pitched* and *bought,* just like I'm about to do. So I got a *month* to show my ass off now. And after we do this big birthday party, we'll just keep doing bigger and better events to get this money you want. But you also need to invest in real estate with me," he told her. "Because I'm definitely thinking about getting into the property development game. I got a feeling about that."

Lucina told him, "You can't do business off a *feeling* alone, Ivan. You have to *know* what you're getting into."

"You jumped into business with *me* off a feeling," he reminded her. "And all I've done so far is help make you new money."

Lucina hesitated. She said, "I was desperate. And desperate people make *bad* decisions all the time."

Instead of feeling slighted by her sarcasm, Ivan flipped it with a grin. He said, "Well, I'm the best *desperate, bad* decision you've ever made in your life."

WHEN LUCINA HUNG UP with Ivan for the second time that evening, she couldn't stop herself from smiling. *Business only, Lucina,* she had to remind herself. She had led herself into a fit over Ivan before and had to refocus her energies on business. Now she felt it happening again.

She nodded her head in her living room, pacing and thinking as usual. She mumbled, "Very interesting person. He continues to make me smile."

And he's smart, she told herself.

Then she decided to call her girl back.

"So, what did he say? Is he serious?" Maya asked her. She sounded really excited. That made Lucina smile more.

She answered, "Evidently he is. And he has all the ideas that you discussed. He wants to make this party really big. And he wants to send out a big message to San Diego."

Maya said, "I *knew* it. Ivan has it in him. He's the kind of man who wants it all."

Lucina fell silent for a spell. Then she asked her girl, "So how close should I be with him?"

Maya toned down all of her excitement. She said, "Well, we've kind of been through this all before, only *you* were the one to tell *me* to slow down. So this time I'll repay the favor."

Maya warned, "I would see how Ivan treats other women before I get too close to him. You know what I mean? So far he seems to be more about business, but these guys *do* change."

Lucina listened and agreed with Maya's assessment.

"I know. I just needed someone else to confirm it."

IVAN FOUND the main ballroom at the Manchester Grand Hyatt had an open date on the second Saturday of March for nearly half the rental fee Lucina had expected. So he secured the date immediately and went into hyperdrive with all of his staff, friends, partners, and new business associates to begin preparing for his big, breakout event.

All of the website advertisers and sponsors were solicited for sponsorship and gift bag contributions. The liquor sponsors were contacted. The radio station ad spots were bought. The catering menu was set. Security teams were secured. A liquor license was applied for, with a bar staff to be hired. All of Lucina's girls were alerted to spread the word to their contacts in and around the San Diego area. Event tickets were created and set for a sale date, three weeks before the big event online, at selected ticket outlets, and from IDPromotions.com.

On the website, Paul and Jeff set pop-up banners on every page to ask their viewers the questions: "Who Is Ivan David?" "What is an I.D. Promotion?," and "Where is the big party?"—all to be answered through the upcoming interviews Ivan had set up with the print media.

In the meantime, Julio had solidified his Aftermath Entertainment connection in L.A. So Ivan told Lucina they would do two celebrity events as preludes to his birthday party.

"Who do you have lined up?" she asked him over the phone.

Ivan spoke to her while admiring the view from his balcony again. "Eve and Busta Rhymes are both willing to come down," he answered. "You know they both work with Dr. Dre now. Then we can go after Xzibit later. He's real popular with that *Pimp My Ride* show on MTV now. Maybe we can do an afternoon car show with an after-party tie-in and get some of the car magazines, local dealerships, and automakers involved.

Lucina told him, "I have Nelly Furtado and Timbaland. They are supposed to be working on new projects together."

"Okay, so we do an event with them after Eve and Busta."

Lucina paused. She said, "You're spreading yourself too thin before your big party."

Ivan brushed it off. "Naw, what I want to do is make sure we take plenty of pictures with them and get my staff writers to interview them for the website. Then I'll just talk about it all. That'll only make my birthday party stronger. We'll make these other events part of the hype."

Lucina warned him, "I'm just trying to make sure you don't take all of the customers' money before asking them for fifty dollars next month."

Ivan shook it off again. "We're expecting different crowds," he argued. "Now I know how to separate them all. And once they finish this new Padres baseball field downtown, you can get thirty, forty thousand in the Gaslamp Quarter *easy.* All we want to do is find our small percentage of that."

She listened to him and gave in. "Okay."

Ivan had made up his mind.

* * *

IVAN HAD LEARNED the party game quickly. But he wasn't too quick to brag about it to the press. He wanted to sound as humble about the process as possible. He understood that the rich would be more attracted to humility. So he focused his comments to appeal to the established and the upwardly mobile who were already used to making money.

"I just try to make sure I do my part to make San Diego a more interesting place to live, love, and party in," he told the reporter at *944,* the San Diego regional magazine.

When asked what made him a unique promoter, Ivan responded, "Sometimes you can't answer that question, you just do what you do. That's for others to figure out. I just happen to have a lot of people who like me and like doing business with me."

After being pressed to explain his character, Ivan answered, "If I had to nail it down, I would just say that I always try to be fair to people and pay them what I owe them."

Accepting Lucina's advice to use his certain look to cross over, Ivan finally broke down and had his left ear pierced before he bought one of the most colorful diamond studs that he could find to match his eyes. The idea was to allow his good looks and humility to create a following on their own without him trying too hard to sway people.

"The real sex symbols are the guys who never talk about their looks," Lucina commented.

Ivan still wasn't sure about the earring in business, and definitely not the sex symbol thing, but he did realize he needed to sell himself to the fullest for his plans of attraction to work. The catch for the *944* magazine article was getting the cover story.

Lucina told him, "You let me handle that."

In the *San Diego Union Tribune,* Ivan wanted to express more of his human side. He knew that more people would read it who were not business related or steady participants of the nightlife.

So in the interview, set up by Eddie K., Ivan told the reporter,

"I'm just a kid who had a dream to try and create events for people to have a good time around me."

In the *Tribune* article, the reporter did research on Ivan's background as an African-American out of South Central Los Angeles. When Ivan was asked about growing up there, he was quick enough to put a spin on that as well.

He said, "The city of Los Angeles has a lot of different cultures and economic classes, and I've always been one to blend in well with everyone. That's why I love living here in San Diego. The city's diversity gives you an opportunity to enjoy and learn from a lot of different people."

Asked what his ultimate goal would be in the San Diego area, Ivan answered, "I would love to just be that guy who you can count on to bring everyone together."

Ivan did a third interview for the *San Diego News Link.* In none of the conversations did he push his website, promote his birthday party, or talk about making money. Eddie K. had helped put together a strong press release with bullet points that did all of those things for him, and without Ivan needing to toot his own horn, including his employment at Hutch & Mitchell Accounting. Each publication had the information handy to plug right in, including the list of sponsors who supported his IDPromotions.com website, and his upcoming birthday party at the Manchester Grand Hyatt, which spoke volumes all by itself.

When Ivan had completed all three interviews, with radio spots and flyers still to come, closer to the week of his big event, he told himself, "The setup is all done. Now it's time to work my plans to perfection."

Fourteen

Celebrity Status

IVAN CONTACTED the West Coast Travel Agency, a contributing advertiser on his website, to secure the best flight rates for round-trip tickets and hotel rooms for the celebrities he planned to bring into the San Diego area, starting with Eve, the rapper, fashion designer, and movie star. Busta Rhymes, another multiple-career entertainer, made plans to drive down from L.A. on that same weekend in late February.

Ivan and Lucina secured the location, travel, and hotel plans, and got back to their promotion to make it work. Only now, Ivan figured he had a lot more showing off to do to live up to the hype of the articles about him that would hit the public soon.

"I gotta upgrade my wardrobe and show up in style now," he told himself.

Lucina advised him to let her girls select his new clothes.

Ivan joked, "Naw, I'm not trying to spend a million dollars on a wardrobe. Your girls all got expensive tastes."

"Ivan, you simply take them with you wherever you go to shop, and they will pick out the things that they like for you."

Reluctantly, Ivan went along with the program and ended up having pretty girls of all nationalities surrounding him after work.

"This looks good on you, Ivan."

"Ivan, you just *have* to have this shirt."

"Oh, those shoes are just *you*."

"This sports jacket really sets off your eyes."

"I just *love* this color on you."

But as Ivan had already guessed, their personal tastes elevated the costs quickly.

"What about a Rolex watch for your wrist?"

"And a diamond-studded bracelet for the other one?"

"Ivan, you really need to upgrade your *car* more than anything."

He asked them, "Why? I'm not even in a car most of the time." *Especially since moving downtown,* he added to himself.

"Yeah, but when you are, and you step out of a hot car in your new shoes and clothes, it will really make a statement."

"And everything you do needs to make a statement now," the girls told him.

They all sounded like mini-Lucinas without the accent. Nevertheless, in the public imagery game, the sights and scenes of a superstar traveled a long way. So Ivan bought nearly half of the items Lucina's girls advised him on, including a gold, silver, black, and blue Rolex watch with small diamonds that replaced the numbers. However, he held off on the expensive bracelet and car. He figured the noticeable bling on one wrist was enough. And he could always utilize the limos he would rent for his celebrity guests instead of using his own vehicle.

I'll just have the limo driver pick me up first and take me wherever I need to go, he reasoned. *Especially if I'm paying for it by the hour.*

Lucina had her own deals with the limo companies. So on their first celebrity-attended event, she and Ivan picked up Eve and two of her girlfriends at the Imperial Hotel in a black stretch limo, dressed to impress and ready to show off. Ivan wore his party uniform, a classic sports jacket, and Lucina wore hers, a one-of-a-kind designer dress.

"Hi, Ivan," Eve greeted him with an open smile as soon as he stepped out of the limo. She wore a tasteful skirt, heels, and a short jacket with her long, frosted blond hair.

Ivan didn't know whether to hug her or shake her hand. He went for the handshake to be safe.

"How are you doing?" he asked her.

She said, "I'm good. I'm just looking forward to hanging out with you guys in San Diego. I really like what you got going on in the Gaslamp."

"Okay, that's good," he commented. "We're trying to do it up. But let me introduce you to my partner."

Ivan helped Lucina out of the limo.

Eve nodded to her and said, "Hey, how are you doing?"

"Oh, I'm good," Lucina responded. "I'm Lucina Gallo." Instead of shaking hands, she held Eve by the arms and gently kissed her on her right cheek.

That's a hell of a lot smoother than me, Ivan thought, grinning to himself. *Girls can get away with that kissing shit a lot easier.*

Eve looked over Lucina's dress and commented, "That is *real* nice. Where'd you find it?"

Lucina told her, "My design secrets will *cost* you. We'll talk about that later."

Eve grinned and nodded. "Okay." She introduced her two girlfriends before they all climbed inside the limo. The driver closed the door behind them.

"So, Ivan, you're from L.A., right?" Eve asked him. She sat directly across from him.

He nodded. "Yeah, South Central." He didn't need to concern himself with putting a spin on his background for Eve. She was from the hip-hop culture, which respected urban roots.

Ivan asked her, "What's Philly like?"

"Man, Philly is hectic, but I love it," she told him. "So, every once in a while, when I need to feel, you know, that realness of my people, I take a trip back home."

"*Or* she can just bring her people out west to chill out here with her," one of her girlfriends commented.

Lucina nodded. "It's always good to have your friends around you to make you feel at home."

Eve asked, "Where are you from, Lucina? Gallo's an Italian name, right?"

"Yes, but I'm from Brazil. Brazil has a lot of Italians."

"Yeah, that's the land of the hot models now," Eve's second girlfriend commented with a nod. They were both as mellow as Eve was.

Eve said, "You know I have a new fashion line I'm working on, called Fetish. Would you be interested in modeling for us?"

"Yeah, girlfriend definitely got the look," both of Eve's girls agreed.

Ivan looked at Lucina to see how she would take it. But his partner quickly blew the attention off.

"Oh, no, no more modeling for me. I have plenty of girls you will like for that at the party. You just let me know which ones you like."

When they reached the Gaslamp Quarter, Ivan told the limo driver to head straight through Fifth Avenue for the weekend sights.

Eve said, "This reminds me of South Street a little bit back home."

"Oh, this is *way* more ritzy than South Street, girl," one of her friends commented.

"Dig it," the other friend agreed. "South Street is *way* longer than this, though. And you're always stuck in traffic there."

Eve said, "Well, you know what I mean, just one straight street with a lot of nighttime stores on it."

Lucina said, "This is nothing compared to the streets in Italy, Paris, Amsterdam, and Japan."

"Oh, yeah, I fell in love with a lot of those places," Eve commented. "I love to travel."

"International travel gives you a lot of places to fall in love with," Lucina agreed.

Ivan had nothing to add on the subject. He was out of his information range. He hadn't traveled much at all.

He smiled and said, "I'll be able to travel like that sometime next year."

"Oh, we *will*," Lucina promised him.

Eve's girls looked at each other and wondered if they were a business couple and a private couple. Ivan and Lucina looked like a perfect match. Even their outfits were complements of each other. But Eve and her crew held their comments to themselves.

When they rounded the corner of Sixth Avenue and headed back to the downtown club, a long crowded line had gathered outside on the sidewalk.

Now, this is what I am used to seeing, Lucina told herself.

It was no big deal to Eve. She had been used to seeing large crowds for years.

Ivan asked her, "You don't mind if we take pictures for the website, do you? We'll make sure that they all look good."

Eve grinned. She said, "I've seen the website. I already know you use good pictures. I'm fine with it."

Ivan told her, "That's good. My photographer's ready to set it all up as soon as we arrive."

When they pulled up to the curb, Ivan's photographer was eager, waiting, and ready with his ideas. He popped his head inside the limo with his camera in hand and started directing.

"Okay, we need Eve to sit in the middle, with Ivan and Lucina on both sides."

They rearranged their seating inside the limo to accommodate the photographer before he snapped several pictures of them.

"Okay, now I need to get pictures of you guys climbing out."

One by one, they climbed out of the limo while the photographer took several shots of it all. Then he took shots of them posing out on the sidewalk in front of the limo. That's when the line took notice and got to talking excitedly among themselves.

"That's her, right there. It's Eve."

"She's taller than I expected."

"Yeah, she has heels on."

"Yo, she's sexy as hell."

"Is that her real hair color?"

"No, you know that's all dyed."

"I wonder if she's just gonna stand over in the VIP section all night."

"When is Busta Rhymes supposed to get here?"

"That's Lucina Gallo with her, isn't it?"

"Yeah, and, um . . . Ivan David."

"Oh, he's the one who runs I.D. Promotions?"

"Duuhh. I.D. Promotions, like in *I-van Da-vid.*"

"Shut up!"

When they finished taking pictures outside the club and headed toward the entrance with security surrounding them, one of the guards stopped Ivan and stuck his hand out. "I had no idea who you were a while ago. But I've been watching you grow. You keep it going, man."

Ivan shook his hand. It was the same security guard who had teased him about his double first name nearly a year ago, outside the Padres party.

Ivan told him, "It's no big deal. I don't sweat it. That was the first night I decided to get involved. And it's been a lot of late nights and hard work since then."

"Well, you're making it all happen for yourself now, Ivan. So you just keep it up."

"Oh, I plan to," Ivan told him as he walked inside.

Daphne and Maya were inside the door with the cash boxes, email lists, and more security behind them.

"Looking good, Ivan," Maya told him, admiring his total package that evening.

He smiled and asked them, "Are we near capacity yet?" It was close to midnight, and Ivan was thinking all business.

Daphne looked down at her hand counter. "Mmm, it's about sixty, seventy percent full now."

"What about the VIP?"

"Oh, that's less than half."

Ivan nodded and said, "All right, keep announcing the VIPs cut line for forty dollars. Busta and his crew should be here soon so we can pack it all in."

Maya and Daphne both nodded to him. "Okay."

They opened the door at twenty-five dollars that night, with a capacity of nearly two thousand in the club, two hundred of which included the VIP section. Ivan and Lucina had to pay a ten-thousand-dollar bar guarantee for taking over the club's Saturday night, but they looked to cover that and break fifty thousand from the door.

As soon as Ivan walked into the party, Red Face Lion spun the popular Eve and Gwen Stefani song "Let Me Blow Ya Mind."

The crowd grew frantic with Eve's arrival and danced hard to her song, while singing along with the lyrics.

Ivan watched them and grinned, before walking into Julio.

"Hey, Ivan, man, I told you we could do it!" he yelled, with a beer in his right hand. He wore a yellow VIP wristband. He said, "You just tell me who you want me to get, and I'll ask my cousin to try and get them down here for you."

Before Ivan could respond, one of Lucina's girls commented on her way past him, "Hey, Ivan, you look great tonight. That diamond stud is really shining."

"Yeah, thanks to you guys," Ivan stated.

Julio looked at him and held up an OK sign with his free hand.

He said, "Man, the women in here are *gorgeous*. You got my two lined up yet?"

Ivan looked at him and asked, "They haven't been treating you well in VIP?"

"Oh, yeah, but I want my two to stay with me."

Ivan knew he couldn't allocate any of Lucina's girls to babysit Julio all night with Busta Rhymes and his crew on their way. So he told him instead, "Here's what I'll do. You point out any two girls you like who are not working the club with us, and I'll give you two more VIP wristbands to invite them over with you. But it's up to you to make them want to stay there."

Julio had plenty of drink money to afford company that night. So he nodded and looked around. "Any two?"

"As long as they're not working," Ivan repeated to him. "Just come get me for those wristbands when you find them. But I have to get over here with my guests."

"Oh, go do it, man," Julio told him. "And I'll do me."

As Ivan headed toward the VIP section to join Eve and Lucina, he could feel the eyes of the room glued to his back.

"That's Ivan David?" the crowd whispered as he passed by. And it felt good.

A couple of attractive white girls grabbed him before he could reach his destination.

"Can we take a picture with you, Ivan?"

He looked them over and was pleasantly surprised.

He joked, "You know who I am?"

"Yeah, we love your website. We were only wondering if you were as hot in person as you are on your pictures."

"Yeah, and now we know you are."

Ivan laughed it off. "All right, well, let's hurry up with it. Eve is waiting for me."

"Oh, okay. Excuse me, can you take this picture for us?" they asked another girl dancing beside them.

When the girl took the picture with their small digital camera, other girls in the crowd looked on in curiosity.

"Isn't that Ivan David?" someone else asked.

"Oh, yeah, it is."

"Can I get a picture with you, too?"

The next thing Ivan knew, he was crowded by picture requests.

He finally backed off and said, "All right, all right, I gotta get back to what I'm doing here."

"Please, Ivan, just one more picture. I wanna put it up on my MySpace page."

EVE AND LUCINA watched the public struggle Ivan had found himself in from where they stood in the VIP section.

Eve chuckled. She said, "The girls give Ivan their full attention here, hunh?"

Lucina looked on and grunted, "Hmmph." *Not yet,* she told herself. *But wait until after his articles come out for his big birthday party.*

She told Eve, "I just hope he doesn't grow a bigger head than the one he already has."

Eve laughed and said, "Tell me about it. That's how they all get. But it's hard to stop it when the girls act so crazy sometimes."

Lucina agreed with her. "Yeah, they do."

By the time Ivan had made it back over to them, the word had passed through the crowd that Busta Rhymes and his crew had arrived. The crowd grew insane with energy.

Ivan told Lucina, "Shit, we need to go get these pictures." He had just made his way through the party.

Lucina hesitated. She didn't particularly feel like running around all night just to take pictures for his website. So she told him, "You go. I'll just take pictures with him in here with Eve."

Ivan quickly grabbed one of the bottles of champagne from their liquor sponsors and headed back toward the front door.

BUSTA RHYMES and several members of his Flipmode Squad stepped out of exotic luxury cars to congregate on the sidewalk. The security team immediately guarded them.

"What's up, dude?" Busta addressed them. "Is my man Ivan David up in the house tonight?"

Busta stood out from his crew, wearing a black leather biking jacket with tattoo designs all over it.

Ivan's photographer told him, "He's on his way out right now. We want to take some pictures of you guys out here before you all go in."

Busta looked around at the honeys in the line and said, "Aw'ight, dude, but I see some pictures I wanna take right now. How many of y'all wanna take some pictures?" he asked the young women waiting in line.

The security team had to prepare themselves as several desperate girls ran over from the line in Busta's direction.

"Oh, my God! I want a picture!"

"Hold up! I look good enough!"

"Busta, you're just who I came here to see tonight!"

"All right, well, let's get these pictures, then," he told them.

Busta's entourage was just as prepared as the security team to pick out which girls and how many would take pictures with him.

Ivan walked out of the club in the middle of the commotion, holding the champagne bottle in hand.

"Hey, hey, hey, keep your cool, ladies," he told them.

Nearly fifteen girls were surrounding Busta and his guys on the sidewalk, while the security team tried to keep order.

"Ivan David. What's up, dude?"

Busta recognized him and stepped up to stick his hand out for a shake. Ivan made his way through the chaos Busta had caused on the sidewalk in front of the club and shook the man's hand.

"Sorry, it took me a minute to get out here, man. I had to fight through the crowd."

"Oh, that's a *good* thing," Busta told him. "And I can already see you got the women and the bubbly up in here."

Four of Lucina's girls had followed Ivan out to help escort them all back in.

Ivan bragged, "Yeah, we got plenty of that."

The photographer jumped right in to get the pictures. "Can I get you two guys shaking hands again?" Busta and Ivan posed for the picture. "Now can I get you standing out in front of the cars with some of your guys around?"

The crew seemed to move a little too slowly.

Busta told them, "Come on, y'all, this is for the website. We gotta make sure everybody knows that we were here. Let's just get it and get on up in the party."

Finally, some of the guys surrounded Busta and Ivan, with a Rolls-Royce Phantom, a Bentley, and a Maybach Benz parked against the curb in the background. Ivan chose to stand in front of the Rolls-Royce Phantom.

He looked over at the cars and said, "Y'all rolled up in style."

The parking spaces had been reserved for them.

"Come on, dude, you know how we do it. It's rock star status over here."

Finally, Busta posed for a few snapshots with the anxious female fans he had left standing by.

"Come on, Ivan, get up in here," Busta commanded. He spoke to Ivan as if he had known him for years already.

Ivan walked into the picture and posed for a few photos with Busta and his eager female fans. Then they headed inside the club.

The security cleared a pathway for them to enter, led by Lucina's girls.

Ivan stopped by the front door with Maya and Daphne on his way in. He said, "All right, forty dollars to get in, or they go home. So let the security know. Either they're coming in for forty or we're closing the doors."

Maya and Daphne looked at each other and said, "Okay." The boss had spoken.

Once Busta and his crew walked in, Red Face Lion immediately began spinning classic Busta Rhymes songs.

The crowd sang along with them line for line: *"If you really wanna party with me / . . . Put all your hands where my eyes can see . . .*"

Busta Rhymes walked through the crowd, bobbing and weaving to his music on his way to the VIP section. The crowd was ecstatic at his presence.

"BUSTA, WE LOVE YOUUU!" a group of three girls screamed out at the top of their lungs.

"And I love you right back!" Busta shouted in their direction.

The security guards and Busta's crew had to push women back in order for them to walk.

Yeah, this is crazy, Ivan mused, following behind them. *The Chargers football players definitely created a crowd, but they never caused this much delirium.*

Eve and Lucina watched it all from the VIP section.

Eve turned to Lucina and said, "You see what I mean? That's all day, every day."

Lucina was used to handling the athletes and their groupies, the movie stars and theirs, the rock stars and theirs, but hip-hop music seemed to create the most powerful energy. It was the pulsations of the music that made you move *right now!* Especially Busta Rhymes's music. The extrathumping kicks, bass lines, and verbal chants drove the crowd into a frenzy.

"Hey, Ivan," a few of the girls called out. They were able to grab on to him because he had no security protection. Ivan didn't figure he needed any.

"Hey, calm down," he told them.

"Are you gonna bring someone to San Diego every weekend? We hear you got Timbaland and Nelly Furtado next week," they asked. They had done their homework.

Ivan told them, "Yeah, so just stay tuned for the next one," as he moved on.

The guys were giving him an extra nod of attention as well.

"What's up, Ivan? Keep doing you, man."

"Thanks," Ivan responded with a nod.

"Hey, nice party you got here, Ivan."

"I'm just trying to work it," he commented.

Other guys looked on and nodded to him.

When Ivan made it over to VIP, he noticed a few of the Chargers making small talk.

"Hey, Perry, I didn't see you in here, man. And how could I miss you, right?"

Perry Downing was a heck of a human specimen to miss, over six foot five and two hundred eighty pounds.

He said, "Naw, you were doing your thing in here, man. I figured you'd see me sooner or later."

"Well, come jump in this picture with us," Ivan told him, leading Perry over to Lucina, Busta, and Eve, who were all chatting it up in the crowd of VIPs.

"Okay, let's all get these pictures for the website," Ivan told them.

The photographer was right there to begin snapping pictures in front of the bar.

Busta faced Ivan and said, "Yo, you know how to party, dude." Then he pointed to Lucina behind her back and gave Ivan the OK finger signal.

"That's a good partner, too," he commented.

Ivan smiled it off, while Lucina's girls flooded the section for all sorts of celebrity catering.

Ivan heard one of Busta's squad members comment, "I feel like I'm in another one of them videos, with so many bad women around me up in here."

"Who you fuckin' tellin'?" his partner responded with a giggle.

Ivan grinned himself, wondering how many girls would get out of there that night without being hit on a bunch of times.

I hope these girls are all ready for this, he told himself. *But Lucina probably has that all handled already . . . I hope!*

Julio approached Ivan and told him, "Hey, man, I found two girls I like. You got those wristbands for me?"

Ivan smiled, dug into his sports jacket, and handed over two yellow wristbands.

"Don't do anything that's going to embarrass your wife and family, man," he warned his old neighbor.

"Aw, naw, man, this is business. And have your photographer take a few pictures of me with all you guys so I can show my cousin for more parties."

"Good idea," Ivan told him. They gathered everyone together and took more pictures before Julio dashed off to retrieve the two girls he wanted to invite into VIP as his special guests.

"You need anything, Ivan?" another assistant asked. It was the same Filipina from Zee-Dog's birthday party in October. She had interrupted Ivan while he'd been speaking to Catherine.

Ivan noticed her and asked, "What is your name again?"

"Ashley."

"Yeah, I haven't seen you in a while, Ashley. Where have you been?"

Ivan didn't remember getting her name before, and he hadn't seen her around in a while. She still looked good, though. And when he studied her glittery, form-fitting dress, he couldn't find any bra straps or panty lines.

Either she's not wearing anything under that dress, or she just hooked it up real good, Ivan told himself. *Either way, she got my attention tonight.*

Ashley looked surprised by his inquiry. "You remember me?"

He said, "Yeah, I remember you. I thought you were one of the best-looking girls at the football party."

She smiled and said, "Thank you."

Ivan told her, "Well, I don't need anything right now, but I'll let you know later, if that's all right with you."

She nodded. "Yeah, that's okay. Just let me know."

Ivan studied her eyes for a minute. She was focused on him, regardless of all the activity going on around them inside the room. And she refused to move until he told her to.

Ivan was curious about that. He asked her out of the blue, "Is your boyfriend up in here somewhere?"

Ashley smiled again. "No, I don't have a boyfriend."

Ivan told her, "Well, we need to talk about that later on."

"Only if you promise," she told him.

Ivan wasn't expecting that. That told him everything he wanted to know.

He nodded and said, "You make sure I give you my private number before you leave here tonight. You hear me?"

She nodded back to him. "Okay."

"All right, well, let me get back to things," he told her.

She held up a hand and said, "Later," as she faded away.

Ivan watched her disappear into the crowd like a mirage.

Yeah, I'm definitely gonna see what's up with her tonight, he promised himself. Then he got back to enjoying the VIP crowd. Busta and his squad were chatting things up with plenty of eye candy, and Lucina looked on, seemingly pleased with it all.

"Hey, man, I'm glad you're into friendships in this promotion game and not just closing people out," one of their promoter friends commented.

Ivan and Lucina had teamed with Joe Proctor to promote at least seven smaller parties downtown. They had not made anywhere near what Ivan and Lucina planned to make that night, but they were still profitable events.

Ivan told him, "It's all about strategies, man. If we help you out, you help us out, and vice versa."

Joe nodded to him. He asked, "So, what do I need to pay to get in on one of your parties?" That was a more detailed question, one that Ivan needed more focus to answer.

He said, "Give me a call this week and we'll talk about it." A few other promoter friends were enjoying themselves in the VIP section as well. It was a perk Ivan would utilize to keep their loyalty to him.

Joe said, "By the way, man, that's a nice new watch you got there."

Ivan looked down at his handsome Rolex and smiled.

"Thanks, man. It took me a lot to decide to finally break down and buy it. But you only live in this world once, right?"

"That's what they say," Joe agreed.

Ivan said, "So, you may as well bling, just a little bit, whenever you get a chance to do it. As long as it don't hurt you too bad."

AT THE END OF THE NIGHT, the Eve and Busta Rhymes party fell just short of the fifty-thousand-dollar goal. The late price increase after Busta's arrival allowed them to get close. But they would net less than half of it. The payout for the party was nearly thirty thousand, including Julio's fee.

"Now they're gonna want to hang out and eat and shit, like vampires, but I'm tired," Ivan told Lucina with a chuckle. It was ten minutes to shutdown at 2 AM.

Lucina smiled and said, "Ivan, that's what you have to do in this business, especially when dealing with *stars*. You can't go back to being an early bird."

Ivan said, "Well, maybe I'll just let you hang out with them. That'll make me more of a mystery man, right?"

"No, it'll make you *rude,*" Lucina warned him.

"Well, we'll just play it all by ear. Maybe they might want to do their own thing," Ivan suggested. "Somebody needs to take this money home, anyway. And I live down here now."

Lucina shook it off with a grin. "We'll see, Ivan."

He really wanted to get out of there to see if Ashley would call him back in thirty minutes, like he had told her to. He had some more private plans for them that evening.

When they all walked out to shut down the party at two o'clock in the morning, Busta's crew were ready to take off and enjoy themselves. A pack of pretty girls surrounded them outside in front of their cars, with security still on a careful watch.

Busta walked over to shake Ivan's hand again.

"Ay, yo, we out, dude. We about to go find something to eat. What are you getting into tonight?"

Ivan answered, "I'm about to get into bed, man. It's been a long day and night for me. I'm just happy everything went well tonight."

Busta joked, "Oh, yeah, how many you getting into the bed with? Because I know you a ladykiller out here. You throwing the big parties, looking good, got all the nice young ladies coming out, the fly website popping off, diamond stud up in your ear, a beautiful partner."

He said, "Oh, I *know* you doing it well out here. You ain't even gotta tell me."

Ivan laughed at Busta Rhymes's assessment of him in his customized rapid-fire tongue, while Lucina walked out of the club in front of Eve and her girls.

Ivan quickly changed the subject. He said, "Hey, man, I meant to tell you, that 'Truck Volume' song on your last album was an inspiration to my hustle. *'Truck shit now / . . . Turn my music up / . . . Truck volume . . .'"* Ivan chanted to him.

Busta laughed. He said, "Oh, shit, let me find out you been studying the album."

"Yeah, I got it. I had that song on replay. But y'all have a good time in San Diego and get your eat on. This was a good money event," Ivan told him.

Busta and his guys had room left in every vehicle for a couple of girls to climb in, while other girls followed in their cars. But none of them were Lucina's girls.

When the limo pulled up afterward for Ivan, Lucina, and Eve, Maya was there to join them.

Lucina said, "Since Ivan is so tired already, we can make this an all-girls night out now."

Eve nodded and said, "That's cool. You had a lot of cool girls in there tonight."

"And I'll have the ones you pointed out for modeling Fetish, too," Lucina told her.

That was all fine with Ivan. He was getting off the hook easy to enjoy his own night. So they dropped him off at his apartment building right before his cell phone went off.

He smiled and told himself, "Perfect timing."

But when he looked down at the number, it was Christina calling him instead of Ashley.

"What the hell?" he asked himself as he walked inside the lobby.

"Good evening, Mr. David," the night security guard greeted him.

"Hey, have a good night, man," Ivan responded.

He didn't answer Chris's call until he made it into the elevator.

"Hello."

"Is your party over with? I know it shuts down at two o'clock."

Ivan said, "Yeah, but now everybody wants to go out and eat and everything. I'm just taking the cash boxes home. But where were you?"

She said, "I decided not to go tonight. I'm just trying to pull myself away from the whole party thing. But I missed you tonight," she told him. "And I couldn't sleep."

Ivan hadn't touched Chris since he agreed to think about her school sponsorship. He had called her after their initial disagreement about it and told her he would see where her finances stood once that time arrived. But he wasn't expecting to hear from her once she failed to show at the party that night.

He said, "Yeah, but you know how this party game is. And now we got celebrities in town. So I might be up with them all night."

"Yeah, I know," Chris responded. "I just thought I'd call you and see. But I wish I could just . . . I don't know, stay over there and spend the night in your bed for when you come back."

Oh, shit! Ivan thought. *That's some sexy shit to say to a guy.* But it was the wrong night for it.

His cell phone buzzed from the other line. It was Ashley calling.

Ivan said, "That's nice, but hold on for a minute," and clicked over. "Hello," he answered on the other line.

"Hi, it's Ashley."

"Are you still downtown?"

"That's where you told me to be," she reminded him.

"Are you by yourself?"

She said, "I *came* by myself."

Ivan smiled. The girl had a seductive wit about her.

He asked, "And are you tired yet?"

She paused. "Umm, it depends. I mean, I don't feel like walking around or anything. I have to get out of these shoes. They're killing my poor feet."

Ivan thought, *Fuck it! What am I waiting for? She's down already.*

"So you wanna just relax for the rest of the night with me?"

"Are you inviting me to?"

"That's what it sounds like," he told her.

"Well, in that case, I accept. But you'll have to answer one question for me when I see you."

"What's that?"

"I'll tell you when I see you," she teased.

"Hold on," Ivan told her. He had left Christina on hold long enough. He clicked back over to Chris and said, "My bad."

She told him, "Go do what you need to do, Ivan. I understand. Just call me tomorrow."

"You sure?"

"No, but what can I do? You're busy. So just go ahead and go."

Ivan got back on the line with Ashley and told her, "My bad, I'm still in the mix of things tonight."

"Okay, so . . . where am I going?" she asked him, cutting straight to the chase.

Ivan gave her his apartment address and prepared his place for her arrival with freshly lit incense. Twenty minutes later, when he opened his apartment door for her, she walked in and immediately asked him her question.

"So, Ivan David . . . are you gonna tell on me?"

Ivan frowned and said, "Tell on you? About what? To who?"

"To Lucina about me coming to visit you. She's so . . ." Ashley twisted up her lightly tanned face, with her dark eyes, and said, "*Controlling*. That's why I took a break for a while. No offense, but I had to get away from her."

"So why are you back now?" he asked her. Now she had him on guard. What was her motive?

She paced his living room and answered, "Well, first of all, I could use the extra money. And I missed being around some of the people."

She kicked her shoes off and asked, "Oh, do you mind?"

Ivan shook it off. "Naw, go ahead and get out of your foot killers."

When he looked down at her feet, he could see the imprints on her skin from her shoes. Other than that, her small feet were unblemished and pretty.

"Nice place," she told him. "Did Lucina help you to decorate, too?"

"You know it."

"Did she get you to change your look, with the low-cut hair, the diamond earring, and the expensive Rolex watch?" She had heard the rumored talk about it.

Ivan began to feel like the prize in a catfight. He smiled and said, "It sounds like you have some kind of competition thing going on."

"Well, it's obvious that Lucina tells everyone to stay away from you."

"Because she doesn't want to mix the business with complications," Ivan responded. It made sense to him, although he planned to ignore it on occasion.

Ashley shrugged and said, "But I like you anyway. I've *always* liked you." She stared right into his eyes when she said it.

He asked her, "Really?"

"Yeah. I just thought you were a cool person to be around. And I know you didn't pay me any mind. You were just focused on what you needed to do," she told him. "But I understand the business part of it, too. So I had to make sure that *we* could come to an understanding first."

When she said that, all Ivan could concentrate on was her body in that dress again without noticeable bra straps or a panty line.

He joked, "So, what about you telling her on me?"

Ashley walked up close to him, close enough to be held and kissed. "Tell her that you did what?" she asked him.

She was a great tease. Ivan was ready to grab her and strip her clothes off right there, and give her what she was asking for. But before he could make a move on her, she made her move instead and kissed him on the lips. Then she slid down to her knees in front of him.

She said, "I'm not gonna tell anybody I did this," and began to undo his pants.

Ivan hesitated to stop her. *Should I let her do that?* he asked himself. By the time he made a move to stop her, she had taken him into her mouth.

"Wait a minute," he said, as he hardened inside her mouth.

"Mmmm," she moaned back to him. "Wait a minute for what? You're ready down here."

It felt too good for him to stop her. So he began to massage his hands through her thick, dark hair and row his body into it. But before he could reach a climax, she stopped and stood back up to face him, with his manhood hanging around in midair.

"You need anything else?" she asked him like a servant.

Ivan stood there feeling ridiculous. He chuckled and said, "I need you to finish what you just started."

"Of course you do," she responded to him. "But I need all of your clothes off to do that." She started taking off his pants and shirt.

Ivan said, "You didn't need all my clothes off to start it."

She grinned. "I was just checking out the goods first." She started to take off her own clothes before Ivan stopped her.

"No, let me do that. I wanted to see if you had anything on under this."

She laughed and said, "You were staring?"

"I couldn't help it."

"Good. Then it did what it was supposed to do," she told him.

Ivan spun her around so he could feel her breasts through her dress.

"So, you *don't* have a bra on," he noted.

"Well, that's obvious," she told him. "It's clumsy to wear a bra with this kind of dress."

Then he checked down below for her panties. "And you're wearing a thong."

She said, "I don't feel comfortable having nothing on down there. So anything that feels good is better than wearing nothing. At least it is for me."

Ivan stripped off her dress and kissed her smooth shoulders. Then he spun her around to face him so he could suck her beautiful breasts. They were the perfect, ripe size that stood at attention to be catered to.

"Nice," Ivan told her as he kissed them.

She bragged, "It's *all* nice. Every part of me. Inside and out."

Ivan stopped for a minute to think about that, with her naked splendor on display in front of him.

He told her, "I would have never figured that, you know, you were like this."

"Like what?" she asked him.

He said, "That you would be down like that."

She studied his face with inquisitive eyes. She said, "You thought I was a good girl who wouldn't do anything, didn't you?"

"Until you used that word 'promise' tonight," he responded to her. "After you said that, I had a big feeling about you."

"What feeling was that?" she asked him.

"That you might have wanted to be with me."

Ashley grinned. "Well, your feeling was right," she told him. "I had a feeling about you, too . . . especially after you asked me about a boyfriend."

Ivan chuckled again. He said, "Yeah, I like to know what I'm getting into before I leap. But enough of all this talking. Are you ready to get into this or what?"

Ashley looked into Ivan's colorful eyes, caressing his manhood in her hands. Then she asked him, "Which way is the bedroom?"

Fifteen

It All Comes Together

As Lucina's surprise to her partner, San Diego's *944* magazine published Ivan's photo as the front-cover story with his article running the same weekend as their second celebrity party event downtown. They were hosting hip-hop and R&B producer Timbaland and his protégé, the Canadian/Latina pop artist Nelly Furtado.

The *944* cover story called Ivan "Mr. Likability," with a great close-up shot of his face, eyes, teeth, and diamond stud earring, all shining and looking good.

Lucina called him up on it only after she knew that he had seen it. "Did you see your article, Ivan? You look *great*. And they're willing to let us distribute extra copies at your birthday party in two weeks. They know it will be a great promotion for them."

Ivan said, "Are they coming out to cover the event with a reporter and a photographer, too?"

"Of course they are. Nobody wants to miss it now. They all want to see how you pull this thing off."

Ivan said, "Yeah, well, we got a hundred tickets allocated for business friends, sponsors, the media, future advertisers; we need to get them all in there. The more the merrier. And by the way," he told her, "that magazine cover story looks good."

Lucina chuckled. "I told you I would take care of it for you."

With sponsorship money included, Ivan was able to cut their budget expense from nearly twenty-five thousand dollars to just under ten thousand. The tickets were set to go on sale the Monday after the Timbaland and Nelly Furtado party.

Ivan also teamed with their promoter friends to have them sell tickets on commission. It was another effort to keep them loyal. With a team of sponsors involved and the local buzz-building, projections looked very positive.

In fact, Ivan and Lucina were guaranteed to make a profit after selling only 10 percent of the tickets, a mere two hundred and fifty out of a possible twenty-five hundred that would go on sale. Including the expected bar money, a sellout crowd would make them more than a hundred twenty thousand dollars, or sixty thousand each.

"Shit, this party is looking real good now," Ivan told himself from his living room sofa. He continued to flip through the *944* magazine. The *Tribune* and the *News Link* articles would be published the week of the party.

Ivan had to admit that the bigger party idea was a lot simpler if you could work out the details. He and Lucina had a lot more leisure time, and they would make a lot more money than they did with the constant grind of the smaller parties.

"I guess Lucina was right," Ivan mumbled to himself, grinning. "As long as it works."

He wasn't even counting the party with Timbaland and Nelly Furtado yet. He and Lucina hoped to net another twenty grand each from that one.

BACK AT the Hutch & Mitchell Accounting offices, Chip Garrett was dying to get in on Ivan's action.

"Hey, man, when are you gonna invite me out to meet those hot girls from your parties? You told me you would a month ago now."

"They'll both be at my birthday party coming up," Ivan told him. He wanted to save all of his corporate-level friends and associates for his bigger, better, and more professional event.

Chip argued, "Ivan, on your website I see you've already partied with Eve and Busta Rhymes, and now you got Nelly Furtado and Timbaland coming to town. And you're telling me that neither one of those girls will be there? Do they even still work with you?"

One of the girls was scheduled to be there. Gretchen.

Ivan asked Chip, "Which one do you like the best?"

Chip answered, "That's easy: the one who likes me the best. I don't believe in chasing women around who don't want to be caught."

Ivan told him, "Well, the one wearing the white hat will be there this weekend. But I don't know if she'll like you."

"Just put in a good word for me," Chip told him. "And I'll do the rest on my own."

Ivan had no idea of Chip's flow with women. He looked like a cool enough guy, but . . . Then again, if he made Chip out to be a high roller . . .

But how would that float with Lucina? he thought. *I don't think she wants me playing matchmaker.*

Ivan told him, "I'll see what I can do."

Everyone at the office knew Ivan had a lucrative side gig by then, and none of them could do anything about it but wish him luck, attend his functions for themselves, or become envious. In the new year, another eight new clients had signed on for accounting work because of Ivan, including Jeffrey Morefield, Thomas Jones, and the young DJ, Red Face Lion. As far as the bosses were concerned, Ivan was company gold.

"Just keep doing what you're doing out there, Ivan," Barry Mitchell told him. He and John planned to attend the big coming-out party themselves and to see Ivan in action. Even Dwayne Bellamy planned to attend.

* * *

BEFORE THE TIMBALAND and Nelly Furtado party that weekend, Ivan's brother Derrick arrived back in San Diego and jumped right into the mix of things.

Ivan was hesitant to have him there, but as usual, Derrick didn't give him a warning that he was coming. So Ivan met him at a downtown hotel with a room key in hand.

As soon as Derrick saw him, he said, "You got an earring now, too? What your job say about that?" He had already gotten used to Ivan's low haircut from the New Year's event the last time he had visited.

Ivan grinned at him. "They said, 'Keep bringing us money, Ivan, and you can look any way you wanna look.'"

Derrick smiled and asked him, "Can you look like me?"

His hair was still long on top, with a week-old stubble around his face, but he still looked healthy, attractive, and approachable. However, Derrick was forever in street clothes.

Ivan told him, "You just need a trim, a shave, and a suit, and you're good."

Derrick shook it off and said, "Anyway, man, thanks for the hotel room this time around. You must have read my mind."

Actually, Ivan didn't want his brother to see his new apartment and start getting too many ideas about his finances. He'd already decided to hide his Rolex watch in his pants pocket. But with Derrick staying for the party, Ivan wouldn't be able to hide anything much longer. So he went ahead and handed his brother a flyer.

Derrick looked at it and said, "So I came into town on the right night, then."

"Evidently so," Ivan told him.

Derrick studied the flyer. "Nelly Furtado's looking good on here. She a little skinny for my taste, but I'll find a way to work with her."

Ivan shook it off. He said, "Yeah, I gotta go get ready for this party now. And you can ask anybody at the hotel where it is. The club's in walking distance from here. Your name'll be on the VIP list at the door."

"So where's your new place?" Derrick asked his brother before he walked off. He knew Ivan had moved, he just hadn't been there yet.

Ivan told him, "I'm down here, too," and left it at that.

Derrick said, "Well, thanks for looking out last month with that little extra," and he reached to shake his brother's hand.

Ivan was hesitant about that as well. He shook his brother's hand and said, "Okay." He didn't want to say anything more than that. He assumed he would have to wire his brother extra money soon again.

He's really gonna start acting up once he sees this party tonight, Ivan predicted. *Maybe I shouldn't have even told him about it. But how long am I gonna be able to hide it from him? I'm just gonna have to tell my brother what time it is. He has to learn to carry his own weight.*

WHEN IVAN ARRIVED back at his apartment to get dressed and ready for the party, his cell phone began to ring with steady urgency.

"Hello."

It was Christina again. "I'm thinking about coming out tonight, just to see it. Should I? I still haven't seen you since I called you last week."

Ivan asked her, "Are you working?"

"No, not really, I just . . . wanna come," she answered. She said, "And I read your article in the magazine. It was nice. So everybody likes you, hunh?"

Ivan smiled. He said, "Hey, don't read too much into that, that was just my spin on things to get more people *to* like me. If you say it, it'll happen," he told her.

"Well, with that picture they had of you on the cover, I can believe it," she hinted. "That's why I don't wanna wait until after the party this time. You'll have me standing in line to take a number to see you now."

She had Ivan laughing, but he didn't want to respond to it. Ashley had been over his place a few times already, and she had pleased him well. Plus, she wasn't asking to be "sponsored" yet.

Ivan said, "Well, you know, it does get busy during these parties, so . . . I mean, if you're not even working with us tonight, then what would Lucina think?"

Chris paused a second. "I don't really care what Lucina thinks anymore. She has her own ideas about things and I have mine."

"So, who would put you on the guest list?"

"If you're concerned about that, Ivan, then I would pay my own way."

"Just to see me."

"Why, is there a problem with that? Is somebody else in there to see you?"

Ivan joked, "Twenty-five percent of the girls in there are coming to see me." He then caught himself quickly and said, "Naw, I'm bullshitting."

"No, you're not," Chris responded. "That's why I'm coming, just to see."

Ivan didn't know how to respond to that. Was she bluffing him or what?

He said, "Well, don't get your feelings hurt in there, because you know I still like you. But when I'm doing my business, I'm doing my business."

"I know that already," she told him.

His cell phone rang with another call. "Hold on."

"Hello," he answered.

"Ivan, the limo is ready," Lucina told him on the other line.

"Shit, I'm still getting dressed."

"Take your time, but not *too much* time."

"All right, I'll be ready in less than a half."

"Please make it *less.*"

Ivan paused. "I thought you said to take my time."

"Well, I didn't mean it," Lucina stated.

Ivan laughed it off. "All right, man, I'm coming."

"Ivan, I am *not* a man," she corrected him.

He paused again. *Yeah, she needs to loosen the hell up,* he told himself. *No wonder these girls are not liking her.*

He responded, "What, you haven't had any in a while? Loosen up a bit."

As soon as he said it, he regretted it. *Aw, shit! Now, what is she gonna say to that?* he thought.

Lucina told him, "We'll be waiting for you out front," and didn't respond to it at all.

That made Ivan curious about what she was thinking. *She'll let it out on me sooner or later.*

He clicked back over to Chris. "Hey, I'm sorry, but I gotta get ready for this party now."

"Was that her?" Chris asked him.

"Her, who?"

"You know, Miss Gallo."

Ivan smiled. *They all have a competitive thing for Lucina, hunh?*

He said, "Yeah, but I needed to get ready anyway."

"All right, well . . . don't be surprised to see me there."

Ivan was silent again. He wanted to tell her not to come. He just didn't need the extra confusion that night. But once Chris hung up on him, he decided to let it slide.

He made it down into the limo, dressed, ready, and smelling good in closer to fifteen minutes.

"See, that was faster than I thought," he stated to his partner in the back of the limo.

Lucina remained silent. Ivan read her sulking attitude and told himself, *All right, let me get this over with.*

He looked into her face and said, "Lucina . . ." He waited for her undivided attention. When she turned to face him, he told her, "I apologize. I didn't mean to say that. Okay?"

She looked into his eyes for his sincerity. Once she read it from him, she nodded. "Thank you. So, you've been getting a lot of great feedback on the magazine article," she commented. She went right back to business as if nothing had happened.

Ivan said, "Yeah. That 'Mr. Likability' thing was a great touch."

Lucina told him, "You'll get a lot more attention tonight, too. So make sure you keep it moving."

She didn't even look at him when she said that. Ivan began to feel the strain of an attractive man and an attractive woman in a lucrative partnership again.

It would be a lot easier if it was just two guys or two women in business, he assumed. *Then again, a whole lot of men and women don't get along with each other like that. Or maybe it would be easier if one of us was ugly.*

Lucina caught Ivan smiling to himself at his thoughts and asked him about it.

"What is so funny?"

"Nothing, I'm just, ah . . ." He changed the subject and said, "Thinking about my brother being at this party."

"What's wrong with that?"

Although Derrick was nowhere near the businessman that she considered Ivan to be, Lucina didn't have any particular problems with him.

Ivan said, "We'll see," and left it at that.

NELLY FURTADO didn't have as many hot club songs on her résumé as Eve or Busta Rhymes, so Red Face Lion was forced to play mostly Timbaland-produced songs from Missy, Aaliyah, Ginuwine, Jay-Z, Tweet, and new ones from Justin Timberlake.

Nelly was reserved in the VIP crowd, while Timbaland danced in the midst of blissful women on the club's dance floor, jamming to Missy "Misdemeanor."

"Go, get your freak on . . . / . . . getcha getcha getcha freak on . . ."

Ivan slid up beside Nelly near the bar and commented, "That guy's put a lot of hits out."

She smiled and chuckled. "Yes, definitely," she responded in her light accent. Ivan was surprised at how tiny she was. But her look fit right in with Lucina. She could pass for Lucina's little sister.

"Hey, let me get a picture of that," the photographer barked, catching them smiling together.

Ivan posed with Nelly next to the bar. They had all taken photos earlier inside the limo, outside the club, and over in the VIP section. But they could never get enough quality pictures to post on the website. And in San Diego, the Latino community was thick.

Julio popped up again and posed in a picture with Nelly for himself.

He said, "Hey, Ivan, she brought out the Spanish crowd for you tonight."

Ivan nodded in agreement. "That's good. I wanna party with everyone."

"And everyone wants to party with you," Julio told him. "I can't wait until your birthday. I'm gonna bring my wife to that one."

Ivan didn't comment on that. Julio was all over the Spanish women in there. Ivan guessed that he would behave himself with his wife around.

At close to midnight, the club was jam-packed before Derrick ever reached the door.

"I'm on the VIP list," he told security. "I'm Derrick David, Ivan's big brother."

"Oh, okay. Come on in. We can see the resemblance in the eyes," the security guard stated.

Derrick said, "Yeah, these eyes run in the family. And they're good for the women, too."

The security guard laughed and said, "Yeah, we know."

Derrick walked in ahead of Christina, who had just arrived at the party herself. She followed him in with forty dollars in her hand to pay.

Maya looked at her and frowned. "Hey, Chris, you don't have to pay. But how come you're not working with us anymore?"

Christina smiled it off. She said, "I will. I'm just being a little lazy right now. And if I'm not working, I get to come to the party late and be nosy."

They shared a laugh.

"All right, well, enjoy it. But I'm still working," Maya told her.

Christina walked in behind Derrick and continued to observe him. He seemed to have three times the swagger of Ivan. Derrick willed the women to wonder about him as he walked by them on the dance floor. And he dared the guys to get upset about it.

He walked through the room, feeling it, with a Timbaland-produced Jay-Z classic blasting through the speakers:

"Jigga what . . . / Jigga who . . ."

Derrick felt as if the song were his own personal anthem for a minute. He looked over and saw Timbaland enjoying himself in a circle of pretty girls, and immediately searched for Nelly Furtado.

She must be in the VIP, chilling, he assumed. *She can't get out there on the dance floor like a guy can without needing bodyguards with her. But Timbaland's big enough to get away with that shit.*

Derrick found the VIP section and immediately spotted Nelly, Lucina, and his brother, all swaying to the music.

"Oh, my God, if he heads this way to go to the bathroom or *anything,* I'm just gonna reach out and grab him. He is so *hot,*" an attractive blonde stated to her girlfriend.

Derrick winced and wondered who she was talking about. He even asked the girl. "Are you talking about Timbaland?"

Money can hypnotize a girl that damn much? he mused. He didn't see Timbaland having it like that no matter how many great records he produced.

The blonde frowned at him and shook her head. "Oh, no, I'm talking about . . . someone else." She stopped and studied Derrick's face and eyes in confusion. She asked him, "You're not, like, related to, ah, Ivan David, are you?"

Her girlfriend was watching, waiting, and wondering herself.

Derrick told them, "That's my little brother."

The two girls looked at each other and lost it.

"Oh, my God, you look like him, I mean, with the eyes and everything."

Her girlfriend asked him, "Can you get him to take a picture with us?"

Derrick studied both of them and wondered how far he could take it. First he looked to see if they had drinks in their hands. In his opinion, a drunk white girl was a down white girl, but a sober one he couldn't count on. However, when he looked at their hands, he noticed that they did have drinks. So he smiled at them.

"Yeah, I'll go see what he says. But don't move, I'll be right back. All right?"

"Okay."

Derrick stopped and asked them, "Y'all need anything else to drink?"

The girls looked down at their glasses, filled mostly with ice. And they nodded to him.

"Yeah, we could use more drinks."

"Aw'ight, one minute."

Christina watched the whole scene from a distance as Derrick walked up to Ivan in the VIP section and whispered into his left ear.

"Looks like you stepped up your game now, Ivan. These girls are all in here buzzing for you. You got a drink tab?"

Ivan turned and looked at his brother. He asked him, "A drink tab for what?"

"For more damn drinks, man, I'm thirsty."

"Well, spend your money, then," Ivan told him.

"Look, man, I wasn't gon' spend my money if I didn't have to."

Ivan looked in the direction his brother had approached him from and spotted the two girls, watching and waiting. They even smiled and waved to him.

Ivan asked his brother, "Did you promise somebody something?"

"They just wanna take pictures with you. You're more of a star to them than Timbaland. I just happened to hear them talking about you as I walked up."

Ivan said, "They always wanna take pictures, but I can't bother with that too much. I got other things on my mind to take care of."

Just as he said that, he saw Christina walk right past the two girls who were still waiting for a response from him.

Aw, shit, here we go, he thought. Ashley was off to his right and heading back in his direction at the same time as Christina.

Then he spotted his coworker, Chip Garrett, searching through the party.

Ivan shook his head and thought, *Too many things are about to go on at once.* So he moved to counteraction.

He told his brother, "Aw'ight, get your drinks and handle them two. Tell them I'll take pictures with them in a minute."

He moved straight toward Christina.

"Hey, you came out," he said to her with a smile.

"So did your brother," she told him.

Ivan mumbled, "Yeah." Then he addressed the two girls standing nearby. "How are you ladies doing? I'll take those pictures with you in a minute."

They both looked shocked by the suddenness of it all.

"Oh, okay. Thanks."

"No problem," he told them. "Come on," he told Chris. He headed in Chip's direction before his fellow accountant could find him.

"Hey, Chip, you made it out in the eleventh hour. I thought you had changed your mind," Ivan addressed him.

Chip smiled and said, "Yeah, I got tied up in a prior engagement and had to rush over here to make it." He wore a light-colored sports jacket, casual blue jeans, and a button-up shirt.

Ivan said, "Okay, that happens sometimes." Then he turned to Chris. "Christina, can you do me a favor and find, um . . ."

"Gretchen," Chip reminded him.

"Yeah, he wants to meet Gretchen. Have you seen her in here?"

"No," Chris told him. "I wasn't looking for her."

"Well, can you be a sweetheart and find her for me?"

Chris gave him a resentful eye and took a deep breath. *I don't believe him,* she told herself.

She warned Ivan, "I will, but it's gonna cost you."

Chip heard that and grinned. As soon as she walked away, he said, "Wow, I've seen her on your website, too. But she's even more stunning in real life."

Ivan said, "They all are."

Ashley reached them before he could get out another word.

"Is there anything you need, Ivan?"

"Naw, not right now. I'm trying to give my friend here a private tour of the party."

Ashley grinned and said, "Oh, well, have fun with it. And let me know if I can help."

"Naw, I got it," Ivan told her.

Chip was grinning his ass off. He asked, "How does that feel, man?"

Ivan told him, "Don't get it confused, it's only business. They're great at giving me the illusion of being in control. When in actuality they're all getting paid to make it look that way."

Chip said, "I wish I could pay a bunch of girls to act that way with me. I'd surely take it."

"Hey, I-vaaannn!" a couple of girls yelled out from the dance floor.

Chip looked at him said, "You paid them to do that, too?"

Ivan laughed it off. "Naw, that's, ah . . . the regulars. They just know me by now."

"Hey, Ivan David, we want to thank you, man," a Latino couple told him in the middle of the dance floor.

Ivan said, "Thank me for what?"

"Your 'San Diego Spotlight' page at IDPromotions.com got us together," the guy told him.

The young woman added, "Yeah, we were like a perfect match, same hobbies and everything."

"Yeah, so I emailed her, and we've been going out now ever since."

Ivan looked at them both, and they certainly looked good together. He smiled and said, "Well, make sure you invite me out to the wedding."

They laughed and told him, "We will."

"Seems to me like they all know you in here," Chip commented.

"Not all of them, just a lot of them." He then pointed to Timbaland, who was dancing his heart out with a group of delirious girls around him. He said, "More of them know that guy right there. I'm just playing my position."

Christina found Gretchen and brought her back to them. Gretchen wasn't wearing her white hat that night, and her hair was cut short and stylish with blond highlights.

She said, "Hey, what's up, Ivan?"

Ivan wasted no time with his introductions. "Gretchen, this is Chip. Chip, this is Gretchen."

Gretchen nodded and smiled to him. "Nice to meet you."

Chip said, "The pleasure is all mine. After I saw your picture on the website, I told Ivan that I just had to meet you."

Chip was giving too much information for Ivan's taste. *But to each his own.*

"Now you owe me," Christina told Ivan.

"And Chip owes me," Ivan joked.

"I have nothing to do with that," Chris argued.

Finally, Ivan pulled her aside. He said, "Chris, you asked for it, but I got a lot of shit going on in here. I got my brother running around, Nelly Furtado and Timbaland to cater to, the crowd, my money . . ." He stopped himself short and said, "Look, come with me for a minute."

He led her to the bathroom area and pulled out the key to his apartment.

He asked her, "Remember you talked about waiting up for me in my bed?"

She said, "Of course."

"All right, go do that. And let the security know that I gave you the key. All right?"

Chris smiled at him. "All right."

When Ivan made it back to the VIP area alone, Lucina pulled him aside and told him, "Your brother was trying to hit on Nelly. Can you talk to him about that?"

Ivan said, "What, she complained about it? And you didn't tell him yourself?"

Lucina shook her head. She said, "He's a little too much to handle. And I don't have the energy right now. So you handle it."

Ivan took a deep breath and thought, *This is gonna be a long-ass night.*

He walked over to his brother, who was serving the two friends more drinks.

"Oh, can we take that picture now?" they asked Ivan.

Derrick beat his brother to the punch. "With clothes *on* or *off*?"

They laughed and responded, "Whatever," with their new drinks in hand.

Ivan pulled his brother aside and asked him, "What the hell are you doing, man? Is that what you wanted the hotel room for?"

Derrick said, "I'm a grown-ass man, Ivan. And I'm having a good time in here. What do you *think* I'm doing?"

"I think you already got *three sons* from *three* different women, that's what *I* think," Ivan snapped at him.

"Yeah, and my sons are all nearly teenagers now. So what are you saying? I don't get every girl pregnant. If that was the case, I'd have a *hundred* kids."

Ivan said, "And you're trying to holler at Nelly, too?"

Derrick chuckled. "Aw, man, I just said a few things to her to see where her head was at, that's all."

Ivan shook it off. He said, "Sometimes you gotta stop and think about how that shit's gonna reflect on me, man. Just for a fucking minute."

Derrick ignored it and said, "Look, are you gonna take pictures with these girls or what? They called you 'Mr. Likable' or some shit like that. And they came out here just to see you. So you can't let these girls down, man."

Ivan told his brother, "Don't embarrass yourself with them tonight, D. Let it go." And he walked away from him.

"Well, what did he say?" the girls asked Derrick when he returned to them.

Derrick shrugged. "My brother's not being 'Mr. Likable' for y'all tonight. But I am," he told them.

The girls giggled at Derrick's humor, while becoming irritated with Ivan's rudeness. "Well, what's wrong with him? He thinks he too *good* now or something?"

Derrick shook it off. He didn't want to take things that far. Ivan was still his brother. He said, "Naw, he's just busy right now. But y'all let me know if you need some more to drink. And I can make sure that all is forgiven tonight."

"How are you gonna do that? You're gonna get him to apologize to us and take a picture?"

Derrick said, "I don't know about all that. But if you're too slow, then you'll never know. So, if you both like having a good time, then we can all make a nightcap out of it."

"Is Ivan going to be there?"

Derrick stared at the girl. It was time to lay down the law and cut the bullshit. He said, "How much does it matter? Do we really need my brother there? He might be busy for the rest of the night. So don't waste *my* time if *I'm* not good enough. Maybe y'all both too good for me."

"No, we didn't say that."

"Good. Then let's agree to drink and have a good time tonight. Agreed?" he asked them.

"Agreed," they accepted.

Derrick said, "Well, let's go ahead and take *our* pictures, then."

BY THE TIME the party wound down at two o'clock, Ivan was exhausted, and Derrick was nowhere to be found again. The door take broke another fifty thousand that night, and with the budget slightly over twenty thousand, Ivan and Lucina cleared another fifteen apiece.

"You're going to bed again, early bird?" Lucina teased Ivan.

"Yup," he told her. And he meant it this time. *Chris will just have to be disappointed until the morning. And I'll just tell Ashley that I'm tired tonight, too,* he plotted.

When he broke Ashley the news over the phone, she said, "I understand. You were working extrahard in there tonight to please everyone. People are really feeling what you're doing now. And next up is your big birthday party. Are you excited yet?"

Ivan said, "Ask me about that in twelve more hours."

Ashley laughed and said, "Okay, I will."

Ivan made it up to his apartment and had to wait for Chris to open the door for him.

"Thanks for coming straight home tonight," she told him, wearing only a T-shirt. It was after two thirty, and Lucina was still hanging out and showing their guests a good time in San Diego.

Ivan told Chris, "Well, you'll have to get that thing from me in the morning, because I'm beat right now. That's on the real."

She nodded to him and didn't sweat it. "Okay, as long as I'm the one who's here with you."

* * *

DERRICK DROVE back up to L.A. after spending a reckless weekend in San Diego, leaving Ivan at peace to prepare himself for the upcoming party of his life. When the *San Diego News Link* article hit the press, asking the question "Who is Ivan David?" followed by the *San Diego Union Tribune* feature, "Ivan David: The Party Promoter," he started getting inquiries about his big event from everyone. The tickets sold briskly, while the IDPromotions.com website jumped from an average of twelve thousand unique hits a day to close to *thirty* thousand, boosting the daily impressions to more than *three hundred* thousand.

Thomas Jones called Ivan at his apartment office excitedly. He asked him, "Do you know what you're about to do, Ivan? You're about to graduate to a whole new level of business, young brother. I don't even think you realize it yet."

Ivan told him, "All I know is that I'm tired, man. This shit is wearing me out."

Thomas laughed and told him, "It's all about momentum, Ivan. You *deserve* to be tired now. But you've already done most of the work to receive the fruits of your labor. And you're not even twenty-nine yet. That's how you do it right there."

He said, "I'm still working on the property sales. I'm just trying to hold out a little longer to get our prices. But we just might be able to do it after this big event. We can just call it 'celebrity-owned property,'" he joked.

But Ivan didn't laugh at the idea. He stopped and said, "Well, we should put it on my website, then. I didn't figure it would take you this long to sell."

Thomas said, "Ivan, I could have sold them *both* at two-eighty three weeks ago. But I'm holding out for three-*twenty*, at least. And when you got the money, you can afford to do that."

Ivan said, "Yeah, but let's get rid of them after this party, man. Then we'll have enough to go shopping for these development deals. I got a football player asking me about it now. He's ready to invest."

"You got it, partner."

Ivan called to check up on his website team over at the office.

"Everything is falling right into place, my friend," Eddie K. told him. "The phones are ringing off the hook over here." He said, "This birthday party was an *awesome* idea. Now we have all of corporate San Diego wondering who else is going to be there."

When he talked to Jeff and Paul, they had news for him on another note.

Jeff told him, "Ivan, you're crazy popular now on the personal web pages of San Diego, dude. People are taking pictures of you and posting you up on their sites."

Paul added, "And a whole lot of girls, too," from the office speakerphone.

Jeff said, "Yeah, and some of them are, like, listing freaky fantasies and shit. So you may want to watch out for who you take pictures with now."

Ivan shook his head. He said, "You see that? Now I gotta have a bodyguard snatching cameras."

"Hey, man, the superstars have to live with that every day. And you're on your way now," Paul told him. "But just look at it this way: the traffic that we're generating now is just *crazy.*"

Jeff joked, "All you have to do now is let your lawyers know you didn't do any of the things these girls may brag about."

Ivan laughed and blew it off. He said, "Well, make sure you guys run out and get your suits tailored for the big event."

"We need to wear suits?" Jeff asked him.

"Well . . . if not a full *suit,* then at least a nice *jacket,*" Ivan told them.

"You mean like you do?" Paul commented.

"Yeah, I want you guys to try and look like mini Ivans," he joked.

They shared a laugh.

Jeff said, "Sure, then we can get a percentage of the women you get."

Ivan told them, "Don't believe the hype on all those women. I've only had a select few."

Jeff and Paul got real quiet at the offices. That claim sounded unbelievable.

Paul said, "Ivan, we're not the judge and jury here. You don't have to lie about that to us."

Jeff broke out laughing. He said, "My sentiments exactly."

Catherine called Ivan up and had her own laugh about his articles. She quoted, " 'I've always been one to blend in well with everyone . . . That's why I love living here in San Diego . . . I would love to just be that guy who you can count on to bring everyone together.' "

She laughed and said, "You are so full of *shit* now, Ivan. You could care less about bringing people together. You're all about bringing your *pockets* together. But I have to admit it, though, that website is *banging*. Those computer geeks are working that thing out."

Ivan smiled and corrected her. "They're my creative executives."

"Whatever. So your birthday party is *fifty* dollars?"

"And all the money people can afford it," Ivan told her.

Catherine paused over the line. She said, "It's crazy how people choose to spend their money. And no offense, Ivan, but who would have ever thought that you could charge people *fifty dollars* just to come to a birthday party to see you?"

"It's not just a birthday party, though," Ivan explained. "It's a networking extravaganza. And we'll be spotlighting all of our sponsors, advertisers, business friends, and associates."

"Oh, *please,* save me the hype machine, Ivan. This is *me, Catherine.* I've even talked to some of our old classmates from San Diego State about it, and they couldn't believe all of this, either. It's all just overnight. Then you got the whole bald-headed, earring thing. I mean, come on."

Ivan no longer liked the tone of her conversation.

He said, "First of all, I'm not bald headed. It's a low haircut. And it may seem all overnight to some, but I've been working my ass off to get here."

"So have other people, Ivan. And they've all worked a lot longer than you. But they can't charge people *fifty* dollars for a damn *hyped-up* birthday party."

"Well, that's *them*," Ivan snapped at her. "Some people can't get sixty thousand fans to pay to watch them play football every Sunday. But the Chargers can."

"You're not the Chargers," Catherine told him.

Ivan said, "Yeah, well, it sounds like you just need to get used to the name 'Ivan David' meaning more than just your old college boyfriend. That's all that is. And I have nothing else to say about it, because I can't afford this negative energy."

He continued, "My gas tank for bullshit is on *empty*. And we got nowhere else to go with that."

Catherine was stunned. She said, "I don't even know why I keep trying to talk to you."

Ivan told her, "If you come the right way, it's cool. But if you're gonna keep coming at me with this college shit, then I can't help you. We're not *in* college anymore."

She said, "Okay. Well, go on back to your business, and I won't bother you anymore."

When Ivan hung up with her, he was *pissed*.

"She said that same shit the last time," he told himself. "She needs to get a grip on her damn emotions. How is she gonna get mad at me for blowing up now?"

He stood up from his desk and stated, "That shit is petty. Jealousy comes in all packages."

ON HIS ACTUAL BIRTHDAY, Friday, March 5, 2004, Ivan had another minor dilemma. Both Christina and Ashley wanted to spend it out on the town with him. Lucina even called herself to ask him how he planned to enjoy his birthday.

Ivan told her, "I don't know what I want to do right now, Lucina. I feel like just staying in and having a good old-fashioned dinner at home. But what woman is gonna cook for me on a Friday night?" he hinted.

Lucina responded, "Hmm . . . what woman do you *want* to cook for you?"

Ivan paused. It sounded as if she were giving him an open invitation. So he went for it.

"Would you cook for me tonight?"

Lucina heard him and laughed. She said, "I can bring you some delicious Italian food from my good friend's restaurant here in Coronado, but I am not in the mood to cook."

Ivan asked her, "But will you be dressed for a formal dinner?"

Lucina paused. "As long as it does not include the wrong ideas about what goes on *after* the dinner."

That comment made Ivan laugh. He said, "Okay. I can call someone else over after dinner. And they can finish up with the dessert."

"I don't believe you said that," Lucina told him.

"Well, it is my birthday. And I wouldn't mind having a girl jump out of a cake naked, either."

"Well, that won't be me."

"All right, well, let's just get dressed and have a candlelit Italian dinner at my place for my birthday, and talk more business."

"Agreed," she told him.

That surprised Ivan. "Around what time?" he asked her.

"Eight thirty."

So Ivan prepared his dining room table with plates, glasses, candles, and dim lighting. He freshened up, dressed in elegant evening clothes, with a dark blue jacket, and awaited his partner's arrival by eight fifteen.

In the meantime, he called Ashley and Christina back. He called Chris first.

He said, "I know you wanted to spend my birthday with me, but, um, Lucina kind of owes me that."

"Owes you what?" Christina asked him for clarity.

Ivan answered, "For business. But it's not a sexual thing at all. We're just gonna talk about where we are and where we're going. And afterward, if you still want to celebrate with me . . ."

Christina cut him off and said, "Wait a minute. You're gonna have a birthday date with *her* for *business,* and then do *me* for *pleasure?*"

Ivan stopped to think about it. It may have sounded ultracocky, but it was what it was.

He asked her calmly, "How else do you want me to explain it?"

Christina failed to answer him. She sighed heavily over the line and told him, "I don't believe you. I mean . . . what do you want me to say to something like that, Ivan? You're gonna make me want to hate Lucina."

"Hate her for what? She's the reason why we even know each other."

Christina was silent. She said, "I don't . . . I just don't know about that."

Ivan told her, "Well, you call me back and let me know later."

Chris still didn't want to respond to it. She wanted Ivan to stop and tell her that he was bullshitting, that it was only a birthday joke to get her going. But Ivan was ready to hang up the phone with her and move on.

"All right," she mumbled. What else could she do? Ivan had made up his mind already.

When he hung up with Christina, he called and said the same thing to Ashley.

She responded, "What? That's crazy. I don't believe you asked me that."

"It's only a dinner with her, Ashley. We do that all the time."

"Yeah, and then you'll have *me* for dessert. Well, no, I'm not

gonna do that," she said. "And you can call me when *I'm* the dinner date. I'm not taking *seconds* to Lucina."

Ivan told her, "You take seconds at all the events. What's the difference?"

That caught Ashley off guard. She stated, "That's exactly why I left her. I want to be my own person. I don't wanna feel like I'm lining up for her all the time."

"You're not," Ivan told her. "You're lining up for me now."

"Oh, like *that's* supposed to make a difference. And what do you *mean* I'm lining up for you, anyway?"

Ivan told her, "It means exactly what I said. I mean, I like you, but everything falls in line where it falls."

Ashley went silent. She said, "Can I ask you a question? And I don't expect for you to answer this, but I want to ask you anyway."

"What?"

"Have you ever done anything with Lucina?"

"Done anything like what?" Ivan asked her.

"You know what I'm talking about. Have you ever had sex with her?"

Ivan told her, "Like I said, it's *business*. It's *always* about business with her. And that's what it is tonight," he answered. "So, if you still feel like you want to give me a birthday present, wrapped in whatever, then you make up your mind to do that."

"Hmmph," Ashley grunted. "You must think I'm *that* desperate for you, but I'm *not*. I'm really not."

"All right, well . . . it's still my birthday tonight. So wish me a good one."

Ivan figured he needed to get used to losing out on women who couldn't stick with him through his plans. There was still too much he wanted to get accomplished to slow down. And Lucina continued to make him too much money to be second fiddle to anyone.

"They'll get over it," he told himself of Christina and Ashley. "Or maybe they won't."

Lucina arrived at his apartment with two brown bags of prepared Italian food at exactly 8:37. She was wearing a long, beige overcoat that nearly reached her pink heels.

"You're seven minutes late," Ivan joked. "And what's up with this coat you're wearing? Is it supposed to rain tonight?"

"First I had to park," she told him as Ivan set the bags of hot food down on the kitchen counter. "And this coat, I wanted to surprise you with."

Ivan looked at it and smiled at her. "So, you got something hot on under that, right?"

Lucina smiled back at him and undid her coat to reveal a pink knee-length Christian Dior dress, decorated with colorful gems.

"Happy birthday, Ivan David."

He chuckled and said, "Thank you." He stared at her and nodded, admiring it all. But his dark blue sports jacket and baby blue button-up shirt failed to complement her dress. "That's nice," he told her. "But now I feel like I need to change into a lighter-color jacket to match you."

"A light earth-tone color," she told him.

Ivan scampered to his bedroom closet to change his jacket.

Damn, I can't take this, he told himself. *I want this girl bad, but the business is just too good to chance it. But . . . Lucina doesn't even talk about guys. Are she and her girl Maya closet dykes or what?*

By the time he walked back out to join her, wearing a camel-colored cashmere, Lucina had already started to set the table with food. She looked him over and grinned.

"That's a much better choice of jacket."

"Only because you're wearing pink," he told her as he helped her set the table. She had ordered veal, steak, chicken, shrimp, spaghetti, salad, vegetables, garlic bread, and a bottle of red wine.

"Are you sure you brought enough food to choose from?" Ivan joked.

Lucina smiled and poured the wine into a pair of wineglasses from his cabinet. "Shall we eat?" she asked him, sitting in the comfortable chair across from his.

"Definitely. I didn't eat anything tonight while waiting for this."

As they dug into the various samples of Italian-prepared food, Lucina asked him, "So, are you ready for your big party next week?"

Ivan chewed his steak and asked her, "What should I wear?"

"A black jacket and white shirt," she answered. She had already thought it over for him. "But no tie or handkerchief because you want to look *loose*. You can also go with dark blue dress jeans and a very nice pair of black shoes. You might even want to buy a new pair."

Ivan said, "Dress *jeans,* at a *fifty*-dollar party at the Manchester Grand Hyatt? I've been telling everyone to dress to impress."

She said, "And you *should* tell them that. But for *you,* you will stand out more by looking classy yet casual."

"Well, what will you wear?"

Lucina smiled. "I have something very special planned."

"And you just want me in black and white with dress jeans?"

She said, "You should look like a more urban James Bond. And they must all know that you can mix well in any circle, like you said in your interviews."

"But wouldn't dressing down make it look like I'm not on their level yet?" he questioned.

Lucina told him, "Ivan, this is *your* party. And the fact that they are even coming puts you on their level already. So now you want to show them that you can be the middleman between their companies and the customers. That's what your website does, right? It makes the link of promotion."

Ivan argued, "Yeah, but there's still a certain look that they expect."

Lucina only smiled at him. She countered, "Just like you know how rich people are through your business of accounting, I know how they are through my business of throwing parties. And at the parties, you no longer work *for them,* you work *with them* to show them how to have a good event. So you want to show them that in *this* arena, you are your *own* man, and you make your *own* rules, including the clothes you choose to wear."

Ivan listened to her and nodded. And he wondered if Lucina would be right again.

Part VI

Million-Dollar Deals

Sixteen

Bingo!

AFTER A GREAT DINNER, a surprise birthday cake, relaxation, and further talk about their plots and plans for future business, Lucina left Ivan alone to indulge in the rest of his birthday pleasures however he pleased that evening, just like she said she would. And both Christina and Ashley called him back to fulfill his wishes. Nevertheless, with his cell phone on silent, Ivan never bothered to answer or return their calls.

"I guess I got 'em both hooked," he commented to himself, grinning. But after the spoils of Lucina's productive company, he was no longer in the mood for their dessert. He preferred to linger in thought about his smart and beautiful partner instead.

Once the time had passed midnight without him returning their calls, he imagined, *Now they'll definitely think I'm involved with Lucina. But what can I say? She's still sexy like that. And sooner or later, I'll deserve to have her.*

IVAN WENT ALONG with Lucina's dress code plan and bought a black-sheen Calvin Klein dinner jacket; high-grade, dark blue denim jeans from Sean John; and quality black shoes from Kenneth Cole.

He had plenty of white shirts to choose from in his wardrobe already.

To make sure the look would do the job, Ivan tried it all on at his apartment and stared into the full-length mirror inside the walk-in closet of his bedroom.

"A more urban James Bond, hunh?" he told himself in the mirror. *Damn! Look how bright this diamond shines in my ear with this black jacket on,* he noted.

He nodded and stated, "Another good look, Lucina. Another good look."

ON SATURDAY EVENING, March 13, 2004, the main ballroom of the Manchester Grand Hyatt Hotel opened its doors to accept the well-dressed and buzzing crowd of the "IDPromotions.com CEO Birthday Network Celebration." It was promoted as a who's who network party of corporate San Diego, with Ivan David at the center of attention as the host with the recent birthday.

Black, white, and gold balloons littered the air, held down by golden bags of Hershey chocolates, with various sponsor business cards attached to the strings. Tall standing tables were spread around the room, covered with white tablecloths trimmed in gold. Plastic wineglasses were set out on each table, with bottles of red and white wine delivered from wine sponsors. Each table had sponsorship name tags and website addresses for added promotional value. Between each set of five tables stood a waiter or waitress in black pants, shoes, vest, and bow tie, with a white button-up shirt. Two long tables of catered foods were spread along the far left and right walls of the fine, chandelier-lit, decorated room. The DJ booth and speakers were set at the front of a large open dance floor area.

Maya and Daphne, both wearing golden dresses, worked the doors as usual, backed by security men dressed in black suits. But instead of collecting money, the girls punched holes in black and gold tickets that the guests were allowed to keep as souvenirs.

"Welcome to the 'IDPromotions.com CEO Birthday Network Celebration,'" Daphne told each group of supporters who approached the ballroom entrance with their tickets in hand.

"The first *annual* network celebration," Maya added, handing out the first of five hundred black and gold gift bags.

"So you mean you're gonna do this once a year?" an older white gentleman asked. He and his wife were both well dressed for a gala affair.

Maya said, "If everything goes as well as we expect it to, then why not?"

The husband nodded. "I agree. Well, you got us interested."

His wife smiled and didn't say anything until she commented in passing, "Those gold dresses you two are wearing are very nice."

"Thank you," Maya responded. Lucina had told all sixteen of the girls who worked the event to find and wear tasteful gold dresses.

Four of Lucina's girls were still on probation status. She still had to determine whether or not they were professional enough to be paid at future events. "You can never have enough new interns," she explained to Ivan. "These girls are gonna come and go every day."

More than two thousand tickets out of twenty-three hundred were sold prior to the event. An extra hundred were held at the door, and a hundred tickets were given away to special guests. The grand party idea was already a success and had broken more than a hundred thousand dollars.

Outside the hotel, the uniformed valet staff were already counting their extra dividends from the expensive luxury cars they began to park.

"It looks like a good night in store for us," one of the valet guys commented.

"I wouldn't mind an event like this *every* weekend," another valet joked. Six of them were all busy on duty that night as the luxury cars of well-dressed passengers continued to drive up.

* * *

At his apartment, less than ten minutes away from the Hyatt hotel, Ivan squirted Giorgio Armani cologne onto his wrists and rubbed it into both sides of his neck before his cell phone rang from his hip.

He looked at the phone call and read Lucina's number. It was a quarter to ten. She wanted them both to arrive at the hotel no later than ten, after the opening of the doors at nine. Several of her more experienced girls would do the hosting until they arrived.

"You're right on time again," Ivan commented.

"Yes, of course. Are you ready?"

"Yeah, I'll be right down in a minute."

"Okay, because we only have a *minute* to waste."

Ivan shook his head and hung up. Lucina could be as anal as a drill sergeant.

Down in the parked limo in front of his apartment building, she sat patiently in the backseat, wearing a black and gold Oscar de la Renta dress and gold and onyx jewelry, with a Gucci watch, a small black purse, and black heels.

Ivan climbed into the back of the limo in his own impressive clothes and looked Lucina up and down.

"Damn," he told her, "now you got me looking all underdressed."

"You do not look underdressed, Ivan. You look very nice," she assured him.

He said, "I don't look nothing close to you."

"Yes, you do, we both have on plenty of black," she told him. "And we're not *supposed* to look too close. We want to look like a partnership, but not a couple. So you have your style of dress, and I have mine."

Ivan looked at her and frowned. He said, "Shit, Lucina, this is *all* your style. You picked all of this shit out."

"Ivan, you watch your mouth before you step out of this car and walk into this big event," she warned him. "It's good to be yourself, but never be too brash."

Ivan looked at her and deadpanned, "Fuck 'em all, baby, we don't need 'em. We can take the world, just me and you."

Lucina stared at him and told him that it was not funny. But when he refused to look away from her, she cracked a smile.

"Unh-hunh, there's the smile. I knew you had it in you," he teased her.

She said, "Because you're crazy."

"Well, like you told me on my birthday, this is my big party, so I make the damn rules here, right? And my rule is to have a good time in here and get this bigger money out of everybody's pockets. And you doubted if I could even do it. Now what?" he asked.

Lucina kept her cool. "Now we get the bigger money that we both want," she told him.

It was a subtle moment for Ivan, sitting there dressed up with Lucina Gallo in the back of the limo, while heading to a top-flight affair. Less than a year ago, he could only dream about such a thing. So he lost his wits for a minute and went after her.

"So, Lucina . . . once we get all this money together, and we're seeing eye to eye, *rich* and all that good stuff . . . are you gonna let me touch you like I've always wanted to?"

Lucina immediately looked away. "We should not have this conversation before business," she answered him sternly.

Ivan said, "Well, when can we have it?"

Lucina blew him off. "We're almost there, Ivan. Behave."

She refused to look at him.

Ivan stared her down for another minute and laughed it off. *Yeah, she likes me, man, she's just constantly fronting. She can't even look at me,* he told himself. *But I'm gonna have her sooner or later.*

When their limousine pulled up to the front entrance of the hotel, the valet staff were still parking cars with zeal.

Ivan looked out at them and noticed one of the guys who had worked there when he visited the hotel with Catherine. He smiled immediately.

That's the guy I told I was coming back that night, Ivan reminded himself. *I wonder if he'll remember me telling him that.*

When the chauffeur helped them out of the limo, Ivan got the valet's attention.

"Hey, man, I doubt if you remember me, but I came here one night in May last year, the same night as the Padres party downtown, with a pretty brown girl, and I left earlier than you thought I would. And you asked me why I was leaving so early. And I said I would be back."

The valet listened to Ivan's story intently, wanting to remember it. And by chance, he did remember. He had wondered why the man was in such a hurry to leave the hotel, with such a pretty girl staying there.

"Oh, yeah, yeah, I do remember that night," he responded. "You ran across the lot like you were in a hurry to get somewhere. That was you?" Ivan no longer looked the same.

"Yeah, I was rushing to get to the Padres party that night, and the girl didn't want me to go," he told him with a grin. "But I've made a lot of changes since then. I cut my hair down, got my ear pierced, started throwing parties, a bunch of things." He said, "But I told you I would be back."

"Yeah, you did," the valet commented with a chuckle. Then he looked over Ivan's style of dress, with Lucina standing behind him, waiting. They had just stepped out of the limo.

"So, you're part of this party here tonight?" the valet asked him.

Ivan smiled slyly. He answered, "Yeah, I'm a part of it. I'm a *big* part."

"A big part who's gonna be *late* if you don't come on, Ivan," Lucina told him from behind.

The valet overheard her and put two and two together to make four.

He said, "Wait a minute, you're not Ivan *David,* are you?"

That made the other valets stop and wonder for a minute.

Ivan tried to hold in his grin, but it felt good to have a recognizable name.

He said, "Somebody has to be him," and started walking off toward Lucina. "But I'll see you if you're out here later."

"All right. I'll be here."

The valets didn't need any convincing after that. Any man who had a woman as beautiful as Lucina waiting around for him had to be worth something.

"Hey, man, you know him?" one of the other valets asked, once Ivan and Lucina had walked into the hotel.

The valet was still stunned. "Ahh, no, not really," he answered. "He just, ah, ran out of here late one night a while ago."

He thought, *But I wish I did know him. He's throwing big, fancy corporate parties, and I'm still out here parking cars for tips. Shit!*

"Your people skills are special," Lucina noted to Ivan on their way in. "You have a way of maintaining your humility with everyone."

Ivan smiled it off and said, "Not everyone. But I'm just starting this. You gotta give me five more years before you can say that."

As soon as they walked into the grand lobby, two of Lucina's interns were there to greet them in gold dresses. Both of them were exuberant white girls who could make the men's magazines as pinup poster models: one blond with gray eyes, the other brunette with greens.

"This is Ivan David, the boss," Lucina told them. "You are both to take *great* care of him."

She didn't have to tell them that. They both realized how important Ivan was as soon as he walked through the door with her. His name was only posted on every part of the ballroom. But being meticulous with her help was Lucina's way with things.

Before they could even reach the bubbling event, businessmen of all nationalities and ages were ready to greet Ivan with their wives and significant others at their side as they all approached the ballroom doors.

"Mr. Ivan David, we all look forward to a prosperous event tonight," an East Indian man in his early forties stated as Ivan and Lucina passed him by in the line.

"And we intend to give you one," Ivan told him. He then held one of Lucina's two helpers by the hand and told her, "Make sure you get his business card and the proper pronunciation of his name for me."

The Indian man laughed. He said, "Yes, that is very important."

"Indeed it is," Ivan told him with a nod. "We'll talk later, my friend. But right now my partner and hostess, Lucina, wants me to address the crowd inside before they all become angry with me."

More of the businessmen waiting in line with their tickets out began to laugh.

"We'll see you inside, Ivan," another businessman commented. "And congratulations."

Ivan nodded to him as well. "Thank you."

As they made their way inside, greeting Daphne, Maya, and the security men at the doors, two more of Lucina's interns approached them: another beautiful Filipina, and an equally enticing Mexican.

Where the hell does Lucina find these girls? Ivan thought.

She said, "I need *all* four of you to collect the business cards and remember the names of each and every potential client who Ivan speaks to tonight," Lucina told them.

Ivan pulled Lucina aside and asked her, "Are you sure you want them doing that if they're all new? I just said that to be polite to the guy back there. That was all part of me working this business crowd with your girls."

Lucina said, "Yes, I realize that, but I would rather have my experienced girls working the room where we are not there. But with the new girls, we can keep a better eye on their mistakes if they are close by you."

Ivan thought it over and agreed with her. "Okay. That makes sense."

They then made their way to the center of the room through the curious crowd of onlookers, buzzing with safe jazz music in the background. Red Face Lion was even forced to wear a business jacket at his DJ booth for the evening. And the versatility of his musical tastes came in handy.

"You're looking good tonight, Red," Ivan told him as Lucina secured the microphone in hand.

"I'm just trying to be like you, man," Red responded.

"We're ready to address the crowd," Lucina stated.

Red faded down the music and raised the volume on the microphone.

Lucina walked out into the middle of the floor to address the business crowd, with Ivan beside her.

"Greetings, everyone," she opened. "We thank you all for coming out this evening to the first annual IDPromotions.com CEO Birthday Network Celebration of executives and entrepreneurs. And for those of you who have never met me before, I am Lucina Gallo, cohost and promotional partner of the birthday man, Ivan David, who has brought us all together here this evening at the luxurious Manchester Grand Hyatt."

She said, "But our purpose this evening is not only to celebrate, but to discuss a *million* ways, I'm sure, to make San Diego an even greater place to live and do business than it already is."

The crowd was impressed with Lucina. They began to clap, nod, and toast her accented opening speech.

Ivan watched and admired her delivery himself, wondering if she had practiced it all.

Now what the hell am I gonna say? he asked himself. He had gone over a few things, but since he had not practiced or prepared with Lucina's address in mind, he had to rethink it all.

Lucina went on to talk about all of the networking opportunities and a chance to share business ideas and knowledge, before she prepared to introduce Ivan.

"And without further ado, I give you the man who we all came here to see tonight, Mr. Ivan David."

The crowd began to clap, nod, and toast again as Ivan stepped forward to secure the microphone from Lucina.

He smiled and decided to address everyone with humor. "Well, I don't know if we all feel comfortable enough to share our business ideas and knowledge—a solid advantage is everything—but I think that we can at *least* meet and identify our business competitors who showed up tonight."

The crowd promptly loosened up and began to smile and chuckle at Ivan's timely candor. Lucina even spotted Randy Sterling and his partner, Ralph Collins, in attendance. They had decided to use the free tickets she had sent to their office.

Ivan added, "However, I would love for all of you to feel open enough to tell *me* everything that you would like, and I promise to keep all of our secrets between you, me, and my banker."

The crowd laughed harder. Even Lucina smiled.

Ivan said, "But seriously, I'm not going to spend too much of my time in front of this microphone, because I would like to meet . . ." He stopped and looked around the room at the large crowd and continued, ". . . at least *half* of you one on one, to discuss how we, at IDPromotions.com, may be able to help bridge the gaps between your company's ideas, products, and services and the San Diego community. So just look at us as the tall bridge that connects the companies to the customers and clients, while also connecting the customers and the clients to your companies."

Ivan looked out at the crowd and spotted his friends from the San Diego Urban League, the Chargers, the Padres, Hutch & Mitchell Accounting, Raymond's Hot Spot Lounge, his attorneys, the Wine Cavern, and plenty of other business establishments, advertisers, sponsors, clients, new friends, and associates from the past year of party and website promotions. They were all there to continue to see him do well, including Ida and her mother, Carol.

Ivan concluded, "I believe that the purpose of networking is all about positioning ourselves for progress. So please, pull out your pens, business cards, and your best conversations, and let's all make this a productive night."

When Ivan finished his address to the audience, Lucina nodded to him and commented, "Well done."

Ivan said, "Not without you. You made me have to work harder for it."

She grinned and said, "A woman who knows how to make a man work harder is always a good thing to have."

Ivan grinned and didn't comment. They had far too much meeting and greeting to do, while Red Face Lion blended more safe music, spinning the classics of Miles Davis, Louis Armstrong, John Coltrane, Thelonious Monk, Herbie Hancock, Wynton Marsalis, and many others. He even mixed in some Frank Sinatra, Nat King Cole, Stevie Wonder, and Lionel Ritchie.

Ivan and Lucina greeted bankers, Realtors, travel agents, car dealers, doctors, dentists, professors, lawyers, artists, musicians, painters, pet care shop owners, managers of tourist attractions, venture capitalists, computer software makers, chefs, chamber of commerce officials, media professionals, publicists, military officers, contractors, architects, filmmakers, television executives, and the list went on. Many of them had ready suggestions of how Ivan's business could help theirs.

"I noticed your website has nothing for San Diego pet care."

"Well, with a pet care sponsor, we can put that right up for you. Just email my sales executive at EddieK2003@IDPromotions.com and let him know what you would like to suggest."

Ivan took a business card and wrote Eddie's email address and position on the back of the card. He would let his sales staff handle it from there.

"Thank you. I'll do that."

"What about a health-care page?" a female doctor asked him.

"Good idea," Ivan told her. "And we could spotlight the different San Diego doctors in different fields. All we would need is for three to five of you guys to show genuine interest, or just have a lone sponsor for the page."

"How much is a page sponsorship?"

Ivan wrote Eddie's email address on the back of another business card. He had brought a box of a thousand that evening, and Lucina's assistants had them ready in hand for Ivan each time he reached for one.

"Email my sales executive and he'll work with you on the rates."

"Have you ever thought about promoting a San Diego car show?" a luxury car dealer asked him. "With the beautiful young ladies you have working here for you, the professional athletes you know, and the successful parties you throw around town, I'm sure we should be able to talk about some kind of promotional car show."

Ivan looked at the well-dressed dealer with perfectly groomed dark brown hair and brown eyes. He said, "In fact, we've already thought about that idea." He wrote his personal cell phone number on the back of another card. "Call me up personally on that and we'll go over the ideas and numbers."

The dealer took the card and put a firm hand on Ivan's right shoulder. "You got it, my friend."

Ivan smiled at his four assistants and asked them, "What do you guys think about that? Would you be willing to wear something hot and sexy for a car show with Xzibit?"

They responded immediately, "Oh, yeah, definitely."

The blond-haired girl looked a bit confused. She asked, "Xzibit?"

The Mexican girl had to fill her in. "You know, the guy from *Pimp My Ride* on MTV."

"Oh, okay, you mean the *rapper* Xzibit."

Ivan just looked at her and grinned. *That's why they're rookies,* he told himself.

"What about a recruiting page on your website?" a military officer asked him.

Ivan paused. He honestly wasn't in agreement with sending young guys into the military. And he didn't agree with the president's support and promotion of an Iraqi war.

He said, "We would need the military's permission to do that, right?"

"I'm gonna get you permission," the officer told him.

Ivan remained hesitant. He said, "Well, we would have to think that over."

"What's there to think about? Don't you agree with the need to support the security of our country?"

Ivan stopped and looked to his assistants again. They all grinned and looked apprehensive. How would the boss handle the patriotic military officer?

Ivan said, "We all agree to support American security. So we'll see what we can work out."

"Can I have one of those business cards?" the officer asked.

"Oh, sure," Ivan told him.

Two of his assistants handed the officer a card at the same time.

He nodded and told them, "I'll keep the extra for my higher rank."

When he walked away, the girls teased, "You better not disappoint him."

Ivan smirked and shook his head. *Fuck him,* he thought. *I'm not sending these kids off to war through my website. President Bush can kiss my ass!*

On Lucina's side of the room, she received suggestions for business of her own.

"So, these are, ah, all your ladies in here, helping out with the gold dresses?" a peculiar man asked her. He looked to be staring too hard. He nursed a glass of dark wine in his hand.

Lucina studied his forward-leaning posture and was quickly put off by him. He seemed untrustworthy and plotting.

"Why?" she asked him.

"Are they, ah, for hire?"

She didn't like the man's line of questions, either.

She answered tartly, "No, they only work for me."

"Well, how do I hire *you*?" he asked.

Lucina promptly looked around the room to escape from him by greeting someone else who gained her attention.

"Hi, how are you?" she asked, with her hand extended to a more jovial and tactful businessman.

"Hi, Lucina. My name is Seth Gardner and I represent a marine brokerage group that specializes in the sales of large yachts and ocean cruise liners."

"And we can throw parties for the right kinds of clients on all of them," Lucina responded to him.

Seth laughed. He said, "You must have read my mind."

"Yes, I have to use all of my skills," she told him. "So, what are your ideas?"

As she spoke to him, she watched the other gentleman walk away in the background.

Good riddance! she told herself while Seth continued to speak.

He said, "My idea is to build a more knowledgeable client base by having events, like you say, that would introduce much larger groups to the excitement of not only being out on the ocean, but *owning* the vehicle that takes you there." He said, "And even if some of them may not be able to afford to buy a boat tomorrow or next year, they may remember us and want to buy a boat in the next *two* to *five* years, including you or Ivan," he added.

Lucina nodded and told him, "Good idea."

All around the room, Ivan's staff and business associates engaged in business conversations. Eddie K. talked with newspaper professionals about the experience of internet advertisement. Jeff and Paul spoke with other computer company reps and website developers about new intellectual media. Lucina's girls spoke with everyone about everything. And Thomas Jones, Henry Morgan, and Ava Tate spoke to several members of the African-American press.

"So, what's Ivan's whole program here? Is he trying to do a full crossover thing or what?" asked a representative from the *Voice & Viewpoint,* one of the leading African-American publications in San Diego. "He didn't even contact us for an article."

"Well, you can do one now," Ava told him. "I could write it up for you myself. And we're gonna have plenty of photos to choose from tonight." She had freelanced for the newspaper several times before.

"Yeah, but how come we didn't have a story *before* this event?" the representative argued.

Thomas didn't want to get into a war of words with him, but he didn't see where their paper not having an article had hurt Ivan any. The place was *packed.*

Thomas said, "Ivan's still a young guy, Nathan. He's not going anywhere. You still have plenty of time to write articles up on him."

Nathan said, "Yeah, but now it looks like we missed the boat on the first one."

"Not if you let me cover this event for you, you won't. But it's all on you," Ava repeated.

Henry had nothing to add. He only heard everyone out while bobbing from left to right to left, as if he were watching a tennis match.

Back inside Ivan's circle, an older woman complained, "Ivan, I am very sad that I did not arrive early enough to receive a gift bag to remember you by."

Ivan smiled and told her, "I'll have one of our lovely assistants run and grab you one of the extras."

They had prepared an additional hundred gift bags just for the left-out latecomers who would ask for them.

"Oh, thank *heavens,* and bless your *soul,* young man," she responded. "Also, happy birthday. And congratulations on all of your success. I'm sure that your mother is very proud of you."

Ivan heard that and froze. He nodded and said, "I'm quite sure she is. Can you take her with you to get her a gift bag?" he asked his new Filipina assistant.

"Oh, sure."

Ashley was there that night as well, working the crowd on the far left side of the room near the catered food. Money was money, so she chose to work that night. She remained upset with Ivan for playing her second to Lucina, but what could she do about it? Ivan and Lucina were partners, while she was only a part-time employee.

Lucina looked over in Ivan's direction to see how he was doing and noticed Randy and Ralph headed in her partner's direction. She saw that and panicked.

Should I intervene to steer the conversation, or stay out of it and see where it goes on its own? she asked herself. She quickly decided to stay out of it. Ivan could handle himself. And she would ask him about their conversation later.

"Hey, Ivan, I'm Randy Sterling, and this is my partner, Ralph Collins, from Randy and Ralph Entertainment."

Ivan heard the name and nodded to them. "Yeah, I've heard about you guys. You're always doing big things in the city." They were two of the few people not dressed to impress that evening. Outside of their sports jackets, they looked pretty casual in their blue jeans, soft leather shoes, and button-up shirts.

"Yeah, I hear you've been doing your thing as well," Randy commented. "We used to partner up with Lucina ourselves."

"Yeah, whatever happened with that?" Ivan asked them. He had never talked with Lucina in detail about it. He wondered what their views of her would be.

Ralph, standing a little shorter than Randy and with darker hair, answered the question. If Ivan had to guess, he would assume that Ralph was the numbers man, while Randy was the people person.

"Well, we just started to cater to different clientele, and Lucina felt that she just wasn't, ah, getting her full value's worth." He said, "But we're glad to see that she's working out well with you now. We're happy for her."

Ivan nodded, wondering how much the two of them were worth. He estimated seven to fifteen million. They were among the lead concert promoters in the city. But they mainly dealt with pop and rock music, leaving the urban and ethnic crowds alone.

Ivan projected, *We probably can't touch them on concerts right now. We still have a lot of work to do.*

Randy asked him, "So, who came up with this idea? Lucina?"

Meeting face-to-face with these guys was the exact competitive situation Ivan had alluded to in his speech. He wanted to be extra-careful with everything he said to them.

"Lucina has a lot of great ideas, but the network that I've been able to build through Hutch and Mitchell Accounting, the *Tribune* newspaper, the Urban League, all of my personal friendships, and the website has allowed us *both* to make the bigger ideas fly," he told them. He added, "This is just the tip of the iceberg. We're just getting started now."

Ivan wanted to protect himself and Lucina right away by name-dropping his accounting firm, the local media, and a well-established African-American business group, and hinting at his own friendships, website vehicle, and the fact that they planned to increase their promotional power within the city limits of San Diego. He wanted to establish a solid base.

Ralph nodded and said, "That's good. It looks like you're building a strong team. So you guys will be doing mostly urban and R&B crowds? We hear you had Busta Rhymes, Timbaland, and, ah, Eve in town a few weeks ago."

Ivan smirked. He said, "You guys are paying attention to us like that? They were pretty much just hangout parties."

"Well, those hangout parties cause a lot of noise w throw them in the Gaslamp," Randy stated with a chuckle.

Since Ivan was still relatively new to most of the club owners in the Gaslamp Quarter, he wanted to create an illusion of distance on those deals to see what would happen. Were Randy and Ralph friends or foes?

"Well, I actually don't decide on who comes in and where we have them. Lucina and the other promoters we work with are usually the ones who tell us what the crowd would like here, and I just follow their lead," he told them.

Randy nodded, comprehending everything. He figured Ivan was more of a freelance investor who was willing to drill in whatever direction he could to find some oil.

He asked, "So, what are you thinking about going in on next? You know, we may be able to include you in on some things."

"Lucina, too?" Ivan asked them. It sounded like they wanted to be friends.

Ralph said, "Are you guys, like, *full* partners, or do you just partner up on different projects? I mean, does she, like, own a piece of IDPromotions.com, or is that question getting too personal?"

That's the good old divide-and-conquer technique, Ivan told himself. *Looks like they're not friends with Lucina.* He was nearly ready to smile in amusement. These guys were tremendously obvious. And if they could be that blatantly disrespectful to his partner, then why should he trust them?

He answered, "Yeah, that is a little too personal there. But, you know, if you guys have something coming that's big enough, where you feel that we could all make something off of it, then call me up and let's talk."

Ralph looked around at Lucina's girls and decided to hold his comments until they could have a more private meeting of the minds later.

"All right, well, we'll talk then," he stated before handing Ivan his card. "I have my personal cell number on the back."

When they turned to walk off, one of Lucina's assistants offered them each one of Ivan's business cards.

"No, we know how to get in touch with him," Randy said, rejecting it.

Yeah, fuck those guys, Ivan told himself. *They're typical white boys trying to snatch up all the marbles off the table.*

Before Ivan could even turn around, Lucina was right there beside him in a flash.

"I want to talk about them later," she commented, and walked away.

Ivan grinned and chuckled. *I can't blame her,* he told himself. *It looks like the next level of business is about to get anxious now.*

Zee-Dog, Perry, Emilio, and some of the other Chargers and Padres players had formed their own huddle inside the room.

"Yeah, this shit right here is definitely Jeffrey's kind of party," Perry grumbled. He watched as his teammate made business talk around the room with his fiancée in tow. He said, "They don't have the right kind of music for me, or even dark enough lights in here."

Zee-Dog laughed and said, "It's a network party, man. Folks wanna be able to see who they're talking to."

"Well, as long as nobody's asking me to sign any damn autographs in here, I'm cool," Perry said.

Emilio only listened to them and smiled. He dreaded not being able to bring Audrey, but she refused to come. She wanted to keep her distance from Lucina, Ivan, and the whole clan. She considered Emilio to be her protected prize now.

"So, how do you guys feel about Ivan?" a bank executive asked John Hutch and Barry Mitchell in their own huddle.

"He's obviously a brilliant young man," Barry commented. "Look how he's brought so many of us together."

"And how long do you plan on being able to keep him under wraps?" the bank executive asked them with a smirk.

John Hutch nodded. He said, "Now, that's a good question. You don't pull off a grand event like this and plan to stand pat. We haven't tried anything major like this for ourselves."

Barry said, "I'm sure we'll be able to work something out with him. He seems to be quite a reasonable guy."

John grinned and responded sarcastically, "Yeah, we'll see real soon how that goes. But we can at least expect another twenty-five clients out of this that we'll owe him credit for."

Chip, Mike, Dwayne, and a few of the other accountants from the office huddled near their bosses.

"Can you believe this? Ivan was setting all of this up right under our noses," Chip commented, as his eyes continued to follow Gretchen in her gold dress, as they had all evening. Mike and Dwayne took in everything in silence.

Dwayne mused, *There's no coming back down from this. Ivan has put himself out there now.*

Carol, from the soul food restaurant in Old Town, whom Ivan continued to promote on his website, looked at her daughter Ida and asked her, "Are you sure you can't work anything out between you and Ivan?"

"Stop it, Mom," Ida told her. "Now, I support what Ivan is doing for himself in business, obviously, but it stops there. And I have nothing else to say about it."

Carol heard her daughter out and shook her head. *She'll learn ten more years from now when she still feels lonely with a man at her side who doesn't have anything in order.*

Just before midnight, the hotel catering staff wheeled out an enormous birthday cake with twenty-nine candles to light.

Red Face Lion then made an announcement calling everyone together at the center of the room to sing "Happy Birthday" and watch Ivan blow out his candles.

"Are you sure you want me to go through with this birthday cake thing?" Ivan whispered to Lucina. The idea seemed ridiculous to him. He wasn't so sure he wanted to promote his age to everyone, either. Twenty-nine still seemed too young to be taken seriously.

Lucina told him, "Ivan, trust me. You do this correctly, and it can easily become a yearly ritual. Singing 'Happy Birthday' is a big moment for everyone, especially at a large party like this one."

So Ivan went through with the ordeal, with the lights turned down low and everything. Red Face Lion led the song through his microphone.

"Hap-py birth-day to you . . . Hap-py birth-day to you . . . Hap-py birth-day dear I-van . . . Hap-py birth-day to you."

Ivan took three big breaths to blow out all twenty-nine candles spread out on an extralong cake. It was decorated with his name, the *IDPromotions.com* logo, and their familiar website survey questions: "Who are you? What do you do? Let us know."

At the end of his big night, one of the gray-haired business guests, on his way out with his wife, shook his head at Ivan. He mumbled, "Twenty-nine years old. You got a long road of success ahead of you, son. You keep at it."

He added, "It took me to nearly *thirty-nine* years just to figure out what was going on. By that time I had made a hundred and three mistakes."

Ivan told him, "But the key is that you still found your way. I could have been doing this years ago myself. But I wasn't supposed to be. I was supposed to be doing it now."

The older businessman nodded. He said, "That's a very mature way of looking at it."

"It's the truth," Ivan told him. He smiled and added, "I needed to meet Lucina first."

WHEN IVAN AND LUCINA made it back out to the limo after one o'clock in the morning, his valet friend was still gathering cars for the many guests who were returning home.

"All right, Ivan. Good luck with everything," the guests continued telling him.

"Thanks again for coming out," Ivan told them back.

His valet friend made an extra effort to make sure that he walked over to shake Ivan's hand before he climbed into the limo behind Lucina.

He said, "You've been a big inspiration to me tonight, Mr. David. I'll always remember this for when I start to make my own plans happen."

Ivan said, "Do what you gotta do, man. Just don't rush it. You let it all come to you the way it's supposed to."

"I'll make sure I will."

When Ivan climbed into the car with his exhausted partner, Lucina smiled at him meekly.

"So, what are you planning to do now with the thousand business cards we collected tonight?" she asked him.

Ivan said, "I'm gonna make a thousand business calls and see if I can pull together *two thousand* dollars from each business. That would be, what, *two million*?"

Lucina winced and answered, "I think, yes."

Ivan said, "Well, that's my new short-term goal. I wanna be a millionaire before this year is out."

Lucina said, "Well, if you make *two million,* that means that I'm a millionaire, too."

"Yeah, if you get involved in real estate with me," Ivan pressed her. "But it's not gonna happen through parties alone. Your guys Randy and Ralph have a big head start on us in that department."

"Yes, what did they say to you?"

Ivan took a deep breath and told her, "Basically, they wanted to know the extent of our relationship, and if I was willing to break away from you to do things on my own. But I pretty much told them that I get all of my ideas from you and then shell out the money to back your genius. And at that point, they wanted to see if I would be willing to back them."

Lucina stared at him. She concluded, "So, you made yourself out to be the moneyman, while I would be the idea girl."

Ivan nodded. "Yup. That's about it."

Lucina said, "Clever. So now you make us *both* valuable in different ways."

Ivan told her, "I couldn't have done any of this without you."

Lucina shook it off, too tired to argue. It had been a long evening for both of them.

She said, "You already had your website before I met you. You had your charm, good looks, drive, ideas, a following, intelligence, Hutch and Mitchell Accounting, *and* the Urban League."

"And none of that would have meant anything without the Chargers party, impulsive girls, my new look, confidence, game plans, and the pocketfuls of cash that you allowed me to share with you," he countered with a smile.

Lucina smiled back. "And you *listened.*"

"And so did you," he told her.

Just that fast, they had pulled up to the front of his apartment building.

Ivan looked over at Lucina and said, "You really don't feel like going home yet, do you? The night is still young. Don't be an early bird on me," he teased her.

Lucina chuckled wearily. She said, "Tonight, I will *have* to be an early bird. I'm *exhausted,* Ivan. I don't remember meeting this many important people in one room, in one night, in my life. I mean, I've met more *wealthy* people before, but not all at once."

Ivan reached out to hold her hand in his anyway.

He said, "Are you sure you don't want to lie down and rest with the birthday boy?"

"Ivan, your birthday was last week. And I did come over and share it with you." She said, "Have you forgotten my company already, and the pink dress that I wore just for you?"

Ivan acted as if he had amnesia. He frowned and answered, "Pink dress? Birthday last week? What are you talking about?"

"Nice try, Ivan. But I'm going home now to go to bed. I'll call you when I get home."

Ivan sighed. It was no use. Lucina refused to break down for him.

"All right, so, call me when you get in," he told her as he climbed out of the car.

"I will."

"Good night, Mr. David," the chauffeur told him.

Ivan nodded and said, "Good night," but he was hardly finished yet. He had energy still left over. So as soon as he made it to the elevator doors inside his apartment building, he called up Ashley.

"Hey, are you still down here?" he asked her.

"I don't know, why? I *shouldn't* be," she pouted.

He said, "But you are. So stop complaining and come on over here and see me like you know you want to."

Ashley paused and thought it over. But there was no hiding her true feelings. She said, "I felt really proud of you tonight. That was really a special event for you. I just wish that I could be the one at the center of attention."

Ivan told her, "You are. I mean, just think about it. Out of all those people there to see me tonight, you're the only one who gets to spend the night with me."

She joked, "You would spend the night with other guys?"

Ivan said, "Come on, now. Don't turn something special into something silly."

Ashley said, "But that's just it, I don't feel special with you, Ivan. I'm always the side chick. And I don't like that."

Ivan took another breath and lost his patience with her. He rubbed his temples with his free hand and said, "Man, after all this shit I put together tonight, I still gotta beg a pretty girl to spend the night with me. Is that how I'm living? Because if it is, then I'm about to take a nice walk downtown and find somebody who wants to give a handsome young man a birthday present."

Ashley chuckled at him. She said, "You're *spoiled,* Ivan. That's what *your* problem is."

"Yeah, well, let me know what you're gonna do," he told her.

She said, "I'm parking down the street from your apartment. Okay? Are you happy now?"

Ivan smiled. He said, "A man is always happy to see a pretty girl when he's feeling it late at night."

"Yeah, whatever. So . . . I guess I'll be there in a minute."

Seventeen
The Bosses

IVAN CALLED an emergency staff meeting at his IDPromotions .com office for Sunday evening. Once everyone had gathered there after eight PM, he made a short, informative speech about his objectives for the week.

"Okay, as I explained to everyone last week, or for the last couple of weeks, our big networking event last night was not just a birthday party but a gigantic key to a big door of new opportunities. We have nearly a thousand business cards and email addresses from the event, and we need to work hard and fast all this week to connect the dots for new advertisers, sponsors, spotlight stories, and new business associates."

He said, "We want to hit it and hit it hard with plenty of sugar. That means we want to make sure that everyone enjoyed themselves *first,* and then we reiterate all of our strengths and services here at I.D. Promotions. Eddie K. will guide all of our sales staff on the ad and sponsorship rates, as well as our availabilities for the month, the quarter, and for the year. Ava Tate will guide all of our new editorial content. And Jeff and Paul will design up to six new web pages, as well as upgrade our existing pages."

"*Whew,* sounds like a whole lot of work this week," Jeff commented.

Ivan said, "And we may not be able to finish everything this week, but since it is such a heavy load on all of us, I've forced myself to allow the idea of giving everyone a thousand-dollar bonus."

That idea cheered his staff up immediately. They exclaimed it in the room.

"Yeah! All right! I can surely use it!"

Ivan added, "Now, some of us are going to be doing more work than others, but it's up to *all of us* to work together as a *team* to make sure that everyone gives the proper *effort* that we'll need to pull this week off."

After his staff address, Ivan had a few private words with Eddie upstairs in his back office.

Eddie smiled and said, "That was quite another speech from you, Ivan. You're impressing me more and more every day."

Ivan didn't thank him for the compliment. Instead, he told him, "I've been thinking all day about the possibilities of this company, Eddie. And it's time to jump on this fast horse and ride it all the way now. So, for the people who can't take the pace, I need to know who they are as soon as possible."

Eddie K. nodded and understood him. He said, "I guess this'll be the last paycheck for a lot of them, hunh?"

Ivan just stared at him. His motives were obvious to a sales veteran like Eddie.

Ivan said, "I'm just being fair with them, *more* than fair. And I'm also being realistic. This is a serious company now. So I need people who are really ready to work."

Eddie grinned and said, "I know."

"You also know that I can't continue to serve two masters," Ivan confided in him. "I need to get out there and make these bigger deals happen all day long now. I can't do it just over lunch hours.

So I'm trying to figure out how I can create a consultant position with Hutch and Mitchell, like you did with the newspaper."

Eddie told him, "You just ask them for it. And after what you just pulled together last night, I can't see how any company in their right mind could turn you down. So you simply give them an offer that they can't refuse." He said, "But honesty is the best policy."

Ivan thought it over and nodded. "Thanks, man. That's exactly what I need to do. The time is now."

MOVING ON from a position of employment that Ivan had held over the past six years of his life was not an easy thing to do.

What if they tell me no? he pondered at his Hutch & Mitchell desk that Monday morning. *Then I'll be out on my own with no big name protection behind me . . . But if I'm really ready to take my company seriously, then my own name should mean something.*

He then looked around at his surroundings and realized, *Here I am, sitting at a damn cubicle, when I just brought together billions of dollars all in one room. What the hell am I doing here?*

He continued to daydream at his desk as the executive secretary passed behind him. Ivan was so deep in thought that he never noticed the older white woman spying on him that morning. Once she witnessed the evidence she needed, she walked right up to John Hutch's closed office door and knocked before he responded to her.

"Who is it?"

"It's Edith."

"Come on in."

When she walked in, Barry Mitchell was already in the room, discussing the pressing issue with his partner.

"So, what does Ivan look like today?" John asked her.

Edith took a breath and said, "He looks like he's on cloud nine. He's definitely thinking about something other than tax laws this morning."

John nodded to her. "Thank you very much, Edith. Can you close the door on your way back out?"

"Oh, certainly."

As soon as she left the room, John suggested to Barry, "So, we both take him out to dinner, and we get everything out in the open."

Barry took a breath of his own. He said, "I still think we're jumping the gun a bit, but I guess we don't have a choice now, do we?"

John said, "All it is, is a conversation. And if you're right, you're right. But if *I'm* right, then we need to have a plan ready."

IVAN MET with his bosses for dinner at a sushi restaurant in Poway, a far northeast section of San Diego. They sat in a dark booth near the back of the restaurant to limit the amount of noise and traffic around them. Ivan sat on one side of the booth, and his two bosses sat on the other.

John Hutch, with his light brown hair and cold blue eyes, figured they would move ahead of the game before Ivan could solidify any future plans. Barry Mitchell, with his warm brown eyes and darker hair, only wanted to hear what Ivan had to say for himself. And by the time they had met him for dinner that evening, Ivan had already come up with plenty of ideas of his own to discuss with them.

"Let us begin by saying that you put on a fabulous event this weekend, Ivan. Fabulous!" Barry commented first.

John only nodded in silent agreement.

"Thank you," Ivan told them. "It was a real stretch trying to pull it all together on such short notice. But everything seemed to work in our favor, so I just went with it. They call it momentum, right?"

Ivan intended to speak openly with them while remaining friendly and loose. He wanted them both to know that he still liked them. They had been very fair to him.

John said, "Ivan, Barry and I will be in some very serious talks to close deals on at least *eight* new major clients from your event on

Saturday evening. Now, we both understand that you'll likely be bringing in your own list of new clients from the event as well. But it gets to a certain point where we all have to ask ourselves, 'Is Ivan more important to us at the office, or out there closing deals?'"

They were taking the conversation exactly where Ivan needed for it to go. So he became cautious. He wanted to see what John and Barry would come up with on their own.

He looked over the table at Barry Mitchell to hear what he had to add.

Barry looked at him and shrugged. In his opinion, John was being a little too anxious.

"Well, you're gonna make a lot of money off of these deals, Ivan, that's for sure," he commented with a chuckle. And he was saved by the food. At least five different sushi dishes arrived at their table, including white rice.

"Perfect timing," John stated to their server. He said, "All of this talk about money makes me hungry. What about you, Ivan?"

Ivan was still trying to configure his angle. Big business was a chess game. He wanted to make sure he made all the right moves.

So John is pushing for a new deal, and Barry is pushing the brakes, he assessed of his two bosses.

Ivan smiled and reached to gather some of the sushi for his plate. He said, "Being hungry is natural. But we always want to make sure we eat the right foods. And I hear that sushi is good for you."

He slid a piece of raw salmon into his mouth and chewed it down.

John and Barry began to fill their plates to eat as well.

Barry looked at a piece of fish before he ate it. He said, "Well, you have fish that swim in schools, and other fish who swim out on their own. Which one are you, Ivan?"

Ivan felt more comfortable with an assertive approach from Barry than a passive approach. A passive boss was much harder to read. But he could respond to the assertive approach with intellectual confidence.

"Well, every fish has to learn how to swim first. But I believe a dolphin is the most cooperative. They can swim in a school, a small group, in a pair, or break off and swim by themselves when they need to. So I would consider myself to be a dolphin."

John frowned and said, "Dolphins are considered mammals, aren't they?"

Ivan kept his poise. He said, "If they are, then I guess I'm not a fish at all. I'm just a mammal who happens to swim fast."

After they shared a laugh, Barry said, "Actually, dolphins are a very social group of animals. And they are considered to be one of the most intelligent, dolphins and, ah . . ."

"Killer whales," John filled in before taking another bite of raw fish. "The orcas."

That wasn't quite the answer Barry had been searching for, but it fit. Killer whales were known as the masters of the sea. Nevertheless, Ivan didn't like the reference. So he tried to tone things down a bit.

"I'm definitely not one of those," he commented.

"Not yet," John argued, eating another piece of fish.

Barry said, "Well, killer whales can be social, too. By the way, they're my favorite part of going to SeaWorld."

On that note, Ivan had to get away from the table for a minute. He chuckled and stood up to excuse himself. "Yeah, let me go use the restroom."

As soon as he walked away, Barry asked his partner, "What are you doing, John? Relax."

John snapped, "Relax? Look, Barry, we need to get this kid to be honest with us. He's not a damn dolphin, he's a killer whale in training. So we're either gonna feed him what he feels he's worth, or he's gonna eat up everything in the tank."

Barry shook if off. He stopped and asked, "So, what are we gonna offer him now, a full partnership, John? This kid isn't ready for that."

"Well, we're gonna have to offer him something, and *fast*. He's already thinking about being in on the much bigger deals, I can assure you of that," John insisted. He said, "This kid is looking at the whole ocean now. He's just sitting over there biding his time."

Barry didn't have anything else to say. In his gut, he felt that Ivan could be a real star, but he had to see it first to believe it. He had gotten burned before by young businessmen who had not reached their full potential. So Barry now preferred to preach, pray, and wait, but not necessarily to believe.

John, on the other hand, was already sold on Ivan's mastery. The straight numbers added up. He admired the young man, even. And he wasn't done talking about him.

He said, "Think about it, Barry. Ivan pulls together over a billion dollars' worth of executives for his *twenty-ninth* birthday, and then he comes back to work for us at a *cubicle.* Are you kidding me? I would be daydreaming, too, about my last damn days at work here."

John stated, "So, Barry, when he comes back out of the restroom, I'm gonna ask him what he wants, and if he doesn't tell us, then I don't trust him anymore."

Barry heard his partner loud and clear and kept his silence. The rest was up to Ivan.

INSIDE THE RESTROOM, Ivan zipped up his family jewels, walked away from the urinal, washed his hands at the sink, and took a deep breath before he stared at himself in the mirror. He then dried his hands with brown paper towels.

The truth is the best policy, he reminded himself. *And since they're out there waiting for me to give it to them, that's what I need to do.*

He took another deep breath and stated, "Let's just get it over with."

When he walked back out from the restroom, the restaurant looked twice as long and twice as wide, designed with Asian architecture and decorated with Asian artwork.

These Asians sure love some dragons and tigers. Ivan amused himself to lighten up his mood. He paced back toward his booth while taking everything in. *Maybe I should try a full-blooded Asian girl next. But Filipinos are Asians, too, right?*

All I know is Ashley got some wet shit, he told himself. *I wonder if they're all wet like that, with that extramoist skin of theirs. Even Chris is part Asian. I guess that's my thing now.*

By the time Ivan returned to his booth to face his bosses, he was completely loose again.

"So, what were we talking about?" he asked them.

Barry spoke up before John could. "Dolphins and killer whales."

"Oh, yeah," Ivan mumbled. *Look, just go ahead and get it over with,* he repeated to himself. He said, "But you know what, to be honest with you guys, over the past six months or so I've been thinking more like a businessman than just an accountant. And I'd be lying if I said I wasn't thinking about following up on a lot of the business conversations I started on Saturday. But while I'm at the office all day, there's just no time for me to do it. So what I came up with is a way to continue to represent myself as well as Hutch and Mitchell Accounting on a marketing and consultant basis."

John looked straight at him. "Which is?"

"I'll spend the majority of my time out in the field closing deals, while using the Hutch and Mitchell brand name just like I do now," he explained. "But since I'm trying to close a lot more deals now for IDPromotions.com than I am as an accountant, I would like to borrow a strong tax and accounting advisor to take with me from the office."

John winced and looked at Barry. Barry then looked back at Ivan.

He said, "So . . . you want us to allow you to do business deals for your own company, while one of our accountants advises your clients on the best tax benefits?"

"That way we introduce new clients to the excellent practices of Hutch and Mitchell, while I make them money in business," he told them. He said, "That's how I've *been* getting new clients. They know who I work for. And when they see me making money and protecting it, they naturally want to make money with me and protect theirs as well. And we don't want them just thinking about April before they decide to use a good accountant."

John and Barry looked at each other and began to laugh. Ivan was being honest and vicious, and there was nothing they could do about it. His methods had obviously worked.

"A killer whale," John insisted. "And just out of curiosity, what guy at the office would you want as your personal tax advisor?"

"Mike Adams," Ivan answered. "He's the sharpest. And Mike being out in the field will eventually make him more valuable to the company. He'll learn how to close deals for himself soon."

John shook his head and said, "He's our best auditor, and April's right around the corner."

"We'll do it after April, then," Ivan told them.

Barry asked him, "Why not take Chip on as your personal advisor? You two seem to get along well at the office."

Ivan stopped and shook his head. He said, "Chip is . . . well, I could use Chip in other ways, but I'd rather have Mike for what I need. He'll do more listening and analyzing."

John just stared at him again. He agreed with him, of course. Chip Garrett was a slacker who needed to be supervised every step of the way. But Ivan was giving them a whole lot to think about.

Barry read John's look and said, "Give us a few days to think this over."

John then asked him, "And how much is this, ah, new position gonna cost us?"

Ivan said, "The twenty percent commission is still good on the new clients, but four hundred twenty thousand in base salary would earn me twenty-four thousand a month *after* taxes to cover my twenty-four/seven marketing and branding of Hutch and Mitchell Accounting out in the field."

John looked at Barry and smiled. "Four hundred twenty thousand dollars?"

"That's twenty-four thousand a month after taxes. Plus you'll need to double Mike's salary."

John frowned and said, "Hell, you can pay him the extra out of your business. What, you're negotiating for him, too, now?"

Ivan grinned it off and thought about it with a nod. "Okay, that's fair."

Barry repeated, "Give us a few days to think it over. In the meantime, get back out there and try and close out these deals before April."

John smiled. He said, "It looks like we have some new hiring to do. But I'm gonna tell you something that's very important for your career, Ivan. You learn to be who you are," he told him. "If you're a businessman, you be a businessman. If you're a closer, you be a closer. And if you're a killer whale, you be a killer whale."

He continued, "I've been around quite a few people who try hard not to be who they are, and it usually doesn't work. So when you're out there deal-making, you remember to keep your integrity, but you do what you feel comfortable with doing. And that means that you may not close all of the deals that you want, but at least people know exactly who you are and where you stand. And that's the way business is, Ivan. We don't like surprises. We like to know exactly what we're getting into and exactly who we're dealing with."

John was basically reiterating the honesty-is-the-best-policy approach. So Ivan nodded to him. "Thanks. I'll make sure to remember that."

A WEEK LATER, Thomas Jones had finally sold Ivan's two real estate properties: one for $320,000, and the other for $310,000, netting Ivan $250,000 after Thomas's 10 percent and additional closing fees.

The sales staff at IDPromotions.com closed on nearly a third of their new potential advertisers and sponsors, and went to a two-week ad rate of $1,200 to replace their monthly rate of roughly

$1,700. The sponsorship rates rose from $1,500 a month to $2,000. Jeff and Paul added four new web pages: the "San Diego Auto Dealership" page, the "Medicine, Health, and Diet" page, the "Law Services" page, and the "Pet Care" page.

The added web pages, combined with the two-week rates, increased their advertisement and sponsor capacity from eighty businesses each month to two hundred, and increased their potential revenue to $240,000 a month. With Ivan pulling in roughly half of the revenue, minus an estimated $25,000 in monthly expenses, IDPromotions.com was set to earn close to $100,000 a month and would make him a first-time millionaire by the end of the year.

The increased revenue would earn Jeff and Paul more than a quarter of a million a year each as creative executives, and as the veteran sales manager, Eddie K. was set to earn more than a third of a million. So they all had plenty to celebrate.

Nevertheless, their progress was not made without hard decisions.

Eddie called up Ivan excitedly and explained to him, "Our U.S. military officer is offering us a one-hundred-thousand-dollar sponsorship for the year to design a recruiting and military news page to incorporate all of their divisions: Army, Navy, Air Force, Marines, the U.S. Coast Guard, ROTC, you name it."

Ivan, however, was not as excited about it.

He said, "Yeah, well, we can't take all of this money, man. I don't necessarily agree with sending kids off to the military. What if it was *your* son?"

"Actually, my son thought about going into the Air Force at one time," Eddie revealed to him. "But who are we to determine their choices, Ivan? All we're doing is posting up their page on our site, and then we update their information for them. We're not actively involved in recruiting kids just because we agree to host a page." He said, "Do you know how many ads the newspapers would turn down if they made specific judgment calls? I mean, this is the American military we're talking about. What could be more patriotic of us?"

It was another occasion where Ivan's personal opinion conflicted with his business decisions. He didn't agree with training kids for war. He always imagined college and trade school as better options. But someone had to serve and protect the country.

Then again, I've been taking this liquor sponsorship money for these parties until the cows come home, he reminded himself. *I'm training these kids to drink. That's hypocritical.* Yet he was hesitant to budge on it.

"Let me think about that a little while longer, Eddie," he told his sales manager. He was on his way to meet with the luxury car dealer in La Jolla, one of the wealthiest areas of San Diego.

"Well, what do you want me to tell them in the meantime?" Eddie asked him. He couldn't believe that Ivan would balk at an instant six-figure deal.

Ivan said, "Tell him that we're investigating the space availability on the site right now."

Eddie paused. He said, "Ivan, he's already talked to me about the new pages we've put up since your birthday network party. He also told me that you had some hesitancy about his idea when he spoke to you personally about it. Now, I want to remind you, Ivan, that this is a heavy military area, and we definitely don't want the word to get out that we have some kind of bias against the U.S. military. That is *definitely* not the kind of press that we need right now, nor at any time in our business future, especially while you're still based here in San Diego."

Ivan heard all of that and thought, *Shit!* Eddie was right, of course. However, Ivan hated the feeling of being pushed into a corner. *Fuck these military guys!* he wanted to shout. But he knew better than to voice it. Businessmen had to do things they didn't like sometimes.

"All right, well . . ." He was still hard-pressed to say it. Finally, he said, "Do what you need to do, Eddie. I'll talk to you about it later. I have a two o'clocker with this car dealership."

Eddie chuckled and said, "It's about time you upgraded that car of yours. Give that Altima away as a bonus to one of the interns on staff or something."

Ivan told him, "I'm not going to buy a car. I'm headed over there to talk about doing a promotional car show."

Eddie laughed again. He said, "You are one *serious* business machine, Ivan. I guess your accounting job was holding you back more than I imagined."

"Definitely," Ivan told him. "The sky is the limit now. So I'm going right after it." He felt he had all the time in the world without his office job. John and Barry agreed to his marketing and consultant position with a few changes. They would allow a three-hundred-thousand-dollar deal instead of four hundred and change, and Ivan had to include the creation and promotion of at least two major networking events for the company each year. They also agreed that Mike Adams could join him as his personal accountant and tax advisor after the busy month of April.

AS SOON AS Ivan pulled up to the World Wide Luxury Cars dealership in La Jolla, he spotted the Bentleys, Rolls-Royces, Lamborghinis, Aston Martins, Ferraris, Bugattis, and other expensive cars that they advertised. They were all parked behind a large, shatterproof-glass showroom.

When he parked in the customer spaces outside, driving his mundane Nissan Altima, some of the younger salesmen had no idea what to make of him. Was he there to buy a car or to sightsee? So no one rushed to the door to greet him until they noticed his classy and casual style of dress, his air of importance, and the diamond stud earring that twinkled in his left earlobe.

"What's your preference, the Ferraris or the Lamborghinis?" one of the older salesmen asked Ivan on his way in. The full-gray-headed man beat the younger guys to the punch, figuring that he would ignore the Altima that the man drove up in. Plenty of their wealthy clients had decided to splurge after living more budgeted lifestyles. New millionaires popped up in America every day, and from all walks of life.

Ivan looked the cars over inside the showroom and remembered the yellow Ferrari that had driven past him in the Gaslamp Quarter nearly a year ago.

I was too slow back then, he remembered. *I wonder what I am now.*

They had two different models of yellow Ferraris inside the showroom, and also a yellow Lamborghini. But they weren't Ivan's taste. All of the sports cars screamed for too much attention. Only the black ones would work for a more humble customer. Then again, once Ivan spotted the Continental GTs from Bentley, he figured that maybe a sports car could work for him.

"Damn," he expressed of a cranberry-red Continental with shiny twenty-inch rims. Ivan walked over near it and noticed the two-tone brown leather interior. The older salesman followed him.

"Oh, yeah, she's a beauty. That's your dinner and breakfast car there," the salesman commented. "You take a woman to dinner in that, and you get to have her around for breakfast the next morning."

Ivan smiled and chuckled. When he turned and faced a younger salesman in his twenties, the younger man noticed him.

"Hey, you're Ivan David, aren't you, from IDPromotions.com? You just had that big birthday network party a few weeks ago at the Grand Hyatt, right?"

It still felt good. He knew Ivan's whole rundown.

Ivan kept his cool and nodded to him. "Did you make it out there that night?"

"No, but our owner did. You remember meeting a Roman Zemeckis?"

Ivan said, "As a matter of fact, I do. And I think he told me to meet him here today at two o'clock. Is he around?"

The younger salesman laughed it off. He caught on to Ivan's sarcasm. But the older salesman was still lost.

He asked Ivan, "You have a two o'clock meeting with Roman? Well, how come you didn't say so? I would have gone ahead and gotten him for you."

"I wanted to check out the cars first. I'm still a little early," Ivan told him. "Besides, you were showing me great courtesy."

"Well, that's my job," the older salesman stated. "Courtesy is a lost art of good service these days. Well, let me go get Roman for you. And it's, ah, *Ivan,* right?"

"Yeah, Ivan David."

The older salesman walked back over to shake his hand. "I'm Frank McMichaels. It's a pleasure to meet you."

"Same here, Frank. But let me sit in this thing for a few minutes while I wait."

"Be my guest." Frank went ahead and opened the car door for him. "By the way, this one is a limited edition."

Ivan sat inside the driver's seat and felt heaven come down to earth. *Damn, this is plush,* he told himself. The Bentley felt more like a private jet cockpit than a car. Ivan was waiting for the wings to shoot out from the sides so he could fly it.

"Enjoy. I'll be right back with the boss," Frank told him.

"Take your time," Ivan responded.

The old salesman chuckled and walked off.

Ivan relaxed inside the luxurious two-door coupe and wondered aloud, "How much of a setback would this be?"

Based on the Bentley brand name alone, he estimated two hundred thousand and change. *Adding in a car note payment for four years would put me somewhere in the range of . . . five thousand a month,* he calculated. *But I could pay this whole thing off in one year and have it over with. Then again, I could buy it through the company and make it a business expense. Bigger business needs bigger props for marketing purposes,* he reasoned.

"Is this the one you like, Ivan?" the boss's booming voice rang into his ears from the passenger-side door.

Roman Zemeckis climbed inside the passenger seat, dressed as impeccably as he had been when Ivan first met him at the network party. He wore great-smelling cologne as well.

Ivan even commented on it. "I want to learn how to dress like you when I hire a professional tailor one day," he joked.

Roman laughed and said, "Your style of dress fits you, though, Ivan. You're the middleman between the customers and the owners. So you want to be able to squeeze somewhere in between. And you do that well. But come on upstairs, Ivan. Let me show you my office."

Ivan climbed out of the Bentley to follow the boss toward the stairs at the back.

Roman told him in a lowered tone, "I can give you the limited GT for two-forty at my own discount."

Ivan smiled and kept his silence. He still had to figure out how he wanted to get it. But he definitely wanted the car. It just wasn't in his budget at the moment.

Once they reached his office upstairs overlooking the showroom, Ivan noticed that all of the other offices were on the bottom-floor level.

There's no question who the boss is in here, he told himself. Ivan felt special even being upstairs with the man. Then he looked to his left and through a full twelve-foot window. Roman Zemeckis had a complete view of the green and brown mountains, the vast ocean waters, and the light blue sky, all framed in the window like a giant portrait.

Ivan nodded and said, "Now, that right there is nice. That's what I want before a car, a house in La Jolla that has a view of everything you have right here." He said, "I've been thinking about that ever since I came to San Diego eleven years ago."

Roman said, "Don't let that be enough for you, Ivan. I've been here a little longer than that myself, from the Miami area. Most of my family's still involved there with the boats and shipping business. But I wanted to do something different. So I came out west and got involved in selling exotic cars."

He continued, "No sense in having toys that you can't trade and sell, you know. And sure, you keep some of your favorites for yourself, but the real fun is in trying to see how many of them you can move."

Ivan nodded, still hypnotized by the astounding view at the window. But he did manage to hear everything that was said. What Roman was telling him was that he had nothing to lose. His family had long money already. So his exotic cars were nothing more than a kid's trading-card game.

Ivan asked him, "Do you invest in the different car companies that make the brands and models?"

Roman stared at him and thought about it with a pause. He said, "Ivan, you're one of the few people who ever asked me that question."

Ivan shrugged it off. It only made sense to him. He said, "If you like cars that much, and you got the money to be a part of the real competition, then why wouldn't you want to invest in the companies?"

Ivan wanted to see what his investment tendencies were like before he tried to pitch him on anything. He took a seat in the deep leather office chair that sat in front of Roman's open desk. He had several wooden file cabinets against the wall behind his chair. The setup reminded Ivan of how he had created open space for Paul and Jeff at his own office. Only Roman's office was ten times more plush, with an Oriental rug that covered the center of his shiny hardwood floor.

Roman asked him, "Do you invest in everything that you like?" He wanted to test Ivan's investment ideas as well.

"If it's gonna make me a profit, yeah," Ivan told him. "But if not, then I'll just admire it from a distance."

Roman chuckled. He said, "You don't mince words much, do you?"

Ivan told him, "Honesty is the best policy. So I try to be as straightforward as possible."

"So, what's your honest take on the success of a car show here?" Roman asked him.

Ivan said, "That depends on what your goals are. If you're just trying to sell more cars, then we do an invitation-only event that stays near the showroom with your staff ready to sell. But if you're trying to do a grand-scale promotion to let more folks know who you are and what you have to offer, then we would do a much bigger public event *away* from your showroom. Then we can throw a big after party with exotic car images around the room. But the catch with the more public event is that, even though it'll make your dealership more popular, it may not necessarily sell you more cars. You'll get a lot more people who just like to look, dream, and talk. But they *will* know the name of your company."

Roman told him, "And what if I decided to do both? What if we wanted to be more popular *and* sell more cars? I may even be interested in opening up a second dealership in the area that sells less-expensive vehicles: an economy trade."

That caught Ivan off guard. He didn't expect the auto dealer to be that hungry. He was expecting an either-or situation.

He must be really bored with his time and money, Ivan thought. *But he could corner the market that way, too.* So he rolled with it.

He said, "Well, in that case, that's even better. Then you'll have both of your bases covered, and we can go all-out on both sides of the coin. I'll have plenty of ideas if you wanna do it that way."

"Well, I'd like to see your proposals. And if your ideas look good, we can talk about getting you behind the wheel of that limited-edition GT you like."

Ivan asked him, "Is that a part of the deal?"

Roman Zemeckis paused. He said, "I like you, Ivan, but I don't like you that much. That's a hell of a car we're talking about."

"And we want to put together a hell of a promotion for you," Ivan countered. He said, "Just look at it this way: if I can call you my friend with the dealership and let everyone know where I bought the car, then that's twenty-four/seven promotion for you. And I'll make sure I drive it everywhere with your license plate frames on it."

The car boss began to shake his head and chuckle. He said, "How old are you again, Ivan, twenty-nine going on *fifty*? You just get those proposals together for me, and we'll see what we can do."

Ivan nodded and smiled to him. "Okay. That's fair."

HIS NEXT BIG MEETING was with Lucina and Seth Gardner, the marine broker, who specialized in the sales of large yachts and ocean cruise liners. Seth wanted to meet with them out on a yacht to show it off and let his promoters see what they would be working with.

When they made it deep out into San Diego Bay and headed toward the Pacific Ocean, Ivan thought back to his elevated view from the window of the Manchester Grand Hyatt Hotel room with Catherine.

This is insane, he told himself of his lightning-speed progress. *In less than a year, I'm out here on a big private yacht already. And I don't own this shit yet, but I'm out here,* he mused.

He had to stop from smiling the whole time, while forcing himself to think about the business. On the other hand, Lucina had been on plenty of boats around the world. She was cool, calm, and collected, with the sea breeze blowing through her radiant two-toned hair. And as they stood out on the front deck of the boat, admiring the yacht's luxury, their unobstructed view of the ocean, and their comfortable place in the world, Ivan couldn't help but notice how every part of wealth fit in perfectly with his partner. Lucina's poise and beauty made her seem to deserve it all. So Ivan was sidetracked into watching her.

Man, I feel like that movie, Titanic. *I just want to hold her and kiss her right here at the front of this boat,* he mused. *I want her to open up to me.*

Ivan was locked in his daydream, which had nothing to do with business.

"What do you think, Ivan?" Lucina asked him, breaking him out of it.

"Oh, ah . . . it's all good. It's nice. This is good money." He said, "But we would need a bigger boat for an all-out party, though. This would be more of a private invitation party."

Then he stopped and looked back at Seth, who idled patiently behind them. He wasn't into overselling the product. He preferred to let the boats do the talking for him. And while they were out there in the middle of the bay, they couldn't rush away anywhere.

"Or . . . we could do *both,*" Ivan suggested to him, taking a page out of his meeting with Roman Zemeckis. If it worked once, then make it work again.

Seth nodded and thought it over, remaining calm. He said, "Whatever size you need, or whatever event you come up with, I can make it happen."

His calm demeanor spoke of experience. He wasn't fazed by much of anything. That made Ivan think even bigger. Seth could handle whatever he had to propose. In fact, Ivan assumed the man felt more comfortable with the bigger ideas as opposed to the hassles of the smaller ones. After all, the man made a living selling multimillion-dollar boats. So why would a mere party rattle him? All Ivan had to do was come up with ideas to increase the popularity of his business and products, and Seth would be willing to do it.

Ivan caught on to that and felt a rush of energy overtake his body. He felt light-headed. Too much knowledge was traveling to his brain at once.

Yo, making these bigger deals is fifty times easier than that small shit, he realized. *He's ready to sign the check already. So I can just relax and give him the proposal next week. SHIT!*

Lucina looked at Ivan for his lead again. Her quick-thinking partner was flooded with ideas, and she began to expect it from him.

"So, what do you think, Ivan?" she asked him again.

Ivan fell into a cool pose. In *his* mind, the deal was *done*. He didn't even want to think about it anymore. He wanted to enjoy the boat ride now.

So he nodded and told Lucina calmly, "We'll just think about all of our ideas and get back to him. Okay?" Then he joked, "We should have all of your girls wear something from Versace out here. The bright colors would all shine under the moonlight and bounce their images off the water."

He looked back at Seth and asked him, "Does that happen out here at night?"

Seth smiled. He said, "You can only imagine how beautiful the nighttime is while out on a full moon."

Ivan said, "I can imagine it. I can imagine it right now."

He felt gleeful and happy, like dancing across the deck. He thought, *I'm about to be a multimillionaire! It's already in my cards. But I need to be bigger than just parties and a website. I need to form, like, Ivan David Enterprises or something: parties, promotions, marketing, website, real estate, cars, boats, accounting, and whatever the hell else I decide to get into.*

Ivan walked over to the edge of the boat and breathed deep, inhaling the ocean air.

He said, "It feels real good out here, Lucina. It feels *good.*"

Lucina looked at him and smiled in front of Seth. But in the back of her mind, she thought, *He's getting a big head again. I know that look.* And she began to feel distant from him. He was a blessing and a curse.

Eighteen

Only the Strong & the Smart

"I NEED TO FIND the best business plan and proposal writers in San Diego," Ivan told Thomas Jones over lunch at a small Mexican restaurant. They had met up in the Chula Vista area of the far southeast to look at the wide-open property available for new home and commercial development.

Thomas said, "You know Henry was a business major. He can write business plans and proposals."

Ivan raised a tortilla to his mouth and asked him, "Is he any good at it?" He started munching down his food and mumbled, "I need the best."

Thomas scooped up some Spanish rice from his plate and said, "I don't know about all that. But you can't write a business plan?"

"Yeah, I can write 'em," Ivan mumbled, still chomping down his food. "But I don't feel like spending that much time doing it. And I can't shortcut it, with bigger money at stake. So what I want to do is form a small team that does nothing but write my business plans and proposals, and let them hammer out my ideas with the numbers, then I'll go back over it to make sure it's right before I present it."

Thomas nodded. "That's what the big dogs do. They're not sitting around slaving over paperwork. But the paperwork still has to be done."

When they finished their food and walked out to their cars in the parking lot, Thomas looked over at Ivan's black Altima. He joked, "Haven't you made enough money to buy a new car yet, Ivan? Or you need a business plan and proposal for that, too?"

Ivan laughed. "Yeah, I'm working on it."

Even Thomas had a luxurious silver Infiniti Q45 model.

As they opened their separate car doors to climb in, a woman yelled out Ivan's name with urgency.

"Ivan! Ivan!"

He turned and looked behind him, spotting Carolyn Padilla, one of Lucina's gorgeous Mexican girls. She had all the right curves in her black jeans and tight, colorful shirt, with good height to boot. She looked overwhelmed to see him there in her neighborhood.

"What are you doing in my turf?" she asked him. She pushed her thick dark hair out of her face and eyes with both hands.

Damn! Ivan thought to himself of her smile and presentation in the bright sunlight. He had been around Carolyn plenty of times, but she always looked more reserved in the party settings.

"I'm out here checking out new properties," he told her.

"Oh, you're gonna buy a new house here?"

Ivan teased her and said, "Yeah, then you can come see me and cook breakfast for us in the morning."

Carolyn studied his kissable lips, his rainbow-colored eyes, and his diamond-studded ear, all glimmering in the sunlight, with his low-cut hair, stylish clothes, shoes, and sports jacket. She took in the pleasantness of his cologne rushing into her nose, and all of it together made her heart race with excitement.

She laughed and placed both of her hands over the cleavage of her chest.

"Oh, my God, you mean that?"

Ivan was surprised. He had expected for her to smile and laugh, not for her to take him seriously. Or maybe he did expect it and was impressed by the instant results.

He shook it off and said, "Naw, you might tell Lucina on me. I'm sorry I even said that."

Carolyn's face reflected horror as she denied it. "I would *never* do that," she told him. "I wouldn't do anything you wouldn't tell me to do."

Ivan was stunned. He had no idea what to say next. She had obviously considered him for a while. There was no other way to explain her exhilaration.

However, Spanish women had a knack for being overdramatic in romance. So he blew it off with a chuckle. He said, "You're gonna get yourself into trouble with your jealous boyfriend if you keep talking to me like that."

Carolyn dropped all of her giddiness and asked him, "How jealous are you?" She stood poised like a grown woman who knew what she wanted.

Ivan saw that and told himself, *Okay, I've gone way too far with this shit, and I have things to do. But the next time I see this girl, it's definitely on.*

In the background, he noticed two of her girlfriends or family members, who were waiting patiently for her with wide grins of their own.

He said, "Well, I don't want to hold us up, I got property to see, and you got people waiting for you. But I'll tell you what . . ." He looked into her dark, steady eyes and said, "The next time we see each other, if you respect my business and privacy, then we can have that breakfast. But if not, then we'll just keep doing business the way we do it. Is that okay?"

Carolyn nodded. "Yeah, okay."

"You sure?" Ivan asked her. He wanted to make certain.

"It would be just between me and you," she answered.

He said, "You got a problem with that?"

She shook it off. "No, I know how Lucina is. She wants all of us to be . . . I don't know, unapproachable. But you know, a girl is a girl."

Ivan teased her again. "What does that mean, any guy can have you?"

Carolyn frowned hard at him. She said, "No. I am *very* unapproachable when I want to be. But, you know, I still choose who I want to choose."

Ivan heard that and read her eyes on him. Nothing else had to be said. She was obviously choosing him.

She said, "So, after the next party, you make sure you don't forget about me. Okay, Ivan?"

He nodded to her. "Okay."

She reached out and squeezed his right arm to indicate her sincerity. "Bye." And when she walked off, she displayed all of her curves to give him another look.

Ivan watched her return to her friends before he climbed back into his Altima. He sat behind the wheel a few seconds and mumbled, "Yeah . . . I definitely need to upgrade my car."

IVAN AND THOMAS drove around the Chula Vista area, looking at several properties that had already started development, as well as wide-open areas that had yet to break ground. Ivan also asked to see a few commercial areas.

"You thinking about setting up for business down here, too?" Thomas asked him as they walked around.

Ivan said, "Well, it's obvious we're gonna be dealing with plenty of Mexicans in this area. And they like to party like everybody else. So, if I just bought the property and had the construction guys build a big enough box on it for a club, I could package the club idea to some of these other owners, finance it, and keep a piece of the ownership, while I help them to pack it out with Spanish talent each month."

Thomas looked at him and shook his head, amazed. He said, "That lightbulb in your head never goes out, does it?"

Ivan grinned. "That's why I can't be sitting around working on proposals and business plans all day. I need to be out here sucking things up to have ideas to work from. You said that about me a while ago," he reminded Thomas.

He went on, "I didn't leave Hutch and Mitchell's offices just to lock myself up in an office of my own. I like being out here rolling around." Then he added, "And you're right. It's time for me to use more upscale cars for my everyday image."

TO IVAN'S SURPRISE, Lucina helped him hammer out every detail of his first proposals for the luxury car and boat parties. The big and small, public and private combinations helped to make the process a lot easier for them to design.

For the big luxury car show, the idea was to utilize Xzibit to host a free-to-the-public event out at Mission Bay Park, with plenty of sponsors involved to appeal to the general public of San Diego. Roman Zemeckis would display his cars out on an elevated platform at the park, while Xzibit asked his sales force to explain the luxuries, prices, and design histories of each car, helped along by the eye candy of Lucina's girls, all wearing tasteful summer dresses.

"I don't want them in swimsuits," she told Ivan. "We want to use this event to partner with fashion designers and retailers to display their summer lineup of dresses."

Ivan couldn't argue with that. It was a solid idea. The San Diego retailers already knew who Lucina was, so including her girls to push their new fashions was good business. Lucina even started her own website ideas to begin pitching to the fashion designers regularly.

"Shit, we should have done that for you a while ago," Ivan told her.

"It's okay," Lucina responded. "It's better late than never."

The public car show idea was to have Red Face Lion spin the latest Top 40 music with a supersized sound system out in the park, while security held the crowd at bay to dance and enjoy themselves. They would record the entire event with a professional video staff to edit down for local television, news shows, IDPromotions.com viewers, and DVD copies for future marketing and proposal purposes.

After the public event, they would send out private invitation packages to a select group of two thousand, including professional athletes who could afford to buy the cars, to attend an upscale private party a month later at the showroom.

The price tag for both events, including a dedicated IDPromotions .com web page, local media marketing, city permits, sound equipment, an auto stage, insurance, security, and Xzibit's appearance fee, reached beyond the six-figure mark. But the plans were too enticing for Roman Zemeckis to turn down.

"We can then make this an annual event as new luxury cars hit the market and San Diego's millionaire population continues to grow," Ivan explained to him at his office. "And your dealership will sit right at the center of the attention every year."

Lucina sat at Ivan's side, wearing a gray St. John business suit and skirt that was extremely professional. She added the feminine touch of a pink silk shirt to soften her image.

Roman smiled at them across his desk and was impressed. He stood up and reached out his hand to congratulate them. "I look forward to doing a lot of business with you guys," he stated.

After they all shook hands on the deal, Roman added, "Now, what about a new car for you, Ivan? You still like that cranberry-red GT?"

Ivan told him, "As a matter of fact, I do. So I wrote out a check for sixty-five thousand as my down payment. I plan to make four more payments in the same ballpark amount to pay it all off this year." He said, "But here's what I'd like to do. Instead of me driving the same car or limousines to our events, we'd like to borrow different luxury cars from you and make World Wide Luxury Cars a regular sponsor of all of our events and promotions like Hutch and Mitchell Accounting agreed to."

Roman considered it with a pause. "So, you'd like to rent my cars—"

Ivan cut him off and said, "We can borrow from your personal collection if you let us. But I'd love to drive up in a Rolls-Royce at a yacht party, or a Bugatti at a Padres or Chargers promotion, or an Aston Martin in the Gaslamp. And each time, your company gets the credit for supplying the car." He added, "And if anything happens to them, you take my GT back as collateral. In fact, we can even designate one of your sales staff as a personal driver and a watchman for the cars."

"What if it's only a two-seater and you have to pick me up?" Lucina asked Ivan with a smile.

He shrugged it off. "Then his driver follows behind us in another car, and we give him the keys once we arrive at our events like a personal valet."

Roman heard all of that and laughed out loud. Ivan was obviously pressing to have access to all the cars. He asked Lucina, "He's not gonna let me turn him down on this, is he?"

Lucina grinned. "I don't think he is," she answered.

Ivan said, "It's better than just leaving them in the garage. You need to at least keep the engines working, right? Think of it like taking a pet for a walk."

Roman said, "Yeah, but *I'm* usually the one who takes the pets for a walk. After all, they're *my* pets."

"Yeah, but you're also trying to sell them. And if you let us show them off in front of our crowds of thousands, along with the VIPs who can afford to buy them, then it all leads to good business for you," Ivan noted. He said, "You already know they're gonna ask us about the different cars. But if it's the same car every time, then they only ask us once."

With that, Ivan reached inside his dark blue sports jacket and pulled out his check to set on Roman's desk. Then they fell into a momentary stare-down.

Finally, Roman grinned and nodded to him. "It's gonna be interesting working with you, Ivan." He picked up the check, read the amount, and nodded again.

Ivan didn't drive off behind the wheel of his Bentley Continental GT on the first day. After filling out all of the paperwork, he told Roman he'd be back to pick it up the following day. So the boss offered to have one of his salesmen pick him up from his apartment downtown.

When they left the showroom in her Mercedes, Lucina asked Ivan, "What made you think he would allow you to borrow his cars? That was very presumptuous of you, don't you think?"

Ivan shrugged it off. "All you have to do is ask," he told her. "And he can either say yes or no." He smiled and added, "*Just* like you do. You tell me no all the time. *He* just didn't."

That caught Lucina off guard. She smiled out the window and refused to comment on it. She mumbled, "It looks like I'm the only one telling you no these days."

Ivan was hesitant to comment on that. Was she referring to his business or his personal life? Did she know about his relations with Christina and Ashley? Sleeping with two of the twenty-five or so girls he had met through Lucina's camp was hardly excessive, in his opinion. Nevertheless, Ivan was curious enough to ask about it.

"What do you mean, you're the only one telling me no?"

"I mean that a lot of things have come far too easy for you," she answered.

"Is that a *bad* thing? It's not like I'm not *working* for it."

Lucina held on to her silence for a moment. Then she answered, "I don't know."

Ivan said, "Just look at it this way. *My* good fortune has been *your* good fortune, right? So why complain about it? Let's just keep rolling sevens and elevens."

* * *

For the large yacht and cruise ship promotions, Ivan and Lucina copied the basic ideas of the luxury car show events, but with a few major changes. Since a cruise could never be as public as a park, they created a hundred-dollar cruise party, open to the paying public and hosted by MTV's Ananda Lewis, who had moved on to host her own television talk show. They also solicited a celebrity guest appearance from Latina movie star Jessica Alba.

The hundred dollars would include a six-hour celebrity-hosted cruise, with a dinner buffet, two free drink tickets, a $25-off cruise coupon, and a main ballroom party for an eight-hundred-capacity crowd. Red Face Lion would DJ, and Ivan, Lucina, and their staff would do their normal thing to keep the cruise lively. Since Ivan no longer moved without the San Diego media and corporate sponsors involved, they expected another major turnout, even at the steeper price tag.

"Then we'll do radio and website promotion giveaways. But we can't select a whole random cruise. We have to make sure folks take it seriously," Ivan suggested. "Cruises aren't cheap."

For his media and website promotions, Ivan stated, "We at IDPromotions.com are known for our unique qualities, and we view all our events as an investment well spent for first-class experiences."

The smaller yacht promotion would be an invitation-only package for a select two hundred wealthy individuals who could actually afford to buy or rent a boat. The added marketing value of both the celebrity-hosted cruise party and the exclusive yacht cruise would be prerecorded videos of several different yachts and cruise ships that Seth Gardner represented. The videos would be displayed on several television screens on constant replay around the boats.

The total price tag was another six figures.

Ivan let Lucina know that he would also ask Seth Gardner about private rentals of yachts from his list of clients.

"We could book regular yacht parties from people who own

boats, where they could make good money off these things instead of them just sitting around at the docks all day."

"Ivan, those are private people using their boats for private purposes," Lucina argued. "They don't want everyone on their boats."

"You don't know unless you ask them," Ivan countered. "A few of them could have a couple of bills that they need to pay, and a private cruise broker like us could help them to pay them. All I have to do is advertise it on the website, work out the prices and availabilities, make sure the owner has people available to navigate the boat, and we go from there."

Lucina considered Ivan's vainglorious idea and grinned. She had gotten used to troubleshooting with him just to see how he would figure his way out of obstacles. And Ivan never seemed to lack answers.

He is truly amazing, she told herself. *I had no idea he could go this far with things. And we have yet to start promoting concerts. But we are surely on our way now.*

WHEN THEY MET at Seth Gardner's office overlooking San Diego Bay, he read through their proposal and agreed to everything. The promotional videos were what sealed the deal for him. He told them, "I've been meaning to produce promotional videos myself. But I could never find the beautiful young ladies that you have to do them with."

Ivan said, "Man, I thought boats attracted the prettiest women in the world."

"Oh, they do," Seth responded. "But usually they are women of leisure and not women who know how to pitch."

Ivan looked over at his partner and said, "Oh, well, you can't work for Lucina without knowing how to pitch. There are no women of leisure with us. They all know how to work it, or they don't work," he stated.

Seth laughed and told them, "Well, just let me know when you'd

like to begin filming. As for you having access to boats for your own business purposes, I'm sure we'll be able to work on figuring something out as long as it would be profitable for my clients."

"That's all I needed to hear," Ivan told him with a grin.

Lucina looked over at him and shook her head, smiling herself. They were all feeding a growing monster named Ivan David.

IVAN SAT DOWN with Thomas Jones over lunch again in the Chula Vista area. He wanted to explain the numbers and terms of real estate development deals to the San Diego Chargers football player Jeffrey Morefield, who had joined them there across the table.

Jeffrey summed up the terms after understanding it all. "So, basically, we double our money," he commented.

"In nine to eighteen months," Thomas filled in for him. "And this is just to get your feet wet. Once you do it a few times and qualify for a line of credit from the banks, you can do several of these development deals at the same time."

Ivan said, "I'm plotting to make even more money on *commercial* real estate. But it's riskier."

Jeffrey eyed him and asked, "You planning on sharing the wealth?"

"You interested in hearing it?" Ivan asked him.

"I'm here, right?" Jeffrey answered with a grin.

Ivan nodded to him. He said, "All right. Well, here's my idea. White boys rarely invest in black, Mexican, or Filipino establishments unless they have famous names attached. So, they'll do a Michael Jordan restaurant, Junior Seau's place, Keyshawn Johnson's. You know, establishments where they believe they can make some money off name value." He said, "But with the power of my website, I can make any place popular, like we did with Raymond's Lounge and Carol's Soul Food. They're both doing extremely well now."

He continued, "With that in mind, my idea is to jump on com-

mercial properties and create hot spots to serve the people who live there. Like right here in Chula Vista. I'd hook up with Mexican promoters who know the clientele and all of the hot Latin performers. Then we bring them in, make them all grand-scale events, push the event through the Latin radio stations, post it up on my website, and we can't lose. All we need to do is find a Mexican partner willing to be the face of the establishment."

Thomas loved the idea and knew that it would work. Ivan had already spoken to him about pitching the Padres rookie Emilio Alvarez on the idea. Ivan also had a solid connection with his friend Julio and plenty of other Mexican-Americans he had become friends with through their various parties. But Jeffrey was still hesitant.

He warned, "Those nightclubs never seem to last long, Ivan. I've seen them come and go all the time."

Ivan said, "Exactly. But you know who always makes money on these new club and restaurant deals? The builders and smart owners of the property. That's what I'm setting up to do now. We want to build the spots, make them hot for the investors, and then sell them."

He continued, "But if you don't feel comfortable with that, then I'll give you a hundred percent return on your money *immediately,* once I close out on other partnerships. And I can have my lawyers write up paperwork for you on that right now. So, each time that we establish a new hot spot, you know that you'll at least double your money with no more risk involved."

Thomas listened to the deal and wondered if Jeffrey would bite on the wrong end of the bread. Ivan could easily make up to *ten times* his initial investment if he promoted grand-scale events on a hot property. The only risk was inviting in partners who would be game enough to establish it. And Thomas was certain that Ivan would find people who would be. Thomas would be helping in the search himself. Like he had said, he was on Ivan's team now.

Jeffrey continued to think it over. He said, "So, your idea is to de-

velop clubs and restaurants that would serve a certain area, then you would put all of your promotional weight and ideas behind them, turn them all into cash cows, and then sell them to the highest bidders."

Thomas listened to that and was surprised. Jeffrey Morefield understood the idea exactly. The table was now open for Ivan's response.

Ivan took a sip of his Pepsi and answered, "I can't afford to be that cut-and-dried with my partners, though. I want to keep a good name. So I'll always make myself available as a consultant marketing and promotions man to keep the place hot. But if they decide not to use me in that capacity . . ."

"If it falls apart, it's on them," Jeffrey filled in for him.

Ivan shrugged and said, "That's as fair as I can make it."

Jeffrey began to smile. He said, "You're about to be, like, the Warren Buffett of the restaurant and party crowd, hunh?"

Over the past forty years, the billionaire stockbroker Warren Buffett had made quite a living and reputation off of knowing what's hot and what's not to invest in in America. So Ivan grinned at the comparison.

"That's a good analogy," he responded. "But I'm not into stocks and bonds yet. I'm into making money that I can *see* right now. But you give me a few more years for that," he joked.

They all shared a laugh as their hot plates of food arrived at the table.

As soon as their server left and they began to dig into their lunch, Jeffrey told them, "Well, count me in as a silent partner and let's see where it goes. But I don't want my name out there at all. I just want to find a quiet way of flipping some of my money."

Ivan nodded to him. "You got it, man. That's the same thing I want to do. I just can't afford to be quiet about it," he joked again. "I need people to want to look me up and talk business, twenty-four/seven."

Jeffrey told him, "And that's how you *should* be as a businessman.

But I'm still a football player right now. So let me just learn the game by watching you. And once my career is over with, I'll see how deep I want to get into it."

"That's a good money deal," Ivan told him. "I can respect that."

Thomas witnessed it all from the table. He told himself, *I'm in the right damn place to be. This boy Ivan is a gold mine.*

WHEN THOMAS WAS ALONE with Ivan inside of his new Bentley luxury car, he wanted to advise him on a few things. He said, "Ivan, I know you like explaining everything as a part of closing out your deals, but as you start to hire your business plan and proposal writers, you wanna get in the habit of letting the numbers do the talking for you. Because you'll find yourself in shark waters soon, with plenty of people who may bite your ideas and take them somewhere else to eat. You catch my drift?"

He continued, "Now, I know that Jeffrey is your own personal connection, but when you start pitching these real money people who you don't really know like that, you might want to stay close-mouthed and let them sign letters of confidentiality before you talk about too many details."

Ivan listened to him without response. He was beginning to like other people's opinions. Opinions gave him more information to make his own decisions from.

Thomas added, "So what you want to do at this point, as superficial as it may seem, is use your new car, your appearance, your reputation, references, good-looking women, and whatever the hell else you need to sell the business before you even speak." He said, "In fact, it's that time now where only the serious people should even be allowed to get in your ear."

Ivan finally smiled at him. He asked, "So I'm a made man now, Thomas? Is that it?"

Thomas grinned back at him inside the extravagance of the car. He said, "You're driving a quarter-of-a-million-dollar car now, ain't ya? That speaks *volumes* for itself. Now you have to learn when to shut up and let everything else do the talking for you."

Ivan grinned and laughed it off as they cruised back toward the interior of San Diego. Gawkers watched him in his Continental GT at every turn now. It was a serious upgrade from driving his Altima. Other drivers even gave him extra space to avoid accidents and fender benders. No one wanted to come close to hitting a car that they couldn't afford to repair.

IVAN'S MOVE UP the ladder was not a positive occasion for everyone. Plenty of friends, family, and associates would have loved to have shared more of the wealth with him. However, Ivan could never expect to climb to new heights with excess baggage attached to him. Something had to give. And it did.

First his brother, Derrick, popped up on him from Los Angeles without warning again. He was posted on the sidewalk outside of Ivan's downtown apartment building, smoking a cigarette. Obviously, someone had informed his brother of his new pad's location.

Ivan strolled up from a dinner meeting in the Gaslamp Quarter and paused. He spotted his brother in the distance and grumbled, "Shit!"

He recognized Derrick's cocky stance with a cigarette in his hand a mile away.

Ivan stopped and wondered if he should dodge him by finding something else to do for another hour. He didn't feel like having a one-on-one with his brother that night. Then his cell phone went off.

While Derrick looked out into the street in the opposite direction, Ivan slipped around the corner of the apartment building to escape his brother's view. He then looked down at his cell phone and read Christina's number. He took a moment before he answered it.

"Hello."

"You've been really busy lately. Is it all business or part personal?" Christina asked him. Ivan hadn't been around her in a while.

"A sure way of finding out would have been for you to keep working with us. Then you could see me in action instead of having to ask about it," Ivan answered.

She said, "You know how I feel about that."

They were going nowhere positive, so Ivan changed the subject.

"Well, how have you been doing?"

"Just trying to stay afloat with two jobs."

That didn't make much sense to him. *Why give up an easy grand a week working parties to slave at two jobs for more hours and less pay?*

Ivan asked her, "You still planning on going to school this summer?"

"You still gonna help me to do it?"

He hesitated. He thought, *Why should I do that when she obviously gave up on her hustle? She could have paid for her own school while working for us and saving.*

Ivan reminded her of their first argument about it.

"I mean, Chris, you're making how much a week by working these two jobs now—three, four hundred dollars? And that's, what, barely two thousand a month? You were making that working on *weekends*." He told her, "That logic just don't add up for me. And then I'm supposed to pay to help you to go to school. For what? So you can graduate and make bad decisions all over again? That would be a waste of my money."

Chris snapped, "You know what, Ivan, you are the cheapest man I've ever met in my *life*. Audrey was right about you. That's why *she* stopped working when *she* did. And to tell you the truth, I have a new friend now in the Marines, and he doesn't make anywhere *near* as much as you do, but he tries his best to take care of me when I need something. But you have all the money you could ask for, and from the first day I met you, you've always been *stingy* about it."

"Yeah, and that's why I'm gonna *keep* it for a long time, too," Ivan snapped back at her. "I'm not out here to take care of you. You're a grown-ass woman."

As soon as Ivan spoke it, a young white woman walked by and overheard him. Ivan was so incensed that he even asked for her opinion.

"Excuse me, you think a guy still needs to take care of a woman these days? What ever happened to women's rights and equality?"

The young white woman was stunned. "Ahh, I guess it all depends on the person."

"Does your guy take care of *you*?" Ivan asked her.

"Well, we, ah, both chip in to take care of each other," she answered.

"Now, that sounds like a better idea to me. I need a woman who can *chip in*."

Ivan believed in what he was saying, but he didn't need to say it out loud like that, especially in front of a stranger. It was severely harmful to Christina.

Her voice cracked with pain when she told him over the cell phone, "You know what, Ivan, you'll never have to worry about me calling you *ever* again. And I hope you burn in *fucking hell* with your money!" before she hung up on him.

Ivan was actually surprised at her outburst. Christina had the coolest of temperaments. So he looked around and wondered which way was up.

Was I wrong for that? he asked himself. He shook it off and mumbled, "Hell, no! I'm not obligated to pay for her."

But he couldn't help thinking about how easily he could write a check for twenty-five thousand dollars to pay for all of her schooling. He had written a check for a car that more than *doubled* that amount.

That's for business purposes, though, he argued to himself. *And if I wrote a check for her like that, then why not do it for the interns who work at my office? They work hard for* free!

Ivan was so worked up about it that he decided to approach his brother with reckless abandon in front of his building.

I'm tired of appeasing Derrick, too, he told himself. *He needs to get his own life together.*

After he had finished smoking his third cigarette outside the apartment building entrance, Derrick spotted Ivan walking up the sidewalk in his direction.

"So, you can't call to tell me what's going on down here no more, li'l brother?"

"What's there to say? I'm doing good," Ivan told him.

"I can see that. But you haven't asked how *I've* been doing."

Ivan eyed him and said, "It looks like you're doing good to me. You're still getting that consulting money, right?"

Derrick nodded. "Yeah, that's still coming through. But family is more than just that, man. I figured you might want to see your nephews soon."

Ivan stopped and stood out front with him at the entrance to his apartment building.

"Are they getting everything they need?" he asked his brother of his three nephews. Ivan hadn't seen much of Derrick's kids. It wasn't as if they had ever lived with him. Derrick was too much on the go to keep his kids longer than a day or two.

"As much as I can offer them when I have it," he answered.

Ivan said, "Wait a minute, they're not getting the child support payments we set up through my lawyers?"

"Yeah, they're getting that," Derrick told him. "But I'm talking about pocket change and something extra for my sons for when I'm out in the city with them."

Ivan couldn't believe the repetition of the same two culprits attempting to dig into his pockets, Chris and D.

He did the quick math on his brother and said, "You know I increased your check amount since the last time you were having money problems, right?" Ivan had figured he would be proactive instead of reactive. So he raised the four-thousand-a-month fee to six thousand just for Derrick being his brother. Nevertheless, it didn't seem to matter.

Derrick stared at him and smiled. He said, "I thought the bank was making a mistake with that automatic deposit shit and gave me more money than I was supposed to have."

Ivan said, "So you took the money right out and spent it before they could correct the mistake, right? That's typical," he snapped. "Now, hypothetically speaking, what if they came after you for that?"

Derrick started to chuckle. He said, "I wouldn't have had the shit. They can't get back money that I don't have. But you didn't tell me you were gonna do that. How come you didn't tell me that?"

Ivan answered, "I wanted to see what you were gonna do with it first. And you went right ahead and proved my point. The more money a broke motherfucker has, the faster he'll find a way to spend it."

Derrick looked surprised by his brother's abrupt candor. He said, "Oh, it's like that now? You saying I don't know how to hustle for mine?"

"It ain't about hustling at this point, D, it's about *working*. And you don't know how to *work*. Period!"

Derrick said, "Yeah, whatever. You down here smelling yourself now. You hanging out with these rich white folks, thinking you got something going, but it can all change in a heartbeat, Ivan. Then we'll see what kind of work *you do* to get it all back."

Ivan didn't feel like arguing with his brother anymore. The argument was frivolous. There was no way in hell he was going to lose his living. He was all legal, and the groundwork for his continued success had already been set. Even if his IDPromotions.com offices burned to the ground, his equipment was all insured, and the popularity of his website would continue. He could throw a party now and pocket thirty thousand dollars at a drop of a dime on any given weekend.

Once he solidified more of his real estate operations, Ivan planned to build million-dollar properties to sell. And none of that included the wages or commissions he still collected from Hutch & Mitchell Accounting, nor the six-figure party plans that he and Lucina had mapped out for late spring and then summer.

Derrick was out of his mind! He just didn't know any better. So Ivan ignored him.

He said, "So, you're down here again to do what, man? What do you need from me now?"

His brother paused. He said, "What if I just came back down here to hang out with you, man? Has that idea ever crossed your mind?"

Ivan said, "You haven't done that before. Why would I think that now?"

Derrick shrugged and told him, "Everybody can turn over a new leaf, man. Even me."

That comment got to Ivan. It showed a little bit of sincerity on Derrick's part. So Ivan took a breath to calm himself.

He said, "Well, we don't have any parties this week, D. We don't have anything set up until May. I'm just promoting other people's parties through the website right now."

Derrick said, "It don't matter. I'm just down here for another weekend to clear my head from L.A. for a minute, like I always do."

Ivan asked him, "You need another hotel room?" He was still hesitant to have his brother stay over at his place. He figured it would be too much of a tease.

Derrick said, "Naw, man, let me just crash at your place. I don't wanna spend no more of your money," he joked.

"I'm having company over tonight," Ivan lied to him.

Derrick leaned back and said, "Oh, okay. What, you got two, three of 'em coming over tonight? You ever had a *ménage* yet? You be around enough women for plenty of 'em."

Ivan shook it off and said, "Naw, I don't get down like that."

Derrick said, "Shit, well, you don't know what you're missing, Ivan. The last time I was down here . . ." He stopped in midsentence and just smiled.

Ivan told himself, *Yeah, that's the kind of shit that I'm afraid of with him. I've kept all of my moves safe and sound and with no drama.*

Ivan moved on from it. He said, "Well, since you snuck down here on me again, I already got plans for the night. So what are you gonna do?"

Derrick shrugged. "I'll take that hotel room, then. The same one you hooked me up with the last time."

NO MATTER WHAT, Ivan couldn't seem to shake the family loyalty to his brother. But not everyone was family to him. When the word hit Chip Garrett at Hutch & Mitchell Accounting's offices that Mike Adams had been chosen to do out-of-office accounting work under Ivan's new negotiation instead of him, he wasn't too pleased about it.

The first thing Ivan asked him was, "Who told you that?"

"Mike told me," Chip answered, nearly screaming over his cell phone on his lunch break.

Why would he do that? Ivan asked himself. He was cruising on his way across the Coronado Bridge to pick up Lucina in his GT. *Mike is so damn honest he doesn't even know when he needs to keep his mouth shut,* he thought. *I'm gonna have to work on him with that.*

Ivan told his fellow accountant, "Different people ask for different things, Chip. You asked me to set you up with one of my partner's girls from a party, and I did that. Now you and Gretchen have been going out together."

Chip told him, "Come on, cut the bullshit, Ivan. You think I want a girl over a new job position? I hear you're gonna be doubling Mike's salary now. And by the way, that girl Gretchen is expensive as hell, let me be the first to tell you."

They all are, Ivan reminded himself. *If not, then they're not impulsive enough for Lucina to keep them around. They're all there to make a guy spend on purpose.*

Ivan decided to level with him. He said, "Look, the bottom line is this, Chip. You were already complaining about the workloads we were getting at Hutch and Mitchell. So what makes me think you're not gonna do the same with me?"

He said, "This is hard work out here, man. I don't get any easy money. I have to be on the numbers every day, even *more* so now. That's why I wanted help."

Chip told him, "And you're just gonna assume that I can't help you and leave me hanging to pick up Mike? Some friend you are, Ivan. And after all this time of me looking out for you, that's how you repay me."

Ivan said, "What do you mean, looking out for me? I always did my own work."

"I mean that I was there when you first got *hired,*" Chip answered. "I was the one who helped you to become comfortable with the job, the managers, the workload, and everything at the office. You still remember any of that?"

Ivan said, "I would have done the same thing for *you.* But you didn't really advance since then, man. And you need to ask yourself why. It's not *my* fault."

Chip became silent for a minute. Ivan had no idea how he would respond to that. So he waited it out.

Finally, Chip asked him, "Are you sure you don't have any other positions?"

Ivan paused to think about it. He needed more time to do so, and while his mind was not on other ideas and issues.

"Give me a few days to think about that."

Chip said, "Yeah, I could use a new job away from this place."

Ivan responded, "Well, give me a call back next week sometime."

When he hung up the phone with him, Ivan smiled to himself.

He could really feel the weight of his new authority. In less than a year, he had become an official boss.

"Well, how 'bout that?" he questioned himself. *Guys I used to work with want to work for me now.*

He arrived at Lucina's stone-built home and was practically walking on air.

Lucina met him inside of her doorway.

"Can a guy at least ring your doorbell?" he teased her.

"You could have if you were not late," she told him.

Ivan smiled it off. "Here we go with that again."

She walked toward the passenger side of his car. It was parked behind her Mercedes in the driveway.

"How do you like how it handles?" she asked him.

Ivan stopped and said, "Lucina, this car is worth a quarter of a million dollars. She better handle me like a woman in love or I'm taking her back in a week."

Lucina was not amused. She stopped at the passenger-side door and stared at him. She said, "How come everything you say to me now has a sexual overtone? I don't like that. And you didn't used to talk to me that way."

She wanted to keep her same level of respect from Ivan no matter how big he got. That was Lucina's way. Respect was pivotal.

Ivan stared back at her. He didn't even mean it like that. But Lucina would not climb into the car until he had something to say about it.

She is such a tough-ass, he told himself. *She's like a damn ice goddess.*

He took a breath and said, "Okay. I apologize." Then he paused and added, "I'll just save all that for the other girls."

Lucina shook her head as she climbed into the car with him. She said, "Anyways, I have a lot of plans to go over with you for this year. And I have a whole list of performers and celebrities that I would like for us to bring in."

"Any Latino folks on that list?" Ivan asked her. He had already told her about his club development idea in Chula Vista.

Lucina answered, "Of course. I even want to invite Brazilian models here to San Diego to enjoy Café Seville. I also met the Chargers' star running back, LaDainian Tomlinson. We can throw a birthday party for him next."

That got Ivan's attention. He asked her, "You met L.T.? I've been meaning to ask the other guys to introduce me to him, but I didn't want to offend any of them by making them feel less important or anything, you know."

"Like you say, you just ask them," Lucina quipped.

"So, when did you meet him?"

"Two days ago."

All of a sudden Ivan felt a wave of jealousy come over him. LaDainian Tomlinson was a huge name in San Diego. He was young, flashy, and popular. Ivan immediately wondered what his partner thought of the running back.

"So, what was he like?" he asked.

Lucina told him, "He was very polite and down-to-earth, a good Southern guy."

Ivan hesitated before he took the wheel. He asked her, "What does *that* mean?"

"That means he's not from L.A. or New York. He's more soft-spoken and respectful."

Okay, just leave that shit alone, Ivan told himself. *It's only business for her.*

He even decided to play her all-business motto against her. He started the smooth purr of the Bentley engine and commented, "You know what, I've never even seen you with a guy outside of business before."

Lucina stared back at him. She said, "And I haven't seen *you* with a *woman* outside of business, either."

Ivan knew for a fact that Lucina suspected he had been intimate with Ida during her brief period of working the doors with them.

But outside of that, she had a point. Both of them seemed to be all business. However, Ivan had been intimate with two of Lucina's girls on the low.

And when I see that Carolyn Padilla again, that will be one more in the bag, he plotted. *If I would have asked for her phone number when I talked with her the first time . . .*

Ivan decided to leave the business-and-pleasure conversation alone. They had nowhere to go but rocky roads with it. So he nodded and told her, "Okay. You're right."

He drove up the street toward McCain Boulevard and their destination for a business lunch date in Coronado.

Lucina admired the car on their way. She said, "Look how far you've come already, Ivan." She sounded proud of him.

"Look how far *you've* come," he bounced back.

"No, I've already *been* where you're going," she teased him.

Ivan doubted that. Lucina may have traveled more, attended more big events, and seen more luxury, but Ivan considered himself nowhere near a finished product yet.

"Are you sure?" he asked her.

She stared into his colorful eyes with hers and challenged him. "I don't know. You tell me."

Ivan looked away and laughed. He said, "You just hang on in there with me. You'll see how far I plan to go in a minute."

Part VII

The Bottom Line

Nineteen

It's Lonely at the Top

IN THE LATE SPRING of 2004, business transitions happened rapidly for Ivan and Lucina. Ivan hired his team of business plan and proposal writers to focus exclusively on deal-making as his new strength. He added Mike Adams to his team as his personal accountant to double-check all figures and validate Ivan's position with the respected firm of Hutch & Mitchell. And Ivan offered to cut Chip and Perry Downing in as silent investors in Gaslamp parties, where he continued to market events with smaller promoters on his website.

"It's the easiest money you could ever make," he told them separately. "The only thing I ask you to do in return is always promote my name and brand in a positive light. Is that a deal?"

Perry Downing was all in. Chip Garrett, on the other hand, would rather have been a paid accountant for Ivan's company like Mike. Nevertheless, flipping a few extra thousand dollars a month on parties was nothing to complain about. So he agreed to it.

Ivan's powerful website at IDPromotions.com stepped up its viewer growth and support another notch online by strengthening its search rankings.

"We want to make sure that if anyone even types up the name

'San Diego,' they end up going through our site whether they like it or not," he told his staff.

So each week they would create new traffic-driving web pages, like "San Diego's Hottest New Talents," where they spotlighted the best new singers, rappers, producers, actors, dancers, filmmakers, poets, artists, skateboarders, and athletes. They also created "San Diego Wants You!" a voting page for who the people of San Diego would love to see the most in person. Ivan created that idea from Lucina's wish list of performers and celebrities.

Ivan's staff promoted blog competitions to post the best articles on subjects involving the people, places, and events of San Diego. They all worked tirelessly to build I.D. Promotions into a standalone brand. And with the steady blossoming of ideas, sponsorships, and advertisement, ad sales manager Eddie K. kept his eyes focused on their increasing company value.

"We may want to extend our reach past just San Diego and include everything between here and Los Angeles at some point," he suggested to Ivan. But Ivan was adamant about maintaining their dominance in the San Diego market before they expanded.

He responded, "We have that to look forward to, Eddie. But I don't see the point in doing that right now. We're still increasing our share first in San Diego. We need to keep our ship steady a little while longer," he advised his veteran salesman.

By midsummer, he estimated that the company would pull in more than three hundred thousand dollars a month, a thousand percent more than their overhead. So Ivan saw no reason to disturb their gain with hasty expansion.

In Ivan's growing real estate interests, Jeffrey Morefield joined him to invest in a Chula Vista housing development, while they continued to search for prime commercial property to build a Latino nightclub.

However, his baseball friend Emilio Alvarez was not as ready to join in on the deal.

Ivan told him, "It's a simple plan, E. All you need to do is to talk about representing the Spanish-speaking community every time the media sticks a microphone in your face. The team is getting a lot more attention this year with the new PETCO Park downtown. They're really pumping the Padres up this year. And once the Latino community knows that you're looking out for them, as soon as we open up this club with your name on it, it'll be like herding cattle."

At Emilio's three-bedroom home, located in the Poway area, Audrey warned him against it.

"Ivan is nothing but a user," she told him. "He'll do anything to get what *he* needs, but what about when you ask him to do something for *you*?"

Christina had told Audrey all about her falling-out with Ivan and how he had left her to dry. But Emilio argued, "Ivan's not that bad. He was the one to introduce us."

"Emilio, he only introduced us to get you to come to his parties," she admitted. "That's what made his parties more popular. But he didn't know that I really liked you, and I didn't want to keep being used by them while he and Lucina made all of the money."

She continued, "*Now* he's trying to use you again by opening up a nightclub in your name. I mean, it's obvious."

"But I will be making money off of this club, too," Emilio countered. "It's better than having my money sitting around doing nothing. And what about if I became the main owner, since it has my name on it?" he questioned.

Audrey said, "That would be a much better idea. And then I can help you to run it."

Nevertheless, Emilio remained hesitant, so Ivan began to discuss ideas with other Spanish-American promoters who would be more willing to jump at the opportunity.

On Lucina's end, with Ivan's guidance, they launched her own website, LucinaGallo.com, to create stronger ties to the fashion and retail industries, using her girls as models. It was another way to increase revenue, while dipping Lucina's feet back into the modeling industry as an agent. They linked the site prominently to IDPromotions.com, with pop-up buttons for fashion, retail, and a "San Diego's Best Dressed" page.

As their wealth, power, and imagery continued to increase within the San Diego market, Ivan began to engage in more flamboyant behavior. His rotation of exotic luxury cars from Roman Zemeckis made a loud splash outside the parties in the Gaslamp, and Ivan's celebrity stature drew noticeable responses from the crowd.

"What the hell kind of car is that?"

"It looks like one of those new Maseratis."

"How much is this guy worth now, anyway?"

"I don't know, but it has to be at least *millions.*"

"Oh, my God, he's so *sexy*!"

"Yeah, and he's standing right there like he doesn't know it."

"Oh, he *knows it.* He's just trying to *act* like he doesn't."

Where Ivan had previously been too busy in business to entertain most of the beautiful women who eyed him at parties, as his status continued to elevate, with more associates to handle his operations, the most enticing women were no longer ignored. And at any given moment, he would disarm them with sudden invitations to join him in the VIP, where some of the sexiest women in San Diego would become tongue-tied in his presence.

"I don't even know what to say to you. I'm just like . . . *surprised* that you even picked me."

Ivan told them, "Just relax and enjoy yourself. And anything you want, you just let me know."

Instead of him making any hasty moves on them, he would collect a competition of three to five women and have them decide—through their words and actions—who was more eligible to keep him company. And before the night would end, they would always reveal themselves.

"So, Ivan, what are you doing after the party?"

Bingo!

"Whatever you ladies allow me to."

But in all of his looseness with women, Ivan managed to stay away from any more of Lucina's models. He spent less of his time around her crew unless it was an event where his presence was requested. He explained to Lucina that it was time for her to build up her own brand again. He noticed that IDPromotions.com had begun to overpower her. Nevertheless, a partnership was a partnership. So Ivan was forced to appear at Lucina's Black Eyed Peas promotion, where he met back up with Carolyn Padilla.

"Ivan, why have you been hiding from me?" she asked him at the event for the crossover rap group. They were making their first visit to the Gaslamp with Fergie, their new female member. They were one of the many performing groups on Lucina's wish list.

Ivan told Carolyn, "We just haven't been in the same places lately, sweetheart." He had to remain careful of Ashley, who was also working the event that night.

He thought, *It's a hell of a lot easier to deal with women who are not in Lucina's circle now.*

Carolyn hinted strongly, "Well, I look forward to seeing you tonight, if you remember what you promised. So don't forget about me."

When she walked away, Ivan turned to his right and met eyes with Lucina.

Shit! She caught me looking, he panicked. He could feel it. But he hadn't done anything incriminating. It was just a stare-down. So he blew off Lucina's look of caution. As he turned back to his left, he spotted Ashley heading right in his direction.

"What was that all about?" she asked him.

"What are you talking about?"

Ashley just stared at him. "What, you don't like me anymore? You don't *call* me."

Ivan shook it off and told her, "Look, go on back to work. Nothing's going on here," and walked away.

He told himself, *I don't have time for this shit. I need to leave all of Lucina's girls alone.*

Lucina continued to watch him from a distance as Ivan separated himself from the crowd. He then caught up with Perry Downing sitting by himself at the VIP bar.

"Hey, Ivan, I need to talk to you, man," he mumbled through his drink. He looked as if he had downed more than the legal limit already.

"Go ahead and shoot," Ivan told him. He had nothing better to listen to. He didn't even want to be there. His mind was on much bigger business.

Perry said, "I'm kind of like . . . in a bind right now, man. I don't know if the Chargers are gonna sign me to a new contract this year. They haven't talked about it this whole off-season."

That got Ivan's attention. "Your contract is up?"

"Yeah, this is the year to do something. I just finished five years with the Chargers after coming over from the Rams."

Ivan didn't realize Perry was that old, but he was sure that he could find another team who would want him. Nevertheless, Ivan would miss all of Perry's bravado and support.

"So, what do you need? You're not asking me to try and negotiate a new contract, are you?" Ivan joked with him.

Perry chuckled. "Naw. I still got an agent for that. But I *could* use some bigger things to invest in until I get a new deal or something, man."

He continued, "I hear you're buying and selling houses in real estate with Jeffrey."

Jeffrey must have told him. Ivan nodded and said, "Yeah, we can definitely talk about that. But that's a lot more money than parties," he warned.

Perry nodded. "I know."

Ivan stared at him to read if he was serious. And he was. So he said, "All right, call me up first thing on Monday."

Perry stuck out his huge hand and said, "You got it, man. And be safe in here tonight. I see the women are all in here looking for you."

With that off his chest, Perry stood up and walked off toward the exit.

I guess that's all he was here to talk about, Ivan told himself. *But maybe he should let someone else drive him home tonight.* Perry didn't look too stable that evening. So Ivan continued to think about him.

"You seem to have a lot on your mind tonight, Ivan," Lucina commented.

She startled him from his thoughts. "Oh, yeah, I guess I do." He said, "Too many people, too many things, too many thoughts are all on my mind at the same time."

Lucina nodded and kept her comments about her girls to herself. She figured she would talk to him about it later.

"You can handle it, Ivan," she told him instead.

At the end of the night, not only were Carolyn and Ashley eager to see him, but a few other hot girls were hanging around the party to catch him for a nightcap as well.

"Hey, where's the after party, Ivan? Any invitations?" a couple of pretty blondes asked him. They looked as close as cousins. Every guy in the party had watched them dancing with each other that night. But they had apparently waited up for Ivan.

"Is this a family resemblance I see going on here?" he asked to avoid their question.

"No, but we can all *make it* a family," one girlfriend responded, producing an alcohol-laced giggle.

"What did you drive in this time? Can we get a joyride somewhere?" the other one asked.

Obviously, the two of them had peeped Ivan out. He grinned and told them, "I don't know about that. I got a lot more to do tonight."

"Aww, all work and no play?"

That was the last thing Ivan heard before he walked away from them.

"Somebody looks real popular tonight," Maya teased him. She noticed girls paying a lot more attention to Ivan than they did the members of the Black Eyed Peas that evening.

Ivan told her, "Yeah, well . . . they'll get over it."

As usual, Ashley disappeared early to call him later. Ivan had told Carolyn to do the same. However, when he walked out of the club with Lucina, she changed her normal program on him.

Instead of hanging out and entertaining the Black Eyed Peas, Lucina told him, "I don't think I'm gonna make it home."

He studied her face and asked, "What do you mean?"

"I mean that I'm tired and I need to talk to you."

Ivan said, "All right. We can do that tomorrow." He was already thinking about Carolyn speaking seductive Spanish to him from under the sheets. She was *asking* him for it.

"No, I need to talk to you *tonight,*" Lucina insisted.

"What about?" Ivan pressed her. "It can't wait until tomorrow? I thought you said you were tired."

Lucina took a breath. "It's personal, Ivan," she told him.

He had no idea what that meant. He took a breath of his own. "All right, Lucina, but I'm tired, too. I'm always tired after these parties," he lied.

"Are you really?" she asked him. She knew damn well Ivan had stores of excess energy. She had been around him for nearly a year, and they had spent some long hours together.

Ivan ignored the question. He didn't even look tired. At the start of the evening he had been dropped off in front of the crowd in a white two-seater Aston Martin. So he had no room for Lucina to ride back with him. And as his driver waited for him at the curb, with eager women still waiting and watching, Ivan told Lucina the deal.

"Well, I only have a two-seater tonight. And it looks like you let the limo drive off already."

She said, "I told him to. And I'll have Maya drop me off at your apartment building behind you."

Ivan looked confused again. "And how are you gonna get home tonight?" He surely wasn't taking her.

"You can drive me home in the morning," she told him.

Ivan grinned and shook his head. He didn't even think about trying Lucina anymore. At that point, he figured she was only getting in the way, cock blocking.

All right, so I guess it's just not meant for me to have Carolyn tonight, he assessed for himself. *I didn't need to go there anyway.*

He shrugged and said, "Okay. You got it your way, then."

AS THEY RODE UP the elevator together at Ivan's apartment building, he still didn't know what to expect from Lucina. All he knew was that he needed to keep his cell phone on mute and never attempt to answer it while she was still with him that night.

When they entered his apartment, Lucina walked straight over to his living room sofa and crashed on it in instant sleep mode.

Ivan had upgraded nearly everything at his apartment, including his sofas. They were quality dark brown leather now.

What the hell is that? he wondered of his partner. He walked over and dropped the bag of money in front of her on the floor before he stepped behind her to stand and wait. He didn't want her to read all of the plotting on his face. But he was tempted to abandon her there and retire to his bedroom. He even thought about going back out to catch up with Carolyn at a downtown hotel and go on about his business. Lucina's blocking was only making him want the Mexican beauty more.

Then Lucina grumbled from the sofa, "Ivan . . . I know all about you and Christina. She called me up and told me about it."

Since they had their falling-out, Ivan would put nothing past the girl. But he was still surprised she had told Lucina. So he had no comment. He only listened, while standing there behind her.

Lucina continued, "She said she could no longer work for me because she could not stand being between us."

Ivan heard that and smirked. *That's bullshit,* he thought. *Now she's trying to make herself look like a victim. And you think you know somebody.*

Lucina went on, "Plenty of people have told me lately about seeing you out with different women all over San Diego. What is going on with you, Ivan?" she asked him.

Ivan paused to gather his thoughts before he spoke. He asked her, "Do you *care*?"

Lucina sat up from her position on the sofa and turned to face him. "Ivan, of *course* I care. You have a *reputation* that you cannot afford to ruin by running around like . . . like . . . like you've never been with a *woman* before."

Ivan had never heard Lucina choke on her words. He found that to be surprising. He even smiled at it.

That only made her snap at him more. "Do you think this is a *joke,* Ivan? You sleeping around is not good for business," she told him. "Have you slept with *Carolyn* now too? Ashley? Daphne? Audrey? How *many* of them?"

Ivan cracked a grin and shook his head. She was going overboard. He said, "Now, you're gonna believe everything that Chris tells you, right, and start jumping to conclusions?"

"She told me you tell everyone to keep it to themselves," Lucina accused him.

Ivan snapped, "That's what *adults* are supposed to do. It ain't everybody's business."

"Especially when it's not *right,*" Lucina snapped back at him.

Ivan told her, "First of all, I haven't been with a lot of your girls. I stay away from them on *purpose.* But what do you want me to do, leave everybody alone?"

Lucina stared at him. She said, "You need to find someone who really *means* something to you."

Ivan countered, "Well, what if I have, and she's not interested?"

Lucina heard that and looked away from him.

She mumbled, "I'm sure she would not make up her mind by watching you sleep around."

Ivan said, "Well, she needs to admit that she's attracted, then. Can she at least do that?" He had no idea they would end up in this kind of discussion. All of a sudden he no longer cared about seeing Carolyn. Lucina Gallo was his number-one priority again.

"I mean, I don't know how *she* does it, but a man's gonna act like a man out here," he told her. "And the last time *I* checked, I was still *single."*

Lucina told him, "That doesn't mean you have to be a *whore,* Ivan. That's what I don't *like* about America. You have *no* real romance here. And you don't know what *real love* is."

Ivan stared at her. Now she had reverted back to the cultural differences. He said, "Look, it's too late at night for this. So you tell me how you feel about it in the morning. And I'm going to bed."

"I'm gonna feel the same way I do now," she told him as he moved toward his bedroom.

He stopped and said, "Then there's nothing else to talk about. We're still partners. We're still making money together. We still care about each other. But I'm gonna do *me*, and I gotta let you do you. Case closed."

He said, "And my thing for women is *not* bad for business. I'm a sex symbol now, right? That's what happens to attractive men when they get money. You told me that yourself. You even set me up for it," he reminded her, pointing to his diamond-studded earlobe. "But now you wanna sit there and complain about it."

With that, he walked off toward his room and left Lucina speechless.

She sat there on the sofa with close to fifty thousand dollars in front of her on the floor and felt miserable.

I can trust him now with money, she mused. *Ivan has been a very fair partner to me . . . But I can't trust him with my heart,* she concluded. Lucina was not used to mixing business with pleasure. Few men had ever gotten close enough to her for intimacy. However, she had rarely found much pleasure in men who were not about business. And Ivan David was *surely* a young man about the task of capital gains. So he was definitely attractive to her in an intimate way. The two of them were just intertwined in a complicated dance of emotional hesitancy.

Lucina rubbed her temples with both hands to relieve the stress. And as she sat there alone on Ivan's comfortable sofa, she thought, *Maybe too much business has ruined my own capacity to trust love.*

IN HIS BEDROOM, Ivan looked down at his cell phone and read the missed phone calls of four separate women, including Carolyn Padilla. He could already imagine her calling him Papi. He shook his head and bit his bottom lip in frustration.

"Yeah, she just fucked my whole night up," he grumbled of Lucina's timing. Nevertheless, he figured she had a point. He had been reckless because he *could* be. His recent behavior was similar to his brother's.

He thought about that for a minute as he stretched out across his bed, fully clothed, and kicked off his shoes.

What if I just . . . picked out the baddest woman I could find in San Diego and made her my new showpiece? he questioned. *I wonder what Lucina would say about that.*

That led him to think about business again.

"The Executives' Club," he told himself out loud. "Nothing but the best: women, cars, boats, airplanes, properties . . . like in the *Robb Report.*"

Ivan smiled up to the ceiling and calmed his nerves. Lucina had sparked another business idea for him. He thought about it more and couldn't wait to get back into his office to have his guys post up his latest creation on their website.

However, in the morning Lucina woke him up with other pressing news.

She knocked hard on his bedroom door and screamed, "Ivan, hurry up and see this! A report about Perry Downing is on the news!"

Ivan jerked up from his bed and looked over at his alarm clock on the tall dresser. It was 7:43 AM. He had gone to sleep sometime after four, with another stream of ideas running through his mind.

He mumbled, "Perry's on the news for what?"

"He was in an accident last night in Balboa Park," she answered.

Ivan froze and remembered how toasted the football player had been before he left the club.

"Shit!" He leaped up out of bed and ran out into the living room, where Lucina was watching the morning news. But by the time Ivan had made it out, the newscasters were finishing their report.

"Perry Downing was reportedly in *stable* condition at the Naval Medical Center. His unidentified *passenger* was reported in *critical* condition."

When they went to other breaking news stories, Ivan looked at Lucina for what he had missed.

She said, "He was driving with a woman in his car and swerved into the other lane, causing a three-car wreck. And it sounded like they were doing something they were not supposed to be doing in the car. Neither one of them had their seat belts on," she concluded.

Ivan didn't hear the whole report and so he couldn't begin to speculate on it. But he could verify that Perry was probably past the legal driving limit. However, he hadn't seen him leave the club with any woman.

He could have picked a girl up at any time, Ivan reasoned. He was already thinking about damage control and going to visit Perry at the Medical Center.

"Shit. He needs to start negotiating a new contract," he informed Lucina. "He was even ready to invest in some real estate deals with me."

Lucina didn't like the sound of that. Ivan's continued thoughts about business were insensitive.

"How could you think about real estate and new contracts at a time like this?" she asked him.

Ivan said, "You think *he's* not thinking about it? Because I can tell you right now that he is, *especially* now. Tragedies make your need to have your business in order *more* important."

"Ivan, he needs to think more about getting well again. And I hope the woman is okay, too," Lucina countered.

Ivan was already thinking about what the breaking news might do to Jeffrey, Zee-Dog, and the rest of the guys on the team, once they knew that Perry had been hanging out at another party promotion before the crash. The Chargers might start to believe that Ivan and Lucina were bad influences. And just when he was trying to open up his own cash-cow club for Mexican-Americans. How would Jeffrey respond to all of that after Perry's accident?

IVAN DIDN'T have to wait long to find out. Soon after he had dropped Lucina off at home that morning, Jeffrey Morefield called him up on the cell phone to talk about Perry.

"Did he get a chance to talk to you about real estate yet?" Jeffrey asked him.

"Yeah, right before the accident," Ivan told him. "He was over at our party, man. I told him to call me Monday on it. But I didn't see no woman with him."

There was no sense in Ivan lying about it. It was what it was.

Jeffrey said, "Well, you know how he is with women. That don't take much for him at all. But it took a lot for me to talk him into doing something with his money before he runs out of it."

He said, "You know they may not re-sign him this year. It's new-blood time. Either that or they'll tell him to take a big pay cut. That's just the nature of the business we're in."

Jeffrey wasn't turned off of his project with Ivan by his teammate's misfortune at all. In fact, it only made him more determined to invest his money in something worthwhile, just as Ivan had hoped for. So Ivan took the added energy with him to his office.

"So, you want us to build a web page now for San Diego Executives' Club?" Paul repeated while jotting the ideas down at his desk.

Ivan answered, "Yeah. Then I'll have Eddie redirect the ads from our more upscale advertisers—World Wide Luxury Cars, Classic Furniture, the Pacific Yacht Club, and our premium liquor sponsors—to the page. We can also link Lucina's upscale fashion pages to it."

He went on, "Then we'll add another photo gallery of the Hutch and Mitchell Golf Tournament, the car shows, and the boat parties. I also need to start talking to private jet companies. I'd like to fly in one of those things myself now."

Jeff walked into the office and said, "Who wouldn't?"

"So, we'll get them to advertise their private flights," Ivan planned.

He was all pumped up with energy that morning. Jeff and Paul just looked at each other and smiled. Their young boss's enthusiastic ideas kept them on their toes, forcing all competitor websites to keep eating their dust with envy.

IDPromotions.com was approaching fifty thousand unique hits per day, with plenty of outside tourism traffic helping them to close in on a half million daily impressions, including national U.S. military viewers. Ivan had to give that credit to Eddie for talking him into allowing the recruiter pages.

"By the way," Ivan added, "outside of Lucina's girls, who's, like, some of the hottest new models sending us spotlight pictures to post?"

Paul looked up and said, "As a matter of fact, there's this Native American girl who's, like, *awesome*. She's getting all kinds of hits now."

Jeff nodded his head and grinned. "Yeah, man, she's, ah . . . she's something else."

"Oh, yeah? Let me see her. How come we didn't spotlight her yet?" Ivan asked them.

Jeff and Paul both looked confused.

Jeff said, "We did spotlight her."

Paul chuckled. He said, "Ivan doesn't have time to look at all of the things we're doing now. I forget about a lot of the things we post up now myself. That's like expecting a publisher to read everything in his newspaper. It's impossible."

Ivan said, "It's not impossible, but I get what you mean." He felt bad that he couldn't keep up with it all. But Paul was right. Ivan couldn't meet everyone at his promotions and events, either.

When they showed him the girl online, Ivan studied her long dark hair, almond-shaped eyes, perfect features, pert breasts, medium-sized lips, olive-toned skin, and teasing smile. She looked about twenty-one, just barely legal for club and party work.

Ivan nodded and said, "Yeah, she's about a nine."

Jeff said, "A *nine*? Are you *crazy*? Dude, she's an *eleven!*"

Ivan chuckled. He was only being modest. He didn't want to seem as excited as they were about her. He said, "So, this girl is the best we have to offer, hunh?"

"We think so," Paul reiterated.

"All right, well, tell her I want to meet her in person. Does she know who I am?"

Paul and Jeff gave each other another look.

Jeff told him, "Of *course* she knows who you are. We're not going back to you being Mr. Invisible. You *are* the brand now. People have been writing blogs all about your exotic cars, outfits, and everything."

Paul nodded and said, "Yeah, it's good for the business. You're the man of San Diego for real now."

Ivan grinned. He said, "I tried to tell Lucina that last night. But I don't know how much she likes the idea," he hinted.

Jeff shook it off. He said, "Aw, she likes it. She may not want to *admit* it, but she *likes* it."

Paul added, "I don't think she's gonna like Jacari, though, if you're asking to meet her personally."

Ivan grimaced and said, "Who?"

Paul pointed back to the Native American beauty queen on his monitor with the name Jacari posted on the edges of the page.

"Shit, I forgot about her already," Ivan admitted.

"You won't forget her when you meet her," Jeff told him. "And do remember that we told you that."

IVAN VISITED Perry Downing with Lucina at the Naval Medical Center to check up on him. From his hospital bed, through all of his bandages and medication, Perry didn't want Ivan feeling guilty about him.

He forced himself to mumble, "Ivan . . . keep doing what you do, man. One injured player don't stop the game." And he smiled.

Ivan smiled back at him and accepted his endorsement. It took a lot of the strain off his shoulders. With all of his plans for the year 2004, he had no time to slow down.

IDPromotions.com went on to hold the luxury car show with Xzibit, the boat party with Ananda Lewis and Jessica Alba, and the Hutch & Mitchell Golf Tournament with NBA basketball legend Charles Barkley and San Diego Chargers quarterback Drew Brees.

After the car show events, Lucina was able to set her feet for a major push into the fashion industry. Her fashion ideas were considered tasteful, practical, and innovative.

The boat promotions allowed Ivan to make legitimate friendships to pitch yacht and cruise ship owners on his plans to promote more cruise events and private yacht rentals, which also led him to conversations about private jets.

He found that the same wealthy individuals who bought and

owned expensive cars and private boats also owned or had access to private jets.

"Now we're right where we need to be," he told his team of business plan and proposal writers. They worked overtime to win the confidence of new business friends and associates, including the new and long-standing clients of Hutch & Mitchell Accounting. They were all reintroduced to Mr. Ivan David as the marketing guru behind their first annual golf tournament, along with other professional networking events in the works.

Barry Mitchell pulled him aside at the tournament and asked him, "How does it feel now to come face-to-face and speak on equal par with the CEOs, Ivan?"

"I'm not on equal par *yet*," Ivan told him. "But I'm okay with it. It just takes some getting used to, to know when to pitch business or when to just relax around them."

Barry patted him on the back and said, "You're right. But I'm sure you'll figure it out soon enough. Generally, you have to wait until they ask *you* first."

Ivan said, "Yeah, I figured that. And that's what makes me a little anxious about it. I'm ready to pitch them every hour now."

SUCCESSES IN various San Diego business arenas allowed Ivan to engage the San Diego Chamber of Commerce to organize and promote a large business expo event at the downtown convention center in 2005. Ivan figured a business expo at the convention center would open the door to other events and concerts there.

"Once the convention center management knows who we are, we can walk back in with other proposals," he told Lucina.

It didn't take long for Randy & Ralph Entertainment to reach back out to them for partnerships on concerts. They started off by offering to team up for Justin Timberlake, Usher, and Carrie Underwood, believing that Ivan and Lucina would be able to help them sell the younger pop and urban crowds.

"I told you how it works," Ivan reminded his partner. "Now you can get your respect back, if you still wanna deal with these guys. *Or* we could wait to set up our own concerts for next year."

He added, "All it takes is our relationships now. We got access to all the money we need, as long as it's gonna be a big enough gain for everyone."

On the strength of his website alone, Ivan was set to cross the millionaire mark by late September. He was already thinking about making his second million before the year was out. Lucina was halfway to a million herself through her share of their party and event promotions.

In the meantime, Thomas Jones had found a plot of commercial property that was big enough for a three-thousand-capacity nightclub in Chula Vista at a reasonable price. But with Emilio Alvarez still stalling and Julio's cousin in L.A. uninterested, Ivan went with the working title of "Latino Club" and pitched it to investors without a Latino celebrity attached.

"I'll just push the club on my own, hire a popular manager, and send my guy Mike Adams in there to make sure the numbers are right," Ivan explained to Thomas and Jeffrey. "Then we'll invite folks like Ricky Martin, Carlos Santana, and get Nelly Furtado back. And if we ask for Mark Anthony, we may even get his wife Jennifer Lopez to come with him."

By the time the new football season was in full swing, Perry Downing had made a full recovery from his injuries, and the Chargers' management had forgiven him for his misjudgment during the off-season. They had decided to offer him another two-year stint to help the team in their quest to win an NFL Super Bowl, but with less money. Perry accepted it on Ivan's advice. And he was forced to pay an undisclosed amount for the injuries of the passenger. Fortunately, she survived it.

Jeffrey was in the third year of a five-year contract, and Zee-Dog was in the second year of a four-year deal. And they all decided to back Ivan in his commercial real estate and nightclub plans after he guaranteed them all a hundred percent return on their money.

Thomas told him, "Ivan, if you can make these club and restaurant deals work, you're setting yourself up to make a *killing*."

Ivan smiled and told him, "That's just what I'm counting on."

The man was on a sweet roll of momentum. By the end of his second year in business, he had earned more than two and a half million dollars before taxes and officially established himself as the CEO of Ivan David Enterprises, the parent company of his diversified interests in websites, real estate, accounting consultation, promotions and events, brand marketing, club and restaurant development, yacht and luxury car rental, tourism packages, and private jet travel.

However, as Ivan refocused on making his first millions, his private life had all but evaporated. He had not had a chance to meet Jacari before her sudden popularity in San Diego earned her a trip to the fashion and modeling capital of Manhattan, where she quickly signed with an agency and began work in her dream career.

Ivan did get a chance to speak to her for a brief moment. And when they got her on the line over the office speakerphone, she exclaimed, "Oh, my God, it's been so unbelievable! I thank all of you guys *so much* for giving me this opportunity to make it all happen. And I promise to stop by the office and visit you guys as soon as I'm able to break away from my work and get back home to San Diego."

She continued, "But right now I'm just, like, *swamped* with so much modeling work. I'm doing an *Elle* magazine spread, and we're in talks for the next *Sports Illustrated* swimsuit issue."

Ivan heard all of that and didn't have much to say. She sounded like an overexcited kid.

I can never imagine Lucina sounding like that for anything, he thought. *Lucina's been there and done that already.*

"Okay, well, don't forget about us," Ivan told Jacari.

"Oh, I won't, I won't, but I have to go now," she told them.

Ivan looked at Paul and Jeff before they all grinned.

When they hung up the line with her, Jeff said, "It sounds like she's really happy."

Ivan said, "Well, I'm glad we were able to do that for her." But he didn't feel anything special toward her. *Maybe next time,* he thought of her. He never attempted to slide back to home base with Carolyn Padilla or roll in the hay again with Ashley, either.

Ivan had toned down all of his looseness and flamboyance to concentrate on making more millions. In his mind, two million was only a few deals away from four, four million was only a few more deals from ten, and ten million was a few more deals from a hundred.

Nevertheless, as he and Lucina remained hesitant to become anything more than business partners, all of Ivan's new wealth and continued aspirations left him with an unsettled feeling of emptiness.

He told himself, *Okay, I'm rich! . . . Now what?*

Twenty

Business Never Stops

About a half mile out from the Pacific Beach of San Diego in the early summer of 2005, Ivan cruised southward while sitting at the back end of a small yacht that had been loaned out to him from clients of Seth Gardner. It was a perfect sunny day in the high seventies, with soft winds in the air. Dressed in a light blue Polo tennis shirt and beige khaki pants, Ivan looked eastward and up at the mansions that were spaced out on the hills of La Jolla. He felt he needed a day off from the hustle and bustle of his new eighth-floor office space in the Mission Valley area. So he sailed out to think for a few undisturbed hours on the beautiful blue waters of the Pacific.

Ivan was so focused on his thoughts that he barely noticed his alluring companion approaching him from the right side of the boat.

She studied the intense glare in his eyes as the sunlight hit them and made them sparkle. "What's on your mind, Ivan?" she asked him.

Her soft, feminine hand, with perfectly manicured nails, met his right shoulder. She sat down beside him in her yellow, orange, and red dress, with no shoes.

Ivan barely acknowledged her. He shook off her question and shrugged. "I'm just, ah . . . thinking," he answered.

The woman, in her midtwenties, looked similar enough to be a distant cousin. She had the same light brown skin and light-colored eyes, with thick, wavy hair that fell past her shoulders.

When Ivan began to promote a creed of "nothing but the best" for the San Diego Executives' Club, he meant it. His companion was definitely exclusive company: only millionaires and up needed apply for her attention. Nevertheless, Ivan paid her no mind. She was another expensive prop, like the cars, boats, jewelry, and private jets that he began to utilize for personal pleasure and company business.

She said, "Well, I can see *that*. But what are you thinking *about?*"

Ivan wondered if she could follow his eyes and spot the multimillion-dollar houses that held his attention up on the hills. That would be the easiest answer for him to give her. Outside of that, he could not even begin to explain all the issues that were running through his mind at that moment. Nor did he want her to know about them.

His brother, Derrick, in his determination to prove that he could still make his own living, decided to sell exotic strains of marijuana, only to be busted when a teenage girl flipped out in her high on Redondo Beach and started pointing fingers when the medics, police, and her parents questioned her about it, which eventually led all the way back to Derrick.

"Man, how the fuck am I supposed to know who these assholes are sharing the weed with?" Derrick had argued in private with his brother back in L.A.

Ivan had snapped, "But why would you sell that shit in the first place, especially while I still have you on the damn payroll? That's all somebody needs to say, my money is dirty, and you'll fuck up everybody's meal ticket, including your sons'."

He said, "You know how many jealous white boys are waiting to jump on some shit like that and try to ruin me? They're already wondering how I did all this shit. They *always* think we're illegal."

Derrick's marijuana case became an easy misdemeanor that Ivan paid his team of lawyers to beat in L.A., but he was more concerned about the negative publicity his brother might cause him in the future, particularly in regards to Ivan's finances.

So with Derrick's self-destructive immaturity in mind, Ivan thought of every way to cut his ties, including paying Derrick a lump sum of cash under the witness of his lawyers and a notary public that would hold Ivan not accountable for how Derrick chose to spend it. He also started paperwork to set up trust accounts for his three nephews that would take care of them regardless of their father, because the man could no longer be trusted to do the right thing with money.

That issue led Ivan to consider the offers he began to receive in reference to the value of his website. His small start-up brand continued to grow, reaching as high as two million impressions per day and an email list that was approaching a hundred thousand names. The IDPromotions.com link to the tourism industry for family vacations, national boat cruises, and airline deals, combined with the rentals and sales of luxury cars, homes, private yachts, and private jets, became a masterful idea.

Ivan had reasoned, "If outside viewers are already looking at San Diego as a tourist attraction, then it makes sense for us to show them other locations and things to do elsewhere, even for the people who live here in San Diego."

He added, "And for our wealthier viewers, who search for news and items at the Executives' Club, if they can afford to buy or rent luxury in one place, then they can rent and buy cars, boats, and planes in another."

Eddie K. loved the idea. His goal had been to make IDPromotions.com a valuable national brand from day one. He saw no use in an internet vehicle having the same limitations as a physical newspaper. The internet had an instant, international reach, and he had continued to view it that way.

The expanded content, marketing approach, and focus of the website also allowed the advertisement and sales force to become more assertive in their efforts to establish regional rates. Ivan even began to think of taking the company public, but he was unsure if his brand was as strong as he would like it to be yet. Nor was he sure if he was personally ready to stomach the emotional roller-coaster ride of the stock market numbers game.

Whenever you take your baby public, you can end up losing a bunch of sleep, while being dictated to by public company numbers, he pondered. *And that's when the shit stops being fun.*

He learned that from the executive clients he had worked with at Hutch & Mitchell.

He thought, *But I'm already making good money. I'm set to bank ten million this year after taxes. But how much more could I make if we go public . . . ?*

To keep the excess money working for him, Ivan acquired three new commercial real estate properties. Outside developing, branding, and selling a percentage of the Latino Club for a sizable gain in Chula Vista, he developed the three new properties into the Ice Mountain Brewery, Club Paradise, and Jock Nation Bar & Grill.

"The setup is simple," he had told his investment groups. "You give the customers flyers and website maps for the locations, and we keep working a dedicated crowd with special guests and events until you get tired of making money. And if you ever do get tired, I can either buy back your percentage or find another investor."

Ivan no longer bothered to overpitch his projects and services. His momentum of success allowed him the confident luxury to take or leave money as it came. With Mike Adams continuing to double-check the accounting numbers of his business plan and proposal writers, just as Thomas Jones had told him, Ivan allowed the numbers to speak for themselves. And the influence of his website allowed him to continue to push whatever pet project he chose to.

However, his idea to utilize the allure of sexy young women in all of his nightclub properties caused a strong rift between him and Lucina.

"Are you trying to copy what Hooters does? I find that to be *very* distasteful," she told him at his downtown apartment.

Ivan grinned at the suggestion. He remembered the competitive struggle Catherine Boone had had with the women who worked at the Hooters chain when he first started.

He said, "Naw, we'll keep them dressed way more tasteful than that. And their dress codes would fit the themes of each club. So, just like we have our Hispanic theme at the Latino Club, we'll have a ski lodge theme at the Ice Mountain, a cheerleader theme at Jock's, and a colorful island theme at Paradise."

It all made sense to Ivan. He liked developing a variety of ideas just to see which one would earn the most support from its dedicated customer base. But Lucina *blasted* the idea.

"That all sounds very generic and degrading," she told him.

Ivan argued, "Well, welcome to America, Lucina. Generic is what works for regular guys drinking beers all night. Not everybody's gonna be impressed by that upscale shit. It intimidates them. But these regular pretty girls, who still need someplace to work, can find steady employment with us with plenty of tip potential."

It was another argument of quantity versus quality, and Lucina was not going for it.

She snapped, "Well, I don't want to be a part of that."

In fact, she was not a part of many of the new projects Ivan was developing. And he didn't want to be a part of throwing concerts with Randy & Ralph. He still didn't trust them. They began asking too many intricate questions about his website operations for them to be trusted, especially since they had their own website. Ivan felt they were trying to duplicate some of his marketing ideas. He figured he could make the same amount of money as he would from concerts by promoting the various club properties he had invested in. He was also more in control of the numbers there. However, Lucina was eager to deal with her old partners.

Nevertheless, without Ivan's website promotions, Randy & Ralph remained cold to Lucina's inclusion in their plans. That led Ivan to think of other ideas where he and Lucina could find common ground. He came up with brand-building events where they would focus less on the paying crowds and work more on sponsorship vehicles. They would be paid to create the support of a large section of the population, while being backed by strong product branders. Lucina would then have limited economic risk, and she could continue to earn from fresh ideas and a strong supportive following.

"That's the wave of new big business anyway," Ivan had told her. "The bigger companies can afford to sponsor any- and everything now."

"Yes, but they often take much longer to pitch," Lucina argued.

Ivan thought, *There she goes with her impatience again*. She didn't have a proposal-writing team like Ivan had. Nevertheless, he figured that *his* team was *her* team.

He told her, "All we have to do is sit down and explain everything to my guys, just like how we worked on the proposals for the events we did last year."

"Yes, and they took *forever* to happen."

"But they *did* happen, and they all went over well. We just tap into the same sponsors, like we did with my second birthday network party this year. I mean, do you want to keep making money with me or what?"

Lucina seemed to be fighting against him more than working with him. Ivan couldn't understand it. She was losing out on major deals and income in the process.

Finally, she told him, "Ivan, you don't know everything. And I can't *stand* that you think you do. You've only been out here for a *couple years* now, and already you think you're some kind of *tycoon*."

Ivan grimaced. He said, "You know what? I went through all this before with you, and it's the same fucking jealousy over and over again. You do this every year. It's like you only want to do your own ideas, but business don't work like that, man."

"I told you before, I'm not a *man,* Ivan," she nitpicked.

Ivan paused. He said, "Well, maybe if you *were* a man you wouldn't *bitch* about so much of this small shit! And maybe that's why you lost so many of your partners before. But all I've been trying to do is work with you."

Those were hard, chauvinistic comments for him to state to her, but Ivan felt he needed to say what was on his mind whether she could handle it or not.

Lucina paused and stared at him. She took a breath and said, "You know, I look at you now, and I tell myself, *Lucina, you've created a masterpiece.*" She said, "But I don't even think that I like it anymore."

Immediately Ivan thought of defending himself by reminding her that his ideas were just as profitable and innovative as *hers* were, and even more so. He had generated more long-term money for them. But he quickly realized that the argument would have been frivolous. It didn't matter. Lucina had been a major contributor to the entire mentality of his success. And without her, he had no idea how far he would have gotten in the first place. He could have been locked into throwing small black network parties for years.

So he allowed her to walk away without a response from him. In business, he could do just fine now without her. He knew plenty of pretty party girls of his own now. He had his own brand name, his own marketable ideas, a monster of a website, a hardworking staff, a business team, executive-level friendships, and access to plenty of personal capital as well as investor support. But on the social side, even though he had never touched Lucina intimately, he felt a great void in her absence.

She doesn't even care about that part, he mused. *I'm just a damn busi-*

ness partner. And now she's made enough connections of her own to do her own thing, too.

The reality of Lucina moving on from him had hurt Ivan the most. And in the end, he felt he was only a *prop* for her. But how much, if any, of his thoughts could he expect to share with a relative stranger on a boat ride?

So Ivan answered his companion's question on the yacht with simplicity. "I'm just thinking about how I still want to buy one of those houses up there one day."

"Are any of them for sale?" she asked him.

Ivan nodded. "That's a good point. I guess I need to find that out."

I should just buy one now, he thought. *I got enough to afford it now.* However, he didn't want to share that much information. He didn't want to cloud the woman's mind by having her naturally include herself in his future plans. Because there would *be* none between them. Ivan didn't feel anything for her.

She smiled at him anyway. "I would love to see what one of those houses looks like up there myself."

I know you would, Ivan thought with a grin. He saw no point in expressing that to her, either. He just planned to enjoy the rest of his peaceful boat ride away from the office.

WHEN IVAN RETURNED to the eighth-floor office of Ivan David Enterprises in Mission Valley that next morning, Jeff and Paul had breaking news for him. Ivan had mimicked the setup of Hutch & Mitchell Accounting by renting an entire floor with cubicles out in the center with main offices and conference rooms surrounding them. Jeff and Paul shared a corner office with their computer equipment, Ava Tate had a second corner office for editorial, Eddie K. had a third corner for sales, and Ivan's executive office was in the final corner at the farthest end from the receptionist booth. In between the corner offices were smaller spaces for all of his business team members, including Mike Adams.

Thomas Jones had sold their close-to-campus hub for four hundred thousand dollars to a fraternity organization, who liked the setup so much that they had the furniture included in the sale price.

Ivan stopped by Jeff and Paul's office that morning to hear their urgent update. Both of them had upgraded their wardrobes since their move into a more professional building. They both wore sports jackets and button-up shirts themselves now, and without Ivan asking them to do so. They just figured it was time for them to look the part of creative executives. With the remarkably increased revenue of the website, they would earn nearly a million apiece before taxes that year. And for their first full year out of college, they would do tremendously well for themselves.

Jeff told Ivan, "Jacari contacted us while you were out of the office yesterday. She said she has a break to come back home soon. She's just getting back to New York from a month over in Italy."

Ivan nodded and said, "Damn. So she's really blowing up with this modeling thing."

"Yeah, she's a San Diego superstar now," Paul commented. "But there was some flack recently over her name. A lot of Native American bloggers were saying that "Jacari" was not an authentic tribal name. They were saying that her real name is Kaya."

Ivan shrugged it off. "Does it really matter? She took up a one-word model name, that's all. What's wrong with that? People do stuff like that all the time in L.A."

"Yeah, well, she said something about her father wanting to meet you, too," Paul commented.

Ivan looked at Paul relaxed behind his fine wood desk and repeated, "Her *father* wants to meet me? About what? I haven't met or even *touched* his daughter yet," he joked.

They all laughed.

Paul said, "No, I think he wants to talk to you about doing something with the website. She told him she owes her popularity all to us."

"Yeah, and she said her father owns a casino on the reservation or something," Jeff filled in.

Ivan nodded again. "A casino, hunh?" He smiled and began assuming things. "So, he must want us to give them the big IDPromotions.com brand treatment."

"Maybe so," Jeff commented.

"Well, when is she supposed to be heading back this way?"

"She said in a couple of weeks," Paul answered. "She said she needed to get back to her apartment in New York and make sure everything is in order there first."

"All right, well, just let me know when she gets back out here," Ivan responded. With that he left their office and walked down the hall toward his own.

"How are you doing today, Mr. David?" a college intern addressed him as he headed to his office. Natalie was a communications major in her sophomore year, with dark brown skin as smooth as satin and ultra-white teeth. She had a bright Colgate smile. But Ivan grinned at the idea of her calling him "Mr. David." He was the official boss more than ever now, at thirty years young.

He said, "Don't call me that, you make me feel like a college professor. Just call me, ah . . . *boss,*" he told her with a shrug. He didn't want them all calling him Ivan, either. It was too informal. At least calling him boss had a slight angle of sarcastic humor to it. And he could deal with that.

Natalie laughed and said, "Okay. Well, how are you doing today, boss?"

On second thought, Ivan didn't like the sound of that, either. Calling him "the boss" was a privilege that Jeff and Paul often used. However, they had built up the company brand with him from its inception. He figured he owed them that right. But with his new employees and interns, the sarcasm was not earned.

Ivan grimaced and said, "Ah . . . on second thought, 'Mr. David''s not that bad. Let me hear you say that one again."

A few of the other staff members overheard the awkward discussion from their cubicles. They began to hold in their laughs. Ivan was still trying to work out his position of power inside the office. He felt much more comfortable with it while directing his staff on the execution of new ideas. But acknowledging his leadership in a basic walk down the hallway to his office was different. He had rarely spent much time in the previous off-campus office, so being around his staff on an everyday basis was an experience he was still getting used to.

Natalie laughed and repeated, "How are you doing today, Mr. David?"

He said, "I'm good. How are you today?"

She giggled and said, "I'm fine."

The whole scene made some of his staff members laugh out loud. They loved working for Ivan. He was loose, fair, and organized. And he paid them well, with plenty of party and retail perks from advertisers, sponsors, and club and event promotions.

"All right, everybody back to work," he said to his amused staff.

When he reached his far corner office, he sat back in his high, comfortable chair and returned a few phone calls to potential investors.

"Yeah, Vance Wellings here," his first contact answered over his speakerphone.

Ivan had expected a secretary to answer. But when Vance picked up the line himself, Ivan switched over to the receiver for more privacy between them.

"Hey, Vance, it's Ivan."

"Hey, Ivan David, the man with the million-dollar website," he hinted.

Ivan chuckled. He said, "I think we're worth a *dollar* more than that. That sounds more like a *penny*."

Vance paused. He said, "A *hundred million dollars*? That's what you think your website is worth?" He sounded surprised by it.

Ivan was only joking to him with random numbers. But once he thought about it, with his website well on its way to generating fifteen million dollars that year, and still based mostly on a San Diego market, a hundred million dollars was hardly a stretch for IDPromotions.com's national potential.

Ivan said, "Maybe I spoke too soon on that number. Give us another year to expand past our Southern California region, and I may have to ask for two or three dollars."

Ivan had become a pro at pitching the numbers. And he liked to stay above the strike zone. But Vance figured he was throwing a pitch ball at him.

He laughed out loud and said, "You won't get any hits with that one. You got the catcher's mitt waaay up high."

Ivan laughed with him. He said, "That's why I'm going back to the dugout to warm up. In the meantime, I gotta work on raising your strike zone."

Vance laughed it all off. At least the young guy had a spirited personality.

Ivan asked him, "So, what's the rest of your week look like?" to change the subject. It was his new philosophy to make investors chase him down with their intentions.

"I got a network event I need to fly to in New York at the end of the week," Vance answered. Vance Wellings owned a military uniform supply company. He was an ironic contact from Eddie K.'s insistence on adding the U.S. military recruiter pages to the website. Vance was now attempting to invest in more civilian products for international marketing. He was nearly a billionaire who had not quite made it onto the Forbes 400 list.

"That's a crazy coincidence," Ivan told him. "My guys and I were just talking about New York less than three minutes ago."

"Yeah, what about? You ever been there?"

"As a matter of fact, I haven't," Ivan answered. "But we got one of our biggest website stars ready to fly back home from New York soon." He had no idea what day or week Jacari planned to return home. However, if he could offer her a private jet plane ride, he seriously doubted that she would turn the opportunity down.

Vance said, "Is that right? And you want me to be a private taxi for him, is that it? Well, how much are you offering to pay for his seat?"

Despite his first reservations about U.S. military connections, Ivan liked the straight shooting from those guys. There wasn't much beating around the bush with the military types. They said exactly what they wanted to say.

Ivan responded, "Well, if you have room coming back in the jet for two, I'd like to meet her over there in New York and bring her back with us."

What the hell, just go for broke, he figured.

Vance said, "So it's a *she*? And now you wanna make a hot date out of it in New York. Is that it, Ivan?" he insinuated.

Ivan was rarely shy about asking. He chuckled at his nerve and said, "I figured I had to at least ask you, since you're headed that way and back. You *are* coming back after a few days, right?" he questioned to make sure.

"In *exactly* a few days," Vance answered. "But I'll tell you what . . ." And he paused. "Okay. I'll make a deal with you. You're a networking kind of guy. That's your business. And what better way for me to gauge what you're gonna be worth than to see how you perform in New York's Big Apple crowd?"

He went on, "Now, they're definitely a different crowd over there. So you may want to get a pair of your best suits and ties out, preferably dark suits. And let's say you bring your date to my network event at the Waldorf-Astoria in Manhattan on Thursday evening. You do that and I'll fly you guys back with me."

Ivan said, "That's a go. I'd like to feel out the New York crowd for myself."

"Good. Then you're gonna need a room there. I'll set it all up for you."

Just like that, Ivan was on his way to New York for a network party with a nine-figure man, and to meet up with an international model whose father wanted to meet him.

He sat back behind his desk and couldn't believe his luck. Then he shook it off.

He told himself, "It wasn't luck. It must have all been in the cards." He didn't even feel like making more phone calls after that one. Everything else would seem anticlimactic.

Nevertheless, he received a phone page in his office from his secretary.

"Ivan," he answered.

"Yes, Mr. David, you have a call from Ida Stewart on line two. Would you like to take the call?"

Ivan hesitated. He hadn't heard from Ida in a while.

"Ah . . . yeah, put her through."

"Thank you."

When Ida got him on the line, she said, "Hey, Ivan, it's been a long time, right? My mother told me you stopped by the restaurant for a bite to eat last week."

"Oh, yeah, I'll always support," he told her.

"Just not on your website anymore, right?" she hinted.

Ivan paused. He said, "Those weekly rates have gone waaay up."

"Even for the people who started you off?"

Ivan felt the trap coming. Immediately he felt he had made a mistake by answering her call.

So, I guess she hasn't healed, he mused. *She's calling me up for a marketing war.*

To nip the argument in the bud as quickly as possible, Ivan asked her, "What do you guys need? I'll pay for it myself." She had Vance Wellings to thank for that. Ivan figured he would pass on the generosity.

Ida said, "Well, it would be nice if we could have a three-year anniversary event at my mother's restaurant, especially since we were your *first* successful promotion. And I see you've been lining up second and third annual events everywhere else. What happened to *us*?"

Her assessment was only half right. IDPromotions.com was repeating only the major events: his second network birthday party, a second luxury car show, a second summer boat cruise, a second Hutch & Mitchell Golf Tournament, and other events that were heavily supported.

Ida's suggestion was a bit more than he expected, but he figured she was right. He *did* owe them continued support through an annual event. It wouldn't take much to pull off. And he liked the idea.

He said, "Yeah, we can work that. That'll work. All I need is a good date."

"Just like that?" she questioned.

Ivan grinned. He said, "I'm the boss. If I say it, it's done."

"Are you sure? You must no longer be with, um . . . *Lucina,* then," she jabbed. Ida just couldn't let the opportunity slip by her.

Ivan only chuckled at it. He said, "As a matter of fact, she's her own boss now. I think that's how all new power women want it. Even Hillary Rodham Clinton couldn't wait to run for senator of New York as soon as Bill was out of the office and out of her way. Next she'll run for president," he joked.

"She should," Ida commented. "I'll vote for her. But how many votes can a sister get from *you* now, Ivan? I look at your website now and don't see *any* black people anymore, sisters *or* brothers."

That comment hit Ivan harder than the first. It was well below the belt. He had stopped paying attention to the racial makeup of his website. The money was all talking too loudly, and it wasn't *black* money. So Ivan didn't have an immediate response for her.

Ida caught on to that and asked him, "What's wrong, Ivan? A white woman got your tongue?"

He quickly remembered how "pro-black" Ida was when he had first met her. She was a real "power to the people" sister, who supported him early on, only for him to scorn her for a Brazilian/Italian hustler, who had left him out to dry. So what could he say about that to redeem himself?

"Actually, no," he responded meekly. "I haven't been going that way."

"You *haven't*? Are you sure?"

Ivan had rolled in the hay with a few white women by then. It was practically inevitable in the crowds that he was in, but he never dated one seriously enough to say that he had crossed over. Nevertheless, his preference had not been all black, either. He had landed somewhere in between. Ida fit the script herself. And Ivan told her so.

He said, "Well, you're not exactly the *darkest* black woman in the world yourself, Ida. But I'm embarrassed to even get into this conversation."

"Well, we're definitely *in it,* Ivan," she told him. "And I just wanted to *remind you* where you started off. Because you didn't start off over *there,* and I thought you would have enough *strength* to fight the right fight. But lately it sure doesn't *look* that way."

She was kicking Ivan's ass and leaving him speechless. She even had him thinking about what Catherine Boone had been up to lately. Then he thought about his connection to Thomas Jones as his real estate partner, and all of his Urban League contributions. He thought about the Black Contractors Association and how he had utilized them to work on remodeling his club acquisitions. He thought about the National Bankers Association, whom he was presently working with for access to lines of credit to develop more residential homes in the underserved areas of San Diego. He even included the African-American Chamber of Commerce in his business expo event at the convention center.

Thomas Jones had made certain that all the proper connections were served in the African-American community, even though many of their businesses and organizations were not pressured to advertise with IDPromotions.com or sponsor any of Ivan's web pages. So Ivan calmed his nerves and realized that he had been more of a team player than those who liked to do the talking.

He calmly told Ida, "Well, looks can be deceiving. Ask Mr. Thomas Jones. He'll tell you all about what I've been doing." He said, "In the meantime, ask your mother to give us a date, and we'll make another event happen for her. And tell her I thank her again for having the courage to start me out. And I thank *you,*" he added. "I have no hard feelings about anything."

But on Ida's side, she *did* have hard feelings. She was tired of the successful black man's rejection of black women and culture.

She told him, "It may be all well and good for you to give to the cause on the sly, Ivan. But sometimes it goes a long way for you to represent out in the public. You should *think* about that for a minute."

After Ida hung up the phone with him, Ivan did think. He thought about how hard and long a road he might need to drive alone to get to where he was going. The picture was crystal clear to him now.

He asked himself, *What am I supposed to do, stop making money doing what I'm doing and then struggle trying to do something more righteous? That's crazy! Somebody gotta make this money. Period! And if it's right there in front of me to be made, I don't care if it's white, Asian, or Mexican, I'm trying to make it. So if they wanna hate me for that, for not choosing to be down, dirty, and broke in the trenches, then so be it . . . And maybe they'll just have to forgive me when I'm done. But I'm not stopping my hustle for nobody. They couldn't pay me to do that. And that includes the women I choose.*

ON WEDNESDAY MORNING, Ivan pulled up to the Gillespie Field Airport on the far east side of San Diego, just north of Interstate 8, in a white Bentley Arnage from Roman Zemeckis's private collection. He wanted to make a statement of his wealth to Vance Wellings immediately.

He climbed out of the black leather interior of the backseat in his sharpest dark blue suit, a powerful blue-and-gold-striped tie, and immaculate black shoes, and had the driver carry his luggage behind him to the private jet. He had kept his diamond-studded earring in his ear for the trip.

If Michael Jordan can do it in both ears, then I can surely do it in one, he told himself defiantly.

Vance Wellings, a tall and solid linebacker of a man with a slight belly and full, dark brown hair, looked on with his two tall, no-nonsense male assistants, along with the pilot and copilot. They were all standing out in front of the plane before boarding, and they were impressed with Ivan. He had outdone their expectations on arrival.

Vance shook his head and chuckled. He said, "You sure know how to make a first impression, don't you?"

Ivan kept his cool. He said, "It's my first trip to New York. And I want to be invited back."

Vance nodded. "I don't think you're gonna have too much of a problem with that."

They boarded the eight-seat plane of plush leather luxury seats, wineglasses, individual ice buckets, headrests, foot and back massagers, cloth curtains, a full-sized bathroom, small tray tables, four flip-down TV screens, and a bloodred carpet symbolizing deep wealth.

"Nice plane," Ivan commented, taking the second seat to his right.

"Glad you noticed," Vance joked. He took the open seat next to Ivan's. His two assistants sat in the two seats in front of and to the left from them.

Ivan got comfortable and asked him, "How long is the flight?"

He had flown a few hours to Hawaii, Los Angeles, Dallas, and up to the San Francisco area in private jets with Seth and Roman. But New York was a much longer trip.

"We got a good five to six hours before we touch down," Vance answered.

Once they got up in the air good and leveled the plane off, heading northeast for America's business capital, Vance poured them each a glass of wine before he began to ask Ivan some of his big questions.

He reclined his chair back halfway for the long flight and asked his guest, "So, Ivan . . . what is your ultimate goal in business? Do you just wanna make enough big bucks to settle down with? Or do you have designs on trying to take over the world?"

Ivan grinned at the question. Vance was being slightly dramatic. Ivan answered, "I'm like thirty years old right now, so I can honestly expect to see a lot of different changes going on in my future. It's only natural."

Vance nodded with his drink in hand. He asked, "What do you see as your strengths and weaknesses at this point in your career?"

Ivan continued to grin. He really didn't want to answer such a revealing question for the man, but he figured Vance had practically *paid* for his answer. They were on a five-to-six-hour flight to New York. So there was no way he could dodge it.

Ivan told him, "My strength . . . is definitely fast thinking. It takes me no time at all to come up with new ideas and figure out how to make them work. I'm also a good manager of talent. I find the best people for the job, I give them direction, and I step out of their way unless they need me for more guidance. And with me being a trained accountant and consultant with the Hutch and Mitchell firm, I'm always tight on the bottom line. It's always about squeezing the most orange juice into the glass."

He continued, "But my biggest *weakness* . . . that would probably be . . ." Ivan honestly couldn't think of anything. His two-year run had been nearly *flawless*. But he knew he had to say *something*. So he came up with, "My *age*. While you're still young, you got such a big learning curve to go through, you know. Fortunately, I haven't made a lot of mistakes yet."

Vance listened to him, took a sip of his wine, and nodded again.

He said, "A young age can also be a *huge* advantage. You get a head start on the competition. It's like getting up early in the morning for war. You capture your enemy before they're even awake."

Ivan took a sip of his own wine. He said, "Let me ask *you* a question."

Vance looked at him and said, "Go ahead."

Ivan asked him, "What nationality are you, you know, your bloodline?"

Vance grimaced as if it were a hard question to answer. "Ah . . . Scottish, German, Dutch, some Native American. Why do you ask?"

Ivan smiled when he said "some Native American." Did that make him nonwhite, like the one-drop-of-African-blood rule?

He said, "I'm just curious to know if you believe that it's harder, easier, or about the same for a black man to become a millionaire in this country as it is for a white man."

As his two assistants sat deathly still in their chairs up front, overhearing Ivan's question, Vance answered, "Well . . . if you look at the percentages of black people who live in this country as compared to whites and others, I would say that there's a *lot* of black millionaires in this country, who surely started out with much less. But you can also say that for some Mexicans, Koreans, and Filipinos. But I think the key for any race or gender to become wealthy in *any* country is to have an undying *drive*. It's just a never-say-die mentality, you know. You gotta have that in your makeup. Or you'll never make it."

Ivan nodded back to him and said, "Yeah . . . I know."

Vance asked him, "Is that it?"

Ivan closed his eyes and reclined in his chair. He answered, "Yup." There was no more overselling, only basic small talk with Vance on the jet plane ride. Ivan planned to do the majority of his work at the Waldorf-Astoria Hotel in New York. And he couldn't wait to see what kind of business opportunities would present themselves there.

Twenty-one

Let's Do It Again

JUST AS THE PRIVATE JET reached the New York city skyline, Vance woke Ivan from his rest and told him, "You don't want to miss this if you've never been to New York before."

Ivan raised his chair forward and opened his window curtain to look out at the view. Tall New York buildings were everywhere. The downtown skyline looked like a game of Monopoly on steroids. And the sunlight was just beginning to fade west.

The first thing Ivan thought was, *Somebody owns every last one of these buildings. And thousands of people are paying them rent.*

As they descended to the airport away from the overpowering buildings of the downtown area, Vance asked Ivan, "So, what do you think?"

"I think there's a whole lot of business going on in that city," Ivan answered.

"Oh, yeah, you bet. You got plenty of millionaires in New York. You can get twenty or thirty of 'em all living in one building."

"And who *owns* that building?" Ivan asked him with a grin.

"Exactly. That's the right way of thinking, my friend. Who owns the damn buildings here?"

Ivan smiled and thought of calling Jacari on her cell phone as soon as they touched down. Like clockwork, she had informed Jeff and Paul that she was free for the rest of the week and that she was looking forward to meeting Ivan, hanging out with him in New York, and then flying back home to San Diego in the private jet. She had already agreed to his surprising offer.

The private jet touched down at New York's LaGuardia Airport, where a black stretch limo was already waiting at the gates for their arrival.

When they all reached the limo, with Vance's two assistants handling the luggage, Vance asked, "So, are you hanging out with us tonight, Ivan, or are you planning to pack it in with your lady friend until tomorrow?"

Ivan hadn't called to talk to her yet, so he didn't know.

"Let me find out right now," he answered. He dialed Jacari's New York number and wondered how long it would take before she answered the phone.

"Hello." It only took her two rings.

I like that so far, he mused. *I want to see this girl in person as soon as possible. Let's get it all out of the way. Then I can get back to business.*

He said, "Hey, this is Ivan in New York. We just arrived at the airport."

"Oh, okay, which one?"

"LaGuardia."

She said, "Okay, well, it'll take you about thirty-five minutes to make it into town. And then what do you want to do?" she asked him.

"First, I just need to see you," he told her. "I feel like I'm going out on a blind date here."

"No, you've seen my pictures and I've seen plenty of your pictures," she responded.

Ivan said, "Cameras and makeup lie sometimes."

"Not with me they don't."

Vance gave him a look of confusion. "You haven't even met her yet?"

"Not yet," Ivan answered, grinning. "But I've seen plenty of her on the website."

Vance shook his head and said, "You're a wild guy, Ivan. Your weakness may be wild adventures."

Ivan chuckled. He asked Jacari, "Are you dressed and everything yet?" He now felt overdressed. What if she was only wearing jeans and a wrinkled T-shirt? He said, "You don't have on jeans and a T-shirt, do you?"

"No, you'll see. I came back with a whole lot of things from Italy. And I can't wait to wear some of them."

That made Ivan look forward to it. He said, "Well, here's what I need you to do so we don't lose any time together. Meet me in the Waldorf-Astoria lobby, and then you can wait there for me while I change into something to run the town in."

"Okay. I know where that is. That should only take me fifteen minutes."

Ivan joked, "Well, bring some reading glasses and a book so the guys'll leave you alone while you wait for me in the lobby."

She laughed and said, "That won't work. Then they'll bother me more to find out what I'm reading."

So far, Ivan liked her wit. He said, "Okay. Just come as you are, then."

When he hung up the line with her, Vance asked him, "Does she look like a lot of the other girls I see on your website?"

Ivan nodded to him. "Now I have to see her in person to make sure."

Vance nodded back and joked, "Maybe your weakness is pretty women."

Ivan said, "Oh, now, in that case, that's a lot of guys' weakness."

WHEN THEY PULLED UP to the curb at the historic Waldorf-Astoria Hotel, bellmen promptly approached the limo to collect their bags from the trunk, then escorted the four men to the registration counters. They then piled the bags on the wheeled luggage carts for the elevators.

One of Vance's assistants looked to his right and asked Ivan, "Is that your lady friend there?"

Ivan looked past him and spotted Jacari in a black and brown leather skirt, brown leather flats, an off-white top, a giant brown leather belt around her waist, and a wide, soft brown leather hat that fell over the sides of her long, dark hair.

Vance Wellings eyed her himself. "Good gracious," he commented. "Now, she's a *beauty.*"

"And she's full Native American," Ivan told him.

"Is that right?"

As Ivan moved in her direction to greet her, he wondered how hot she would be in so much leather clothing during the summertime. Did it get that cool out at night in New York?

He approached her with open arms for a hug, as if they had known each other for years.

"Jacari," he greeted her in a warm embrace. Ivan had learned to become a much better greeter with women than he had been in the past. It was all a part of comfortable business.

"Ivan," she responded, embracing him back.

She was the perfect size for him, and the same height as Lucina. He held her there for a second near the registration counters. Then he asked her, "Now, how hot are you gonna be wearing all of this leather tonight?"

She broke away and said, "No, it's really, really *thin*. I wouldn't have worn it if it was thick. Here. Feel it."

She pressed his hand into the bottom of her skirt.

Ivan felt the paper-thin leather and nodded. "Damn. That's barely even there."

"See, that's what I mean. But what about you, Mr. Fancy? You look like you're all dressed to go out to a major event tonight."

Ivan grinned and said, "Yeah, I went a little overboard for the plane ride. But let me introduce you to the folks we're gonna be hanging out with here tomorrow."

He led her over to Vance and his two assistants to introduce them all.

"I hear you're a full-blooded Native American," Vance commented to her.

"Yes, I am."

"I have a little bit of it in me myself," he told her.

As they all made small talk, Ivan thought again about Ida's comments on him not dating black women anymore. But he wasn't dating Jacari. They were only going to hang out for a few days and fly back to San Diego together. Or at least that was the plan.

He collected his key from the counter and told Jacari, "Well, let me get up here to this room and change into something more comfortable to hang out in."

"Okay, I'll wait here," she told him.

"Are you sure you want to leave her alone down here all by herself?" Vance asked him.

He made it sound like a bad idea, but she was right there inside the lobby of a very popular and busy hotel. What could possibly happen to her?

Vance said, "Well, I'll just have my guys wait down here with her while you go up and get yourself together."

Ivan agreed to it with a nod. "All right. That's a good idea. Thanks."

On their elevator ride up to their floors, Vance said, "She's quite a pretty girl, hey?"

She was, but Ivan still wasn't too pressed about it. "Yeah, she's dynamite," he commented.

"I guess you're not looking to settle down anytime too soon, hey? I found that the longer it takes for a guy to settle down, the longer that guy wants to stay away from it all. But I've been married to my wife now for twenty-three years."

Ivan nodded. "That's good. Since your twenties, hunh? That means you got another twenty-three years to go."

"Yeah, we'll have grandkids by then. You don't have any kids yet, do you?"

Ivan was proud to tell him, "No." He said, "I think I *would* want to be married before that happens. That way it won't be a mistake, you know?"

"That's the right idea. You always wanna find the right woman first. But how old is, ah, Jacari? She's pretty young, right? You'll have to wait her out a few years before she's ready."

The twelfth floor arrived for Ivan before he could respond. Vance's room was on the fourteenth floor.

Ivan climbed out and said, "Naw, I'm not looking at her like that. She's cute, but I've already been around the block a few times. I think I may need a harder edge on a woman."

Vance laughed. He said, "I hear ya. You need one who can stand her ground. But be careful what you wish for," he added as the elevator doors closed.

Ivan let himself into his room with his key card and found his luggage already up in his room.

"Damn, they move fast," he commented.

The room was all done up in deep, rich colors with dark wooden furniture and a high king-sized bed. But it was nothing spectacular.

Ivan quickly changed his clothes into his casual dress of dark blue denim jeans, a button-up shirt, and a sports jacket. He sprayed soft-scented Joop cologne, and that was that. But by the time he returned to the lobby to meet back up with Jacari, she was surrounded by admirers.

"Oh, you're so *gorgeous*. Are you having an event here this weekend?" an older white woman asked her.

Jacari was gracious with a smile. "No, I'm just waiting here for a friend."

Vance's two assistants continued to stand by her like a security team. They didn't even talk much. That only attracted more people to stare at her.

Ivan walked over to her and was ready to go. "Thanks, guys."

"No problem, Ivan. We'll see you tomorrow."

Ivan asked Jacari, "All right, where to? I've never been to New York before."

She politely stepped away from the crowd of gawkers. She told Ivan, "Times Square is where all of the tourists go. So let's start there."

She led him out the front door of the hotel to hail a taxi at the curb. A Yellow Cab stopped for her immediately.

"Damn," Ivan commented. "You get instant cabs here, hunh?"

"Yeah, you get used to it," she responded with a chuckle. When they climbed inside the back of the tight cab, she told their East Indian driver, "Times Square," and he took off driving.

Ivan asked, "So, there's no private driver for an international model?"

Jacari frowned. "If you think you *need* one. But I don't think I need all of that. I can pretty much take care of myself. I've been here for a year now."

"Thanks to us," Ivan teased her.

She laughed and squeezed his left arm. "Yeah, thanks to you."

Ivan immediately asked her about the name issue. "So, Jeff and Paul were telling me that bloggers said your real name was Kaya, and that there is no 'Jacari' as a tribal name," he commented.

She smirked and said, "Well, I'm the first one now. And Jacari means 'she who drums to her own beat.' "

Ivan stared at her. "Are you for real? Well, what does Kaya mean?"

"Kaya means 'oldest sister,' which I'm not. But I guess I can act like an oldest sister when I need to."

"So, how was Italy?"

"Great! I loved it over there."

"How many models were over there with you?"

"Waaay too many. I was like, how can they even tell who's up here with the whole catwalk thing? It was just one after another after another. And they try to make us all look the same in pony-tails."

Ivan said, "So, ah, I hear your father wants to meet me."

Jacari nodded. "Oh, yeah, he does. He wants to ask you about your website to inform visitors about our reservation casinos."

Bingo! The man stayed about his business. "Where are they located?" he asked her.

"Northeast of San Diego. But I haven't really lived there since I was ten. I moved in with my cousins in Spring Valley. And I didn't really know how my parents would take the whole modeling thing, especially since I started with posting up my pictures on a MySpace page. So I kind of made up the name 'Jacari' to hide it, but then your guys Paul and Jeff decided to put me up on your spotlight page, and the rest was just, like . . . *wow!* I still can't *believe* it all."

The taxi reached a block full of movie theaters, reminding Ivan of Hollywood Boulevard in L.A., only it was bigger and brighter, with no fake movie stars or film characters posing for pictures with tourists on the sidewalks.

Out of the blue, Ivan asked her, "You want to go to the movies?"

"Sure." Jacari grabbed his hand and pulled him out of the taxi, paying their fare with a twenty-dollar bill. "Come on," she told him.

Ivan felt like a much older man with the girl. He only had her by eight years, but her look and energy made her seem much younger.

"What do you wanna see?" he asked her.

"The new Batman movie."

She whisked him into the movie line before he could even agree to it.

"I can see you're used to having your way with people," he told her.

She smiled at him. "Only with those I like. And I like to make the first move sometimes, too. Which is really different from most Native American girls. But like I said, I like to drum to my own beat. So I guess you can call me the rebel drummer girl."

She continued to give Ivan quick looks, as if she couldn't bear to stare at him. Ivan noticed that a lot from girls as a teenager. They were hesitant to gaze into his eyes sometimes, while others seemed hypnotized by them. But Derrick had used the eyes much more than Ivan had.

Ivan asked her, "Do you have a problem staring right at the camera on photo shoots?"

She flashed a look at him again and stared a little longer. "No, why?"

He said, "You just seem to be a little jumpy around me, that's all."

She smiled. "Maybe."

"Maybe what? Maybe you're nervous around me?"

She smiled again and remained silent. Her elusiveness reminded him of Lucina. Only Lucina was much better at it. She was elusive in a grown woman's way. When Ivan thought about it, he realized that he had never even gone to a movie with Lucina before.

How the hell did we manage never to do that? he questioned. *At least once or twice.* They had surely been around each other enough.

Ivan bought the tickets, popcorn, nachos with cheese, and two medium drinks. Then they chose seats in the middle of the theater to watch the extralong movie. And before it was over, Ivan began to stroke Jacari's long hair with his left hand. It ran halfway down her back, and he couldn't help himself. But instead of thinking about the young model while he did it, he thought more about being back home in San Diego and going after his *real* prize.

I just need to go at her hard and tell her how it is, man, he told himself. *This shit has gone on between us long enough.*

As Ivan continued to stroke her hair, Jacari found herself stimulated by it. So she placed her right hand on his thigh. There was an enticing comfort, having Ivan David so far away from San Diego with her. She had often stared at his pictures on the IDPromotions

.com website and wondered about him. Now they were together in New York in a dark theater. And it felt romantic.

I'm not supposed to feel this way, she told herself. *But it feels good. I want to be with him.*

Instead of an undesirable photographer, an obnoxious businessman, or an ego-tripping ball player, all of whom had lusted to have her company after many fashion shows, Ivan David was someone Jacari felt a warm affinity for. She was impressed with his ability to make local dreams come true with his website. He was a young and touchable power broker on the rise. And even though they had just met in person, she felt much closer to him than to any New York celebrity.

No one has to know if we do anything, she told herself. *We're all the way in New York.*

So her hand remained frozen on his thigh for the rest of the movie. She was too nervous to rub him back, and she was too curious to move it away.

AT THE END of the Batman movie, Ivan knew for a fact that he could have a beautiful dessert if he wanted it. He was no longer an amateur. All he had to do was ask Jacari the right questions. But he was hesitant to ruin her.

It wouldn't be fair, he told himself. *I'm not really feeling her like that. I mean, she's nice, but my mind is preoccupied. Then again . . . we're all the way in New York. I could just act like it's a vacation thing.*

He held her hand comfortably until the end of the night. Then he asked her, as they strolled up the New York street, "Are you looking forward to getting all dolled up for me tomorrow?"

She grinned. "Of course." She sounded more confident now.

"And you got some more Italian clothes you wanna show off?"

"Yup."

"And lingerie?" Ivan couldn't help but slip that in as they walked, hand in hand, outside the movie theaters. They hadn't bothered to hail a cab yet. What was the rush? The New York City lights were beautiful.

Jacari felt all hot and jittery as she failed to answer his sneak attack of a question. All she could do was smile at it.

He's teasing me now, she told herself. *What do I say?*

As a respectable young woman, she felt obligated to back him off.

"I don't know about that," she forced out with a smirk.

Ivan smiled back at her knowingly. *She don't mean that,* he assumed. *But I wouldn't rush it anyway . . . if I even decide to do it.*

However, he *was* thinking about it. So abruptly he stopped walking. Things were getting too clouded in his mind. He said, "I guess I need to get you a taxi back home now, right?"

She nodded, still undecided about them herself.

"Yeah, I guess so. I'll just see you again tomorrow."

Ivan said, "You will." And when he grabbed an available taxi for her to ride home in, he pulled her close to him and kissed her on the lips anyway. He felt like she deserved it.

"That's just because you're beautiful," he told her. "Now I need to see how you'll look for me tomorrow."

Jacari continued to smile and climbed into the back of the taxi. "Okay. We'll see," she responded to him. She gave him a girlish wave. "Bye." And when he closed the taxi door back behind her, she had to squeeze her legs together to knock the edge off her feelings of looseness.

From Ivan's view on the sidewalk, he watched the taxi pull away with her before he decided to look for a taxi of his own. Then he cursed himself. "Shit!" *What the fuck am I doing?* he questioned. *I'm out here about to ruin another girl when I need to be taking this all out on Lucina.*

So he went ahead and called her. "Fuck it. It's only nine o'clock back home."

Lucina answered her cell phone as if she were still upset with him over old business. "Yes, Ivan?"

All of his smoothness seemed to evaporate whenever he was up against her.

He said, "I'm out here walking the streets of New York, and I just thought of calling you to say hi."

"What are you doing in New York?"

Ivan paused. "Thinking about you," he told her.

She said, "Why would you go all the way to New York to think about me?"

"Actually, I'm out here for a business network function with some bigwigs at the Waldorf-Astoria Hotel tomorrow. I'm trying to study how they do business in New York."

Lucina told him, "They do business there the same way they do business everywhere. They pitch what they have to sell, and they buy what they want to buy. But I have a few phone calls that I need to return. So good luck for tomorrow."

Just like that, she was off the line. Nevertheless, Ivan felt at peace with even a small conversation with her. Every time he talked to Lucina, she seemed to ignite his focus and creativity. So he repeated in his mind what she had just told him.

They pitch what they have to sell, and they buy what they want to buy . . . Business is that simple, Ivan told himself. *All around the world.*

He thought about that for a minute, while walking around the downtown streets of New York City, and he began to smile and talk to himself.

"This girl is money in the bank . . . *Damn,* she's money!"

Not that he didn't already know, but the steady reminders she gave him were priceless.

THAT THURSDAY EVENING at the Waldorf-Astoria Hotel in Manhattan, Ivan looked at himself in the full-sized mirror of his room. He wore a fine black suit with a powerful, mint-green-and-black-striped tie. He wanted to look like money in a room of money. And he planned to distribute and collect plenty of valuable business cards.

"It's all about pitching and buying," he reminded himself of Lucina's comments again. "Who's pitching what, and who's buying what?"

His cell phone went off with a call from Jacari. "Are you down in the lobby yet?" he asked her.

"Yes."

"What color dress are you wearing?"

"Turquoise."

Turquoise was not far from mint green, but it was not close enough to consider them coordinated.

"Good," he told her. "Stand by the elevators. I'm on my way down in a minute." Then he called Vance Wellings on the hotel phone. "Hey, Vance, this is Ivan. You guys ready yet? I'm going down."

Vance laughed and said, "Ivan, it's only six o'clock. You're gonna be caught in the early rush. Settle yourself down. We want to arrive closer to seven."

Ivan said, "Yeah, but my date is already here. And you know how women get when they go out of their way to wear something pretty. They want to be *seen* in it."

Vance chuckled. He said, "Okay, I see your point. But that's why I rarely take my wife out on business anymore. It all gets too complicated."

Ivan hung up with him, expecting to see him later. In the meantime, he wanted to find who the event organizers were. As soon as he walked onto the elevator going down, he discovered suits, ties, dresses, colognes, and perfumes were already out in force.

Ivan squeezed onto the crowded elevator and got his charm ready. "I guess we're all here for the big event tonight," he commented to no one in particular.

A few people laughed.

Another guy joked, "What big event? You mean there's a big event tonight?"

Ivan joked back to him, "It's either that or we're all overdressed for dinner."

He got a stronger laugh from the passengers as they reached the bottom floor.

Ivan walked out of the overcrowded elevator and spotted Jacari. Her silky turquoise dress, matching heels, long elegant frame, and dark flowing hair all stood out in the crowd. But with so many older business folk around, her youth made her look like someone's beautiful lost daughter.

Ivan looked young in this crowd himself. He didn't sweat it, though. He greeted Jacari with a hug and a smile, and was ready to do his work.

"You look fabulous tonight," he told her.

She grinned. "Thank you. You look nice yourself."

Ivan took her hand and followed the well-dressed crowd toward the ballroom.

"Ivan David," he told the young hostesses at the sign-in table by the entrance.

They checked for his name. "Table thirty-nine."

Another hostess led them forward and into the room. "Right this way."

Ivan asked her, "Excuse me, do you work with the promoters or organizers of tonight's event?"

"Oh, yeah, I'm an intern with Northeastern Communications, a marketing, public relations, and events firm."

"Is your boss gonna be here tonight?"

Vance Wellings hadn't given him all of the details. Ivan was skeptical about how much Vance wanted him to know. And arriving early to find out more information was one of Ivan's many priorities that evening. He was at business war and on the front lines before daybreak.

The intern began to look around the room in search of her boss.

"Ah, I just saw him a few minutes ago."

Ivan gave her his business card. "Can you do me a favor and introduce us once you catch up to him again?"

She took his card and read it. "'Ivan David Enterprises.'" Then she flipped it over and studied the IDPromotions.com logo.

Ivan decided not to list any services on his new business cards. A list tended to limit the conversations. Or if the list was too long, it could make a business appear unfocused. So Ivan would explain in person instead, his services changing to fit the needs and interests of each client. This also allowed him to add business ideas that were still in development.

"So, what do you do?" the intern asked him, still searching his card for answers.

Perfect! Ivan thought. He wanted them *all* to ask.

He answered, "I'm a brand promotions consultant for people, places, products, companies, and ideas. I'm the guy who makes it all happen."

The intern nodded to him. She said, "Oh. So you, like—"

Ivan cut her off. "I'm like the Super Bowl. I put the biggest spotlight on your commercials, and I make sure everybody knows that you're there."

She nodded and said, "Oh, well, that's like what we do."

Ivan said, "But who promotes *you* to a larger audience? Northeastern Communications? Who are you? What do you do? Let us know. That's where IDPromotions.com comes in. We identify whoever you are for a larger community, whether it's business or personal."

The intern showed them to their table and said, "Wow." She didn't know what else to say.

Ivan told her, "Well, just check out the website for yourself. And make sure you remember to introduce me to your boss."

"Oh, I will," she told him.

As soon as she walked away, Ivan sat at his empty table with Jacari, who was proud as hell to be with him. She had to hold herself together to stop from exploding with energy. She felt she believed in everything the man stood for. He had brought the Super Bowl to *her* and shone light on *her* career. And he had never asked her for anything.

She said, "That's why my father wants to meet you. He wants everyone to know about the Native American casinos."

Ivan squeezed her hand at the table and grinned at her. "We're gonna make that all happen as soon as we get back to San Diego. We can put it on our tourist and family vacation lists."

He asked her, "Can you buy, like, Native American clothes, and belts, and souvenirs there?"

Jacari told him, "Of course. We have plenty of things there to buy."

Ivan said, "Okay. That sounds like a good money deal, then."

The attendees ate a chicken and vegetable dinner with dessert before listening to the usual business speeches, introductions, and comedic efforts from the podium. The room then began to buzz for the next few hours with all of the real meeting and greeting. The soft instrumental music in the background was drowned out by the busy chatter.

Ivan told himself, *Yup. This is just like business everywhere else. Time to go to work.*

Jacari was a perfect companion as she followed him around the room, smiling, nodding, and cosigning his every joke and explanation. Their teamwork was so good that Vance Wellings got a real kick out of watching them, which led him to work Ivan around the room to amuse himself.

"Hey, Ivan, tell my friend Gil here how you plan to turn your company into the next Google," Vance joked, with too many glasses of wine in his system.

Ivan explained, "Our whole goal at IDPromotions.com is to

become the signature branding vehicle, *online,* of all hot companies, products, and services. Right now our focus is in the San Diego region, but as we expand nationwide, the sky is the limit."

Vance said, "Then he'll focus on the *world's* hottest products."

As long as Jacari could collect and distribute business cards, Ivan didn't mind the spectacle. But once his initial explanations were made, he continued to move on. He realized that the business plans and proposals he would create as a result of this gathering were when the business talks would really begin. The network event was about the introductions.

"Well, what makes your company unique from any other website that could essentially do the same thing?" Ivan was asked.

"That's the million-dollar question," he responded. "And the million-dollar answer is *loyalty*. Who has the loyal following to increase and maintain their numbers? That's the same question you can ask of any business. And a lot of that has to do with better products, better services, better ideas, easier accessibility, a faster response to your customer's needs, name recognition, and ultimately, investor capital for marketing and expansion."

He continued, "But at IDPromotions.com, we're more concerned with identifying *you*. What makes *your* company unique? So our strength is in being the strongest *support* system. We don't try to be more important than our clients. Where our clients go, *we go.* And what *we do best* is help to take them there."

Vance Wellings could drink and laugh all he wanted to that night, but Ivan's pitch was *serious.* And he took it that way.

He stated, "When people think about IDPromotions.com, I want them to *trust* that we're going to identify the *best* of everything. And if we *don't* identify the best, we want our customers to let us know what *is.* And we can then start an online survey."

He concluded, "And the result of that information would be valuable to any company."

* * *

NEAR THE CLOSE of the event, Jacari had a purse full of business cards along with aching feet. She told Ivan, "You are very, very *good* at talking about your business."

Ivan said, "I *have* to be." Then he asked her, "Are you all right?"

She was walking slowly and gingerly.

She gritted her teeth and told him, "I have to get out of these *shoes*."

Ivan nodded to her. He had done enough pitching for one night anyway. But was she going back home or staying with him at the hotel? That was the big question. So Ivan asked her.

"Are you staying with me tonight, or . . . do you need another taxi?"

His pause left the question wide open. He had become a man who used words masterfully.

Jacari responded hesitantly, "I . . . I don't know. I mean, I know you're tired and everything by now."

Ivan held her hand again and gave her his undivided attention in the room. He looked into her eyes and asked her more intently, "Do you *want* to stay here with me tonight?"

He *knew* that she wanted to. He just had to ask her better. He had been speaking to so many people in the room that night about business that he failed to address the needs of a woman properly. And when he did, all of Jacari's emotions from the night before resurfaced. She had thought about him the previous night and daydreamed all day about being in his presence again. Now he was asking her if she wanted to stay.

And of course she did. So she nodded and gave him the only answer that she could live with. "Yes." She couldn't imagine saying no and never having that opportunity again. They were still together in New York, and it would still be special there, so far away from home.

Ivan told her, "Well, take off those shoes for the elevator ride. Then I'll carry you down the hallway to my room."

Jacari smiled and chuckled at him. "Okay."

* * *

After Ivan had carried her to the room, he had no more confusions about his intentions with her. He had worked it all out in his mind already. So he held her hands out in front of him while he sat on the edge of his bed and told her the truth.

"Jacari . . . Kaya . . . or whatever I need to call you," he joked.

She grinned and said, "Either one. It doesn't really matter for you. You can call me whichever one you feel more comfortable with. My family still calls me Kaya," she told him.

Ivan heard that and thought, *Damn. I got it good with her.*

He continued, "Well . . . *J* . . ."

She chuckled there, waiting patiently for him to explain himself.

". . . what I want to say is, you're a very beautiful girl. Everybody can see that."

She smiled and said, "Thank you." Coming from him it meant much more.

Ivan said, "Well, with me being a guy and everything, we don't always think *emotionally* like women do. Sometimes we do things because the opportunity is there. And right now I feel like I want to do a lot of different things with you."

Jacari felt butterflies unleashing themselves throughout her body. She looked down at their hands and grinned in her girlishness.

Ivan said, "But I don't want to hurt your feelings when I tell you that I can't be that everyday guy for you."

Jacari stopped her smiling with a nod, and she began to stare at Ivan like a grown woman. She said, "I understand. You got a lot of things that you do. But . . . I'm not gonna be around that much, either."

She stopped and left it at that. Ivan would have to read between the lines.

He read her quickly and asked, "So, what if you see me with someone else?"

That was a harder question for her to bear. She looked downward and took a deep breath. Then she looked back into his eyes.

"I will always care about you anyway, for everything that you've done for me," she told him. She said, "I heard you talk tonight about loyalty in business. Well . . ."—she pulled her hand away and placed it across her chest— "my heart will always be loyal to you."

Damn! Ivan thought. *She's killing me with her softness. That's that Indian-girl shit from the movies. Pocahontas.*

He started smiling about his thoughts. He was even ready to make a joke about it to loosen things up. But instead, Jacari held his head in the palms of her hands and started to kiss his lips, and she kept going with it.

Ivan stopped and told her, "You don't owe me anything because of the website. Somebody was gonna find you eventually anyway. Like I said, you're beautiful."

Jacari responded, "Ivan . . . this is not because I owe you *anything.* I kissed you because I *want to.* And I want to *be* here. If I *didn't,* I *wouldn't* be. Like I told you last night, I can take care of myself."

And she backed up to take her clothes off.

THE FOLLOWING WEEK in San Diego, Ivan called a conference-room meeting at his office, gathering all of the key members of his staff.

He spread the business cards from his trip to New York across the conference table and sat at the head chair. He told everyone, "Over the next few months, our new goal is to document every possible way to expand the company into a national brand identifier. And what that means is that, instead of us just talking about San Diego's restaurants, we identify the best restaurants nationally. Instead of just talking about San Diego's parties, we talk about the hottest parties in the country: East Coast, West Coast, South, all of that."

He went on, "In football, instead of us just talking about Drew Brees and LaDainian Tomlinson, we also talk about Peyton Manning, Donovan McNabb, Shaun Alexander, and Tiki Barber. In other words, everything that we do now for San Diego, we want to create a list that does the same thing nationally."

Eddie K. had to fight to hold back an enormous smile. He had been trying to get Ivan to think outside of just San Diego for a year now. He had hit the jackpot with the company, earning himself over a million in commissions. But if the company expanded nationally, he could earn millions more.

Joining up with Ivan was one of the best decisions I've ever made in my life, he told himself.

As the editorial manager, Ava Tate nodded her head and took notes. By the time they had moved into the new office and increased editorial content tenfold, Ivan had given her a ten-thousand-dollar-a-month salary.

Ava said, "We can use the search engines to expand to national lists and articles easily."

"Then we can add sidebars to list the top ten of whatever," Jeff added.

Ivan said, "But the key here is getting a national audience to *respond* to the list. So we have to start documenting every increase in traffic, and where that new traffic is coming from."

Paul took notes on that. He and Jeff had a staff of four now, who surveyed all of the numbers: the unique visits and multiple impressions, as well as the verification of email addresses.

Paul mumbled, "Got it," as Ivan continued to express their plans of execution:

"Now, with our existing numbers, I want Eddie to work with the proposal writers to pitch all national brands in clothing, automobiles, liquor, cell phones, you name it, on how our company can help them to push their new services and products through advertising and articles on our site, *or* through creating national sponsored events. And we want to be sure to ask them *how* we can help them on a *national* and/or *regional* level, because we can *use* that same information to pitch other clients."

Eddie nodded to his part of the plans. He smiled and said, "That's awesome. I'm right on it."

Ivan added, "Last but not least, Mike, I want you and your team to start an audit of the company to evaluate how much it's worth *now,* and how much it *could* be worth in three years, as compared to all of the website competitors. And I mean *nationally.*"

Mike Adams nodded. "Okeydokey," he uttered. Mike had already thanked Ivan profusely for the opportunity to be a major member of his team. Combined with the new arrangement he had with Hutch & Mitchell, he was making two hundred thousand dollars a year himself.

Ivan looked at the business cards spread out across the table and concluded, "We start by doing research to solicit every one of these businesses on the table. Because if we can break New York, then we can break *any* city."

There was a sudden silence in the room. No one had anything to say. The plans were all thorough.

Jeff coughed up, "Jesus, Ivan, did you eat your bowl of business Wheaties this morning or what?" Everyone in the room laughed to break up the tension. Jeff added, "That trip to New York must have really made an impression on you."

Ivan grinned and said, "It did. So, if anyone runs into any problems or needs explanations on the details, please let me know immediately and we'll work it all out."

When their meeting was adjourned, Eddie K. followed Ivan back to his head office and closed the door behind them so they could speak in private.

He said, "Those are all some wonderful plans you have, Ivan. *Wonderful,*" he repeated. "But am I, ah, *correct* in assuming that you may be looking into selling the company?"

Ivan had never shown that much interest in assessing the company's national value before. Eddie wondered if that meant something. Had someone offered him a serious bid in New York?

Ivan explained, "Not necessarily. If we were gonna take the company public, or accept private investment offers, we would need to know the same information."

Eddie asked him, "But we *are* looking to do *something?*"

Ivan read where his real concerns were. He told him, "Either way, I understand what I owe you and the guys, Eddie. You're safe. My goal would be to protect *all* of our interests under *any* situation, including my *own* ideas for the company. Who's gonna have more interests in where the company goes than me? It still has my initials on it."

Eddie nodded and thought it over a bit more. There was nothing he could do about it but wait the process out and make sure he continued to do his job.

He said, "Okay. We'll see where it all goes, then."

WITH THE IDEA to travel more, while studying the people, places, products, and events of the nation and around the globe, Ivan began to delegate more of his San Diego interests to his teammates.

He told Chip Garrett, "I may need you to step in at some of these club locations and become a name and face for me. I need someone to keep his head in the place and make sure the numbers are adding up they way they're supposed to. You think you'll have enough time on your hands to do that?"

Chip said, "Come on, Ivan, you gotta stop doubting me like that, man. I'm still an *accountant*, you know. I know how to balance the spreadsheets."

Ivan told him, "Yeah, but this is about *more* than you balancing the sheets. This is about you becoming a *personality*. The customers have to learn to *know* and *like* you."

Chip said, "Hey, man, I can do that. I've *always* been more of a personality."

Ivan realized that himself. If Chip was good at anything, it was mingling with the social sets. So Ivan made sure that he would have access to the finest props of cars and girls to raise Chip's public profile. However, to maintain a necessary system of checks and balances, Ivan told the same thing to Joe Proctor, one of his more experienced promoter friends.

He said, "Joe, I know I haven't always been able to include you in some of the bigger events I've done, but now you have a real opportunity to take a lead position at several venues I'm pushing. So you and Chip Garrett can become teammates to make sure these clubs are still hot for business when I'm out of town."

Joe got all excited about it. He said, "Thanks for looking out, man. That's all I've been asking for is a bigger shot, Ivan. You *know* I'll work hard for you."

Ivan said, "I know. Well, now you got your chance." Then he shook his hand and warned him, "Just don't miss that bull's-eye."

Ivan then set up promotional campaigns and website space to highlight several Native American reservations and casinos, including those that surrounded the San Diego area. And he continued to enjoy Jacari's companionship on several travel occasions. Despite her name change dispute, she had become a point of inspiration to her local tribe and to Native Americans nationally, particularly for the younger women.

Ivan joked, "I guess you're 'Jacari' *for real* now. These young girls are happy to see you drumming all over the country."

She laughed and told him, "A little bit of independence is *good* for a girl."

"As long as that girl can handle herself as maturely as *you* do," he commented. He was certain that he and Jacari would maintain their friendship. However, Jacari still served to remind him of a younger, softer, and less experienced version of someone else.

Ivan's long-term and personal plans remained a work in progress, where he made sure to check in on Lucina's continued fashion events and celebrity parties. He wanted to show his support as well as keep an eye on any suitor who might think to take her hand in another partnership, either business or personal.

"Oh, you don't have to worry about that," her girl Maya told him. Ivan had hinted at his concerns to her after dropping by on Lucina's Christina Aguilera party.

Maya said, "I'll be the first to break that up and call you if that ever happens. I'm still holding out for *you* two," she hinted back with a wink.

That made Ivan feel more secure about his wait. He was fortunate that Maya felt that strongly about him.

Just a little while longer, he told himself as another year of emotional chess went by between them.

BY THE SPRING OF 2006, the wait was over. Ivan made sure Lucina had no excuses to stop herself from giving him three hours of her time. That was all that he asked her for.

He picked her up at her house with a driver, wheeling Ivan's own Rolls-Royce Phantom in Pacific blue. The interior was a soft saddle-brown leather.

Lucina sat inside the top-of-the-line luxury car and smiled. "Is this yours or Roman's?"

It was a typical Lucina Gallo response. Ivan was used to it by now. He grinned and said, "I don't borrow Roman's cars that much anymore. But I still make money with him, renting them to other people. It's a good money deal. And I remember you thought he wouldn't go for it."

She glanced at him with a smirk. She still looked as fabulous and as fierce as she had when he first met her. She was wearing a white summer dress from Donna Karan, before season.

She asked him, "So, what are you working on now?"

Ivan seemed a million miles away from where she had first seen him in the Gaslamp Quarter. His potential had been met, many times over. That was how Lucina had always pictured him. He only had to manifest it. But somehow he remained the same man in his dark blue jeans, white shirt, and tweed sports jacket. He was still right there with her, and still searching.

He told her, "Like always, I got a lot of things I'm working on now."

She looked him over and nodded. "That's good. I'm always happy for you."

It sounded like a hint of envy to him. Was he as happy for her? Was that what Lucina was thinking? And if they were trusting partners like they had once agreed, then how come she was not where *he* was?

Ivan smiled it off and ignored her bait. "Thanks," he commented. He wanted to save everything for later. He had other plans for her. So he enjoyed the drive with no further response.

As they headed across the Coronado Bridge toward downtown, Ivan looked out the window and said, "This is really a beautiful city that we live in. But there are so many others out there, you know."

Lucina studied him. She responded, "Are you saying you are already tired of San Diego? Obviously, this city has been very *good* for you, don't you think? And already you want to *leave*."

He was beginning to irritate her more by the minute now. Maybe he *wasn't* the same man anymore. And for the record, Lucina *loved* San Diego.

Ivan grinned, still playing a mysterious game with her. He said, "I'm just wondering out loud what other places have to offer. You never do that? I thought you loved to travel at one time."

"Who says I don't like to travel *now?*" she asked him. "I've just been busy lately."

"All work and no play," Ivan suggested.

Lucina shot him a look and held her tongue. Was he *that* smug now?

He is really bothering me now, she told herself. *And what is his point today? Is he trying to show me how much of an asshole he can be now that he has wealth? Because I am perfectly fine without him. These men are all the same!*

On Ivan's side of the car, he told himself, *I hope we don't get caught in lunch-hour traffic. Because this is killing me! I just want to surprise her.*

They were on Interstate 5 heading north.

Ivan asked her, "You think people can really have what they want at our ages?" He needed to make more conversation with her.

However, Lucina never spoke of her exact age. She refused to allow people to know how old she was. Maya told him that she was only twenty-eight to his thirty-one. That meant she had been twenty-five to his twenty-eight when he first met her. But she always had seemed so much older.

She said, "It depends on a person's appetite. If you have a small appetite, then you can be happy with a little. But if you have a *big* appetite . . ." She shrugged and looked away again. She realized that Ivan's appetite was much larger than she ever expected.

Once she saw that they were still heading north, past SeaWorld, Lucina became anxious, especially since he had irritated her earlier. She didn't know if she had three hours left for him. So she asked him, "Where are we going, Ivan? I still cannot ask you that?"

He had told her the rules in advance, days before she had agreed to it. He was not to tell her their destination. She was to find out. And Ivan would not break those rules.

So he told her, "Nope. Just sit back and enjoy the ride."

Lucina took a breath and held her piece a minute longer. Ivan looked down at the designer ring on her finger and at the bracelet on her left wrist, and he was tempted to reach out and hold her hand as they continued to travel.

No, he told himself. *Just be patient a little while longer. You don't want to alarm her.*

He could have held Jacari's or any other woman's hand without a problem. They would have even preferred it. But they were not Lucina.

Once his driver turned off at their exit and began to ascend the hills of La Jolla, Lucina began to assume things.

He bought a house in La Jolla, she told herself. *Okay . . . now he wants to show off everything.*

Ivan realized the cat was out of the bag once they began to pass the expensive homes that were spaced out to the left and right of the winding road up the hills of La Jolla.

However, he was pleased that she held her thoughts to herself until they arrived. And as they got closer and closer, Ivan had to restrain himself again from reaching out to hold her hand.

I must have gotten too comfortable with Jacari, he thought. *Her affectionate personality has rubbed off on me.*

On Lucina's end, all she could think about was how high they were rising.

Oh, my God, I don't know if I like this, she admitted to herself. *I guess it's easier to look up here than to be up here. Or maybe I just feel that way because this car is so big. I feel like we are too close to the edge of the road.*

She had driven on high mountainous roads in small cars before. Just not any recently. So she forced herself to remember those times and countries, in order to relax. There were plenty of high roads back home in Brazil.

When the Rolls-Royce finally turned in to an extrawide driveway to the right, Lucina was indeed impressed. There was a four-car garage in front of them, and the home above it had a southern view looking back into the downtown skyline of San Diego with no obstructions. The view looked past SeaWorld, past Mission Bay Park, past the San Diego airport, and right into her own Coronado Bridge to the right of downtown.

Oh, my God, this view is heavenly! she admitted to herself.

The driver walked over to open her door and help her out of the car.

"Welcome home, madam," he had been instructed to tell her.

Lucina's side of the car placed her directly in front of the view. She'd heard what the driver had said to her, but it hadn't registered yet. She just wanted to see it all.

Ivan paced over to join her as Lucina walked toward the large, oval-shaped landing beside the garage. The oval, paved with smooth California stone, was big enough to land a helicopter. A three-foot-high stone wall surrounded it.

Lucina stood there by the edge and looked out at the view. To the right was the Pacific Ocean and three of San Diego's beaches: Pacific Beach, Mission Beach, and Ocean Beach. To the left were the homes on the hills across Interstate 5 in Clairemont. There was a perfect view of the highway traffic below, directly across from where Ivan used to drive to the offices of Hutch & Mitchell Accounting. It was the view he had dreamed about for *years.*

When he reached Lucina, standing out on the stone landing, he gave her a set of color-coded house keys: green, red, and gold.

He told her, "The green opens the door from the garage, the gold opens the doors to the house from the outside, and the red is for a secret door inside. You may even want to put that somewhere else."

Lucina remained speechless. She took a deep breath with the keys in her hands and turned to face him. She said, "Ivan . . . what are you . . . what are you trying to say?"

She could barely get her words out. And it wasn't just the house, the view, or the proposition, it was being able to share it all with *him.* Lucina had been so used to selfish men who built storages of wealth around her, or others who attempted to seduce her with preexisting wealth she had not earned, that Ivan's surprise was overwhelming for her. She actually felt that she *deserved* it this time. And more than that, she genuinely *loved* Ivan. She loved his fairness, his determination, his vision, and his courage. She even admired his stubbornness. She just didn't know how she could ever bring herself to accept a relationship with him outside of business. So she had fought off the idea, while maintaining enough proximity to him to continue to monitor his progress. She had played the same game that *he* had played—watch and wait.

Ivan took a deep breath of his own. He told her, "I want us to be partners again. Lately we've been more like . . . *associates.*" He said, "But all of this right here . . . this is *yours* now. I can't see myself sharing it with anyone else. You're the one who sparked a lot of my ideas and forced me to make 'em *work*."

Lucina just stared at him as if he were a statue that had hypnotized her. She still had no words to respond to him with. She needed to hear more to confirm that it was all real.

Ivan asked her, "You don't have anything to *say*?"

She didn't. She looked away in silence, still taking it all in.

Ivan read her silence as confusion and hesitancy. He wasn't used to Lucina not being able to respond to him. So he continued to pitch her.

He said, "I've had this place empty for *weeks* now, just waiting for you to get the time to come over here and see it. But just with you standing here, with no furniture or nothing, it's like . . . your *presence* fills the place up alone. You know what I mean? Just having you here to share it with me is like . . . *everything*. And I want you to live here. Move in. Decorate it. The whole house. Any way you want to. And I'll just watch you. This is *your* house," he repeated.

He went on, "I don't want us to be partners like we were, where we do an event together and you leave me and go home at night. I want to make *this* your home now. I want you to wake up and go to bed here. And we can use your other house as a guesthouse or something. The same with my downtown apartment. That's *your* downtown apartment now until we buy something bigger. Maybe a penthouse condo or something," he told her. "You see all the new spots they're building downtown?"

He continued, "It don't matter to me. Whatever you want. You helped me to come up with all this, and I'm setting up now to do more. And I want you *with me* while I'm doing it so you can do *your* part. That's why I'm talking so much about traveling now." He said, "But I would never take you away from San Diego. I know how much you love it here. I love this place, too. Just look at this," he reminded her of the view. He turned around and faced it all.

Lucina had heard enough. It was Ivan, all right. He was talking like his old, passionate self and was full of ideas. She shook her head and grinned, holding up her right hand to stop him.

"Ivan. Please. Slow down," she told him.

Ivan didn't know what that meant. He asked himself, *Is she still fucking turning me down, with all of this? Shit, she's a hard-ass girl!*

However, Lucina did not have those intentions. At least not initially. She was already imagining what Maya would say once she invited her friend over for lunch. Maya would probably joke with her and ask for her own guest room there.

Nevertheless, it was all too sudden. There was too much to consider first. Lucina could not just move in with him on a whim like that, no matter how nice his new house appeared. They had not even been out on an official date. *Ever!* Ivan had far too many female admirers for her to trust him now anyway. His proposition would also put an obvious price on her head. So ultimately it was an unacceptable deal, as unacceptable as many others had been.

She told him, "Ivan, you are not the first person to offer me a big home."

Ivan said, "I *know* I'm not. But I don't care about those other guys. They're not *me*. That's why you turned them all down. And imagine how many women would love to be in *your* shoes. But they're *not*. And they never will be," he told her.

Before she could get out another word, he said, "Lucina, the bottom line is this: I choose you today, I'll choose you tomorrow, and I'll choose you again next week. In fact, I chose you the first time I ever laid *eyes* on you. And during all of this time that I've been around you, that still hasn't changed. Did you read that from me when you first saw me out on the sidewalk? Be honest about it."

She shook it off and told him, "That's only because you haven't *had me,* Ivan. But what about the girls you've been with? How come *they're* not here?"

It was a good question. But Ivan answered her with poise. "Because they're not *you*. They're not what I want." He said, "But *you*, you're a long-term investment, Lucina. I wanna put you in my retirement fund," and he broke into a smile.

Lucina heard that and chuckled. She couldn't help herself. It was corny but clever. A retirement fund meant old age. And she couldn't see Ivan retiring anytime soon. He loved to hustle too much, a long-term addiction that matched her own fetish for hustling.

Ivan told her, "That's a good money deal right there. I only love my *mother* like that."

When he said that, he stopped smiling. He was dead serious.

Lucina looked into his eyes and read his sincerity. She had heard Ivan talk about his late mother before in his interviews. He held her memory in high regard. His mother had been a strong inspiration for him, as much as Lucina's mother had been an inspiration for her. Ivan even made her think about her mother back home in Brazil, where she refused to leave. She loved it there too much. So Lucina continued to send her love and money to her family back home.

After Ivan had opened up a soft spot in her armor, Lucina became silent while thinking about their possibilities.

We are so much alike, she told herself. *I've known that ever since that first night. I could see it in his eyes as soon as I looked at him. So how long can I continue to run away from him?* she asked. *And he's right. I did feel this that first night. But it was only a possibility then. Now it is a reality.*

Ivan seized the moment and walked over toward her in her silence. He continued to have an urge to hold her. He wanted to wrap his arms around her body and feel her heartbeat against his chest.

Lucina had not trusted the naked intentions of a man in years. Yet it was *time* now, and it had *been* time for a *long* time between them. So she took a step toward Ivan as he closed the gap. And she waited there, hoping he would be able to read her body language.

Ivan read her and understood. She needed affirmation.

She wants to, he told himself. *I got her! Finally!*

He opened his arms to receive her.

He said, "I've been wanting to hold you for a long-ass time."

Lucina just stared at him and said nothing.

Well, do it then, she thought. *I've waited long enough for this, too.*

Ivan gently held her body inside his arms and slowly closed them around her. Lucina reached her own arms around his waist and squeezed him back. Then she leaned her head gently onto his shoulder, taking in the attractive aroma of his cologne.

Ivan asked her, "So . . . I guess this means *yes,* right? You're back in with me now."

She smiled into his shoulder. "I guess so . . . until you act up," she teased him.

Ivan eased his hold on her to look into her eyes. He said, "Lucina, I expect us to disagree on some things. That's just human nature. But at the end of the fight, I'm still gonna be loyal to this company. And I know that we're gonna make a whole lot of *money money* together."

Lucina chuckled girlishly. "You liked that line, didn't you?"

"Oh, that was *classic,"* Ivan told her. "That got me going. I can't even lie. But you're not tired of hustling with me yet, are you?"

She thought about it and said, "No. I'm definitely not tired of that."

Ivan said, "Well, let's do it again, then. I spent a lot of money on this house. So let's get out there and make it all back. I got us set up to be *global* brand promoters now. And we can throw parties around the world, with company jet service all the way."

Lucina responded, "Yes, but I think I want to slow down and see the rest of this *house* first. Can we do *that* for a minute?"

"Oh, yeah, well, right this way," Ivan told her with L.A. swagger. "Let me show you how to use your keys with the alarm system."

They walked hand in hand toward the hillside home in the bright afternoon sunshine. And as Ivan showed her how to enter the house with her keys, he looked forward to throwing more network parties and events with her. Eventually he would make love to her, and offer her everything that came with it, all while they continued to hustle. And with both of them together . . . who could ever stop them?

Closing Interview:

The Voice & Viewpoint

After beginning another unprecedented year of gains at IDPromotions.com, while hinting at the desire to take the company public, Ivan David was able to sell his start-up website brand in the summer of 2007 for $180 million to Dortch Media Group in northern New Jersey. Included in the deal were company stock options, a salaried president of marketing and consultant position, and a commissioned sales agreement. Ivan also negotiated positions of continued employment for several of his staff members.

After the deal was finalized, with payouts to Ivan's key teammates in excess of $50 million, Thomas Jones advised him to break the story with the *Voice & Viewpoint*, the leading African-American newspaper in the San Diego region.

"If I.D. Promotions is planning to focus on more of a national clientele now, then you got nothing to lose by not breaking the story with the *Union-Tribune. The New York Times* and *The Wall Street Journal* will still love you," Thomas joked. "But the story would do a lot more locally to inspire the folks who read the black press by having you break that nine-figure deal on the front page of *their* paper. You know what I mean, Ivan? I'm proud to even know a young man like you my damn self."

He added, "Usually you're reading about some shit like this going down somewhere else. Either that or some young athlete or rap star did the deal. But you're a legitimate entrepreneur and businessman. That's a different *twist* for us."

So Ivan agreed to the interview over lunch, back at his humble beginnings at Carol's Soul Food Restaurant in Old Town.

He arrived early in a pair of fine shoes, a casual beige sports jacket, and a purple tie with his white dress shirt and dark blue jeans. He sat down at a corner table toward the back to avoid too much traffic. But after two in the afternoon, many of the earlier customers had headed back to work as expected.

"Hey, Ivan, what are you having?" one of the young waitresses asked him in her all-brown uniform of pants and a tennis shirt inscribed with CAROL'S SOUL FOOD RESTAURANT on the left.

"Let me try that tuna casserole to keep things light," he told her with a grin. He didn't want to eat anything too heavy or complicated, knowing that he would be forced to talk a lot.

"And your drink?"

"Lemonade. And tell Carol I said hi back there."

The waitress smiled. "And you know she'll come right out to see you before you leave, too."

As soon as his order was made, the *Voice & Viewpoint* reporter hurried through the door her cameraman held open for her. They spotted Ivan relaxed in his corner chair and hustled over to him.

"Oh, my God! You haven't been here long, have you?" the reporter asked him. She was a healthy-sized woman in her midthirties, wearing a lavender skirt suit. She inspected her watch. It was seven minutes after two. She said, "I know we're just a little bit late, but I'm usually ahead of schedule."

Ivan smiled it off. "It's all right. This place is like family. I'm good."

She nodded to him. "Okay, well, I'm Levonia Battle, and this is Nathan Clark, our first-rate photographer."

Nathan was an older black man with long gray dreads for hair. He kept his poise and nodded.

"If you can, just try to imagine that I'm not even here, Ivan. But I will need to set up my light," he commented.

Ivan shrugged it off. "Do what you need to do."

Levonia sat across the table from him and pulled out her tape recorder and notepad. She turned the tape recorder on and took a deep breath.

"Okay . . . so . . . Mr. Ivan David . . ."

Ivan grinned and waited for her first question. She seemed to be a little unsettled.

She shook her head and said, "Wow, I just . . . I mean, how does it *feel?*" She even leaned forward to lower her volume in the room. "A hundred and eighty million dollars? I've never even been around a person with that much money before."

Ivan told her, "Actually, you probably have, you just didn't *know* it. This is San Diego. There's plenty of money around here."

"Oh, well, yeah, walking by, but not sitting down to do an interview with *me.* So how does it feel?" she repeated. "I'm sure that a whole lot of us would just *love* to know."

Ivan answered, "Well, you know, when it first happens, you're excited about it like anyone else would be. But once it's over with, then you start to think to yourself, *Okay, so what do I want to do next?*"

Levonia said, "You relax and enjoy yourself."

"Exactly," Ivan agreed with her. "But I'm only thirty-two years old. How long do you expect me to relax?"

"I know," she told him. "That's what makes it all the more *special*. You did it at such a young age."

Ivan said, "But that's really how it happens, though. Once I started to read up and meet with other wealthy people, they all explained a zone that they fell in where things just *took off.* And you have to be ready for when it happens. My zone just came early."

"Yes, it did," the reporter commented.

By that time, Nathan was set up to take his first pictures.

"So, how did you do it?" Levonia asked Ivan.

"It's really all about hooking up with the right people," he answered.

She immediately frowned at him. "I mean, really, how much of a cliché is that?" It *had* to be more than the who-you-know game.

Ivan smiled and said, "It's true though. I owe everything to the people I teamed up with. And some of the ideas were mine, but other ideas I listened to and went along with."

"Like what kind of ideas, specifically?"

"Well, the I.D. Promotions idea I got from calling the Padres' Emilio Alvarez E.A. So I plugged my initials in as I.D., and it just worked for me."

"So you just happened to have the perfect name, then."

Ivan shrugged. "Whatever works for you. But that's the point. You never know what road will lead you there. And you can't really follow behind other people. That's *their* road. You gotta find your own way."

"Yeah, but how hard is *that*? Seriously."

"It's as hard as you make it," Ivan told her. "It would have been harder for me before I decided to just go for it. But before then, I wasn't even trying. That's how it is with a lot of us. We're not trying. Or not trying to make it *big*. We just talk about it occasionally. But if you talk about it enough, then you need to start *doing it*."

Levonia looked him over and said, "You know, it always sounds so *easy* when successful people reflect. It's almost like all the right things just seemed to happen for them all at the right time. I mean, you hear that movie producer Tyler Perry was once homeless, and then you look at him now and say, 'But was he *really* homeless?' "

Ivan said, "I bet he was. And I bet that when things started to happen for him, it all came together fast. But you work so hard that you don't even have time to stop and notice it. That's the *zone* I'm telling you about. But you have to want to *be there* to get there. And you gotta *work* for it."

She said, "Okay, now, I have to ask you this, Ivan. Since your company was doing so well so fast, then why sell it? Why not ride it all the way to the top? You could have made a *billion* dollars like Bob Johnson and BET."

Ivan nodded. He said, "That's a good question. And what I realized was that *IDPromotions.com* was unique, but not as unique as BET. Bob Johnson had a very specific niche audience, and I had the same with marketing to San Diego. But once my company expands past S.D., I come into a very different world of competition. And where BET is still the only significant black television network on the market, once IDPromotions.com became a national company, there were thousands of other promotional websites to contend with. So I was able to maximize a sale of the company based on the numbers that we were doing locally and the numbers that we projected on the West Coast as a whole. In the meantime, I'm still connected to my brand, I still earn a significant salary, I maintain a very strong voice within the company, I acquired plenty of stock, *and* I get a chance to study how Dortch Media Group carries out business on the East Coast, with stock in *their* company."

Levonia heard all that and nodded back to him. "Wow. It sounds like you know what you're doing, then."

Ivan smiled and told her, "Basically, I'm giving myself a chance to study the larger marketplace by freeing my hands. And as long as I stay smart and profitable with what I learn, I can always buy my company back on a good deal. That's what big business and the stock market is all about. We're all selling and buying. But sometimes when you get greedy without a plan, you can end up losing everything."

"And you obviously have a plan?" she asked him rhetorically.

"Definitely," Ivan answered. "With the fast run that I had here in S.D., I learned a great deal about a lot of things."

He paused for a minute as the waitress brought his casserole and lemonade to place on the table away from the tape recorder.

"I'm sorry," she commented to him.

Ivan raised a hand and shook it off. "I'm good, you're just doing your job. Besides, I'm hungry."

When the waitress walked away with a smile, Ivan took a bite and continued. "I learned a wealth of important business lessons here," he stated. "And what I want to do now is study how all of those dynamics work on a larger scale around the nation, and then globally. How can you apply your business model in Chicago? New York? Africa? China? Brazil? I mean, it's a pretty big world out there."

As Ivan dug into his plate of food, Levonia jotted down his points. She grinned and said, "Well, I guess, with all of that in mind, you pretty much *do* need to have your hands free."

Ivan nodded to her while eating. He mumbled, "The key is not to get stuck by earning only one type of money. That was the first lesson I learned. Expand your marketplace by any means necessary. So I expanded my website and small network parties to include nightclub branding, celebrity events, exotic car rentals, corporate business events, real estate, yacht parties, private jet travel, family vacation packages, U.S. military news. And each time you expand your interests, you end up meeting new businesspeople. That's what led me to meet up with companies on the East Coast, including Dortch Media Group."

He added, "I'm even involved in promoting events at Native American reservations and casinos now."

"Yeah, I heard about that," Levonia confirmed. "And if you're talking about making *global* money like that, then you might have designs on becoming a *billionaire* soon anyway," she suggested.

She wanted to make her story as big as possible for her readers.

Ivan stopped and stared at her, reading through her intentions. As a young African-American man who had become incredibly successful in his goals, he felt he had a responsibility to speak to those in the community who were still trying to find their way.

So he stated, "If you *really* want it, *anything* is possible. But I don't think a lot of people want it as bad as they *say* they do. If they did, they would make all the moves they need to make it happen. But once you start adding up excuses for not moving forward, you've already lost the game. And I've had a good run by surrounding myself with people who do what it takes. That's what I spoke about earlier. It's the people who you surround yourself with."

Levonia said, "Okay, but once you get all of that money, *hundreds* of *millions* of dollars . . . I mean, what do you *do* with all of that?"

Ivan chuckled and said, "When I first started looking at checks with my company name on it, and they got bigger and bigger, it blew me away like that, too. But then you get used to it. And it allows you to take care of the immediate people around you so you can have the peace of mind to continue to do *you*. Then you end up with these countless opportunities on your mind. So you have to actually *discipline* yourself not to go crazy by trying to chase every rainbow."

"And do you get a lot of friends and family members asking you for hookups? I mean, I can just *imagine*," Levonia commented with a grin.

Even the photographer, who had been silently taking pictures in the background, was forced to smile at that one. After their article would hit the San Diego public, Nathan figured Ivan would have even *more* of a problem on his hands with all types of solicitations. He was brave to even do the interview.

Ivan thought specifically about his decision to take care of his older brother and three nephews. He answered, "Well, unless you're the last man on the planet, you're always gonna have to deal with the less fortunate. So you figure out a way to do it in the most . . . *peaceful* way." He laughed and said, "And sometimes you need the help of your lawyers to develop the safest and sanest way to do it."

"And what about your love life when you're a multimillionaire?" Levonia asked him. She smiled and added, "You know I can't let you go without asking you that."

Ivan thought about his long-standing relationship with

Lucina Gallo, business and now personal. And he chose his words carefully.

He said, "The best relationships for people who make big money are with other people who understand how to paddle in that canoe with you. In other words, if she don't understand money, and don't want to learn, then keep her safely separate from your business. But with people you wanna get serious with, you gotta make sure they're in step with where you're going."

Levonia read through his politically correct answer and followed up with, "Yeah, but what about *you,* Ivan? I understand the philosophy of the rich marrying the rich, but what woman has *your* nose open?"

Ivan grinned and answered, "The same one who pulled it open in the beginning." He laughed it off and said, "You'll also learn that a lot of wealthy people are loyalists. Once we feel comfortable with a person, and the relationship is working well for us, we figure, why fuck it up? Especially when you're talking about people who are close to us. So, unless someone else can take their place, you tend to keep coming back to the people you know."

"So even *love* is business with you?" Levonia asked him.

Ivan didn't hesitate. "*Definitely,*" he answered. "That's why I've never made the mistake of getting hitched too early. I've seen what getting married and having kids early can do to people. And I'm not saying that it's *all* bad, because it's not. I know other people who have used family as a motivation to stay focused and busy. But I didn't want that extra burden in my life before I felt I was ready to handle it."

"And now?" she asked.

Ivan rocked back in his chair. "I'm almost ready." Then he laughed again. He said, "But that's a two-way street, so you *both* have to be ready for that next step, you know. But for right now, the immediate goal is becoming recognized as a global brand identifier."

Levonia stopped him and said, "Yeah, I've seen you talk about that before on your website blog. But could you explain what that means for our readers?"

Ivan obliged. He said, "Basically, one of the biggest things I did learn from studying the Bob Johnson deal with BET is that it's very hard to compete with big business by yourself. So Bob had a lot of deals going on even *before* he sold BET. With that in mind, you'll find that the rich continue to get *richer* by buying other people's companies. But that's a hell of a risky game to play. And just a couple of bad moves can *lose* you billions of dollars. So instead of being the *buyer,* as a brand identifier, you become *the finder* of the next hot thing: Google, YouTube, Facebook. And if you can't afford to invest in the company outright, then you do a marketing and promotions deal for a piece of the company and become wealthy that way."

Levonia commented, "Yeah, but it sounds like you would still need money to compete with that. It takes *a lot* to market a new brand."

Ivan countered, "Not necessarily. All you really need is a strong *name* and a desire to *network*. I've already been talking to my football and baseball friends about it. It's the next level of endorsement. You use your name and popularity to make something *else* popular, and then you take it to the venture capitalists or the big deal makers and get your piece of the pie. That's a way in which you keep your personal risk low while making money off the bigger deal."

He continued, "The only risk you take is choosing the right people, companies, and products to get involved with. The rapper 50 Cent did it with his interests in Vitamin Water, which ended up selling big to Coca-Cola. That made him a lot more money than just rapping and selling clothes. But when *I* do it, I'm not just thinking *nationally,* I'm out to identify hot new brands *globally.* I want to become the guy that the big money people can count on. And my partner . . . she's set up to help me to do it," Ivan added.

"You're talking about Lucina Gallo?"

"Yes, I am. And she understands everything I'm doing now.

So, instead of us getting involved in just the local parties, events, and concerts, we're now conversing on *international deals,* while talking to all of the brands who want to be a part of it. That's even the new way of using *music* now. It's not about how the album sells anymore, it's all about producing the big shows, and all of the tie-ins that come with a hit song. All we have to do is know who's hot. And as Kanye West has continued to prove with *his* music, it's not just a *black* or *white* thing. You gotta get out there and get *everybody's* money. So you have to continue to create the kind of products and teamwork that you'll need to compete in a more diverse market."

Levonia was impressed. Ivan was giving her more information than she had expected from him. She couldn't even use that much information in a print article. She would have to link the rest of it to his website.

Again, she nodded and said, "Wow." She then looked at her notes to see what he hadn't answered yet. But before she could ask him her next question, Carol Henderson made her way out of her back office to give Ivan a hug and a kiss on the cheek.

Nathan immediately got the two of them to pose for a picture.

Carol said good-naturedly, "You make sure you write a good article on this young man. And make sure you add that it all started for him right here in my restaurant."

Ivan said, "Yeah, this is one of the many brands that I want to make famous in more than just San Diego." He had made his peace with her daughter Ida. Business was business, and fortunately their brief attempt at pleasure did not destroy it.

Levonia smiled and decided to ask Carol a few things.

"What do you think about how far Ivan has come since throwing his first event here at your restaurant?"

Carol paused before she answered. She said, "When I first spoke to Ivan years ago, right here at this restaurant, he looked me straight in my eyes and told me what he wanted to do, and I *believed* him. Now, I had no idea of knowing if he was lying to me or not," she added with a chuckle. "But being able to *believe* in a person is the first part of business. And Ivan has a gift for making you *believe*."

She added, "But I don't want to take up too much of his interview, just make sure you get some good pictures of him around the restaurant."

"Oh, I got you on that," Nathan promised her.

Before Levonia could ask her anything else, Carol was already making her way back to her office. She was in and out.

"You be good, now, Ivan," she told him.

"You know I will."

Levonia looked at her notes and didn't know where to pick up their conversation. Ivan had said so much already that she could work from.

Finally, she asked him, "Well, is there any advice that you would like to give to a young black professional looking to do anything *close* to what you've been able to do? I mean, just *anything*," she asked him.

Ivan smiled and took a sip of his lemonade.

He said, "You know that old statement 'When the student is ready the teacher will appear'? Well, that's always the case. Sometimes we give people advice before they're ready to use it. And it only becomes important to them *after* we become wealthy. But all of my *real* lessons were learned while I was building my company for four years. But that's now the boring part. We don't want to learn about all the hours of thought and preparation that an entrepreneur puts into building a brand. We just want to know about the after parties: the girls, the cars, the money, the drama. And as long as we think that way, we will never learn what it really *takes* to become rich."

He added, "So I can tell you a *million* things to do right now, and it won't change anything for you unless you're ready to change *yourself* first. That's the first thing I had to do when I got started with this four years ago. I had to change the way I thought about *a lot* of things . . . But I made those changes. And look at me now."

* * *

IVAN WRAPPED UP his interview slightly after three o'clock, as planned, and walked outside the restaurant into the afternoon sunshine. His well-dressed driver waited outside for him with the blue Rolls-Royce parked at the curb, shining.

"How did it go?" the driver asked on their short walk to the car.

"It went perfectly," Ivan told him. "And hopefully it will help to get someone started."

The driver nodded and walked him around the rear end of the car to open the back door for him. Ivan climbed into the backseat. Sitting on the other side was his partner, Lucina Gallo. She wore a beige and white silk dress from Gucci and looked as classy as ever. She was adorned in tasteful diamonds and gold jewelry from her earlobes to her ankles, glistening with stature.

"Did you do good?" she asked him.

First Ivan leaned over to kiss her on the lips. Lucina held his arms gently to balance herself as she kissed him back.

Ivan answered, *"Always,"* as they disengaged.

"And now we're back off for New York," Lucina commented.

"Yup. Let's hit the airport," Ivan stated to his driver.

The driver nodded and started the smooth purr of the Phantom's engine.

Ivan then smiled at Lucina as they held hands in the back.

"You know she asked me the big one, right?"

Lucina played coy with a grin of her own. "What big one?"

"She asked me who I was involved with," Ivan informed her.

Lucina shrugged, no longer concerned about it. She had grown superbly comfortable with Ivan. They were business teammates as well as a couple. She fully accepted it.

"Everyone should know that by now," she countered.

Ivan continued to smile. He said, "Then she asked me about kids and family."

That got Lucina's attention. "And what did you say to that?" she asked him.

"I said it's a two-way street. Both parties have to be ready for that."

Lucina grinned and turned away to look out the window. They were entering Interstate 5, headed north toward the private airport.

She looked back at Ivan and told him, "You keep being good to me and everything will happen in time."

Ivan stared at her, eye to eye. He asked her, "You mean that?"

Lucina stared right back and nodded. "I do," she answered.

Ivan continued to smile, loving the sound of it. *I do,* he repeated to himself.

He then nodded back to her with poise. He carefully squeezed her left hand in his right and told her, "Okay . . . we got a deal." Then he sat back and relaxed in the comfortable leather seat of the Rolls-Royce . . . and he was no longer dreaming.

About the Author

Omar Tyree, the *New York Times* bestselling author, 2001 NAACP Image Award recipient, and 2006 Phillis Wheatley Literary Award winner, has published sixteen novels, five anthologies, a children's book, and *The Equation,* a nonfiction work that describes the four indisputable components of successful business. In 2007, Tyree launched, with *The Last Street Novel,* his first "CinemaStory" of visual mastery, to jump-start an expanded career as a filmmaker. With *Pecking Order,* he continues in his books-to-film transition, while solidifying himself once again as the "godfather of contemporary urban literature." He lives in Charlotte, North Carolina.

To learn more about Omar Tyree,
visit his website at www.omartyree.com.